Dressed To Kill
A Biblical Approach to Spiritual Warfare and Armor

Rick Renner

Albury Publishing
P. O. Box 470406
Tulsa, Oklahoma 74147-0406

Unless otherwise indicated, all scriptural quotations are from the *King James Version* of the Bible.

8th Printing

Dressed To Kill
A Biblical Approach to Spiritual Warfare and Armor
ISBN 1-88008-906-8
Copyright © 1991 by
Rick Renner Ministries, Inc.
P. O. Box 472228
Tulsa, Oklahoma 74147-9994

Published by Albury Publishing
P. O. Box 470406
Tulsa, Oklahoma 74147-0406

Dressed To Kill
A Biblical Approach to Spiritual Warfare and Armor

Eph 1:11-12 trusted in Christ
the heard word of Truth
Gospel = of yr salvation
1. not ashamed = Rom 1:16
2. Power of God to Salvation to everyor
   th
3. Believeth
3 4. after you Trusted I whane
   2. heard you
   3 word of Truth
   4. You were sealed
   5. H. Sp of promise
14. Who is - _payment_ /earnest
   1. our our inheritance
   2. Time until - redemption of
   of - purchased - possesson,   not yr But
   3. To praise of his glory - his
Eph 1:15 - faith w. Lord Jesus and
V 11 & 16 + 18   love to all saints

Dedication

I wish to dedicate this book to Jim and Judy Kennedy, two very faithful friends and comrades in the Lord.

Like others in the Body of Christ, you are growing in your understanding of Satan's defeat, and you are learning to completely rest in the perfect and completed redemptive work of Jesus Christ!

Thank you for your faithfulness and for allowing God to use you to help us take the life-transforming truths of God's Word to spiritually hungry people.

Table of Contents

Acknowledgments

I wish to express my deepest gratitude to Brother Kenneth E. Hagin for his incredible public support of this book and for encouraging me in the work of the Lord. There are no words adequate enough to express my thanksgiving for your words of support. Let me also thank Tony Cooke for being used of God to pass the original manuscript of this book along to Brother Hagin.

I cannot fail to mention my appreciation to Marti Barry, Joella Davies, Louise Norcom, Erlita Renner, Kyle Roach, Elizabeth Sherman and Lori Stout for their editorial suggestions and proofreading. More importantly, thank you so much for taking this project to the Lord in prayer.

Most important of all, I want to thank my precious wife, Denise, for believing in me and my ministry, and for faithfully releasing the godly fragrance of Jesus Christ into our home and into our personal lives. I love you dearly, Denise.

Dressed To Kill
A Biblical Approach to Spiritual Warfare and Armor

Chapter One
Spiritual Warfare Mania

There is no issue more popular or more intensely controversial today than the issue of spiritual warfare. Leaders and people all across the nation are talking about demonic powers and strongholds, and how to pull these horrible, dark, controlling and manipulating influences down and off from our personal lives, nations and cities.

From the widespread popularity of spiritual warfare these days, one would think that spiritual warfare was a brand new revelation to the Body of Christ. Everyone seems to be teaching on it. There is no doubt about it, spiritual warfare is the current "rage" in the Charismatic sector of the Body of Christ. Any person who is in touch with the national pulse of the Church would quickly agree that the Body of Christ is currently experiencing what I have come to call a "spiritual warfare mania."

This preoccupation with spiritual warfare is on a measure which we have never known in our day — which is both *good* and *bad*.

This emphasis on spiritual warfare is *good* in the respect that it has caused us to become familiar with our adversary, the devil, and how he operates. When we understand his mode of operation, then we can foil his attacks against us. This is the very reason that Paul, concerning the devil and his mode of operation, told the Corinthians, ". . . we are not ignorant of Satan's devices" (Second Corinthians 2:11).

On the other hand, this new emphasis on spiritual warfare has the potential of becoming very *bad*. If spiritual warfare is not taught properly, it can be devastating. This subject has a unique way of captivating people's attention to the extent that they end up thinking of nothing else but spiritual warfare. This itself is a trick of the devil to make believers magnify the devil's power to a greater degree than it deserves.

If this trick works, then these imbalanced, devil-minded believers will begin to imagine that the devil is behind everything that occurs — thus paralyzing them from functioning normally in any capacity of life, and eliminating them from future usefulness in the kingdom of God.

Unfortunately, this has been the norm with many people who have focused on the issue of spiritual warfare in recent years.

Everywhere you look, it seems that this subject is surfacing. The pages of our leading Charismatic magazines are filled with articles on spiritual warfare, advertisements for books and cassette tape series on spiritual warfare, and now even video series are available on this subject — not to mention the dozens of spiritual warfare meetings and seminars that take place every month and every week of the year.

Honestly, there are so many conferences on spiritual warfare today, that if you are looking for one to attend, it could be very hard to decide which one to choose. Of the multiple choices available, you could attend a:

Spiritual Warfare Retreat. . .

Prophetic Spiritual Warfare Conference. . .

Worship Warfare Conference. . .

Militant Church Meeting. . .

Prayer Warrior Campmeeting. . .

Kingdom Conference on Spiritual Warfare. . .

Overcoming Faith Warfare Meeting. . .

Kid's Combat Meeting. . .

Aggressive Church Convention. . .

And the list goes on and on and on.

In addition to these various meetings and conferences, now you can purchase Bibles that are specially designed with a spiritual warfare emphasis in the marginal notes, spectacular spiritual warfare posters to hang on the walls of your home, spiritual warfare study guides, spiritual warfare manuals, spiritual warfare T-shirts, spiritual warfare toys for your children, and so on.

The subject of spiritual warfare is sweeping across the nation at an unprecedented rate!

Do not misunderstand what I am saying: *I am not opposed to spiritual warfare. Spiritual warfare is real.* We are commanded in scripture to deal with these unseen, invisible forces that have been marshalled against us. We are commanded in scripture to "cast out devils" (Mark 16:17), and to "pull down" the "strongholds" of the mind (Second Corinthians 10:3-5). This is a part of our Christian responsibility toward the lost, the oppressed and the demonized.

In my own ministry I have had to deal with demonic manifestations on occasions. I remember a time not too long ago, when a young teenage Satanist approached me at the end of one of my meetings in a large church. Realizing Satan's powers had taken his mind captive, he had come forward to receive prayer in the prayer line that evening.

As I continued through the prayer line, praying for this one, and then that one, I could visibly see from a distance that this particular young man was sending forth spiritual signals of a very strong, evil presence. As I came nearer to him, I sensed that he had been involved in some type of occult activity.

When I finally reached the young man, he looked up through eyes that were tightly squeezed together like little slits in the front of his head. When I looked into his eyes, it almost looked like a demon was looking back at me from behind his face. When I saw this, I knew that this young man was serious about being helped — it had taken a great amount of determination for him to shove that manipulating force aside, and forge his way down to the front of the church auditorium.

As I laid my hands on the young man that night, his body began to violently react to the power of God. Trembling under the weight of God's power, he fell to the floor, crumbling down right next to my feet. Lying there under the electrifying power of God that was surging up and down his body, he quietly moaned, *"I'm afraid to leave them* (the satanic group in which he was involved). *They said they would kill me if I left the group."*

I leaned over to pray for him a second time, and as I did, the horrible demonic influence that had held his mind captive immediately released him and fled from the scene. I definitely believe in genuine spiritual warfare!

Spiritual Hostages

There are multitudes of people in the world today who are held hostage by the devil in their minds. "For this purpose," First John 3:8 says, "the Son of God was manifested, that he might destroy the works of the devil."

The word "destroy" is taken from the Greek word *luo* (pronounced lu-o), and it refers to the act of "untying" or "unloosing" something. It is the exact word we would use to picture a person who is "untying" his shoes. As a matter of fact, the word *luo* is used in this very way in Luke 3:16, when John the Baptist says, ". . . but one mightier than I cometh, the latchet of whose shoes I am not worthy *to unloose. . . ."*

Jesus Christ came into the world to "untie" and "unloose" Satan's binding powers over us. At the cross, He unraveled Satan's power, until finally, his redemptive work was complete and our liberty was fully purchased.

Furthermore, Peter told the household of Cornelius, "How God anointed Jesus of Nazareth with the Holy Ghost and with power: who went about doing good, and healing all that were oppressed of the devil; for God was with him" (Acts 10:38).

4

We know from both of the verses above, that setting people free from Satan's power is a primary concern of Jesus Christ. Since this is His concern, then it should be ours also.

In order to free people from demonic oppression, we must learn how to recognize the work of the enemy and how to overcome his attacks against the mind — *and the mind is the primary area which he seeks to attack.* He knows that if he can plant a stronghold of deception in some area of an individual's mind, then from that lofty position he can begin to control and manipulate them.

The Holy Spirit is obviously speaking a strong message about spiritual warfare to us in these days. Leaders and churches all across the nation are awakening to this reality. In light of this, we must give heed to what the Spirit is saying to the Church, *and proceed with the Word of God as our guide and foundation.*

As we proceed in this subject of spiritual warfare, we must be very careful to walk in balance. In addition to dealing with the devil, other major elements of spiritual warfare have to do with taking control of your mind and crucifying the flesh. Let's not forget these elements of spiritual warfare that are just as vital as the others.

The truth is that the devil's attacks against our lives would not work if our flesh did not cooperate with them. If we were really mortifying the flesh on a daily basis (Colossians 3:5), and if we were living lives that were "dead to sin" (Romans 6:2) as we are commanded to do in scripture, then we would not respond to demonic suggestions and to fleshly temptation. Dead men do not respond; they are incapable of responding. Thus, the power of a crucified life!

Living the crucified life is a critical part of spiritual warfare. To write a book on spiritual warfare without mentioning this, would present a view of spiritual warfare that is unrealistic, and it would do a great injustice to my faithful readers.

One can scream at the devil all day long, but if he or she has willfully permitted some area of his or her mind to go unchecked and unguarded — if he or she has an area of sin they are aware of, but have not been willing to deal with — then they have opened the door for an attack on themselves. All their prayers against the devil will be to no avail. In such cases, the devil is not their real enemy; their enemy is their own carnal mind and flesh which must be submitted to the control of the Holy Spirit in order to eradicate these attacks.

If we permit *only* the devil to occupy our thoughts about spiritual warfare and fail to mention other equally important areas, then this emphasis on spiritual warfare can and will be very damaging.

Spoiling Principalities and Powers

While spiritual warfare is real and we cannot ignore it, we must be careful to remember that the real battle with Satan was won at the cross and the resurrection. Now this same victorious Christ who single-handedly defeated the devil lives in us! Thus, the apostle John told us, ". . . greater is He that is in you than he that is in the world" (First John 4:4).

Our view of spiritual warfare must begin with this basic understanding of Jesus' already accomplished victory over Satan. If we do not start out with this as our foundation, then eventually we will be led to utterly ridiculous spiritual conclusions. The victory has already been won; there is nothing that we can add to the destructive work that Jesus did to Satan's domain when He was raised from the dead.

In Colossians 2:15, Paul vividly portrays Jesus' victory and Satan's defeat. It says, "And having spoiled principalities and powers, he made a shew of them openly, triumphing over them in it."

Especially notice the word "spoiled." The word "spoiled" is taken from the Greek word *apekdusamenos* (a-pek-du-sa-me-nos), and it refers to the act of "stripping one's garments off to the point of complete nakedness."

By using the word "spoiled," the Holy Spirit tells us that when Jesus Christ arose from the dead, He thoroughly plundered the enemy. Quite literally, He "spoiled principalities and powers." An even better translation would be, *"He completely stripped principalities and powers and left them utterly naked, with nothing left at their disposal with which to retaliate. . . ."*

Furthermore, when Jesus' sacking and plundering of hell's powers was complete and His mission was accomplished, Paul tells us that He rubbed this defeat in the devil's face by throwing the biggest party the universe had ever seen!

Colossians 2:15 continues, "And having spoiled principalities and powers, *he made a shew of them openly, triumphing over them in it."*

The word "shew" is taken from the word *deig-matidzo* (deig-ma-tid-zo), and it literally means "to display" or "to expose" something. It was used in classical Greek writings to denote the display of captives, weaponry and trophies that were seized during war on foreign soil.

Once the war was completed and the battle was won, the reigning emperor would return home and victoriously "display" and "expose" the treasures, trophies, weaponry and captives that he had seized during his military conquest. This was a grand moment of celebration for the victor — and it was a humiliating experience for the defunct foe.

Now the Holy Spirit has carefully chosen to use this same word (*deigmatidzo*) to let us know what Jesus did after He was finished plundering the enemy. When His resurrection was complete and the enemy was stripped bare to the core, Jesus then proceeded to publicly "display" and "expose" this defeated spiritual foe and all of his defective wares to the hosts of heaven!

But wait. . . there is still more to Colossians 2:15 which we must understand. Paul goes on to tell us that "he made a shew of them *openly. . . ."*

Especially pay heed to the word "openly." The word "openly" is taken from the word *parresia* (par-re-sia), which is used throughout the books of the New Testament to denote "boldness" or "confidence." By using the word *parresia*, Paul declares that when this heavenly party and celebration of Jesus' victory commenced, it was no "quiet" affair.

Quite the contrary! He "boldly," "confidently," and "loudly" exposed and displayed this now-defunct foe to heaven's hosts! Make no mistake! When Jesus made a "shew of them openly," it was not a quiet moment in heaven. Jesus made a display of these defeated enemies and their defective wares "openly," "boldly," "confidently," or you could even translate it "loudly." This was quite a "show!"

Then the verse continues, ". . . he made a shew of them openly, *triumphing over them in it.*"

The word "triumph" is taken from the Greek word *triambeuo* (tri-am-beuo), which is a technical word that was used to describe a general or an emperor who was returning home from a grand victory in the enemy's territory. The word "triumph" (*triambeuo*) was a word used to specifically describe the emperor's *triumphal parade* when he returned home! (For more on this, see pages 227-229, LIVING IN THE COMBAT ZONE).

Colossians 2:15 explicitly teaches that when Jesus' work on the cross was finished, He descended into the lower places in order to take the enemy apart piece by piece. Jesus thoroughly "spoiled principalities and powers" through his death and resurrection. *They were so utterly plundered, that they were "stripped to bare nakedness" and left with nothing in hand to retaliate!*

If our understanding of spiritual warfare does not begin with this as our foundation, then we will eventually move into realms of teaching and experience that are not doctrinally sound. We must approach warfare from this perspective.

Ridiculous and Unscriptural Behavior

The term "spiritual warfare" creates all kinds of images in the mind. Certainly it rightly makes one think about our ongoing conflict with unseen, demonic powers, and this indeed is what spiritual warfare is all about. As Ephesians 6:12 tells us, "For we wrestle not against flesh and blood, but against principalities, against powers, against the rulers of the darkness of this world, and against spiritual wickedness in high places."

But the mind also has the ability to dream up some very wild, unfounded, unbiblical ideas about the devil and our warfare against him. If believers do not have a solid, Biblical understanding of the devil, of our Christ-imparted authority over him, and of our divinely empowered weaponry to be used against him, then they are left wide open to all kinds of wrong thinking, vain imaginations, fears and methods of opposing him that are unfounded.

This is precisely the reason I stated that this new emphasis on spiritual warfare is both *good* and *bad*. It is good because we are learning how the adversary operates. In no way do I intend to convey the idea that all teachings and spiritual warfare conferences are bad; *some are exceptionally good.*

As we approach this topic we must guard against superstitious, homemade remedies about spiritual warfare and base our teachings and actions firmly on what the Word of God has to say — and not on emotions, wild imaginations or an exciting hype that temporarily thrills a frenzied crowd of novice believers.

For instance, some leading spiritual warfare advocates today teach that since demon spirits lived in "high places" in the Old Testament, and since Satan is called the "prince of the power of the air," then we must go high up into the sky in order to do serious damage to the devil.

Therefore, some who specialize in spiritual warfare are currently suggesting that the 30th, 40th, 50th or 60th floors of tall skyscrapers are the best places to hold prayer meetings and to do spiritual warfare!

If victory still eludes you after going into these particular "high places," some have further suggested that perhaps you should rent a plane or helicopter to go up even higher — right into the actual "high places" where the devil dwells — so you can do spiritual warfare even better!

I was dumfounded when I first heard that some were teaching the necessity of having warfare meetings on the 60th floor of buildings, and the necessity of flying over cities in planes and helicopters in order to really wage spiritual warfare successfully. It made me wonder how the Lord Jesus Christ ever got along! He had no 60th floor buildings where He could hold His meetings, and sadly enough, no planes or helicopters were available for Him to get up high enough to do the devil damage. *Yet, somehow in a miraculous way, the Lord was still able to carry on in His earthly ministry!*

Ignorance of God's Word always leaves the Body of Christ in a dangerous position. As Hosea 4:6 says, "My people are destroyed for lack of knowledge. . . ." Where ignorance is rampant concerning the Word, and especially concerning the devil and our authority over him, superstition nearly always prevails — resulting in all kinds of *"spiritual hocus-pocus"* in order to *"shoo the devil away."*

Unfortunately, much of what is called "spiritual warfare" today falls into this embarrassing category of ridiculous and unscriptural behavior. Yet, spiritual warfare is real and we must not ignore this truth. Rather, we must proceed into this new emphasis which the Holy Spirit is speaking to the Church today with the Word of God as our guide.

Why This New Emphasis Today?

Someone recently wrote me and asked, "Why does it seem that everyone across the nation is suddenly talking about spiritual warfare?"

In response to this question, I began to do some research. I spoke to many national leaders about this new emphasis on spiritual warfare, and specifically asked them, "Why do you believe spiritual warfare has become such a central issue these days?"

The answers I heard could be categorized into three different classifications.

The first group of leaders I spoke with suggested the reason for this new emphasis is because Satan is unleashing new hordes of demon spirits against the Church in these last days — perhaps more demon spirits, they say, than ever before. Therefore, they believe this new thrust on spiritual warfare is God's way to teach us how to overcome these masses of innumerable, uninvited nuisances that have been released to destroy the Church in these last days.

The second group of leaders suggested that there has been a new infiltration of demons into the Church in these last days, who have been specifically assigned to destroy individual churches and ministries from within.

As a matter of fact, some leaders even expressed their strong belief that this is the reason so many ministers have failed morally and have fallen into immorality in recent times.

Because they believe demon spirits are working around the clock to do this havoc to the leadership of the Church at large, they say we must learn right now — at this very crucial time — how to combat these foul creatures of darkness that have come to carefully scheme the demise of great men and women of God.

The third group of leaders believed that the reason for this new emphasis on spiritual warfare was because witches and Satanists are uniting together in satanic prayer to cast curses upon the Church of Jesus Christ. In order to combat these curses, they believe the Holy Spirit is bringing to the Body of Christ a new awareness about the necessity of spiritual warfare.

Regardless of whether any of the three scenarios above are right or wrong, spiritual warfare has recently come to the forefront of the Body of Christ.

Regardless of "why," the fact is we need to know what the Word of God has to say on these issues of spiritual warfare and spiritual armor.

11

Nothing New Under the Sun

It is clear from history that innumerable masses of demon spirits were released to attack and victimize the Church of Jesus Christ in its infancy — in the first, second and third centuries. This idea is nothing new.

Because we are the ones living in these contemporary times, it is natural for us to think that our problems are far worse than those of any preceding generation. But even with all of these present problems and the potential difficulties still to come, our problems today are really no greater than those of the preceding generations of believers who have gone before us.

When the Church of Jesus Christ first emerged on the scene on the Day of Pentecost, it was born into a world very similar to ours — nations were in revolt, national boundaries were disappearing, violence in entertainment was popular, and godly morals in the Roman world were nearly nonexistent.

The Roman army was quickly conquering the entire civilized world of the day. Homelands were being seized, plundered and occupied by this Roman army from Italy. The world was being united politically and economically by the prevailing government of Rome. And the occultic paganism of the hour was far worse than any historian could ever state.

Satan used all of these things as a part of his plan to destroy the Church before it could destroy him. Yet, his plan to destroy the Church of Jesus Christ miserably failed. God had another plan! Rather than destroy the Church, the Church arose in the power of the Spirit to meet the challenge — just as we shall rise in our own day to meet any challenge that the enemy would attempt to put before us!

Equipped with "the whole armor of God" (Ephesians 6:10-18), these early believers lived victoriously for the Lord in the midst of the worst predicaments — predicaments much worse than anyone reading this book has ever known. *Satan*

*buffeted the Church with unimaginable torture and outward per-
secution, but he could not destroy her!*

"The whole armor of God" which worked effectively
for these early believers is the same identical set of spiritual
armor that the Church of Jesus Christ still possesses today.
Just as these early Christians were fully equipped with "the
whole armor of God" for the troubles of their day, we also
have "the whole armor of God" to live victoriously for
Jesus Christ during our day. This armor still works very
effectively!

The "loinbelt of truth," the "breastplate of righteousness,"
the "shoes of peace," the "shield of faith," the "helmet of salvation," the "sword of the Spirit" and the "lance of prayer and
supplication" are still vital, effective and powerful weapons
for the Body of Christ today. With these "weapons of our
warfare" (Second Corinthians 10:4) in hand, we are more than
able to defeat any foe that would challenge our faith!

The "strongholds" these early believers faced were real
— they really knew what "strongholds" were all about! They
lived in an environment of paganism, demonism and idol
worship to a measure which we cannot fathom. They were
forced to live with *religious opposition, social opposition* and even
political opposition.

This opposition by the pagan Roman society was so bad
that Christians were regularly attacked and physically assaulted by witches, astrologers and mediums. In fact, it was at
such an event that Timothy, Paul's disciple and the pastor of
the Ephesian Church, was brutally murdered.

Intense hatred for Christians grew so rapidly under the
reign of Nero that they were burned to death at the Circus
Maximus in Rome; they were eaten alive by wild beasts in the
Coliseum; they were publicly mutilated to death by gladiators
in the amphitheaters; and their gruesome, terrible, grotesque
deaths provided the Romans with the most popular form of
entertainment during that time.

The violent deaths of believers became so popular with the Romans that it became necessary to expand the seating capacity of the Coliseum to 87,000 seats in order to accommodate the massive crowds that would assemble for a whole afternoon of Christian martyrdom. Wild beasts would be released into a series of tunnel-like passages, and then Christians were placed into these same passages to be hunted down by ferocious wild animals. They were chased by these hungry beasts until caught, and then, they were eaten alive before 87,000 cheering people.

At first such murderous events only took place once a year — usually during the month of January as a dedication to the gods. However, during the demented rule of Nero, the number of such afternoons of entertainment at the Coliseum increased greatly.

Nero used nearly any excuse he could muster together to see additional Christians die in the Coliseum. His birthday, his anniversary of becoming Emperor, the anniversary of his Predecessors' birthdays, his mother's birthday, perhaps a special religious day, or simply a holiday, was enough reason for Nero to fill the Coliseum to the brim with spectators who would sit on the edge of their seats to watch Christians die in the Coliseum.

The worth of Christians was so low in the Roman world that when the construction of the Appian Way (a road leading from Rome to southern Italy) required the road workers to work into the night, the dead bodies of martyred Christians were strung on poles along the road and were set on fire — like huge lanterns in whose burning light the road workers could continue working and building.

Demonic activity in Rome was rampant! All Roman Emperors from this period consulted astrologers and occult priests for important decisions. These high-ranking mediums were considered to be so vital to the cause of government that they actually held official positions in the administration — and they were held in the highest esteem by the reigning Emperor.

14

In addition to these high-ranking occult spiritualists who held especially prominent positions in the government, there were hundreds of other lower-class occult priests on the payroll of Rome who served as priests for the official religion of Rome. There is no doubt that these official governmental witches, astrologers, soothsayers and mediums must have influenced Nero's sentiments about God-fearing believers.

There were other brands of religion besides the official religion of Rome. The city of Pergamos, the most famous of all Asian cities and the official seat of the Proconsul of Rome, was a city that was filled with idolatry and paganism.

High upon a mountaintop, 800 feet above the city of Pergamos, there sat a great altar to the goddess Athena. Directly in front of this idolatrous temple to Athena, and protruding out on a ledge that was visible to the entire city below, was yet another idolatrous statue. Glistening in the sunlight every afternoon was a huge, polished marble altar that was built in the shape of a giant throne. This was the altar of Zeus.

From every section of Pergamos, citizens could look upward and see the smoke of burning incense billowing out into the sky from this demonic altar. This is the reason that Jesus told the Pergamene believers, "I know where thou dwellest, *even where Satan's seat is. . .*" (Revelation 2:13).

But wait, there is still more! In addition to this idolatrous worship of Athena and Zeus, the city of Pergamos was also the citadel of the cult of Asklepios (As-kle-pios), a demon spirit who took the outward form of a large serpent.

The cult of Asklepios boasted that Asklepios, the serpent spirit, had power to heal the sick. The supernatural manifestions of this serpent spirit eventually became so well known that people traveled from all over the world in order to consult the priests of Asklepios and be healed. Massive altars to Asklepios were erected all over the city, and there were literally hundreds of mediums who were employed as priests in this dark, demonic cult.

As for the morality of Rome... *there was none!* Even non-Christian historians and scholars agree that Nero carried on an active homosexual relationship with many of the men that were close to the imperial throne. Bisexuality was completely acceptable by the standards of the day. Nero was himself a married man when he was cavorting with men.

Like the entertainment industry today, the theatre was full of vulgarities and lewdness and was blatantly sensuous and sexual. It was common for sexual scenes to be fully acted out on stage in front of a carnal Roman audience.

Female believers who refused to renounce their faith in Jesus Christ, and who fell into the hands of Nero's government, were often forced to work in Rome's perverted burlesque as a form of mental and spiritual persecution.

Satan tried to destroy the Church of Jesus Christ at its inception — and we are certain that he will try to attack and victimize the Church as we approach the coming of the Lord. He knows that if he is going to do damage to the plan of God, this is his last opportunity and he must do this damage quickly.

It is emphatically clear that the early Church, just like the modern Church of the 1990s, had to contend with many demonic attacks.

But just as the early Church arose in the power of the Spirit to meet the challenge, so we — *equipped with "the whole armor of God"* — will also conquer the world around us and will live victoriously for Jesus Christ in these last days!

As the apostle John told us, "For whatsoever is born of God overcometh the world: and this is the victory that overcometh the world, *even our faith*" (First John 5:4).

The spiritual condition of the world cannot possibly be any worse today than it was back then. Have any of your friends been burned at the stake recently? Have you recently seen any of your Christian friends eaten alive by wild, hungry beasts? Have you been imprisoned for your faith?

Though spiritual opposition is as real today as it was then, it is not worse. This is the same lost world it has always been, and this lost world system is still ruled by the same "prince of the power of the air" that has always sought to dominate it, and our battles are the same battles that the Church has been fighting since its infancy.

Satan has always sought to destroy the Church through his army of invisible, wicked, lawless spirits. This is not new at all!

Because the devil did this in the past, it should be no great surprise if he *tried* to do this again in these last days. But remember, his early attack upon the Church miserably failed. The harder the devil hit the Church, the faster the Church of Jesus Christ grew and multiplied. If the devil does send forth a new army of innumerable wicked spirits against the Church in these last days as some have suggested, the Church will once again grow, thrive, multiply and overcome!

What About Witches?

The idea of witches and Satanists corporately uniting to cast curses on the people of God is not a new idea either.

In First Kings 18:17-40, the Bible tells us that four hundred prophets of Baal corporately assembled to release their demonically energized power against the prophet Elijah.

Though Elijah stood physically alone on Mount Carmel that day, he single-handedly confronted the prophets of Baal with the power of God and saw their total destruction. These Old Testament Baal worshippers were the equivalent of today's witches and Satanists. Yet, these Old Testament devil worshippers, who genuinely did possess strong satanic powers, did not prevail over the power of God.

In light of this, we joyfully declare that even if modern-day witches and Satanists tried to repeat this scenario again — regardless of how many of them show up to cast curses upon a specific local church, a specific ministry or the Body of Christ at large — like the prophets of Baal in the Old Testament, they, too, will miserably fail.

This very scenario occurred on October 31, 1990, when angry witches and Satanists came out of their closets in San Francisco to cast curses on the work of God. Yet, with all of those hundreds of witches and Satanists who came with spells, potions, incantations and demonic power, they did not even slightly affect the work of God!

They were wroth that Larry Lea and a large band of believers had gathered together to pray in the city of San Francisco. Moreover, they were violently mad that these believers were holding this huge prayer meeting on their unholy night — Halloween. Right on national news, with no shame whatsoever, they declared that they wanted these Christians out of their city.

In protest against these Christians, they came dressed in their traditional witch and Satanist clothing, carrying all kinds of occultic items, shouting obscenities, waving insulting signs, chanting spells, shrieking, and touting about blasphemous symbols of Jesus Christ. They even tried to physically block the buses that were bringing believers to the downtown auditorium to pray.

They minced no words about the reason they had gathered at the Civic Center Auditorium. These witches and Satanists had publicly assembled to cast curses on Larry Lea because he had called this prayer meeting.

There, on national news, witches and Satanists were nationally declaring war on the saints. To begin this assault, they proclaimed that they would destroy Larry Lea by casting curses on him, cursing him to die in the pulpit, cursing him to break his legs, cursing his ministry to fail, cursing his money to fail, and so on.

In addition to these witches and Satanists, a screaming crowd of more than 1,000 from the homosexual community of San Francisco joined in the fray and began openly assaulting believers as they entered the auditorium. At one point, the possibility of physical violence became so serious that dozens of police in riot gear were summoned to protect the Christians as they entered the building to pray.

With all of their planning and scheming, and with all of their incontestable diabolical assistance from Satan, none of these forces prevailed over the power of God or the people of God, *and they never will!*

Every world leader who has attempted to destroy the Church of Jesus Christ has himself been destroyed; and every dark period in the last 2,000 years of history has eventually succumbed and given way to the overwhelming, conquering light of Jesus Christ and His Church.

Though Satan has raged loudly like a ferocious beast on many occasions, he has never devoured the Church, and according to the Lord Jesus Christ, he never shall. In Matthew 16:18, in reference to the Church, Jesus said, ". . . and the gates of hell shall not prevail against it."

In regard to this casting of curses upon believers, Proverbs 26:2 declares, "As the bird by wandering, as the swallow by flying, so the curse causeless shall not come."

What does this mean?

This verse means that just like a bird that flies around, but never locates a nest — and just as a swallow migrates to another place when the season changes, a curse may flutter all around a believer, but it will not find a resting place there. In time, it will return to those who sent it.

Witches and Satanists can cast curses, use potions, incantations and magic spells until they are blue in the face, but their power will never prevail over the people of God or the power of God.

Biblical Spiritual Warfare

Though the Old Testament is replete with illustrations of spiritual warfare, such as the Battle of Jericho, Jehoshaphat and his singers, and David and Goliath, the words "war" or "warfare" only occur *five times* in the entire New Testament. That is pretty remarkable when you consider how much talk there is today about spiritual warfare.

These Old Testament true life stories of how God's army, Israel, defeated both physical adversaries and spiritual adversaries were written for our instruction and admonition. This is why Paul tells us, "Now all these things happened unto them for ensamples: and they are written for our admonition, upon whom the ends of the world are come" (First Corinthians 10:11).

Certainly it is true that by studying the battles of Old Testament Israel, we can ascertain much-needed revelation about conquering the invisible foes that come to attack and try to destroy the Church of Jesus Christ. However, since the terms "war" and "warfare" are used so often today, it is imperative for us to build a doctrinal understanding of how the words "war" and "warfare" were used in the New Testament.

Of the five times that the words "war" and "warfare," taken from the word *stratos*, are used in the New Testament, they are *never once* used in connection with the devil. For instance, both the terms "war" and "warfare" are used in Second Corinthians 10:3-5 to denote *mental bondages* that must be "pulled down."

While it is true that these bondages and strongholds in the mind may have first attached themselves to us in the past, when we were still under Satan's control, we must keep these verses in their proper context. *In context, these verses are about making an immovable decision to take charge of one's mind, and to take "thoughts" of the mind captive!*

The word "war" is used in First Timothy 1:18 in connection with a prophetic utterance that was spoken over Timothy. Paul commanded Timothy to remember the prophecies that had been spoken over him, that by them he might "war a good warfare."

The words "war" and "warfare" used in this verse were meant to admonish Timothy to stay in the fight of faith and to be faithful to the call of God on his life! *Once again, the words "war" and "warfare" in this verse have nothing to do with the devil!*

20

In Second Timothy 2:4, the word "warreth" is used once again. Paul says, "No man that warreth entangleth himself with the affairs of this life; that he may please him who hath chosen him to be a soldier."

The word "warreth" in this verse has nothing to do with the devil either! Rather, *Paul is exhorting Timothy to keep his life clear of clutter, to be single-minded and to stay committed to the call of God on his life regardless of the cost.*

Then in James 4:1, the word "war" is used again — this time to describe the flesh, not the devil. According to James, "spiritual warfare" is primarily about fighting *fleshly lusts* that come to destroy spiritual growth and development.

And in First Peter 2:11, Peter uses the word "war" in the same way to vividly describe "fleshly lusts that war against the soul." Therefore, once again the word "war" is used not to describe the activity of the devil, but rather, *it is used to describe the flesh's attempt to conquer and subdue the mind.*

In light of this, it is abundantly clear that the New Testament usage of the words "war" and "warfare" primarily has to do with conquering the flesh and taking charge of one's mind. Yes, the devil may attack the mind. . . . and he may attempt to energize the flesh to work against us. *However, if the mind and the flesh are kept under the control of the Holy Spirit, then the majority of spiritual warfare you will encounter in life, will already have been settled!*

How Real Warfare Begins

Most ministries who have fallen in recent times would not have fallen if they had not given some kind of place to the devil in their minds. Those who have fallen would be the very first to tell you that they left a door open for demonic attack somewhere along the way, by not dealing with some unseen, private area of their lives.

Demon spirits have absolutely no power to bring about destruction unless they can find an open door into a person's mind. If such an entrance into the mind can be located, then from this lofty position, evil influences and attacks can begin to be waged upon the individual.

The Holy Spirit is sure to convict us of these areas and to urge us to repent and change before the devil builds strongholds in our thinking. However, it is still up to us to see that these opened doors are slammed shut and forever closed.

If we ignore the Holy Spirit's pleading, and allow sin, willfully permitted temptation or wrong attitudes to continue unconfessed and unchanged, we are leaving gaping holes through which the enemy will seek to undo us. Most spiritual destruction is avoidable — if we will reverently listen to the pleading of the Spirit and obey His warnings to us.

Again, demon spirits cannot destroy without an open door into a person's soul — and such an entrance can only be given by way of permission!

Evil forces may try to buffet and hinder us, as they tried to buffet and hinder the apostle Paul (Second Corinthians 12:7; First Thessalonians 2:18), but they cannot destroy you or me without first having something already wrong in us that they can latch hold of and twist to our destruction.

The tendency of flesh has always been to blame personal failure on someone else, or on some external circumstance that was beyond our control. Remember, it was Adam (the natural father of us all) who shifted the blame for his own moral failure to Eve. Rather than acknowledge that he had committed sin when he ate freely of the forbidden fruit of the garden, Adam told God, "The woman whom thou gavest to be with me, she gave me of the tree, and I did eat" (Genesis 3:12). *Shifting blame is as old as the Garden of Eden.*

Likewise, it is an excuse to say, "The devil made me do it." You are shifting blame when you assert, "I failed because witches are praying against me." Furthermore, regardless of how many demon spirits have been assigned to destroy you, you must cooperate with their suggestions in order for temptation to overtake you and ruin your witness. *Ultimately, you are responsible.*

This means you cannot shift the blame to anyone else; you cannot even shift the blame for your failure to demonic attack. In order for that demonic attack to work effectively, you had to cooperate in some way; either through deliberate cooperation, or through negligence by refusing to deal with some unseen, private area of your life.

For instance, you can scream that the devil is after your money until you are blue in the face; but if you failed to balance your checkbook and were irresponsible in paying your bills, then you opened the door to that attack.

You can declare that the enemy is attempting to afflict you with sickness; but if you abuse your body by eating wrong, overworking, and pushing your body beyond its capabilities, then you have opened the door for your body to be attacked.

Similarly, you can cry out that your marriage is under attack; but if you speak harshly to your spouse, never spend any time with him or her, and have not made your marriage a priority in your life, then you have thrown open the door for the enemy to come and destroy your marriage.

And the list goes on and on. . .

Certainly there are genuine surprise attacks from the demonic realm that catch us off guard. Sometimes the devil really does attack our finances — especially if we are using our finances for the kingdom of God. It is absolutely true that at times the enemy comes to steal, kill and destroy a person's health. And it is similarly true that the enemy can come and try to orchestrate failure in a marriage.

In my own ministry the enemy has struck viciously to destroy from time to time. I know the reality of genuine demonic attack. These attacks have usually come at a critical point in our ministry when we were about to do something important in the kingdom of God — they were clear attempts to thwart the plan of God.

When my book, LIVING IN THE COMBAT ZONE, was about to be published, this ministry was thrust into a financial combat zone. In a matter of days, all of our income dried up. For some strange reason which we could not explain, no offerings came into the ministry and our partners stopped writing — our income just dried up.

The enemy knew God was going to use that book in a great way, and therefore, he wanted to stop it before it ever got into the hands of our readers. Obviously, his attack failed and the power of the cross prevailed!

Dealing With the Wind and the Waves in Your Life

Any time you are on the front lines of battle and are doing something significant for the kingdom of God, the enemy's attacks against your life will escalate. (For more on this, see pages 78-81.) Even Jesus came under such an attack when He was preparing to cast a legion of demons out of the demoniac of Gadara (Mark 4:35-41).

Violent and destructive winds seemed to come from out of nowhere to capsize Jesus' boat and drown Him and His disciples in the middle of the lake. The verse says, "And there arose a great storm of wind, and the waves beat into the ship, so that it was now full."

Notice that it says, "And *there arose. . . ."* The phrase "there arose" is taken from the Greek word *ginomai* (gi-no-mai). The word *ginomai* is used more than 200 times in the New Testament, and hence, its primary meaning is well documented. The word *ginomai* normally describes something that happens "unexpectedly" or something that catches one off guard.

For instance, the word *ginomai* is used in Acts 10:9,10 to describe how Peter received his vision concerning salvation becoming available for the Gentiles. It says, "On the morrow, as they were on their journey, and drew nigh unto the city, Peter went upon the housetop to pray about the sixth hour; and he became hungry, and would have eaten; but while they made ready, he *fell into* a trance."

Especially notice the words "fell into." This phrase is derived from the Greek word *ginomai*. The fact that Luke would use the word *ginomai* tells us that Peter did not expect this visitation to occur that afternoon; he was waiting on dinner, when suddenly — *unexpectedly* — he "slipped into" a trance. This was an encounter with God that caught him off guard.

When John tells us how he received the Book of Revelation, he also uses the word *ginomai*. John said, "*I was* in the spirit on the Lord's day."

The phrase "I was" is also taken from the word *ginomai*. Therefore, we know, from the usage of this word, that John was not expecting to have a visitation that day. Unexpectedly and taking him completely off guard, he looked up and found himself standing in the realm of the spirit.

Now this same word, which contains an element of surprise, is used in Mark 4:37 to plainly tell us that Jesus and His disciples did not expect bad weather that night — these winds took them "unexpectedly."

Many of Jesus' disciples were fishermen before they were called into the ministry and they knew the weather of the sea. Had a natural storm been brewing that night, these men would never have taken their little boat out into the middle of that sea. Therefore, you can be sure that when they began their journey that night, it was a perfect night for sailing.

When suddenly and unexpectedly "there arose" a great storm of wind. Notice that Mark tells us that it was "a great storm of wind." The word "great" is taken from the word *mega*, which denotes something of magnificent proportions. It is where we get the idea of *"megabills," "megawork," "megatired"* or the word *"megaphone."* By using this word, we know that this was a *"megastorm."*

And notice what kind of storm it was: it was "a great storm *of wind*. ..." Mark doesn't say that it was a thunderstorm, or a rainstorm; he tells us that it was "a great storm *of wind.*"

The word "wind" is taken from the word *lalaipsi* (la-lai-psi), and it describes a "turbulence" or a terribly "violent wind." Therefore, the storm which came against Jesus that night was an unseen storm; you could not see this storm, but you could feel the effects of it.

This was an attempt of the enemy to destroy Jesus and His crew before they reached the other side. On the other side, in the country of the Gadarenes, Satan had a prized possession: the demoniac of Gadara. The devil knew that if Jesus' ship reached the other side, he would lose his prized possession, and Jesus would work one of the greatest miracles of His ministry.

So when Jesus was on the edge of a breakthrough, when Jesus was on the brink of a major miracle, this unexpected attack of "violent and destructive turbulence" came down upon them to kill and destroy. The devil did not want Jesus to arrive at the country of the Gadarenes. *This was a preemptive strike of the devil to undo the work of God.*

This was a great opportunity for the disciples to learn that Jesus Christ is Lord of the wind and the waves! After exercising authority over this unseen turbulence and speaking to the waves of the sea, the Word says that "the wind ceased, and there was a great calm" (Mark 4:39).

Like so often happens, this attack came right when Jesus was on the brink of a major miracle. This is normally when genuine demonic attacks occur. If such attacks came against Jesus, then we can be sure that the enemy will attempt to do this to us as well. Therefore, we must mentally and spiritually prepare ourselves to deal with demonic attacks; we must "put on the whole armor of God" and take authority over the wind and the waves that come against our lives, our families, our businesses or our bodies — just like Jesus took authority over the wind and the waves that came against Him.

If you have come under such an attack — and you really know that you have been diligent to cover all of your bases by heeding the pleading of the Holy Spirit in various areas of your life — and if, to the best of your knowledge, you have left no doors open for an attack — then you, like the Lord Jesus Christ, must rise to take authority over the wind and the waves. This is your golden opportunity to see a demonstration of God's power in your life.

Let me also point out that when the wind and the waves ceased that night, the Word says that "there was a great calm." Verse 37 previously told us that this storm had been a "great storm." When everything was said and done, Jesus matched a *great storm* with a *great calm!*

If the enemy has created a great financial problem in your life, then Jesus Christ wants to match it with a great financial blessing. If the adversary has created a great sickness in your body, then Jesus Christ wants to match it with a great healing. If the devil has created a horrible marital mess in your life, then the Lord Jesus Christ wants at least to match it with a great marital blessing. *Whatever the devil does, Jesus Christ wants at least to match it in your life!*

However, we must be honest with ourselves when it comes to these attacks: the majority of battles that we fight in life do not fall into this category of "surprise attacks." *Most battles are fought because a Christian soldier was unfaithful to heed the Holy Spirit's warnings to deal with some area of his or her life before it got out of control.*

Spiritual Warfare: A Mental Condition

Spiritual warfare is not a momentary gust of emotion to frighten the devil away in a few moments of time. Quite the opposite! Real spiritual warfare is a mental condition and a life-long commitment; *it is not so much an action as it is a determined and committed attitude of the mind.*

The apostle Paul understood that spiritual warfare was an attitude and a life-long commitment. After being outwardly buffeted by demonic forces who had come against his ministry, Paul prayed three times and asked the Lord to remove this "messenger of Satan" that had been sent to "buffet him" (Second Corinthians 12:7), and to keep him from moving into higher realms of revelation.

Yet, the buffeting was never removed. In response to Paul's request to rid him of this buffeting, the Lord answered him by saying, "My grace is sufficient for thee" (Second Corinthians 12:9).

Why did God answer Paul in this way?

Paul had made a request which was *unrealistic*. As long as Paul was effective for God and was doing damage to the realm of darkness, he was going to be opposed by demonic forces. Rather than offer Paul false promises that he could achieve a life free from opposition, the Lord promised instead to give him the grace and power he needed to conquer each of these attacks as they came.

Though Paul's outward circumstances were a constant challenge, and though invisible, spiritual opposition stirred up horrible community hatred toward him everywhere he went, and though the government of the day stood in his way and sought to block the gospel message, he was never destroyed by any of these outward attacks.

Paul himself said, "We are troubled on every side, yet not distressed; we are perplexed, but not in despair; persecuted, but not forsaken; cast down, but not destroyed" (Second Corinthians 4:8-9).

From his own personal testimony in Second Corinthians 11:24-28, we know that his outward opposition had been intense. In verse 24, he tells us, "Of the Jews five times received I forty stripes save one."

As if this was not enough for Paul to endure, in verse 25 he continues, "Thrice was I beaten with rods, once was I stoned, thrice I suffered shipwreck, a night and a day have I been in the deep. . . ."

Without going into great detail about all of these different persecutions now, we know from these particular methods of persecution that Paul underwent, that his feet had been beaten with rods on three different occasions, his head had been crushed at least once, he had been on three separate shipwrecks, and at some point in his ministry, he spent a night and a day in the deep, a whole twenty-four hours treading water in order to stay alive (for more details on these methods of persecution that were used against Paul, see pages 36-43, LIVING IN THE COMBAT ZONE).

After mentioning these extremely harsh afflictions, he continues to speak more generally about other, lesser afflictions he has endured.

He says, "In journeyings often, in perils of waters, in perils of robbers, in perils of mine own countrymen, in perils by the heathen, in perils in the city, in perils in the wilderness, in perils in the sea, in perils among false brethren, in weariness and painfulness, in watchings often, in hunger and thirst, in fastings often, in cold and in nakedness" (Second Corinthians 11:26,27).

Yet, with all of these challenges and oppositions — and with all of his mental fatigue and physical exhaustion — Paul never fell into any kind of immorality or any type of moral failure.

He never rationalized failure by saying, *"I failed because demons were assigned to destroy me."* Or, *"I failed because witches were meeting in covens and were casting curses on me."* Paul never said, *"The devil trapped me, and made me do this!"*

Similarly, many of the tragedies that occur, occur because of anger, bitterness, wrath, or sometimes through pure slothfulness. It is true that the devil can also strike a believer who is walking in faith and who is walking in the spirit. These "sneak attacks" are real. As I stated before, as long as we seek to do God's will and to obey God's Word, the devil will try to thwart the plan which God desires to accomplish through us. But once again, the majority of such attacks and tragedies occur because of some *omission* on the part of a believer.

Surprise attacks from the demonic realm would not find success if our shield of faith was in place to protect us, and ricochet these attacks back to where they were sent from.

Demon spirits cannot destroy a person unless there is something already in that person that they can grab hold of and twist to their destruction. There were no such places in Paul's life. Though he was outwardly buffeted, he was never attacked to the point of personal failure.

Therefore, Paul's personal consecration to the Lord was his greatest defense against the enemy. This personal holiness paralyzed the devil's ability to make him fail morally; there was nothing in Paul that the devil could use to destroy him. Because he lived the crucified life, he was dead to sin; *nothing in him cooperated with the devil's devices and temptations.*

If not entirely impossible, it is very difficult for the devil to completely destroy a person who lives a sanctified and consecrated life. Most attacks would be totally avoided if sin and wrong attitudes were not permitted to have a place in us.

Spiritual warfare is not a momentary gust of emotion to frighten the devil away in a few moments of time. Before all else, genuine spiritual warfare is a mental condition and a lifelong commitment; *it is not so much an action as it is an attitude of the mind.*

A Warning About Spiritual Warfare

Because of the mindless approach to spiritual warfare that some have taken in recent days, many of our older and more seasoned respectable Spirit-filled leaders — *who truly understand that there is a real spiritual adversary to be opposed with genuine spiritual weapons* — have begun urging the Body of Christ to come back into a proper balance on this issue of spiritual warfare.

Spiritual warfare is most definitely a reality which we must all learn to face at some point in our lives. *The devil, himself a very cunning, wise strategist, would love to sidetrack us from doing him real damage by leading us off into silly spiritual voodoo tactics, weird noises, violent screaming that in reality hurts no one (except our own throats) and other extremely unfounded, unscriptural, so-called "spiritual warfare" nonsense.*

People tend to flock to these weird teachings by the droves because they offer relatively simple solutions to difficult, life-long problems.

Sticking to the Word of God and applying its principles to our lives may seem to take longer; the Word of God requires one to live a crucified life; it demands one to repent from a wrong thought life; and insists that one seek to conform to the image of Jesus Christ.

Therefore, the thought of an instant cure is very alluring to the uncommitted and spiritually immature who are looking for a quick-fix to change their deeply rooted, habitual, and often self-imposed problems.

Again, no one — including this author — would doubt the reality of *genuine spiritual warfare.* We have all come face to face with the enemy at some point in our lives, and we can be certain that we shall face him again at some point in the future.

As long as we seek to live in God's will and to obey His Word for our lives, the devil will do his best to oppose and thwart the plan which God wishes to accomplish through us.

It is for this cause that God has given us a complete set of spiritual armor. We will begin studying, verse-by-verse and word-by-word, what the Bible says about spiritual armor when we come to chapters ten through sixteen in this book. With this powerful set of armor in position, you are ready for the fight. With this weaponry at your disposal, you are **"Dressed To Kill!"**

Chapter Two
Fleshly Weapons Opposed to Spiritual Weapons

L et me say right from the start of this chapter that some people will love this chapter, and others will despise it. Yet, because of the various kinds of teachings on spiritual warfare that are being circulated throughout the nation today, I am compelled by the Holy Spirit to include this chapter.

Instead of magnifying the victorious work of Jesus Christ over Satan and our deliverance from Satan's power, much of what is taught today implies that the work of the cross is unfinished — that the blood saved us, but it did not really free us completely from Satan's power. Though this may not be the intent of some of those who teach on spiritual warfare, it is often the message that is perceived.

The fruit of this is a new form of spiritualized legalism. In other words, what Jesus Christ did was not enough by itself; therefore, you must now do additional "things" in order to gain additional freedom from the devil's control. In reality, this is the equivalent of trading one form of bondage for another — and the second bondage is much more dangerous, for it comes in the guise of spirituality, and at least at first, it is very difficult to discern.

In regard to such man-made fleshly weapons and fleshly techniques, Paul said, "For though we walk in the flesh, we do not war after the flesh: for the weapons of our warfare are not carnal, but mighty through God to the pulling down of strongholds" (Second Corinthians 10:3,4).

Notice Paul says, "For though we walk in the flesh. . . ." The word "walk" is taken from the word *peripateo* (pe-ri-pa-teo), and it is a compound of the words *peri* (pe-ri) and *pateo* (pa-teo). The word *peri* means "around" and the word *pateo* means "to walk." When the two words are compounded together (*peripateo*), it simply means "to walk around" or "to habitually live and carry on in one general vicinity."

By using the word *peripateo*, Paul is making a very strong message about his humanity. The idea is, *"Nearly everything I do, I do in the flesh. . . I eat in the flesh, I recreate in the flesh, I sleep in the flesh, I think in the flesh, I study in the flesh. . . nearly everything I do, I do in this realm of flesh. My life primarily consists in this earthly realm."*

As a matter of fact, the Greek tense used here is *the locative sphere of influence*. This is extremely important! Quite literally, this meant that Paul knew he was "locked into" his fleshly body and he could not get out of it, and neither could he trade it for another! He was "body-bound." This state of being "body-bound" would never change until death, when his carnal, natural body would be gloriously transformed into a spiritual body!

The very fact that Paul said "we do not war according to the flesh" tells us that Paul was aware of the weakness and futility of his own natural man. He knew there was no hope of accomplishing anything good through his carnal man; therefore, he turned toward the spirit realm, where supernatural assistance was available.

Bloodthirsty, Daring and Committed Men of War

He continues to tell us that there is one thing he does not do with his carnal, fleshly, natural body. He continues, ". . .we do not *war* according to the flesh."

The word "war" is taken from the word *strateomenos* (stra-teo-me-nos), and it refers to the "militant attitude of a trained soldier." It was particularly used to denote the committed attitude of a heavily dressed, trained-to-kill Roman soldier.

There is no doubt that Roman soldiers were the finest military machines of their day. These men were the finest soldiers in the history of the world. These men were trained killers. In fact, they were so thoroughly trained in the act of murder and mutilation, that it became instinct to them. They were professionals in the weapons of war, and they knew how to use those weapons against adversaries very effectively. You might say that Roman soldiers had *a taste for blood.*

Furthermore, especially good soldiers requested to be placed on the front lines of battle. Their insatiable desire to draw the blood of their adversary was so ingrained into their disposition, that they were not content to wage war from behind where there was only minimal action taking place. An especially good soldier would request to be placed out on the front lines of battle, so that he might see the enemy first, and have *the first opportunity to strike.*

Extremely brave soldiers frequently volunteered to go on dangerous missions that others did not want to undertake. The idea of penetrating an enemy's camp, and the notion of invading dangerous foreign soil, was a thrilling prospect to these special types of soldiers. *They were bloodthirsty, daring and committed men of war.*

All of these graphic images are conveyed in the word "war" that Paul now uses in Second Corinthians 10:3. Therefore, when Paul says, "we do not war according to the flesh," he is making several powerful statements to the Church.

First, he tells us that, spiritually speaking, his own mental attitude is much like that of a Roman soldier: he is so committed to see victory, that he wants to draw the enemy's blood himself; furthermore, he wants to be placed out on the front lines of battle so that he will have the opportunity to strike first; and he is so spiritually brave, that he is willing to go where no other soldier will go!

This is one of the reasons that Paul declared he wanted "to preach the gospel in the regions beyond. . ." (Second Corinthians 10:16). His desire was to go and minister in places where no other men would go! This is the reason that

he was willing to go into cities like Ephesus and Corinth —
these cities were citadels of sensuality and demonic activity.
Paul was a front-line soldier of the Lord.

But he tells us something else that is also very important
in this verse. In addition to possessing this committed and
determined mental attitude and resolve, he says, "we do not
war *according to the flesh.*"

Remember, Paul was an educated and impressive man
— *naturally speaking!* Yet, when it came to dealing the enemy
a blow, he knew that his intelligence and his education did
not count. *The flesh, regardless of how impressive it looked, or how
loud it roared, would be no match for a spiritual foe.* Fleshly
weapons simply are not suited to fight spiritual adversaries,
and they never will be!

Spiritual Weapons and Spiritual Strategies

Paul continues to say, "For the weapons of our warfare
are not carnal, but are mighty through God to the pulling
down of strongholds."

Pay special heed to the words "weapons," "warfare,"
and the word "carnal" in this all-important verse about spiritual warfare.

In the first place, Paul tells us that we *do* have weapons
at our disposal — they are *spiritual weapons.* These weapons,
both offensive and defensive, can be found in Ephesians 6:13-
18. (We will thoroughly cover these weapons in chapters ten
through seventeen of this book.)

Second, notice that Paul goes on to say, "For the
weapons of our *warfare. . . ."* The word "warfare" is another
major key to defeating the attacks of the enemy.

The word "warfare" is taken from the word *stratos* (stratos), and it is where we get the word "strategy." By choosing
to use this word, the Holy Spirit has told us some very important things about spiritual warfare.

In the first place, the word *stratos* (which means "strategy") tells us that in order for spiritual weapons to work effec-

tively, they must be accompanied with a divine "strategy" on how to use them. To have weapons, but no battle plan, will assure you of defeat.

This, in fact, is the primary reason that most believers do not experience victory in their personal lives. It isn't that they do not have the proper weaponry — *they do!* But they do not have a "strategy" on how to attack, and hence, their weapons are to no avail.

Having weapons, but no strategy, always spells failure. Imagine an army that is fully equipped with weapons of warfare, but has no "strategy" about how to use those weapons against the enemy. Even with all of those weapons and artillery at their disposal, this kind of an army will utterly fail.

Likewise, many believers boast of having "the whole armor of God," but have no idea how the "armor" should be used practically and experientially in their lives. Until God speaks, direction is clearly given, and a battle plan is conceived in the heart, these weapons will do little to drive back the forces of hell that have come against you.

Just as God has graciously dressed you in spiritual armor when you were born again, He now wants to graciously give you a "strategy" on how to pull the devil's lies and deceptions down from your *mind* so that they will control you no more.

In order for you to receive this "strategy," you must hear from the Spirit of God. This mandates that you spend time praying in the Spirit, reading the Word and seeking the mind of God. By yourself, you will never conceive a plan that will deliver you.

When strongholds are rooted into the mind, they are rooted deeply. Only the Holy Spirit can give you a "strategy" on how to pull them down. He will show you how to use those God-given weapons, and He will show you when and what to attack!

The Futility of the Flesh

Then we come to the next point in this verse. Paul continues, "For the weapons of our warfare *are not carnal* . . . ."

The word "carnal" is taken from the word *sarkos* (sarkos), which is the Greek word for "flesh." By electing to use this word, Paul tells us that real spiritual weapons do not come from the flesh realm. As a matter of fact, Paul takes a hard stand on this subject. *He emphatically declares that spiritual weapons have absolutely nothing to do with the flesh or the activity of the flesh.*

Though Paul lived, functioned and walked in the flesh, just like we do today, he did not fall back upon the flesh or fleshly techniques when it came to defeating spiritual adversaries. In order to reinforce the victory which Jesus won at the cross and the resurrection, it would require that Paul move in spiritual weapons. *Flesh can fight flesh, but flesh is no match for the spiritual realm.*

Even though Paul was extremely educated, his education was no match for the devil; neither was his marvelous and genius mind a match for the devil; his notoriety as a well-known Christian leader did not scare or impress the devil; his manner of speech and his vocal style of preaching were not wonderful enough to rid him of the devil's assaults. *Regardless of how good the flesh looks, or how loud the flesh roars, it was never intended to fight a spiritual foe.*

Thus, the reason that God has so graciously given us spiritual weapons such as "the loinbelt of truth," "the breastplate of righteousness," "the shoes of peace," "the shield of faith," "the helmet of salvation," "the sword of the Spirit," and "the lance of intercession!" Without these, we stand naked and defenseless before the adversary.

Weak and Silly Weapons of Flesh

Yet, there are many believers today who are using outward, physical, bodily, fleshly techniques in their attempt to defeat the work of the adversary in their lives and to do so-called "spiritual warfare."

These outward, physical, bodily, fleshly techniques are not what struggling believers need! These will eventually become a new form of legalism in their lives — which means in addition to fighting real strongholds which the devil has sown in their minds, they will also have to fight with the feelings of condemnation for not gaining victory through the so-called techniques that have been taught to them!

Rather than rest in the "redemptive" work of Jesus Christ and use the weapons that are provided in scripture (Ephesians 6:13-18), they move over into a mode of "spiritual warfare" that is totally foreign to any teaching of the New Testament, where they must do additional "things" in order to free themselves from the devil's control.

This new legalism of doing so-called "spiritual things" in order to obtain freedom, has painfully come to the forefront of many Spirit-filled groups in recent years. I feel this tragedy deeply in my heart, for I, too, am a Spirit-filled believer and am primarily called of God to minister to such like-minded people. Therefore, when I see sincere people swallowed up in works of the flesh, that in reality add nothing to their freedom, it grieves me deeply.

Yet, there are many believers today who are using fleshly weapons and techniques to do so-called "spiritual warfare."

I cannot help but sorrow for those dear Spirit-filled believers who are constantly, habitually trying to set themselves free from demon possession when Jesus Christ has already set them free. . .

I feel so sorry for that group of Christians who in recent years have revived an old Gnostic error which teaches they must deliver themselves from demonic control by deliberately making themselves vomit continually, week after week. . . as though vomiting alone would somehow remove demonic powers.

And it is saddening to see so many physically abusing their bodies and hurting their throats with the new teaching that is gaining acceptance today, called "warring tongues."

"What are warring tongues?"

Some think that by screaming, screeching, and violently praying in throat-ripping, loud prayer, they exert more power against the devil. Some even teach that if you pray quietly, then you might as well find something better to do with your time. In their distorted view, prayer exerts no spiritual power unless it is done loudly and is ear-deafening. Somehow they believe their authority is attached to the volume of their voice.

When dealing with the devil, the issue is not the sound level or volume of your voice. The devil is not afraid of noise. Remember, he has created all kinds of horrendous, loud, screaming music during our time. Noise obviously does not bother the devil.

A policeman doesn't yell and scream to stop a crime; he simply pulls out his gun and waves it in front of the offender. There is no need for the policeman to scream, yell and holler — all the screaming in the world wouldn't stop the offender. That officer's gun, on the other hand, carries great authority. With that gun in hand, he can whisper to the offender and the offender will gladly obey.

Likewise, it is the authority of one's spirit that causes the devil to obey. If you know who you are in Jesus Christ, and know how to use that Christ-imparted authority against him, you can whisper ever so faintly to the devil and he will flee. *The issue is not the sound level or volume of your voice, but the authority contained in your spirit.*

The whole idea of screaming violently in tongues is that, because the heavenlies are full of demonic powers, and because we are physically under that dark, demonic cloud, we must therefore attempt to pierce the heavenlies with our loud, screaming noises and try to break our way through that hellish barrier.

Therefore, sincere brothers and sisters are led to believe they must "scream violently in tongues at the devil" for hours on end, day after day, week after week in order to gain freedom for their personal lives.

Having heard of these meetings, I personally attended one some time ago. After hearing the message that night, I could hardly believe my ears. For a whole hour the speaker instructed the people how to yell, scream, "go into weepings" (self-imposed crying) and "go into purgings" (self-imposed vomiting). My heart ached to hear what sincere believers were doing in the name of the Holy Spirit, and to hear what they thought was genuine spiritual warfare.

I have no question as to the sincerity of these fellow believers, or of their true desire to defeat the work of the devil in their personal lives and in the lives of others. Their zeal is admirable, but these actions are not "according to knowledge" (Romans 10:2). These methods are not scripturally based.

Never once does the Bible teach that tongues are to be used against the devil — and the scripture absolutely must be the foundation of all we believe, teach and do.

What does the Bible say about the purpose of tongues?

Paul said, "He that speaketh in an unknown tongue speaketh not unto men, *but unto God. . .*" (First Corinthians 14:2). Notice that when Paul writes about praying in tongues, he makes no mention at all about the devil.

Likewise, First Corinthians 14:2 says the purpose of praying in tongues is not to speak to the devil, but on the contrary, *to speak mysteries unto God!* The end result of praying in tongues is for personal, faith-building edification. Paul said, "He that speaketh in an unknown tongue *edifieth himself*" (First Corinthians 14:4).

By praying in the spirit your faith may be built up so that you can stand against the devil's schemes when necessary. But praying in tongues was never meant to be something which we speak "at the devil" as many espouse today.

There is no scripture for this. Therefore, this popular teaching has no basis in scripture and those who teach it are *wrong*.

If we do choose to pray loudly, let us clarify "why" we are praying loudly. If we pray loudly, it is not because we are not "warring" with the devil, but on the contrary, we are warring with the flesh; trying to break through the strong lusts and desires of the flesh so God can have His way, and speak to our spirits and bring us divine revelation.

This is another deliberate attempt of the adversary to enslave Spirit-filled believers in spiritual nonsense, and to drag them into legalism — where they will never be able to do enough to satisfy or to bring them the freedom they desire. It is only a matter of time before they must do something else, then something else, something else, and then something else in order to procure more freedom. There is no end to where legalism will take people.

One dear brother whom I knew personally became a victim of such works of the flesh. He became involved in such an off-base "spiritual warfare" group. He was attracted to them because of their great zeal. It wasn't long until he had swapped the joy of his salvation for a life of spiritual bondage.

It didn't matter how much he did, it was never enough. If he prayed for hours on end, *it wasn't enough*. If he screamed like the others did, even until he lost his voice, *he didn't scream long enough*. If he induced vomiting to rid himself of demon spirits like others in his group, *he never seemed to rid himself of them all*. There was always more to do, do, do, and do. Enough is never enough with legalism.

In the end, he despaired of it all completely and ended up shattered and broken, feeling that he could never do enough to gain complete freedom in Jesus Christ.

All of these are merely new doctrines and teachings of men, which are not based on scripture, that try to add unto the already completed, redemptive work of Jesus Christ as though it were not enough. Paul correctly asked the Galatians, *"Are ye so foolish? Having begun in the Spirit, are ye now made perfect by the flesh?"* (Galatians 3:3).

Touch Not, Taste Not, Handle Not

Legalism, adding our own works to the already completed, perfect work of Christ, was trying to attach itself to the Church in the region of Galatia. Knowing that legalism was a killer that eventually sapped spiritual strength and joy out of people, Paul commanded the Galatians, "Stand fast therefore in the liberty wherewith Christ hath made you free, and be not entangled again with the yoke of bondage" (Galatians 5:1).

The Galatians were being tempted to go back under the Old Testament law. After receiving Jesus Christ and the promise of the Spirit *freely*, erroneous teaching was now coaxing them back into Old Testament rules and regulations from which they had been delivered.

Their thinking was, "Yes, we received Jesus Christ *freely*, but now in order to maintain and keep that salvation which we *freely* received, we must do our part to 'keep' our salvation. Therefore, we must place ourselves back under Old Testament law to keep its rules and regulations."

For similar reasons Paul wrote the Colossian Church, and told them, "Let no man, therefore, judge you in meat, or in drink, or in respect of an holy day, or of the new moon, or of the sabbath days. . . if ye be dead with Christ to the rudiments of the world, why, as though living in the world, are ye subject to ordinances, (Touch not; taste not; handle not; which all are to perish with the using); after the commandments and doctrines of men?" (Colossians 2:16,20-22).

Then Paul continues, "Which things have indeed a shew of wisdom in will-worship, and humility, and neglecting of the body: not in any honour to the satisfying of the flesh" (Colossians 2:23).

These outward things do indeed have an outward shew of self-abasement, humility and hardness on the flesh. The religious nature of man loves this! He wants to believe he can by his own work and merit, somehow attain a perfection that makes himself acceptable to God.

This is precisely why far eastern religions such as Buddhism and Hinduism require its adherents to live a life of self-denial, abasement and humility. It is a disguised pride of the flesh that says, "I can do this on my own. Thanks for your help, God, but I can also help out in this."

This same religious nature tries to attach itself to Spirit-filled believers, too. The old flesh nature says, "Let me do something to merit my freedom!" "Christ's work alone surely cannot be enough!" "Let me scream for my freedom!" "Let me purge myself of demon spirits!" *"Let me. . ." "Let me. . ." "Let me. . ." "Let me. . ."*

To this we must answer, "Not by works of righteousness which we have done, *but according to his mercy he saved us!"* (Titus 3:5).

We can add absolutely nothing to what Jesus did at the cross of Calvary. It was a total, perfect and completed work! And in that glorious work of redemption (we will cover Jesus' work of "redemption" in chapter three), He also purchased our complete and total deliverance from the powers of the evil one!

In Hebrews 2:3, the writer of Hebrews declares that our salvation is a "great salvation." How "great" is this salvation if Satan's power still controls us? How "great" is this salvation if we are still under his heavy hand and must fight our way out from under him from day to day? How "great" is this salvation if we must scream, yell, and vomit in order to maintain it? I trust that you see how utterly ridiculous the work of the flesh really is!

If it is true that we must do all these outward, fleshly, physical things, it would seem that Jesus' death and resurrection did not really effect a permanent change in the spirit realm, and that our salvation is not so "great" after all. How "great" can a salvation be that doesn't completely and thoroughly deliver?

The good news is, our salvation is a "great salvation!"

By His work at the cross and victorious resurrection from the dead, Jesus Christ completely broke the dominion of Satan and the bondage of sin over us — and in the New Birth He released all of His creative powers in us as we passed from the realm of death over into the realm of life (First John 3:14).

Our goal in life now is not to fight for our deliverance, but rather, our goal in life now is to freely accept our deliverance which has already been procured for us. In fact, scripture commands us to cease from our own works and "to enter into that rest" (Hebrews 4:11) where we may enjoy the wonderful provision that God has made available on our behalf. Entering into that "rest" is what the faith walk is all about — that is, learning to accept and rest in Jesus' finished "redemptive" work!

To enable us to enjoy our salvation and its benefits (healing, soundness of mind, preservation of mind and deliverance from bondages), God has graciously supplied us with faith to believe, and He has given us the Word of God to enlighten us to our inheritance by virtue of the cross.

If Satan does try to wage warfare upon us after the New Birth, and if he tries to afflict us with past bondages, afflictions, poverty, or any other kind of demonic weapon — we have been given divinely empowered weapons to resist these attacks and maintain the blessings of our salvation.

These spiritual weapons are not fleshly weapons like many are trying to use today. On the contrary, they are of spiritual substance, and according to the apostle Paul, they are "mighty through God to the pulling down of strongholds" (Second Corinthians 10:4).

Chapter Three
Resting in Our Redemption

Before we begin studying what the Bible has to say about spiritual armor in Ephesians 6:10-18, first we must back up for a moment and see what the Bible has to say about "redemption." A correct view of "redemption" will clear up many wrong ideas about the devil and spiritual warfare.

There are four different words for "redemption" in the Greek New Testament. All four of these words are extremely important for us to understand as we approach the issue of *spiritual warfare*. The four Greek words that are used throughout the New Testament to denote "redemption" are: *agoridzo*, *exagoridzo*, *lutroo*, and *apolutrosis*.

Agoridzo (a-go-rid-zo), the first of these four words, was a technical term that was used to describe "the marketplace." It was most frequently used to specifically describe "the slave market."

The "slave market" was a dreadful and deplorable place. Such places should have never been permitted. Human beings were paraded in front of potential buyers, and were then placed on the trading block where they were auctioned off like an animal, an old piece of furniture, or an unwanted hunk of junk.

Before this nauseating buying, selling and trading of human debris began, potential buyers were allowed to check out the "merchandise." The slaves' heads were shoved up and backward, their mouths were forcibly jerked open, and their teeth were inspected to see if they were rotten or if they were in fairly good shape. Their value was determined primarily by the condition of their teeth. If they had good teeth, they were probably in good shape and, therefore, more expensive. If their teeth were rotten, then they probably could have been bought pretty cheap.

As if this was wasn't inhumane and degrading enough, slave-buying customers were encouraged to kick and hit the "merchandise" in order to find out what kind of physical shape the slave was in.

To discover what the slave's temperament was, buyers spat in their faces, and slapped them and cursed at them. If a slave could swallow his pride, grit his teeth and hold his temper during such humiliating abuse, then it was assumed that this slave could be used to the point of abuse without giving his owner any kind of trouble.

In short, slaves had no personal worth. They were viewed to be no better than animals. According to the thinking of the day, they were just another kind of workhorse and had no real human value. Their only purpose in the world was to serve the demands that their current owners exacted of them.

By using the word *agoridzo* to describe "redemption," the Holy Spirit has told us something extremely important.

Satan's Slave Market

When Jesus Christ came into the world, the world had become an utterly deplorable place.

The beautiful paradise which God had originally created in Eden was gone, and not even a hint of it remained. In its place, the world had become a global "slave market" where Satan had gripped the hearts of men and filled their natures with violence and destruction. With each successive generation after Adam, spiritual death took people of all nations, tribes and ethnic groups deeper and deeper into slavery and total depravity.

Therefore, the world that Jesus Christ was born into nearly 2,000 years ago was a world of complete captivity.

Through Adam's disobedience, this spiritual death had seized the nature of all mankind. As Paul said, "Wherefore, as by one man sin entered into the world, and death by sin; and so death passed upon all men, for that all have sinned" (Romans 5:12).

By using the word *agoridzo,* we unmistakably know that when Jesus Christ first came to the earth, he came into a disgusting, nauseating spiritual "slave market" where human beings were "slaves" to Satan and to the negative effects of sin.

Our bondage at that time was so complete that Paul states we were "sold under sin" (Romans 7:14). The word "sold" is from the Greek word *piprasko* (pi-pra-sko), and it literally describes a "transfer of property." By using this word, Paul clearly tells us that mankind had been transferred from the hands of God into the hands of a new owner. This, of course, is the picture of Satan's total ownership of us before Jesus Christ came into our lives.

Like slaves in the "slave market," the devil slapped our lives around, hit us, kicked us, spat upon us and abused us. He tried to damage our self-images, kill our bodies with various kinds of sin and vices, and tried to mar us emotionally. When one form of bondage and death was finished with us, we were placed on the trading block to be auctioned off again. Soon, another form of bondage took us and began to make its new destructive mark on our lives.

We were passed from one bondage to the next, to the next and to the next. Each day we lived, this hellish ownership took us further downward into deeper captivity. Lock, stock and barrel, inside out, from beginning to end, head to toe, backward and forward, every inch, and up to the brim, our lives — whether we were aware of it or not — according to scripture, were sinking deeper into the captivity of sin and total depravity.

The Bible says this was our condition before the grace of God touched our lives. This is the very reason that Paul repeatedly tells us in scripture that we were previously "the servants of sin. . . ." (Romans 6:17, 20).

The word "servant" is taken from the word *doulos* (dou-los), which is the most abject term for a slave in the Greek language. One expositor has explained that the word *doulos* describes "one whose will is completely swallowed up in the will of another."

This means that prior to our salvation experience, we were "swallowed up" in the will of Satan. Though we intellectually thought we were in charge of our lives, and though we thought we were calling the shots, in reality, we were abject slaves to sin and our destinies were being temporarily mastered by an unseen, diabolical spirit who wanted to destroy us.

Our prior slavery to Satan was so deep-seated that our nature became intrinsically meshed together with the seed of rebellion, which is at the very core of Satan's nature. Rebellion against God ran deep in our blood and became ingrained into our human disposition. Eventually the gulf between God and man became so vast, that scripture declares we became "alienated and enemies" in our minds through wicked works (Colossians 1:21).

This pervading demonic presence in our lives and in the world around us was so absolute and supreme, that Paul continues to say, "Wherein in time past ye walked according to the course of this world, according to the prince of the power of the air, the spirit that now worketh in the children of disobedience" (Ephesians 2:2).

Short-Sighted, Temporal-Minded People

Paul says, "Wherein in time past ye walked *according to the course of this world*. . . ."

The phrase *"according to. . ."* is taken from the word *kata* (ka-ta). The word *kata* portrays something that is "forceful" or "dominating."

By choosing to use this word, Paul tells us that before we met the Lord, we were completely "dominated" and "manipulated" by "the course of this world." We were not only *influ-enced* by "the course of this world"; the word *kata* emphatical-ly means we were "dominated" and "manipulated" and com-pletely "controlled" by it.

What Is "the Course of This World?"

The word "course" is taken from the Greek word *aiona* (ai-o-na). This is a simple word that describes a "specific, alloted period of time" like an "age," a specific "era" or a "generation." For instance, the decades of this century (such as the 1940s, 1950s, 1960s, 1970s and 1980s) are technically an *aiona* — a "specific, alloted period of time." You could say that this word denotes the influence of one particular gener-ation, and then the next, the next and the next. It denotes a short-lived period of time.

But there is still more to this! The word *aiona* signifies not only a time period, but also the *spirit* of that period. For instance, the spirit of the 1920s was typified as the "roaring twenties." With the advent of rock-n-roll, the 1950s was typ-ified as a "rebellious period." The spirit of the 1960s and 1970s, because of drugs and war, was typified as a time of "experimentation and questioning of the status quo." Each of these individual decades (*aiona*) had a flavor of their own that was unique to their particular time and place in history.

So when Paul declares that we "walked according to the course of this world," the word "course" conveys the idea of being dominated by the popular thinking of our own partic-ular time and generation. Philosophies and ideas come and go very quickly. A lost man or woman, because they have no eternal perspective and no constant Biblical standard to live by, are dominated entirely by these *fluctuating philosophies* and *ideas*.

The word "world" is from the Greek word *kosmos* (kos-mos), and Paul uses the word *kosmos* to convey the ideas of "order" and "arrangement." Scientists use *kosmos* to describe the universe; because the universe, though huge, diverse and ever-expanding, is a perfectly ordered and arranged system.

Thus, they say it is a *kosmos*. The word *kosmos* always describes "order" or "arrangement."

Kosmos was also used during the early Greek period to describe *society* — society, at least in a measure, is a system that possesses "order" and "arrangement." When *kosmos* is used to depict society, it also carries with it the idea of *fashion* and *sophistication* — and this is exactly the idea that Paul presents in Ephesians 2:2.

Before we met the Lord, we were so short-sighted and temporal minded, that scripture says we were totally dominated, manipulated and mastered by the day, hour and society in which we lived.

You could paraphrase the verse, *"you walked around completely dominated by the whim of the times. . . ."* Or you could translate it, *"you walked around controlled by the fashion of the day and the thinking of the hour. . . ."*

Who's Working Behind the Scenes?

Paul isn't finished yet! He goes on to say that we *"walked according to the prince of the power of the air. . . ."*

Now Paul tells us *who* is manipulating the lost world system that is manipulating and controlling lost men and women! In addition to being controlled by the society and world in which we lived, Paul adds that we also formerly *"walked according to the prince of the power of the air. . . ."*

The phrase "according to" is once again taken from the word *kata*, the same Greek word that has already been used once in this verse to convey the ideas of "domination" or "manipulation" and "control."

Thus, to the same extent our lives were formerly controlled by the trend-setters of the world (Hollywood, fashion, the music industry, the educational system, etc.), Paul says we were dominated by *"the prince of the power of the air. . . ."*

Scripture tells us three things about Satan in this verse: (1) *he is a prince*, (2) *he has genuine authority*, and (3) *his power base is located in the lower regions of the air.* Let's look at each of these one at a time.

First, this verse tells us that Satan is a "prince."

The word "prince" is taken from the word *archonta* (ar-chon-ta), and it refers to one who is in "first place," or to one who is in a "ruling position." It describes a "potentate," "ruler," "chief," or "prince."

This shouldn't surprise us! In Matthew 9:34, Jesus told us that Satan was "the prince of demons" and even ascribed a real kingdom to him, which is called the kingdom of darkness. In John 12:31, Jesus called Satan "the prince of this world."

In Second Corinthians 4:4, the apostle Paul specifically stated that Satan was "the god of this world." Paul continues in Second Corinthians 4:4 to tell us that as "the god of this world," Satan has "blinded the minds of unbelievers" so that they cannot see the truth.

In addition to these well-known scriptures that identify Satan as a "prince," Ephesians 6:12 also tells of an entire ordered demonic system that is under Satan's domain. Satan himself is lord over these demonic hosts.

Therefore, Satan is a real prince over demon spirits and exercises real authority over the affairs of lost men and women whom he had blinded.

Second, this verse tells us that Satan has "power."

Paul designates Satan as "the prince of *the power* of the air. . . ." The word "power" is derived from the word *exousia* (ex-ou-sia). The word *exousia* would be more accurately translated "authority." Since Satan is a real prince over a real kingdom, it should not surprise us that his dark kingdom has real authority to back up his wicked reign.

During Jesus' forty-day temptation in the wilderness, the scripture says, "And the devil, taking him up into a high mountain, showed unto him all the kingdoms of the world in a moment of time. And the devil said unto him, All this power [Greek: *exousia*, "authority"] will I give thee, and the glory of them, for that is given unto me; and to whomsoever I will, I give it. . ." (Luke 4:5-6).

Please pay attention to the fact that the Lord Jesus never argued about Satan's claim to possess authority. It is obvious from the passage that Jesus had no argument with the devil's claims; He knew that Satan did indeed possess a measure of authority over the deteriorating lost world system, and that he did possess a measure of authority over lost humanity.

This authority of the devil over believers was eternally broken at the cross and resurrection! However, lost humanity is still being dominated by *"the prince of the power of the air. . . ."*

Third, Satan's power base is located in the "air."

The word "air" is taken from the word *aer* (pronounced "air" in Greek), and it was used by the classical Greek writers to describe the "lower, denser regions of the earth's atmosphere" — as opposed to the word *aither* (ai-ther), which was used to describe the purer and cleaner air that resided high above the moutaintops.

Why is this important? Because it explicitly tells us that Satan's power base is not "high up in the air" as some have suggested in recent days. Just the opposite! The air that is "high above the moutaintops" represents the cleanest and purest atmosphere that we know.

You needn't go out into outer space in order to locate the devil's power base. Satan's power base is located in the lower, denser environment that engulfs the earth. He isn't interested in controlling uninhabited planets and expanses of the universe that are emptied of human beings. He wants to own, control, dominate and manipulate *man!*

This is the reason he is called "the prince of this world" (John 12:31) and "the god of this world" (Second Corinthians 4:4). He doesn't want the Moon; he doesn't want Mars; he doesn't want Jupiter; he doesn't want Venus, Neptune or Pluto. He wants to be "the god of this world"!

Demonically Energized

Paul continues to tell us that Satan is "the spirit that now worketh in the children of disobedience. . ." (Ephesians 2:2).

What a shocking discovery this is! To find that before our life in Jesus Christ, we were demonically energized by the power of Satan himself. Yet, this is precisely what the scripture teaches!

The verse says, "the spirit that now *worketh*. . . ." The word "worketh" is from the word *energeo* (en-er-geo), and it denotes a power that is "operative" or "energizing." This is where we get the word "energy."

Therefore, in this verse the Holy Spirit vividly portrays how destitute our spiritual condition was before we were born again! *This verse declares that prior to our salvation, we were "energized" by demon spirits.* The devil himself was at work in us, energizing us, and was working through us to accomplish his destructive will in our lives.

The Bible declares that this was our condition before Jesus Christ touched us and totally set us free!

It was into this stinking, sinking, deteriorating, death-permeated, demonically energized world that Jesus Christ came 2,000 years ago in order to secure our deliverance from bondage — where our lives were being auctioned off by the devil into various kinds of slavery and bondage.

Agoridzo, translated "redemption" in the New Testament, denotes this horrible, deplorable, abject slavery in Satan's slave market where we used to live! But not anymore!

The word *agoridzo*, fully understood in the context of "redemption," means Jesus came to redeem us from this miserable state of bondage! As Paul told the Corinthians, "For ye are *bought* with a price. . ." (First Corinthians 6:20). The word "bought" in this verse is the word *agoridzo*.

In regard to this same "redeeming" work of Jesus, Paul continued to say, "Ye are *bought* with a price; be not the servants of men" (First Corinthians 7:23).

The word "bought" is once again derived from the word *agoridzo*. Paul's admonition could be paraphrased, "Since Jesus paid the price to deliver you from bondage and slavery to Satan, do not now turn around and make yourselves slaves to people!"

When the four and twenty elders fall before the throne of God and begin to worship, they sing a song about Jesus' work of "redeeming" us from Satan's slave market.

The Word says, "And they sung a new song, saying, Thou art worthy to take the book, and to open the seals thereof: for thou wast slain, and hast *redeemed us* to God by thy blood out of every kindred, and tongue, and people, and nation" (Revelation 5:9).

It is imperative for us to understand the word *agoridzo*. This important word adequately portrays our spiritually bankrupt condition in the "slave market" of the world before Jesus Christ set us free; and it portrays Jesus' "redemptive" work to remove us from that terrible place.

This leads us to the second word for "redemption" that is used in the New Testament.

Purchased "Out Of" Slavery

The second Greek word for "redemption" is derived from the word *exagoridzo* (ex-a-go-rid-zo). The word *exagoridzo* is a compound of the words *ex* and *agoridzo*.

The word *ex* is a preposition that means "out" and the word *agoridzo* (which we discussed in the section above) described "the slave market." When *ex* and *agoridzo* are combined, they form the word *exagoridzo*, which pictures one who has come to "purchase a slave *out of* the slave market." *Exagoridzo* conveys the idea of "removal."

Therefore, it signifies "the purchase of a slave in order to permanently set that slave *free* from that heinous place, never to be put on the trading block of slavery again." The word *exagoridzo* pictures a slave that has been liberated *"out of"* this stinking, nauseating, disgusting, depraved and cursed slave market forever!

The word *exagoridzo* is used several times in Paul's epistles to carry the picture of Jesus' redemptive work *to remove us* from slavery. A perfect New Testament example of this word is found in Galatians 3:13, where Paul says, "Christ hath *redeemed us* from the curse of the law. . . ."

By using the word *exagoridzo* in connection with Jesus "redeeming us from the curse of the law," Paul is telling us plainly that Jesus' sacrificial death didn't only pay the penalty for our sin; His death *removed us* from living under the curse from henceforth!

Paul continues to tell us that it was for this work of "redemption" that Jesus came into the world. "But when the fulness of the time was come, God sent forth His Son, made of a woman, made under the law, *to redeem them* that were under the law, that we might receive the adoption of sons" (Galatians 4:4,5).

Hear this: God's purpose was not only to inspect our condition of slavery, and to locate us in our depravity; His ultimate plan, which He accomplished in Jesus Christ's death and resurrection, was to *"buy us out of"* that miserable condition, and to place us as His own sons — forever removed from under the curse of sin and the law.

However, slaves did not come cheaply. If the auctioneer knew that a buyer really wanted a particular slave, he could demand unbelievably high prices. We must ask, "What price did Jesus pay for our freedom from Satan's power?"

This leads us to the third word for "redemption" that is used in the New Testament.

Paying the Price Demanded

The third Greek word used to describe "redemption" in the New Testament is taken from the word *lutroo* (lu-troo).

The word *lutroo* means to set a captive free "by the payment of a ransom." In order to secure the slave of your choice, a very high price had to be paid. If you greatly desired a certain slave, the auctioneer could demand unreasonably high ransoms.

Because Paul uses the word *lutroo* to denote the redemptive work of Jesus Christ on our behalf, he reminds us that our freedom was not really free. Quite the contrary! Our freedom from Satan's power was *extremely expensive*. In fact, *the price Jesus paid for us was the highest price ever paid for a slave.*

What was the ransom that Jesus paid in order to procure our freedom from Satan's ownership? *His own blood!*

Ephesians 1:7 says, "In whom we have redemption *through his blood. . . ."*

Colossians 1:14 says, "In whom we have redemption *through his blood. . . ."*

Colossians 1:20 says, "And having made peace *through the blood* of his cross. . . ."

Hebrews 9:12 says, "but *by his own blood* he entered in once into the holy place, having obtained eternal redemption for us."

First Peter 1:18-19 says, "Forasmuch as ye know that ye were not redeemed with corruptible things such as gold and silver. . . but with *the precious blood of Christ. . . ."*

It was the shedding of Jesus' own blood that guaranteed our deliverance and lasting freedom from demonic powers that previously held us captive. The word *lutroo* unmistakably means that Jesus paid the ransom that set you and me free! *He bought us with His own blood!*

Titus 2:14 declares that Jesus gave *Himself* as the ransom in order to set us free. The verse says, "Who gave himself for us, that he might *redeem* us from all iniquity, and purify unto himself a peculiar people, zealous of good works."

The word "redeem" used in this verse is taken from the word *lutroo*. According to Titus 2:14, a price had to be paid, and Jesus paid it with His own life and His own blood at the cross.

But wait! There is yet a fourth word that describes Jesus' work of "redemption."

Restored to Full Status

The fourth word for "redemption" that is used in the New Testament is taken from the word *apolutrosis* (a-po-lu-tro-sis).

The word *apo* means "away" and it also often conveys the idea of a "return." In this particular case, *apo* would be better translated "back," as in something that is being "returned back." The second part of *apolutrosis* is taken from *lutroo* (which we just covered in the section above). The word *lutroo* means to set a slave free "by the payment of a ransom."

This fourth word for "redemption" tells us God's ultimate purpose in redeeming us from Satan's slave market. The word *apolutrosis* ("redemption") most assuredly means Jesus "paid the ransom in order to return us" to the condition we were in before our captivity began!

In the plainest of language, this means Jesus paid the price to permanently set us free, and to *restore us* to the full status of sons!

Paul uses the word *apolutrosis* in this very way in Ephesians 1:7. He says, "In whom we have *redemption* through his blood, the forgiveness of sins, according to the riches of his grace."

By choosing to use the word *apolutrosis* ("redemption"), Paul declares that we were forever delivered from Satan's power — we were forever removed from that dreadful place — and now we have been *fully restored* by the blood of Jesus Christ and *placed back into a right state of being with God*. We are fully restored and fully set free from Satan's former grip over us!

This is why Galatians 4:7 declares, "Wherefore thou art no more a servant, but a son; and if a son, then an heir of God through Christ." Romans 8:17 proclaims that we are so entirely restored through the blood of Jesus, that now we have even become "joint-heirs" with Jesus Christ Himself!

The first word for "redemption" (*agoridzo*) tells us that Jesus Christ came to earth to *locate us* in our depravity, and to personally inspect our slavery to Satan.

The second word for "redemption" (*exagoridzo*) declares that Jesus came not only to inspect our condition, but he came to permanently *remove us* from Satan's power.

The third word for "redemption" (*lutroo*) tells us that Jesus was so dedicated to deliver us from Satan's dominion, that He was willing to pay *the ransom price* of His own blood in order to break the devil's ownership over us.

The fourth word for "redemption" (*apolutrosis*) tells us that, in addition to permanently setting us free from Satan's hold, Jesus also *restored us* to the position of "sons of God" — we are fully restored, made joint-heirs with Jesus Christ Himself (Romans 8:17).

This is what "redemption" is all about!

Translated Out of Satan's Kingdom

What do all of these words about "redemption" have to do with spiritual warfare and spiritual armor? *Everything!*

These truths explicitly let us know that the real purpose of spiritual warfare is *not* to fight for freedom from Satan's control over us. This has already been completed by the death of Jesus Christ on the cross, and by his triumphant resurrection from the dead. *We are already free!*

Ephesians 2:6 states that we are not under Satan's power, *but are rather above it.* "And [Christ] hath raised us up together, and made us to sit together in heavenly places in Christ Jesus" (Ephesians 2:6).

Accordingly, Colossians 1:13 teaches that we do not need to break away from Satan's dreadful dominion over us, *because we have already been translated out of it.* "Who hath delivered us from the power of darkness, and hath translated us into the kingdom of his dear Son."

Because of Jesus' redemptive work, we are seated with Jesus Christ in the heavenly places and have been elevated *"far above all principality, and power, and might, and dominion, and every name that is named, not only in this world, but also in that which is to come"* (Ephesians 1:21).

Therefore, Satan has no legal right to control us, our bodies, our families, our businesses, or our money. Though we once genuinely belonged to him (Ephesians 2:2), we are no longer his.

Chapter Four
Why Does the Battle Still Rage?

Someone may ask, "If Jesus' death and resurrection really broke the authority of the devil over our lives. . . then why does the battle still rage?"

"If we have been truly translated out of Satan's kingdom, why does his kingdom still seem to exert influence upon our lives?"

"If Jesus genuinely spoiled principalities and powers as Colossians 2:15 declares, then why do so many believers still have to deal with horrible strongholds in their minds?"

Several years ago, a friend of mine was called by the police in the middle of the night. The police informed him that one of his animals, a goat, had gotten out of the property and had been hit and killed by a car. My friend quickly put his jacket on, and rushed to the place where the dead goat was supposed to be lying.

However, when he arrived at the scene, he discovered the goat wasn't dead at all. Someone had stolen the goat, and had tied its legs up with rope so that it could not move, and then dumped the goat along the side of the road.

My friend reached over, untied the rope that held the goat captive, and then slapped it and said, "Get up!" But the goat just lay there, as though it was still bound and unable to move. Once again, he slapped the goat and said, "Get up!" But the goat continued to lie on its side, as though it was unable to move.

When he began examining the goat, looking for a wound that was possibly keeping the goat from getting up, he noticed that the animal's legs were still tightly clinging to each other as though they were still tied with ropes. It then became clear: the goat thought it was still bound.

He bent over and picked the goat up, set it on its feet, and slapped it again, telling it to "Get up!" Finally, the goat realized its feet were no longer bound and it began to jump and leap.

Most of us are just like the goat in this story. We were previously bound by Satan's destructive power. He tied us up in total slavery and then dumped us, waiting for destruction to completely ruin us.

Then, when we heard the gospel message and were born again, Jesus Christ came to "untie" Satan's hold on our lives! Through His redemptive work at the cross, He legally removed the bondages that held us captive. . . and through His redemptive work at the cross, He legally removed the bands that held us hostage in our minds. But often, even after this freeing work has been done, we may not be able to fully perceive that we have really been set free.

Jesus looks at us and says, "Get up!" Yet we lie on our sides, in our scars, our pains and our mental hang-ups, not realizing that we have really been set free! Therefore, someone must come along and point our freedom out to us! To help us maintain that Christ-bought, Christ-imparted freedom, we must now renew our wrong thinking and wrong believing to what the Word of God declares about our new condition.

Any pastor could verify that people who have just been saved must work to overcome the emotional and mental scars they received when they were still in the world and were under the devil's control. Though the inner man has been born again and made new, the mind and the body must now be conformed to the image of the inner man.

While members of Satan's slave market, individuals received much abuse during their slavery to Satan and to the negative consequences of sin. Perhaps they had a bad marriage, a drug problem, some kind of sexual perversion, a lying spirit, a mental hang-up, or some other type of scar that was laid on their soul before they met the Lord.

If these "residual areas" from the past are not removed by the renewing of the mind by the Word of God, they can and will continue to exert power even in the life of a Christian. Moreover, if these "residual areas" are not attended to and renewed with the Word, these are the very areas that Satan will use to wage warfare against your new life.

When the adversary locates an area such as one of these, that has never been surrendered to the sanctifying work of the Holy Spirit, he may seize that unsurrendered area of your mind and emotions and energize it — filling it with a brand new vitality — and he may then begin to use it to work against the growth and development of your new freedom in Jesus Christ. *Refusing to deal with these areas is where the majority of spiritual warfare stems from!*

Wrong thinking, wrong believing, allowing memories of terrible experiences that happened to us before we knew the Lord to continue dominating our emotions, or fears that were transferred to us by parents or family members or friends, or years of incorrect doctrine that we were taught in our former churches that we must now unlearn and overcome — all of these have the potential of working against the legitimate freedom which we now possess in Jesus Christ.

Spiritual Warfare and Renewing the Mind

The mind is the strategic center where spiritual warfare with the "god of this world" takes place! The enemy knows the importance of the mind; he knows that your mind is the key to controlling your life.

He knows that if he can take control of one small area of your mind, then he can begin to expand outward into other weak areas that need to be strengthened by the Holy Spirit and the Word of God. By poisoning your mind with unbelief and lying strongholds, the devil can manipulate your mind, your emotions and your body. Moreover, he can use you to pour the same kind of unbelief and lying strongholds into the minds of others around you.

There is no doubt about it, the mind is the strategic center for spiritual warfare!

By nature, the condition of the mind is hostile toward God and is bent on destruction. We were all born with an innately rebellious mind and a rebellious nature that was against God. This is why Romans 8:7 says "the *carnal mind* [the natural mind] *is enmity against God. . . ."*

Colossians 1:21 says that prior to our salvation experience, we were "alienated and enemies in *our minds* by wicked works. . . ."

Ephesians 4:17-18 says unbelievers "walk in the vanity of *their mind,* having the *understanding* darkened, being alienated from the life of God through the *ignorance* that is in them, because of the *blindness* of their heart. . . ."

Second Corinthians 4:4 says, "the god of this world hath blinded *the minds* of them which believe not. . . ."

And in Romans 1:28, scripture teaches that the natural mind is so completely contrary to God, that it can become *"reprobate. . . ."*

Hence, we were initially born into this world with a nature that was bent toward self-annihilation and was fully capable of developing strongholds by itself. The natural mind is contrary toward God, and has always sought to fulfill itself in the destructive lusts of the flesh. This is why Paul said, "Among whom also we all had our conversation in times past in the lust of our flesh, *fulfilling the desires of the flesh and of the mind, and were by nature the children of wrath. . ."* (Ephesians 2:3).

If we do not seek to renew our minds, wills and emotions to the truth of God's Word, then the illusion of bondage will continue to dominate our lives. Most often it is through these unrenewed areas of thinking that the devil continues to exert his foul influence upon our lives. He knows that if your mind is renewed to the truth, he cannot wage successful warfare against you or your family!

This is the reason the New Testament epistles earnestly plead with us to give serious attention to the condition of our minds. We are commanded to renew our minds to the truth of God's Word. These scriptures command us:

— "To be transformed by the renewing of your mind" (Romans 12:2).

— "Be renewed in the spirit of your mind" (Ephesians 4:23).

— "To put on the new man" (Ephesians 4:24).

— "To put on the new man, which is renewed in knowledge after the image of him that created him" (Colossians 3:10).

— "To let the Word of Christ dwell in you richly. . ." (Colossians 3:16).

— "Wherefore, gird up the loins of your mind. . ." (First Peter 1:13-14).

Especially notice Peter's admonition to "gird up the loins of your mind." The picture that Peter puts before us is that of a runner whose garments have fallen down, and have become entangled about his legs. He was running a good race and his stride was picking up, when this encumbrance of dangling, loosely hanging clothing hindered his steps.

Likewise, we must "gird up the loins of our minds" and seek to renew our thinking with the Word of God. This consistent renewal of the Word will eradicate wrong thinking, wrong believing, scars from the past, and hurtful, emotional memories that would exert their influence on our new life. *It is these loose, dangling, uncommitted and unrenewed areas of the mind that the devil uses to wage warfare against us.*

This renewal of the mind does not add to the already completed work of Jesus Christ; it simply puts us in a mental state of being that will enable us to better use our faith, and to enjoy the benefits of the redemptive work that Jesus accomplished for us!

Take heed! To deliberately allow wrong thinking and wrong believing to continue will impair your ability to enjoy your redemption. This is equivalent to a runner who deliberately allows his garment to hang down where it will get caught in his legs. Though he is still in the race, he certainly will not win the victory, and he will not experience much joy in running his race.

Therefore, Peter admonishes us to "gird up the loins of our minds." We must tighten up those areas that the devil would try to grab hold of and use against us.

A Life-long Commitment

This is the reason I stress that spiritual warfare is a life-long commitment, and not a gust of emotion to frighten the devil away in a few moments of time. Real spiritual warfare will take much longer than that!

In addition to taking authority over demonic powers, real spiritual warfare also entails taking authority over your mind.

Renewing of the mind, meditating on the Word of God until it gets into your heart and soul, learning to live a holy life, and seeking to be conformed to the image of Jesus Christ on a day-to-day basis and learning how to walk after the Spirit — *all of these are essential elements of genuine spiritual warfare.*

Real spiritual warfare requires a life of commitment, purity, and consecration. Any view of spiritual warfare that fails to include these, is *lopsided* and fails to meet the mark.

Chapter Five
A Menace From Heaven

When the Holy Spirit's power came upon believers gathered in the Upper Room on the day of Pentecost, and with the emergence of the supernatural Church of Jesus Christ in Jerusalem, Satan knew — beyond any shadow of doubt — that his earthly domain was no longer secure.

If Jesus could single-handedly defeat him so thoroughly, how could he now stand against multitudes who were filled with the same Spirit that raised Jesus from the dead?

Now endued with supernatural power from on high, the believers in Jerusalem had been miraculously transformed into a divine army that was equipped with supernatural power and supernatural weaponry to execute the victory which Jesus had already achieved over this supernatural foe.

Satan's worst nightmare had become a reality. His dark, demented, diabolical kingdom that had been secure for thousands of years before Jesus' birth, had now been penetrated, first by Jesus, and now by the Church. In his view, a heavenly menace had entered his domain — in order to execute the victory Jesus Christ won over him at the cross and the grave, and to demonstrate his defeat. God's army, the Church, had been sent from heaven's headquarters to take the dominion away from Satan, and return it to the people of God!

The kingdom of God had arrived! The Church began preaching, teaching, evangelizing, healing the sick, raising the dead, casting out demons and driving back the forces of hell one step at a time. Satan's security was gone forever. The Church had arrived to execute judgment on him and his perverted hosts.

In order to divert his total collapse of power in the affairs of the lost world system, Satan released all of his fury to destroy this heavenly menace from heaven before it could fully execute the judgment already declared concerning him.

An Opportune Moment for the Devil To Attack

When Paul wrote the book of Ephesians in the year A.D. 64, Satan's strategy to destroy the Church was already in full motion.

Paul, a powerful, faithful Christian soldier — even a father and general of the faith — was imprisoned in the imperial city of Rome for allegedly planning the huge fire that had burned down twelve sections of Rome the year before. In reality, it was Nero, the current reigning emperor, who had planned this arson.

Because Nero believed in his own deity and because his demonically influenced mother (Agrippina) urged him on to believe in his own godhood, he went before the Roman Senate in the year A.D. 63 and requested that the city of Rome be rebuilt with idols of himself positioned throughout the city, so that good Roman citizens could worship him at any given point of any day of the week.

When the Senate refused to do this, Nero returned home and placed torches into the hands of his servants and ordered them to burn the imperial city to the ground. His thinking was, "If they won't let me tear it down, then I'll burn it down."

After surveying the city of Rome when the fire was finally extinguished, it became obvious to the Senate that Nero had planned this arson. The only section of Rome that did not burn was the district where Nero had just built his new, famous palace. Upon discovering this convincing evidence, and realizing that Nero was behind this devastating blaze that severely burned their beloved city, the Senate immediately began to plan Nero's trial and execution.

It was then that Nero, empowered and inspired by the devil himself, began to publicly allege that Christians had burned down the imperial city (for more on this, see pages 4-

20, LIVING IN THE COMBAT ZONE). Because of Paul's notoriety as a Christian leader, he was captured and was imprisoned for his alleged part in this fire that Nero had orchestrated, and was now spending the remaining portion of his life chained to a heavily armed Roman soldier in a prison cell in Rome.

This attack against the Church was a part of Satan's plan to thwart the plan of God. The Church at this exact time was growing at an unprecedented rate; it was growing numerically; it was growing doctrinally; it was growing spiritually. Before the entire empire fell from Satan's hands into the control of God's victorious army, the Church, Satan struck fast and viciously to abort the work of God.

As always is the case, in the end this demonic attack, which was meant to destroy the Church, really helped to further the advancement of the gospel.

Demonic Attacks That Backfire!

None of Satan's strategies to destroy the Church have ever succeeded. It becomes evident very quickly, by studying Church history, that each attack which the enemy has waged against the Church has ultimately helped to further the cause of Jesus Christ. *Two thousand years of experience emphatically tell us that the devil has absolutely no winning strategies; he simply does not know how to win.*

By having Paul imprisoned for his faith, the devil thought he could destroy Paul's ministry. This was not a winning strategy for the devil at all! By imprisoning Paul, the devil made the horrible mistake of placing Paul in a situation where he had nothing to do but listen to the Holy Spirit! *This strategy of Satan utterly failed!*

During his confinement in prison, Paul received some of the most outstanding revelations in the entire New Testament — *the books of Galatians, Ephesians, Philippians, Colossians, Second Timothy and Philemon* — all of these are a result of Paul's time spent in prison! Thus the reason Paul said, "Wherein I suffer

71

trouble, as an evil-doer, even unto bonds; *but the word of God is not bound"* (Second Timothy 2:9).

Had he never been bound in prison, he may not have written these vital books of the New Testament. Can you imagine how hectic Paul's ministry outside those prison walls must have been? His ministry was perhaps more demanding than any other ministry in history.

As an apostle, his time was consumed with establishing new churches, discipling new leaders, and helping to correct problems in the local church. Outside those prison walls, Paul's ministry was extremely effective and damaging to the domain of darkness. By binding him in chains and throwing him in jail, the devil miscalculated that his effectiveness would be destroyed. The devil was wrong! His effectiveness increased!

History is full of the devil's miscalculations. Another example of Satan's miscalculations is found in the story of the apostle John.

The devil clearly inspired Domitian, the Roman Emperor, to imprison John on the isle of Patmos. By putting John on this little foreboding island out in the middle of the Mediterranean Sea, he thought he could destroy John's effectiveness in ministry. This was yet another horrible mistake! By isolating John on the isle of Patmos, the devil helped to position John to receive the Book of Revelation!

How about the miscalculation that the devil made about Aquila and Priscilla? This is another extremely dramatic illustration of how Satan's strategies always backfire!

The earliest Church records reveal that Aquila and Priscilla founded the Church of Rome. In fact, the Church in Rome actually met in their home when it was first being established. When the massive persecution against Jews first commenced during the reign of Emperor Claudius, like many other believers who lived in the Jewish colonies of Rome, Aquila and Priscilla were driven out of the city.

Imagine how heart-rending it must have been for them to leave their church family behind! They had founded the church in Rome and had led many of those people to the Lord. They had seen them filled with the Spirit, and they had taught them, discipled them and watched them grow in their relationship with the Lord. The church family of Rome was precious and dear to their hearts. Now, against their wills, they were being forced to leave it all behind.

On the basis of human nature alone, you can be sure that when they were expelled from Rome, they thought it was all over for them. Just think how devastated and crushed their hearts must have been as they packed their belongings and hugged their remaining church family in Rome farewell. Surely they must have thought that their ministry was over and that they were now all "washed up" in the ministry.

Yet, Aquila and Priscilla's greatest ministry began *after* they left Rome! Once expelled from Rome, they traveled eastward and settled in the city of Corinth, where they took up the trade of tent-making. It was here that they met Apollos, an extremely influential and educated Jew from Alexandria who had come to visit the city of Corinth. While on his journey, Aquila and Priscilla "expounded unto him the way of God more perfectly" (Acts 18:24-26).

Apollos eventually became the pastor of the Corinthian Church. Had Aquila and Priscilla been allowed to stay in Rome, they might never have met Apollos and led him to the Lord. This attack that came to destroy their ministry, actually positioned them to help further the gospel of Jesus Christ.

Likewise, had Aquila and Priscilla stayed in Rome, they might never have met the apostle Paul. It was after they were driven out of Rome, that they met him and joined him as one of his associates. This apostolic team ministered to churches all over Greece and Asia Minor for years and years to come.

While the devil thought he was shutting them and their powerful ministries down forever by expelling them from Rome, *he was actually positioning them to do the greatest ministry they had ever done.* Had the devil never attacked them and expelled them from their work in Rome, they might never have left Rome and entered into this greater mission field.

A Closed Door Does Not Mean Failure

Regardless of what the devil tries to do to you, your family, your church or your ministry, if you stand in faith, God will turn it around to work for the advancement of the kingdom of God!

Even if your finances are assaulted, and even if the plan of God appears to come under seige in your life, God is able to take these wicked devices and turn them to work for your good! As Paul said, "And we know that all things work together for the good to them that love God, to them who are the called according to his purpose" (Romans 8:28).

A closed door does not mean failure! If a door slams shut in your face and it looks like everything is over, hold tight, and refrain from making a judgment call about the situation! What the devil did to hurt you, God will use to bless you! *God may be preparing to open the largest, most effectual door of opportunity that has ever been made available to you!*

Paul suffered many blows from the enemy that, naturally speaking, should have mortally wounded him. Yet he was still alive and well and was still in the ministry. Having seen God's faithfulness on so many occasions, he confidently looked trouble in the face and said, "Nay, in all these things we are more than conquerors through him that loved us" (Romans 8:37).

Notice Paul calls us "more than conquerors." The phrase "more than conquerors" is taken from the Greek word *hupernikos* (hu-per-ni-kos), which is a compound of two words: *huper* (hu-per) and *nikos* (ni-kos). It appears that this is the first time the word *hupernikos* was ever used in Greek literature; it was coined by Paul himself.

Why is it important to know this? It tells us there were no words strong enough in the Greek language to express what Paul wanted to say. Therefore, he made up his own word! By joining the words *huper* and *nikos* together into one word, Paul makes one fabulous, jammed-packed, power-filled statement!

The phrase "more than" (*huper*) literally means "over, above, and beyond." It depicts something that is "way beyond measure." We derive the word "super" from the word *huper*. As used in this passage, it conveys the ideas of "superiority": "greater, superior, higher, better; more than a match for; utmost, paramount, foremost." Or, to be "first-rate, first-class, top-notch, unsurpassed, unequaled, and unrivaled by any person or thing."

Now Paul uses this word to denote what kind of conquerors we are in Jesus Christ. We are *huper-conquerors!* The word *huper* dramatizes our victory! It means that we are *"greater conquerors, superior conquerors, higher and better conquerors; we are more than a match for any adversary or foe; we are utmost conquerors, paramount conquerors, foremost conquerors, first-rate conquerors, first-class conquerors, top-notch conquerors, unsurpassed conquerors, and unequaled and unrivaled conquerors!"* This is what the phrase "more than" means.

The word "conqueror" is from the word *nikos* (ni-kos). It describes an "overcomer, conqueror, champion, victor, or master." It is the picture of an "overwhelming prevailing force." The word *nikos* is a dramatic word that depicts one who is altogether victorious! However, *nikos* alone wasn't strong enough to make Paul's point! So, he joined the words *huper* and *nikos* together to make his point even stronger!

By calling us "more than conquerors," Paul tells us that in Christ Jesus, we are "an overwhelming conqueror," "a victor paramount," or "an enormous overcomer." This word is so power-packed that one could translate it "a phenomenal, walloping conquering force!"

In light of this, when Paul says, "Nay, in all these things we are more than conquerors through him that loved us," he is not referring to a small victory, but instead, he declares that we are mighty victors! We are "a phenomenal, walloping conquering force!"

With the power of Jesus Christ at our disposal, we can be certain that "neither death, nor life, nor angels, nor principalities, nor powers, nor things present, nor things to come, nor height, nor depth, nor any other creature shall be able to separate us from the love of God, which is in Christ Jesus our Lord" (Romans 8:38,39).

Regardless of what the devil has attempted to do to you in the past, and regardless of the attacks that have come against you, your family, your business or your ministry, in the end these attacks will utterly fail! Though the devil may try to abort the plan of God for your life, "no weapon formed against you shall prosper" (Isaiah 54:17).

Each attack that comes your way will end up working for your good, because God will make "all things work together for the good to them that love God, to them who are the called according to his purpose" (Romans 8:28).

Over the centuries Satan's plan has always been to destroy the Church. His plan has not changed. He still hates the Church of Jesus Christ, and he, likewise, hates the preaching and teaching of the Word of God.

Rather than allow the Church to demonstrate Jesus' victory over him and execute the judgment that the Word of God has declared over him, he still actively seeks to destroy us. *The Church is still a menace to his domain which he will seek to oppose with all of his might.*

Your Problems Are Not Unique

As you grow in your spiritual walk, you need to know that attacks upon your life may begin to escalate. The good news is that your new growth and knowledge of God's Word will help you to eradicate these attacks.

The adversary doesn't want you to grow. Spiritual growth in your life equals real trouble for him and his kingdom. He would rather that you remain infantile in your spiritual life so that you will do him no serious damage.

Therefore, when you begin to grow and expand in your knowledge of God's Word and in the power of the Holy Spirit, your growth will pose a threat to Satan's domain. This may cause the demonic realm to make a preemptive strike against you to slow down your growth. *Do not be surprised by such preemptive strikes!*

Paul said, "There hath no temptation taken you but such as is common to man. . ." (First Corinthians 10:13). In regard to these attacks from the devil, Peter said, "Whom resist stedfast in the faith, knowing that the same afflictions are accomplished in your brethren that are in the world."

The devil may try to coax your flesh and emotions into believing that no one has ever suffered like you are suffering, or that no one else has ever gone through the difficulties that you are going through right now. *This is a trick to make you fix your eyes on yourself.* If you allow it to work, this trick will ultimately lure you into a maze of self-centeredness, where everything in life revolves around you, your problems, your difficulties, your fears, and so on.

Be assured that when you begin to grow, *you will have an opportunity to use your faith and to resist the devil!* When your understanding of God's Word begins to increase, you will probably have *many opportunities* to use your faith and to resist the devil!

I couldn't begin to count the times someone has told me, "I didn't have any health problems until I saw that healing was included in the atonement! After I started believing and confessing that healing was in the atonement, it seemed like I was hit with all kinds of sicknesses."

Others have said, "I had no financial woes until I believed what the Word of God has to say about tithes and offerings. Everything was fine financially until I started acting on the Word of God. When I began to give tithes and offerings to the Lord, everything seemed to fall to pieces."

These are attempts of the adversary to drive you back from the land of promise. He doesn't want you to obey God's Word and experience blessing. This is exactly why the writer of Hebrews told his readers, "But call to remembrance the former days, *in which after ye were illuminated, ye endured a great fight of affliction"* (Hebrews 10:32).

A fight nearly always follows illumination (for more discussion on this, see pages 232-236, LIVING IN THE COMBAT ZONE). The enemy comes to attack when you have been illuminated concerning some area of the Word of God. Such attacks come almost immediately, trying to steal the Word that you have just embraced; and trying to make you doubt that Word so that you cannot confidently stand on it by faith.

You must know that:

✝ An attack against your finances is not unique.

✝ An assault against your body is not unusual.

✝ A strike against your church is not an oddity.

✝ This is how the enemy works.

He waits until growth has begun and then he strikes with an unrelenting force to shove you back into spiritual despair. He wants you to retreat and back off from the front lines of battle!

By knowing ahead of time how the enemy works, you will be mentally prepared to deal with such challenges. He comes to challenge you when you are growing and gaining new ground. *Your knowledge of how and when Satan attacks will equip you to deal with these attacks more intelligently.*

In regard to these moments of spiritual assault, James said, "My brethren, count it all joy when you fall into divers temptations" (James 1:2). Notice James says to count it all joy *"when* you fall into divers temptations."

The word "when" implies that these assaults *will* come. James doesn't say to count it all joy "if" you fall into divers temptations; he says "when" you fall into divers temptations. The Greek tense used here suggests that these attacks normally come when you least expect them; they usually come from a direction you would have never dreamed of in a million years; and these assaults are specifically designed to catch you off guard and to take you by surprise.

From time to time everyone (even the most spiritual people you know) come under some type of assault. Regardless of whether the assault is from the natural realm or from the spirit realm, the important thing is for you to know how to respond when such attacks upon your life commence.

James doesn't warn us of this in order to inspire fear in us. Instead, he forewarns us of this reality so that when attacks do come, we will not be shocked and taken off guard, and thus thrown into a state of confusion and discouragement. *Such attacks should be anticipated.*

The devil does not want you to make spiritual progress in your life and he will try to stop you dead in your tracks! If nothing else, these attacks prove that you are making headway in your spiritual life and are becoming a threat to the security of the kingdom of darkness. Otherwise, these unseen enemies would leave you alone.

A large portion of spiritual warfare is mental preparation. If you are mentally prepared and alert to how the enemy operates and to the potential of attack, then you have already eliminated half of the battle.

Constant mental preparation is the major key in dealing with potential attacks from the demonic realm. If we are mentally alert to this possibility, and if we understand that these attacks occur when we are becoming more illuminated concerning the Word and our place in Christ, then we will be better positioned to guard against these assaults and to overcome them.

Mental preparation removes the element of surprise, and this will always give you the upper hand.

Attacks Against Churches and Ministries

How many local churches and independent ministries have been struck with destruction just when they were about to accomplish something significant for God?

Think of all the pastors who have come home from their time of relaxation on their vacations to discover sabotage occurred in the leadership of the church while they were away!

I wonder how many local churches have been in the middle of a building program, when suddenly the church family became divided by behavior that was completely out of character for that body of believers?

Or I wonder how many ministries and churches have moved forward in faith toward the fulfillment of their God-given vision, to have the finances of the ministry bottom out on them with no warning whatsoever?

As long as we do nothing for God, then we can be confident of no challenge from the enemy. However, when we begin to do what God has called us to do, and when we begin to have a measure of success in it, we must be mentally alert and aware! Countless churches have been split and destroyed when they were on the verge of fulfilling their vision and accomplishing something important for the kingdom of God.

The devil waits for an opportune moment to strike!

This is why Luke tells us that when Jesus' temptation in the wilderness was over, the devil "left him until an opportune moment" (Luke 4:13, *NIV*). The implication is that the devil would be back to attack again — but he would wait for the moment when an attack was better suited for his purposes.

Remember, the violent winds that came to destroy Jesus and His disciples came at the very moment when Jesus' ship was headed toward the country of the Gadarenes (Mark 4:35-41). When Jesus reached the shores of the Gadarenes, He was going to cast a legion of demons out of the demoniac of Gadara. This would be one of the greatest miracles of His earthly ministry. Knowing that Jesus was going to perform this miracle, and knowing that he was about to lose a prized possession — *the demoniac,* Satan struck with all his fury to abort the miracle-working power of God.

Similarly, the devil loves to strike local churches and ministries when they are about to come to the shores of their own Gadara, where the miracle-working power of God will be unloosed in their lives and ministries. He doesn't want you, your ministry or your church to move into the blessings of God. Therefore, be aware and know that when your vision is finally within your reach, this may be the "opportune moment" the devil will seek to deal a mortal wound to your church or ministry.

Be confident, however, and know that if the devil attacks the leadership of the church, or if an assault is made against the finances of the church, or even if strife and discord erupts in the church, God is able to make these devastating devices work for your good!

By creating spiritual sabotage while the pastor was away, the devil positioned the pastor of the church to discover who he could and couldn't trust! It is good that this occurred now, and not later, when the damage could have been much greater. By acting to disrupt and destroy, *the devil overplayed his hand!*

Likewise, while the enemy attacked your ministry with financial distress that caused you to put your plans of growth and expansion on hold, even this wicked device will turn out to your favor! While things are on hold, God will reveal a plan to you that is a far more expedient way to fulfill your vision. He will show you a method and a plan that will be easier for you to handle, and one that will cost you less money in the end. Once again, *the devil overplayed his hand!*

Satan hates the Church of Jesus Christ! In his view, we are a menace from heaven that has invaded territory that was once secure for the domain of darkness. To discourage us and stop us from making further inroads into this earthly sphere, he will try to attack and destroy the Church.

But regardless of what the devil does in his attempts to hurt the work of God, if we remain faithful and continue "fighting the good fight of faith," none of these things will ever find success in thwarting the plan of God. *God is able to make all of these work for our good!*

A Pattern of Strife and Discord

Attacks of strife and discord in the local church are a tool that the enemy has universally used in the Body of Christ. Concerning attacks of strife and discord in the local church, James says, "For where envying and strife is, there is confusion and every evil work" (James 3:16).

In the first place, notice that James mentions "envy." The word "envy" is from the Greek word *zelos* (ze-los), and it denotes "a fierce desire to promote your own ideas and convictions to the exclusion of everyone else."

In order to disrupt the peaceable flow of things in the local church, the enemy may try to make someone in the local church believe they have a view (or even a "word from the Lord") that *must* be acknowledged and implemented by the leadership of the church. This "fierce desire to promote their own ideas and convictions to the exclusion of everyone else" can become so strong, that they will not relent until the pastor succumbs and agrees with their point of view.

If this carnality persists, it will naturally lead to the next step in this horrible sequence of events. James says, "For where envy and *strife is. . . .*" According to James, this "fierce desire to promote your own ideas and convictions to the exclusion of everyone else" will naturally lead to "strife."

The word "strife" is taken from the word *eritheia* (eri-thei-a). It was used by the ancient Greeks to denote a political party that had become entirely "factioned." This "factioning" eventually became so bad that the political party could no longer function as a whole; hence, because of this internal strife, discord and division, such divided political parties were normally deserted and abandoned. Thus the reason that the word *eritheia* is often translated as a *"party spirit."*

Why is this important to understand? It tells us that if this spiritual attack of "strife" is not dealt with severely and quickly, it is only a matter of time before the church family will be horribly divided and split with internal problems.

Ignoring the fact that the pastor is the God-appointed leader of the local church, a divisive person (not realizing that they are operating under the outward influence of a spirit) will probably begin to gather people around them to see their view of things. This is the beginning of a "party spirit" inside the local church.

One group of people will begin to "take sides" with one person's point of view, and another group may begin to "take sides" with the other. The church then becomes "factioned" into so many different points of view, that in the end, when all is said and done, this particular local body will no longer be able to worship together.

This, then, leads to the next step in this sequence of events! James continues to say, "For where envying and strife is, *there is confusion. . . ."*

The word "confusion" is taken from the word *akatastasia* (a-ka-ta-sta-sia). It was used in New Testament times to describe "civil disobedience, disorder, and anarchy" in a city, state or government.

By choosing to use this word, James explicitly tells us that when situations of strife and discord are allowed to persist in the local church — and when people begin to ignore or bypass pastoral authority, they usurp the authority God has given the pastor and dangerously move into a type of "lawlessness" where "anarchy" and "civil disobedience" and "disorder" begin to destroy the local church.

To make sure we understand where this kind of behavior will eventually lead us, James continues to say, "For where envying and strife is, there is confusion *and every evil work."*

The word "evil" is from the word *phaulos* (phau-los). The word *phaulos* describes something that is "terribly bad" or "exceedingly vile." We derive the word "foul" from *phaulos*. When believers cooperate with this kind of behavior, it always produces a "foul situation" in the local church.

Furthermore, if there is any question in your mind as to where this kind of behavior originates, James tells us! He

This wisdom descended not from above, *but is earthly, ,al and demonic"* (James 3:15).

In order to successfully defeat these attacks of the enemy against us individually or against the local church body, God has provided us with supernatural weapons! As Paul declared, "For the weapons of our warfare are not carnal, but mighty through God to the pulling down of strongholds" (Second Corinthians 10:4).

Heavily Dressed, Trained Killers

In addition to being the most powerful political seat of the world, Rome, where Paul was now bound, was also headquarters for the world's most highly developed, highly advanced military machine — *the Roman army*. From this world-conquering military base, the entire civilized world of that time had fallen prey to the Roman Empire.

Surrounded by this huge military machine, and bound to a heavily armed Roman soldier, it was logical for Paul's thoughts to turn toward the issue of spiritual warfare and spiritual armor. The environment was perfect for the Holy Spirit to begin speaking to Paul in such terms. There, at Paul's side, was a perfectly dressed and fully armed soldier who had been trained in the skill of warfare. This soldier was literally "dressed to kill."

With this image constantly next to his side night and day, Paul began to receive exceptional spiritual insight from the Holy Spirit regarding our own spiritual weapons. He recorded this revelation for us in Ephesians 6:10-18. Yet Ephesians 6:10-18 is not Paul's first recorded thoughts on the subject of spiritual armor.

About ten years earlier, when Paul was writing his first epistle to the Thessalonians, around the year A.D. 54, he also wrote about spiritual weaponry. However, at that earlier time in his ministry, his understanding of spiritual armor was clearly undeveloped. At the time he wrote First Thessalonians, he mentioned only two pieces of spiritual weaponry. He said, "But let us who are of the day, be sober, putting on the

84

breastplate of faith and love; and for an helmet, the hope of salvation" (First Thessalonians 5:8).

It is plain to see that over the next ten years the Holy Spirit continued to expand these ideas and imparted even further revelation concerning the "weapons of our warfare" (Second Corinthians 10:4).

During his numerous imprisonments, Paul was frequently held captive by being bound to a Roman soldier who kept constant watch over him. Hour after hour, day after day and week after week, he lived side-by-side to this heavily dressed, trained killer.

As Paul sat and observed the durable loinbelt of the Roman soldier, the Holy Spirit must have began speaking to him about the "loinbelt of truth." As his eyes moved toward the soldier's bright and shining, tightly woven breastplate of brass, the Holy Spirit began to illuminate his understanding to the "breastplate of righteousness."

When his eyes turned downward toward the Roman soldier's dangerously spiked shoes and invincible greaves of brass, the Spirit began to open his eyes about "shoes of peace." As his sight suddenly caught a glimpse of the huge, oblong shield made of animal hide and saw it there at the soldier's side, the Holy Spirit began to communicate to Paul about the "shield of faith."

As he looked upward and beheld the decorative helmet on the head of the soldier, the Spirit of God began imparting revelation concerning the "helmet of salvation." And as he turned his attention over to the other side of the Roman soldier, he observed his wide, broad, heavy, massive sword, and the Holy Spirit began to speak to Paul about the "sword of the Spirit."

During that ten-year period between A. D. 54 and A.D. 64, his insight about spiritual armor had tremendously developed into a whole system of spiritual weaponry. Now, rather than having only two pieces of armor to use in our fight against the adversary, Paul tells us that we have six pieces of weaponry, and perhaps even a seventh, since there is a possibility of a seventh, hidden weapon found in Ephesians 6:18.

Over the years, Paul's understanding concerning spiritual armor increased. You must understand that a Roman soldier was a killer of the worst order. Once retired from military life, it was not unusual at all for these men to still kill, though now retired as a civilian. Murder and violence were ingrained into them and had become a very intregral part of their natures. Now Paul uses this very graphic, dangerous and murderous example to show us what the spiritual weapons God gives us can do to a spiritual foe.

On an average-sized Roman soldier, these pieces of weaponry (the loinbelt, breastplate, shoes with greaves, shield, helmet, sword, and possibly the lance) weighed approximately 100 pounds. The exact weight of a soldier's armor varied according to the physical stature of the soldier. If he was a large man, his armor was larger and heavier. If he was smaller, then his armor was smaller and, therefore, lighter. Regardless of the size of the soldier, all Roman soldiers carried a very heavy amount of armor.

What kind of man do you think it would require to wear this kind of weaponry? *A strong man!* No small, frail, weakling would be able to stand, walk, run, or function to any degree in this kind of heavy armor. To wear this weaponry and to successfully wage warfare in it, would require that the wearer be extremely strong and physically fit.

Therefore, before Paul goes into any detail about spiritual weapons, he first informs us that God has provided us with supernatural power that will enable us to victoriously contend with unseen, demonic powers! This is a power that will enable us to reinforce Jesus' victory, and to demonstrate Satan's defeat!

Chapter Six
An Important Message
To Remember

Before Paul rushes into his detailed explanation of spiritual armor, he beseeches us, "Finally, my brethren, be strong in the Lord. . ." (Ephesians 6:10).

Notice that Paul begins this portion of scripture about spiritual warfare and spiritual armor by saying, *"Finally. . . ."*

The word "finally" is one of the most important words in this portion of scripture. It is taken from the Greek phrase *tou loipou* (tou loi-pou), and it would be better translated, "for the rest of the matter, in conclusion, or in summation."

The phrase *tou loipou* is used in other secular Greek manuscripts of that same period to depict something that is so extremely important, that it is held until the very end of the letter — so that if nothing else from the letter can be remembered by the reader, they will be able to remember this!

In light of this, the word "finally" in Ephesians 6:10 carries this idea: *"In conclusion, I have saved the most important issue of this epistle until the end of the letter, so if you remember nothing else that I have said, you will remember this!"*

This is a remarkable statement! The Book of Ephesians contains some of the most important and practical instructions given in the New Testament. Ephesians is so powerful, deep, detailed and foundational to our view of Jesus Christ, the Church, ourselves and the devil's defeated position, that it demands our fullest attention!

In chapter one Paul covers the deepest and hardest-to-understand theological concepts in Christianity, such as *"election"* (1:4); *"predestination"* (1:5); *"adoption"* (1:5); *"redemption"* (1:7); the *"seal of the Spirit"* (1:13); the *"earnest of the Spirit"* (1:14); and our complete, glorified *"redemption"* (1:14). And this is only chapter one!

Then there is chapter two! In this powerful section of scripture Paul covers the reality of spiritual *"death"* and its fruit (2:2,3); the intervention of God's *"rich mercy"* (2:4); the doctrine of *"grace"* versus man's works (2:8); the *"redemptive"* work of the cross (2:11-18); and *"the foundation of the apostles and prophets"* in the New Testament Church (2:19-22).

In chapters three, four and five, he deals with *"the mystery of God"* revealed (3:9); *"the eternal plan of God"* (3:10); *"the unity of the Spirit, and one Lord, one faith, one baptism"* (4:5); *"apostles, prophets, evangelists, pastors and teachers"* and their ultimate purpose (4:11); *"renewing the mind"* and *"putting on of the new man"* (4:23,24); *"grieving the Holy Spirit"* (4:30); being continually *"filled with the Spirit"* (5:18); God's plan for *"husbands and wives"* and the corresponding example of Christ and His Church (5:22-33).

Yet when you come to the end of this grand epistle that is jam-packed with all of these marvelous truths, Paul says, "Finally. . . ."

A better rendering of this Greek phrase may be, *"In conclusion, I have saved the most important part of this epistle until the end of the letter, so that if you remember nothing else that I have said, you will remember this. I want this to stand out in your mind."*

Spiritually Lopsided Believers

Considering the powerful content contained in the first five chapters of Ephesians, surely you can now see why I said that it is remarkable that Paul would say spiritual armor was the most important thing he had to say in the Book of Ephesians! At first, this perplexed me greatly. I asked myself,

"How could the issue of spiritual armor be more important than the doctrine of election?"

"How could the issue of spiritual warfare be more important than the doctrine of predestination?"

"How is it possible that it could be more important than the doctrine of adoption?"

"Could it possibly be more important than understanding the eternal plan of God?"

"Why would Paul save this section on spiritual armor and spiritual warfare until the very last of this powerful epistle, and then conclude that it was more important than any of these other things?"

"Why?"

Then I came to see and understand why Paul had made this outrageous statement about spiritual warfare and spiritual armor. The issues of spiritual armor and spiritual warfare are *not* more important than these other Bible doctrines — *generally speaking!* They couldn't be!

These doctrines are *extremely important* for us to know and understand; they are *foundational* to all that we believe about the work of the cross. But, at this specific time and for the specific readers to whom Paul was writing, spiritual warfare and spiritual armor were *temporarily more important* for a very practical reason.

Like so many in the Church world today, the believers to whom Paul was writing had gathered together a vast accumulation of spiritual knowledge, information and facts. Nevertheless, with all of this knowledge, information and facts at their fingertips, they were spiritually defeated in their personal lives. While they could have answered nearly any Bible question which you could have put before them, their personal lives were falling to pieces.

Ephesians 4:25-31 identifies a few of the problems that were afflicting Paul's readers. To mention just a few, Paul commanded them *"to put away lying"* (4:25); *"let not the sun go down upon your wrath"* (4:26); *"neither give place to the devil"* (4:27); *"let him that stole steal no more"* (4:28); *"let no corrupt communication proceed out of your mouths"* (4:29); *"grieve not the*

Holy Spirit" (4:30); and to *"put away all bitterness, and wrath, and anger, and clamour, and evil speaking, and malice"* (4:31).

Does this sound like victorious people to you?

Do victorious people have to be told to stop lying? Do victorious people give place to the devil in their personal lives and relationships? Do victorious people permit corrupt communication to have a place in their conversation? Do victorious people continuously grieve the Holy Spirit with bad attitudes such as bitterness, anger, clamor and malice?

Naturally speaking, the churches that were situated in the Lycus Valley (one was the Church of Ephesus) were more educated in regard to New Testament truth and doctrine than any other region during New Testament times.

We know that the apostle Paul founded the Ephesian Church (Acts19:1-20), and afterwards spent three years of his life raising up the elders in Ephesus (Acts 20:31). Furthermore, at some point after Paul's departure from Ephesus, Timothy arrived on the scene to serve as their pastor (First Timothy 1:3). If we stopped right here, this alone would have made Ephesus the most unique local church in Church history. But there is more!

In addition to the roles of Paul and Timothy in the Church of Ephesus, the apostle John was a member of this church. Moreover, when John moved his ministry base from Israel to the city of Ephesus, he moved Mary — the mother of Jesus — to the city of Ephesus with him, where he cared for her until her death. The mother of Jesus was a member of the Ephesian Church!

I think you can see from this how unusual the local church in Ephesus really was! As the largest church in existence during that day, you can also be certain that other great men and women of God came to minister there. Peter, Apollos and Aquila and Priscilla most assuredly had ministered in this church at some point along the way.

Nevertheless, even with this abundance of excellent ministry and accessibility to spiritual insight and knowledge, they were not experiencing the overcoming, abundant life that Jesus Christ came to offer. Rather, their personal lives were becoming a shambles.

Though the scripture does not specifically say *why* they were experiencing turmoil and defeat in their personal lives, the fact that Paul reserved this text on spiritual warfare and spiritual armor to the end of his epistle implies the reason.

It appears that they were *spiritually lopsided.* They were mature in the realm of doctrine, but had failed to develop in other critically vital areas.

The great bulk of their time and energies had been spent developing doctrine and educating their minds in great and necessary scriptural truth. Because of the newness of the early Church at that time, it was very important for sound doctrine to be taught and analyzed. There was nothing wrong with this. However, while they were growing in their intellectual understanding of the Word, they needed to simultaneously grow in their understanding of spiritual armor and spiritual conflict.

They lived in a world very similar to ours today; it was a world that was full of conflict, violence and upheaval. While they were developing, analyzing and teaching sound doctrine inside the Church at large, they also needed to equip the saints to deal with the hostile surroundings outside the Church.

Studying the Word was an absolute necessity! They needed to intensively search and study the scripture as they began to record doctrine in those early days. This was good! Anyone familiar with me or my ministry knows that I place the highest premium on the study of God's Word! But now they needed to start acting on the knowledge they had obtained.

They needed to take their intellectual understanding of the Word of God and turn it into a *"sword of the Spirit."*

Now they desperately needed to grab hold of that faith they intellectually possessed, and turn it into a *"shield of faith."*

Their knowledge of salvation needed to be forged into a *"helmet of salvation"* and their understanding of God's marvelous grace needed to be transformed into a *"breastplate of righteousness."*

In light of all this, when Paul begins this text on spiritual warfare and spiritual armor, he says, "Finally. . . ."

The word "finally" could be better translated, "in conclusion," or "for the rest of the matter," or *"I've saved the most important part of this epistle until the end, so if you remember nothing else, you will remember this. . . ."*

Comrades in the Fight

As Paul continues on in this verse, he says, "Finally, *my brethren*. . . .".

Now we come to the word "brethren." The word "brethren" is another very significant New Testament word that is overlooked and misunderstood. The word "brethren" is of such tremendous importance to the issue of spiritual armor and spiritual warfare, that we must back up for a moment and study this word before we go any further in Ephesians, chapter six.

The word "brethren" is taken from the Greek word *adelphos* (a-del-phos). It is one of the oldest words in the New Testament. In its most frequent usage the word *adelphos* simply means "brother." However, the word "brethren" has a much deeper meaning than this.

In its very oldest sense, the word *adelphos* ("brother") was used by physicians in the medical world to describe two people who were born from the same womb. So when the early Greeks addressed each other as "brethren," they meant to convey this idea: *"You and me, we are brothers! We came out of the same womb of humanity and we have the same feelings, we have similar emotions, and we deal with the same problems in life. We are truly brethren."*

At least in part, this was Paul's thinking when he addressed his readers as "brethren." By using this word, he was coming right down to the level of his readers and was identifying with their place in life, and with their personal struggles and their victories.

But this is not all there is to the word "brethren." The word "brethren" was not used in a popular sense, like we use it today in the Body of Christ, until the time period of Alexander the Great. Pay careful attention to this important light on the word "brethren."

During the time of Alexander the Great, the word "brother" began to take a new twist; it began to carry a militaristic notion. Considering that Ephesians 6:10-18 is a text about spiritual warfare and spiritual armor, there is no doubt that Paul also has this militaristic notion in his mind when he addresses his readers as "brethren."

Alexander the Great was irrefutably the finest soldier whom the world has ever known. By the age of 18 years he had already conquered the entire eastern empire, and by the age of 33 years, the western empire had fallen into his hands. From Europe to the northern end of Africa, and reaching over into Greece, Asia, Turkey and all the way to the western border of India, Alexander the Great had conquered nearly the whole civilized world of his day. In one single military strike against the Persians, he overcame 40,000 Persian aggressors, losing only one hundred and ten fighting men of his own.

The fame and notoriety of this young and powerful man of war was so widespread and revered, that soldiers from all over the far-flung empire desired to have some kind of personal acquaintance with him. To know Alexander personally, and to have his recognition, was the highest honor that a military man could receive.

Therefore, on very special occasions, Alexander would host ceremonies during which time he would summon hard-working, especially brave soldiers onto a giant platform to stand next to his side. Once on the platform and next to his side, Alexander the Great would ceremonially give public recognition to these special soldiers who had fought so hard and had gone the extra mile in battle.

Before a large audience of adoring military men, Alexander would place his arm around individual faithful fighters one at a time and would publicly declare, "Let all the empire know that Alexander is proud to be the *brother* of this soldier." Therefore, the word "brother" (as it was used during Alexander's time) really carried the idea of "comrade" or a "fellow soldier."

With this in mind, we know that the word "brother" portrays the picture of two soldiers who are fighting in the same fight who, like two brothers born from the same womb, share similar feelings, desires and fears — and yet these brothers have learned how to overcome these emotions and how to gain victory in the midst of difficult attacks and confrontations.

To these men, to be a "brother" meant you were a true *comrade*. Through it all they stayed united together in the heat of the fray, and thus they achieved a special level of "brotherhood" that only soldiers know.

So when Paul addressed his readers as "my brethren," he was imparting a powerful message to his readers. He was saying, *"We are out of the same womb of humanity, and we share similar feelings, struggles and emotions in life — but we have not been conquered by these things. Like myself, you are still in the fight and are giving it your best shot. Therefore, I am personally proud to be affiliated with people like you — we are brothers!"*

Soldiers Who Are Worthy of Your Association

Even though Paul's readers were obviously struggling in their personal lives when Paul wrote them, they had not given up the fight! They were still in there, slugging it out, and plodding along one step at a time. This kind of ongoing commitment to stay in the battle constitutes the kind of believers who are worth knowing and affiliating with.

Regardless of how good or bad they are doing in the middle of their fight, *at least they are still fighting!* Others have given up, but they haven't given up. According to Paul, these are the very kind of people whom we should view as "comrades" in the faith.

This is good news for those who are having a difficult time in life right now. The adversary tries to accuse them of being spiritual failures because they haven't achieved total victory in their lives yet. But as long as they remain faithful to the fight, and refuse to relinquish their stand of faith to the enemy, they are still exceptionally fine soldiers! They are the very kind of soldiers that any of us should be happy to know and associate with!

The word "brother" emphatically means that it's not how well you fight that really counts in life. *What really counts is that you keep on fighting.* This always eventually produces winners!

Chapter Seven
Be Strong in the Lord

Before Paul begins his message on armor, he first urges us to receive supernatural power! In this chapter we are going to see what Paul has to say about this supernatural power that God has made available to us. Ephesians 6:10 continues to say, "Finally, my brethren, be strong in the Lord. . . ."

What does it mean "to be strong in the Lord?"

First of all, the word "strong" is taken from the word *endunamoo* (en-du-na-moo), which is a compound of the Greek words *en* (pronounced "in") and *dunamis* (du-na-mis). The word *en* means "in" and the word *dunamis* means "explosive strength, ability, or power." The word *dunamis* is where we get the word "dynamite."

Taken together as one word, as Paul uses it in this text, the word *endunamoo* describes an "empowering" or an "inner strengthening." It conveys the idea of *"being infused with an excessive dose of dynamic inner strength and ability."*

Because the first part of *endunamoo* means "into" and the second part depicts "explosive power," it is easy to conclude that this word portrays a "power" that is being deposited "into" something; something like a container, a vessel or some other form of receptacle. The very nature of this word emphatically means that there necessarily must be some type of *receiver* for this "power" to be deposited "into." This is where *we* come into the picture!

We are specially designed by God to be the receptacles for this divine power. Thus, the reason Paul urges us, "Finally, my brethren, *be strong. . . ."* The idea is, *"Receive a supernat-*

ural, strengthening, internal deposit of power into your inner man."
God is the Giver of this explosive power, and according to
Ephesians 6:10, we are the receptacles "into" which this
"power" is to be deposited.

The Greek tense used here, in Ephesians 6:10, is the *present passive imperative.* The *present imperative tense* means Paul
was not simply suggesting that they receive this power; he
was *commanding* them to receive this power, and furthermore,
to receive it as soon as possible.

There is no question about Paul's intentions in this verse.
The *present imperative tense* means he was urging them in the
strongest of words; he was commanding them to open their
hearts to receive a brand new touch of God's power into their
lives.

In addition to the *present imperative tense,* Paul also uses
the *passive tense* in the statement "be strong." The *passive tense*
describes the ongoing, lasting effect of this power upon our
lives. The *passive tense* tells us that this special *endunamoo*
power is more than a one-shot experience. On the contrary,
once this special power is released in a believer's life, while
it is true that there will be an immediate "strengthening"
effect, this is a power that continues "strengthening" that
believer for a long, long time to come.

Paul knew that there was an ongoing experience with
God's power that was available for believers. He also knew
that we desperately needed this special touch of supernatural
power in order to successfully combat the attacks that the
enemy would bring against us in this life.

In light of these things, Paul urges us to open our spirit,
soul and body to God so we may receive this supernatural
strength. In fact, his desire for us to receive this power was
so earnest, that he used the *present passive imperative tense.*
Again, he was not *suggesting* that we receive this power; he
was *commanding* us to receive this power, and to receive it just
as quickly as possible.

In a very strong, authoritative tone of voice, Paul commanded all believers everywhere, *"Be infused with supernat-*

ural strength and ability. . ." "Be empowered with this special touch of God's strength. . ." "You must receive this inner strengthening. . ."

Why was Paul so strong on this point? Because he knew believers needed to receive this power before their fight with unseen forces commenced. Without this power, no believer could ever be a match for the witty schemes and devices of Satan, or against the demon spirits that come to war against our souls.

Moreover, without this supernatural power of the Holy Spirit operating in us, we are still no match for Satan's schemes and devices. He is intelligent, keen, brilliant, canny, cunning, quick, brainy and shrewd; he is strong, capable, puissant, influencing and determined; he is a wise strategist, orderly planning and arranging systematic assaults against humanity; and he is the epitome of an opportunist, knowing just exactly when to strike with his destructive power.

Naturally speaking, our physical strength does not even begin to compare to his; our intelligence doesn't begin to touch his brilliancy; and our wittiest moment is thoroughly deficient in comparison to his shrewd methods of thinking and operating.

Satan was a powerful, brilliant angel before he fell into his present distorted condition. And though fallen into his present perverted condition, he has still retained much of his former intelligence which was originally given to him by God.

It is true that Jesus stripped him of his *legal authority* over us, but his *intelligence* is still intact. It is his cunning, keen, sharp, witty, brainy mind that he uses against us today. The devil's power is no match for the all-surpassing power of the Holy Spirit, and the devil knows this. Therefore, he seeks to outwit our natural minds with malevolent strategies that he has composed with his incredibly intelligent mind.

To stop these satanic strategies, we must receive this special "empowering" from on high. It will "empower" us deal victoriously with this archenemy of the faith. Paul commanded the early Church to receive this special power — and now the Word of God is giving us the same specific, urgent command: "Finally, my brethren, *be strong. . . ."*

There is no suggestion here on the part of Paul; this is a *direct command.*

Superhuman Power for a Superhuman Task

The word *endunamoo* ("strong") was frequently used by classical Greek writers to describe very carefully and specially selected individuals who were handpicked by the gods to perform some extra-special, superhuman task.

For instance, writers from the classical Greek period would have said that the legendary character, Hercules, and his superhuman strength was a result of the pagan Greek gods depositing *endunamoo* power into him. *Endunamoo* was perfectly suited to illustrate the kind of supernatural strength that Hercules supposedly possessed. With this enduement from the pagan Greek gods, legend says he performed many extra-special, superhuman and supernatural tasks.

The apostle Paul was an exceptionally brilliant and educated man. From his own studies in classical Greek, he doubtless knew this historical usage of the word *endunamoo.* He knew that this word described very carefully and specially selected individuals who were handpicked by the gods to perform some extra-special, superhuman and supernatural task.

So when discussing the supernatural power which the Holy Spirit gives us to withstand the work of the adversary, Paul chose a word that had unmistakable connotations. This word denotes a power that takes mere men and turns them into champions; individuals who possess superhuman and supernatural power.

Furthermore, *endunamoo* is a power that is bestowed on an individual *when he or she is called to perform some special task at hand that is beyond their natural abilities.* This is a power that is given to an individual when a task before him or her will require that they possess superhuman strength.

That Paul would begin this text on spiritual warfare and spiritual armor with this command to receive this *endunamoo* strength, tells us plainly that Paul assuredly believed that our only hope of reinforcing Jesus' victory and demonstrating Satan's defeat, was with the help of this special, supernatural power.

Paul knew emphatically — beyond any shadow of doubt — that when God's power is released full-force into the life of a believer, that strong stream of power takes normal believers and turns them into spiritual giants!

Therefore, Paul commands us in the strongest of terms, *"Be empowered. . . ." "Receive this inner strengthening. . . ." "Be infused with this supernatural strength and ability. . . ."*

Where To Get This Power

Paul continues, "Finally, my brethren, be strong *in the Lord. . . ."*

The phrase *"in the Lord"* is grammatically called the *locative tense.* Simply put, this means that this special power (*endunamoo*) can be found only one place — and that is *"in the Lord."*

The fact that Paul wrote in the *locative tense* tells us that this power is "locked up" in the Person of Jesus Christ, and that this power cannot be found anywhere else. You cannot obtain this special, supernatural power by reading books, listening to tapes, or through any other such means. Thank God for good teaching tapes and books, but this special power can only be obtained through a personal relationship with the Lord Jesus Christ. This power is locked up *"in the Lord."*

The first chapter of Ephesians also uses the *locative tense.* In fact, this same *locative tense* is used seven times in the first chapter of Ephesians to teach that we are "in Christ" (1:3,4; 6,7,11,13). Doctrinally, this means that once redeemed by Jesus Christ, we are "locked up" in the Person of Jesus Christ forever! As Paul told the Corinthians, "But he that is joined unto the Lord, is *one spirit*" (First Corinthians 6:17); or as Paul told his audience on Mars Hill, *"For in him we live, and move and have our being"* (Acts 17:28).

This wonderful *locative tense* is used seven times in Ephesians, chapter one, to declare that we are perpetually, endlessly, and infinitely "locked up" in the Person of Jesus Christ. He has become our realm of existence and habitation. We are *"in Him."*

The reason this special *endunamoo* power of God is so very accessible to you and me, is because both we and this divine power — this special, supernatural power that takes normal people and turns them into spiritual giants — are both gloriously "locked up" in the Person of Jesus Christ. We, as believers, are locked up *"in the Lord,"* and along with us, this special, divine power is also locked up *"in the Lord."*

Though we may not always be mentally aware of it, we are constantly rubbing elbows with this divine power on a day-to-day, hour-to-hour, minute-to-minute basis. The very fact that we are locked up "in the Lord," and this power is locked up "in the Lord," means we are never far away from a new surge of superhuman power into our own human spirits. A fresh surge of this power into us is as accessible as our very next breath of air.

It's Yours for the Taking

Sometime ago, at a large church in the Midwest, I was preaching about this divine flow of power and its accessibility to the believer. At the end of the morning service, I gave an invitation for people who had never been filled with the Spirit to come forward to be filled with the Holy Spirit that morning. At the conclusion of that particular service, many people came forward to receive the infilling of the Holy Spirit.

As I approached the altar to pray with those who had come forward, the pastor turned to me and said, "This morning I want you to watch the way that we pray for people to be filled with the Holy Spirit. By observing the way it is done in our church, you can flow better with the training that our altar workers have received on how to pray for people to be filled with the Spirit."

As he requested, I stepped back to watch as his workers began to pray for people to be filled with the Spirit. One after another they walked along and patted the backs of the people who were kneeling at the altar, and said, *"You've got to pray much harder than you're praying." "You're not praying loud enough." "You must cry and plead to receive from God." "You must tarry here a little longer."*

I was heartbroken at what was happening. These precious, spiritually hungry people had come forward to freely receive from God, and what could have been a beautiful scene had now changed into a nightmare. These sincere, misinstructed people began to vehemently beat themselves spiritually in order to make themselves feel "good enough" to receive from God and be filled with the Spirit.

What a terribly deplorable thing this was to me! To reduce the infilling of the Holy Spirit into a work of the flesh is disgusting — especially when you know that the infilling of the Holy Spirit is a work of grace, and not human effort. It was one of the most spiritually obnoxious sights I have ever observed in a church setting.

God knew that if He made it difficult for us to receive His power, then the majority of us would never receive it.

Knowing this about us, God made it very simple. He permanently "locked us up" inside the Person of Jesus Christ, and He also locked His divine power up inside in the Person of Jesus Christ. By doing this for us, He placed us in a position to rub elbows with this divine power *continuously.* God graciously fixed it so that it would be very difficult for us *not* to freely receive this impartation of superhuman, supernatural strength for the fight.

To experience this ever-available, nearby power, you must open your heart to it and ask that it be released in your life — and by *faith* you must reach out to embrace this divine

power. Because of your position "in the Lord," you are surrounded by this power *right now*. At this very precise
moment you are immersed in this power. *It is yours for the
taking!*

The only prerequisite to receive this power is that you
are "in the Lord." If you are "in Him," as the first chapter of
Ephesians repeats seven times, then you are in position —
right now — to receive a fresh touch of God's strengthening
power into your life.

Paul says, *"Finally, my brethren, be strong in the Lord. . . ."*

Evidence of the Spirit's Power

How can you tell when when God's supernatural
strength is operating in your life?

Paul answers us by saying, "Finally, my brethren, be
strong in the Lord *and in the power of his might."*

Being a Southern Baptist in background, I heard many
discussions about the Holy Spirit as I grew up in my home
church — discussions about what we believed about the Holy
Spirit, and discussions about what we did *not* believe about
the Holy Spirit. As Southern Baptists, we were adamantly
opposed to the Pentecostal view that speaking in tongues was
the initial evidence of the Spirit's empowering.

From our theological point of view, the Pentecostals
didn't have a leg to stand on. Though they had many scriptures to prove that speaking in tongues was the evidence of
the Spirit's empowering, we could explain those verses away
in just a few moments of time.

We believed that speaking in tongues was a phenomenon
designed only for the Book of Acts, which was a special,
never-to-be-repeated "transitional period" to last only long
enough to help the Church get started. According to our
view, healing, miracles, and speaking in tongues were given
only for this "transitional period" and were never intended
to last indefinitely or to be repeated again.

Rather than believe in what we thought were utterly unintellectual, unintelligible, ecstatic, ridiculous utterances called "tongues," we had our *own evidence* of being empowered by the Holy Spirit. And just like the Pentecostals, we also had scriptures to back up our theological point of view.

We declared that *the real evidence* of the Spirit's power was the ability to be a "witness" for Jesus Christ. The proof text for this was Acts 1:8, which says, "But ye shall receive power, after that the Holy Ghost is come upon you: and ye shall be *witnesses* unto me both in Jerusalem, and in all Judaea, and in Samaria, and unto the uttermost parts of the earth."

On the one hand, the Pentecostals said that *the initial evidence* of the Spirit's indwelling power was the ability to speak in tongues, while on the other hand, my former denomination taught that the evidence of the Spirit's power was the ability to be a witness for Jesus Christ.

To be absolutely fair to both Pentecostals and Southern Baptists, in a measure they were both correct in their views. Both of these external signs are *evidences* of the Spirit's abiding power in the life of a believer.

Speaking in tongues is definitely the initial evidence of the fresh, indwelling presence of the Holy Spirit's power in the life of a believer. The Book of Acts is our pattern for this, and the Book of Acts was never intended by God to simply be a "transitional period" until the Church got her feet on the ground. There is absolutely no scripture for this fictional, man-made, so-called "transitional period." Any honest theologian would agree. This doctrine (which is embraced by many denominations) was designed to excuse the Church of her powerlessness and her lack of the supernatural.

However, it is true that becoming a "witness" for Jesus Christ is a subsequent, bona fide proof of the Spirit's ongoing, empowering presence. Jesus Himself stated this in Acts 1:8. *This scripture is so clear that no one can dispute that the Spirit's power always produces strong witnesses.*

Yet becoming a "witness" is not *the initial evidence* that one has been filled with the Spirit. According to the New Testament pattern recorded in the Book of Acts, the initial evidence is speaking in tongues.

The ability to witness is one of many subsequent evidences that follows after we are *initially filled* with the Holy Spirit. In this same category of subsequent evidences, we would find the fruit of the Spirit, the gifts of the Spirit, etc.

Kratos and *Ischuos* Power

But in Ephesians 6:10, Paul gives another very important subsequent evidence of the Spirit's empowering work in our lives! He continues in the verse to say, "Finally, my brethren, be strong in the Lord *and in the power of his might.*"

Let me first remind you that Ephesians 6:10 is a verse about the supernatural power that God has made available for our fight with unseen, demonic powers that come to war against the soul.

The word "strong" used at the first of Ephesians 6:10, is taken from the word *endunamoo*, which describes a power whose purpose is *"to infuse a believer with an excessive dose of inward strength."* This particular type of *endunamoo* power is so strong, it can withstand any attack and it can successfully oppose any kind of force.

To historically prove the supernatural nature of this word, it was used by early writers from the Greek classical periods to denote special individuals, like Hercules, who had been handpicked by the gods, and who were supernaturally invested with superhuman strength in order to accomplish a superhuman task.

This is the kind of "strength" that God has made available to us!

But now we must continue to see what else Paul has to say about this power. In Ephesians 6:10, he says, "Finally, my brethren, be strong in the Lord *and in the power of his might.*"

Especially notice the words "power" and "might." These two words are extremely important for you to understand as you progress in your understanding of spiritual warfare and spiritual armor.

The word "power" is taken from the Greek word *kratos* (kra-tos), and it describes what I have come to call "demonstrated power." In other words, *kratos* power is not a power that you merely adhere to and believe in intellectually. Rather, this *kratos* power is a power that is demonstrative, eruptive, tangible and it almost always comes with some type of external, outward manifestation that one can actually see with his or her own eyes. This means that *kratos* power is not a hypothetical power; this is *real power*.

Ephesians 1:19,20 declares that when God raised Jesus from the dead, He used this very same *kratos* power. "And what is the exceeding greatness of his power to usward who believe, according to the working of his mighty power (*kratos*), which he wrought in Christ when he raised him from the dead. . ."

The King James sentence structure is a bit reversed from the original Greek. The Greek says, "according to the working of *the power of his might*. . . ."

Why is this so significant?

Because *"the power of his might"* is the same identical phrase that is used in Ephesians 6:10 to denote the power that is working behind the scenes to energize us for our combat with unseen, evil powers. The very same, exact, identical kind of power that God used when He raised Jesus from the dead, is the very same, exact, identical power that is now at work in us — *we have resurrection power!*

This is the strongest stream of power that is known in the universe. In fact, this power is so supreme, that in scripture it is only used in reference to God's power. Man does not possess this kind of power — *unless it has been given to him by God!*

Kratos power is so overwhelming that the mighty Roman soldiers who guarded Jesus' tomb on the resurrection morning, fainted and crumbled to the ground beneath the full load of this power, and laid prostrate on the ground, paralyzed, and unable to move, until the resurrection was complete. . .

This *kratos* power was so indomitable, overpowering, conquering and irresistible, that when it flooded the grave where Jesus' dead body lay, it permeated every dead cell and fiber of His body with divine life until it was impossible for death to hold Him. . .

Had you been present at the resurrection, this *kratos* power was so overwhelming that you would have felt the ground trembling as this electrifying force entered the tomb where Jesus' body lay. This was *kratos* power that raised Jesus from the dead! It was an eruptive power; it was a demonstrated power; it was an outwardly visible power; *it was the strongest kind of power that is known to God or man!*

And now Paul uses this very word to describe the power that is available for our use! As a matter of fact, Paul emphatically tells us that if you have had the experience of being filled with and empowered by the Holy Spirit, then this *kratos* power will be *another evidence* of the Spirit's empowering work in your life.

This is why Paul says, "Finally, my brethren, be strong in the Lord and in the *kratos.* . . ." The operation of this *kratos* power in your life is evidence that you have been supernaturally empowered by the Spirit of God. Only divinely empowered people possess this *kratos* power.

When the empowering presence of the Holy Spirit is operative in our lives, it releases in us the very same power that physically raised Jesus Christ from the dead. *This kratos power is an eruptive, demonstrative, visible and outwardly manifested type of power — a power that you can see, and a power that you will experience.*

Because the word *kratos* is normally used to denote a demonstrated or outwardly manifested kind of power, this tells us that when this power begins to operate in us, it immediately seeks an avenue of release so that it might *demonstrate* itself.

In other words, this power doesn't come to us in order to sit idly by and do nothing. This power comes to accomplish some kind of *superhuman task.*

Before he ever began discussing warfare with unseen forces, or before he could begin dealing with the armor of God, Paul knew that first he had to cover the issue of power. Without this power operational in our spiritual lives, there will be no battle. We cannot stand against the deeds of darkness in our own strength — *this is an impossibility.* Furthermore, we do not have the strength in ourselves to carry the heavy armor of God that we so desperately need in our campaign against the wiles of the devil.

Therefore, Paul puts first things first, and begins this text on armor by first dealing with the *kratos* power of God.

Without this power, we are no match for the adversary, and without this power we cannot function in the armor of God. On the other hand, with this *kratos* power at our disposal, the devil is no match for us, and we are well able to fight with the armor God has provided.

God's Mighty Arm!

Paul continues, "Finally, my brethren, be strong in the Lord and in the power of *his might.*"

The word "might" is taken from the word *ischuos* (is-chu-os), and it conveys the picture of a very, very strong man; a strong man like a body-builder; a man who is "able"; a man who is "mighty"; or a man with great muscular capabilities.

Now Paul applies this picture of a strong, muscular man, not to himself, but *to God!* He pictures God as One who is "able, mighty and muscular." I must ask, "Is there anyone more powerful than God?" "Is there anyone more able than

God?" Or, "Is there any force in the universe equal to the muscular ability of God?"

With one stroke of the hand, God's mighty arm released so much creative power that the entire universe was flung into being. . .

With one stroke of the hand, God's mighty arm unloosed so much power that the Tower of Babel, Nimrod and all his wicked cohorts were scattered across the face of the earth. . .

With one stroke of the hand, God's mighty arm discharged such a force that the civilized world of Noah's day was flooded, and an entire period of civilization was wiped out. . .

With one stroke of God's mighty arm, such overwhelming power was released that the cities of Sodom and Gomorrah were forever wiped out by fire and brimstone. . .

With one stroke of God's mighty arm, Egypt's rebellion against God was crushed beyond recognition, and the children of Israel were set free. . .

With one stroke of God's mighty arm, the turbulent, raging walls of waters in the Red Sea collapsed, and came tumbling down to swallow up the pursuing chariots of Pharaoh. . .

With one stroke of God's mighty arm, the wicked powers of the heavenlies were forcibly shoved aside, and though it was physically and medically impossible, Jesus was conceived and miraculously born from a virgin's womb. . .

With one stroke of God's mighty arm, His power surged into the throes of hell itself, where it ripped Jesus out from the pangs of death, and stripped principalities and powers naked and made a public display of their embarrassing defeat. . .

When the mighty arm of God moved on the day of Pentecost, the Holy Spirit came as a "mighty rushing wind" and filled the Upper Room with His awesome power, supernaturally empowering the disciples to preach with the accompaniment of signs and wonders. . .

And now this same mighty arm of God is still *working, working and working.*

Where is this powerful, mighty, able and muscular ability of God working today? *In you and me!* Paul says, "Finally, my brethren, be strong in the Lord *and in the power of his might."*

The reason *kratos* power is so powerful and demonstrative (as in the resurrection of Jesus from the dead), is because God's muscles (*ischuos*) are backing it up! One expositor has accurately translated Ephesians 6:10, ". . .*be strong in the Lord and in the powerful, outwardly demonstrated ability that works in you as a result of God's great muscular ability".*

All that God is, and all the power that He possesses, and all of the energy of His muscular and mighty ability, is what energizes the *kratos* power that now is at work in believers who have been empowered by the Spirit. All of this is at work in you and me!

Ready for Battle

With this power at your disposal, now you are ready to commence your successful confrontation with unseen, demonic spirits that come to wage war against the flesh and the soul.

For this reason, Paul continues to tell us, "Put on the whole armour of God that ye may be able to stand against the wiles of the devil" (Ephesians 6:11).

In the next chapter, we will see how to recognize *the wiles, devices and deception of the devil!*

Chapter Eight
The Wiles, Devices and Deception of the Devil

Paul continues to say, "Put on the whole armour of God, that ye may be able to stand against the wiles of the devil" (Ephesians 6:11).

The phrase "whole armour" is taken from the Greek word *panoplia* (pan-op-lia), and it refers to a Roman soldier who is fully dressed in his armor from head to toe. Since this is the example that Paul puts before us, we must consider the full dress, the *panoplia*, of the Roman soldier.

Because of Paul's many imprisonments, this was an easy illustration for Paul to use. Standing next to these illustrious soldiers during his prison internments, Paul could see the Roman soldier's *loinbelt, huge breastplate, brutal shoes affixed with spikes, massive, full-length shield, intricate helmet, piercing sword, and long, specially tooled lance* which could be thrown a tremendous distance to hit the enemy from afar.

The Roman soldier of New Testament times basically wore these seven pieces of armor, both offensive and defensive. These pieces of weaponry can be found in our museums today.

First of all, the Roman soldier wore *a loinbelt*. Though it was the ugliest and most common piece of weaponry that the Roman soldier wore, *it was the central piece of armor that held all the other parts together*. For instance, the loinbelt held the breastplate in place; the shield rested on a clip on the side of the loinbelt; and on the other side of the loinbelt was another clip on which the Roman soldier hung his massive sword when it was not in use.

The loinbelt was so ordinary that no soldier would have written home to tell his family about his new loinbelt. Yet the loinbelt was the most important piece of weaponry that the Roman soldier owned because of its importance to the other pieces of armor. Without the loinbelt, these other pieces of weaponry would have fallen off of the soldier (we will cover more on this in chapter ten).

In addition to the loinbelt, the Roman soldier also wore a second weapon — *a magnificent and beautiful breastplate.* The breastplate of the Roman soldier was made out of two large sheets of metal. One piece covered the front of the soldier, and the other piece covered the back, and these sheets of metal were attached at the top of the shoulders by large brass rings. Frequently these metal plates were comprised of smaller, scale-like pieces of metal, causing the breastplate to look very similar to the scales of a fish. Later on, the breastplate was most often referred to as a "coat of mail."

This heavy piece of weaponry began at the bottom of the neck and extended down past the waist to the knees. From the waist to the knees it took on the resemblance of a skirt. The breastplate was by far the heaviest piece of equipment that the Roman soldier owned. Depending upon the physical stature of the soldier, this piece of equipment at times could weigh in excess of 40 pounds. In First Samuel 17:5, we are told that Goliath's breastplate weighed "five thousand shekels of brass," or the equivalent of 125 pounds! (This "breastplate of righteousness" is the topic of chapter eleven).

In addition to this beautiful coat of mail, the Roman soldier also wore a third weapon — *very dangerous shoes.* These shoes were not like the Roman sandals that people wear today. The sandals people wear today are merely a flimsy little piece of twine that is wrapped around their heel and their toe.

The shoes which the Roman soldier wore were primarily made of two pieces of metal. The first piece of the Roman shoe was called *a greave.* This was a piece of bronze or brass that had been wrapped around the soldier's lower legs. Beginning right at the top of the knee, it extended down past the calf of the leg and rested on the top of the foot. Because this tube-like piece of metal covered the lower leg of the soldier, the Roman soldier's shoes looked like boots that were made of brass!

The top, sides and bottom of the foot were decked with a very thick piece of heavy metal. On the bottom, the Roman soldier's shoes were affixed with extremely dangerous spikes. If you were a civilian soldier, the spikes on the bottom of your shoes were approximately one inch long. If, however, you were involved in active combat, the spikes on the bottom of your shoes could be somewhere between one to three inches long. These shoes, which Paul amazingly calls "shoes of peace" in Ephesians 6:15, were intended to be "killer shoes" (These "shoes of peace" will be fully dealt with in chapter twelve).

In addition to these "killer shoes," the Roman soldier also carried a fourth important weapon — *a large, oblong shield*. This massive shield was made of multiple layers of animal hide that were tightly woven together, and were then framed along the edges by a strong piece of metal or wood. (We will cover the "shield of faith" in chapter thirteen).

The fifth weapon which the Roman soldier wore was his *helmet*. This all-important piece of armor, which protected the soldier from receiving a fatal blow to the head, at times weighed 15 pounds or more. Surprisingly, while the breastplate was the most beautiful piece of weaponry which the Roman soldier possessed, the helmet was the most noticeable. It would have been very difficult to pass by a Roman soldier without noticing his helmet (we will see more on this "helmet of salvation" in chapter fourteen).

The sixth weapon of the Roman soldier was his *sword*. While there were many kinds of swords during that time, the sword which the Roman soldier carried was a very heavy, broad and massive sword that was specifically created for jabbing and killing an adversary or foe (the "sword of the Spirit" will be the subject of chapter fifteen).

And seventh, the Roman soldier carried *a specially tooled lance* that was designed to strike the enemy from a distance.

Most have not recognized the presence of the lance in Ephesians 6:10-18, but the lance must be present in the text because we are told to "put on the *whole armour* of God. . . ." There is no doubt that the lance was a part of the whole armour of the Roman soldier. In order for Paul to carry through this illustration about the "whole armour of God," it is absolutely necessary for the lance to be included in this text.

In the chapters to come, you will see that the lance is indeed a very important part of *"the whole armour of God"* (the lance will be thoroughly covered in chapter sixteen).

A New Set of Clothes!

These weapons are clearly taken from the picture of a Roman soldier who is dressed in full armor; he is *dressed to kill!* With this example before us, now Paul gives us a powerful word of instruction. He says, "Put on the whole armour of God, that ye may be able to stand against the wiles of the devil" (Ephesians 6:11).

Especially notice that Paul says, *"Put on. . . ."* The phrase "put on" is taken from the Greek word *enduo* (though similar in appearance to the word *endunamoo* which we studied in chapter seven, pages 97-101, these two words are *not* similar in meaning).

The word *enduo* is frequently used throughout the New Testament. In fact, it is the exact word Luke used when he recorded Jesus, as saying, "And behold, I send the promise of my Father upon you: but tarry ye in the city of Jerusalem until ye be *endued* with power from on high" (Luke 24:49).

The word *enduo* refers to the act of "putting on a new set of clothes." In light of this, one expositor has properly translated Luke 24:49, ". . . but tarry ye in the city of Jerusalem until ye be *clothed* with power from on high." The word *enduo* has to do with the "putting on of a new set of clothes."

Paul used the word *enduo* throughout his writings to symbolically depict the "putting on" of the new man. In both Ephesians 4:24 and Colossians 3:10, he urges us to *"put on the new man. . . ."* By using the word *enduo* in these two particular passages, Paul tells us to "put on" the new man and the fruit of our new life in the same way that one would put on a brand new set of clothes.

Now Paul uses the word *enduo* in Ephesians 6:11 in this same way (i.e., to denote the act of "putting on a new set of clothes"), only now he uses this word in connection with spiritual armor. He instructs us to *"Put on the whole armour of God. . . ."*

Moreover, he uses the *imperative tense* in this text. This means he was not making a suggestion, but rather, he was issuing the very strongest kind of command that can be given. In the strongest tone of voice available, he is commanding us with great urgency to take some kind of immediate action. This action is so important, that when Paul speaks to us, he speaks in the *imperative tense* — commanding and ordering us to *"Be clothed with the whole armour of God. . . ."*

We can reject his command to "Put on the whole armour of God," or we can accept it. If we choose to take Paul's command to heart, then we must learn *how* to put on "the whole armour of God."

How Do You Put on the Whole Armor of God?

Paul describes this weaponry as "the whole armour *of God."* Especially notice the phrase *"of God."* This little phrase is taken from the Greek phrase *tou theo* (tou the-o), and it is written in the *genitive case.*

Simply put, this means this supernatural set of weaponry comes directly *from God Himself; God is the source of origination for this armor.* Thus, the verse could be accurately translated, "Put on the whole armor *that comes from God. . . ."*

Because this weaponry has its origination in God, it is vital for us to remain in unbroken fellowship with God in order for us to continually enjoy the benefits of this spiritual armor. By breaking fellowship with the Lord, we step away from our all-important power source. But as long as our fellowship with the Lord is intact, then our power source is also intact.

I am amazed by people who ignore their spiritual lives and cease to walk in the power of God, and then complain because it seems like all kinds of trouble breaks loose in their lives! They often look for deep, dark reasons for this trouble that has erupted in their lives — when the reason for this outbreak of confusion is simple: spiritual armor has its source in God, and when you temporarily cease to walk in fellowship with the Lord and in the power of God, you are choosing to temporarily step away from the source from which this armor comes!

Just as we draw our life *from God*, and just as we draw our nature *from God*, and just as we draw our spiritual power *from God*, this spiritual armor also comes *from God*.

What happens to your spiritual life when you temporarily cease to walk in fellowship with the Lord? In that state of being, do you enjoy abundant life as you once did? *Of course not!*

While abundant life still belongs to you, this state of stagnation will pull the plug on abundant life so that you cannot enjoy it as you once did. Why? *Because abundant life has its source in the Lord!* When you temporarily cease to walk in fellowship with the Lord, you are electing to temporarily walk away from that flow of abundant life.

What happens to the power of the Holy Spirit in a believer's life when he or she develop a "who cares" attitude about their spiritual development? Does that believer continue to enjoy the power of God in his or her life? *Certainly not!*

While the power of God is still available to that believer, this "who cares" attitude temporarily pulls the plug on their power source. Why? *Because this spiritual power has its origination in the Lord!* When you temporarily stop walking in fellowship with the Lord, you are choosing to temporarily stop the flow of this divine power into your life.

Furthermore, what happens to a believer's ability to walk in spiritual armor when he or she temporarily suspends their relationship with the Lord? Does that believer continue to reap the benefits of their God-given spiritual armor in this state of suspension? *Of course not!*

While this spiritual armor is still accessible for them to use and enjoy, by temporarily suspending his or her relationship with the Lord, he or she is opting to temporarily suspend their ability to walk in the armor of God — the very armor that God gave to protect and defend them. Why? *Because spiritual armor has its origination in the Lord!* By putting your spiritual life temporarily "on hold," you have opted to lay your armor aside until you begin walking in fellowship with the Lord again.

Many people begin each new day by pretending to "put on the whole armour of God." When they awaken and get out of bed in the morning, the first thing they do is to act as though they are actually putting on each piece of their weaponry.

They reach down to their waist, and pretend that they are actually wrapping the loinbelt of truth around them; they reach to their chest and carry on as though they are actually placing a breastplate of righteousness across their upper torso; they manipulate their feet as though they are really putting shoes of peace on their feet; they reach over and act as though they are really picking up a shield of faith to carry throughout the day; they pretend to put on a helmet of salvation; and they simulate the movements of one who is placing a sword in its scabbard along their side.

While this daily routine is fine to do, and may help some people to focus better on their spiritual life (especially children), this daily simulation of putting on a suit of armor *does not* put "the whole armour of God" on anyone.

The armour of God is ours by virtue of our relationship with God! Thus, the reason that Paul wrote in the genitive case. He wanted us to know that this armor originates in God, and is freely bestowed upon those who continually draw their life and existence from God. *Your unbroken, ongoing relationship with God is your absolute guarantee that you are constantly and habitually dressed in "the whole armour of God."*

Also notice that in Ephesians 6:11, Paul says, "Put on the *whole armour* of God. . . ." God has not provided a partial set of weaponry for us; He has provided a *complete* set of weaponry for us. He has given us "the *whole armour* of God."

Again, the phrase "whole armour" is taken from the word *panoplia* and pictures a Roman soldier that is fully dressed in his armor from head to toe. Everything the soldier needed to successfully combat his adversary was at his disposal; likewise, God has given us *everything* we need to successfully combat opposing spiritual forces! *Nothing is lacking!*

It is unfortunate that some denominations and Charismatic organizations have majored only on certain parts of the armor of God. Some teach incessantly on "the shield of faith" and the "sword of the Spirit" and neglect the other pieces of armor which God has given us. Other groups and denominations seem to preach and teach on nothing but the "helmet of salvation" week after week. They have their helmets on, *but otherwise they are stark naked!* We are commanded to "put on the *whole armour* of God. . . ."

Thank God for our loinbelt of truth, *but God gave us more than a loinbelt. . .* Thank God for our breastplate, *but God gave us more than a breastplate. . .* Thank God for our shoes of peace, *but God gave us more than shoes of peace. . .* Thank God for our shield, *but God gave us more than a shield. . .* Praise God for our helmet, *but God gave us more than a helmet. . .*and thank God for our sword of the Spirit, *but we have been given more than the sword of the Spirit!*

We have been given "the *whole armour* of God!" It is this armor that Paul commands us to pick up and use in the course of our Christian lives!

⁺. Maintaining a Strategic Position Over the Battlefield of Your Life and Mind

As Paul continues in this passage, he tells us "why" we need this armor. He says, "Put on the whole armour of God, *that ye may be able to stand against the wiles of the devil.*"

Especially notice the phrase, ". . . that ye may be *able*. . . ." The word "able" is from the word *dunamis* (du-na-mis), and it describes "explosive ability, dynamic strength or power." This Greek phrase could be more accurately translated, ". . . *that you may have incredible, explosive, dynamic power*. . . ." By using this word, Paul declares that when we are equipped with "the whole armour of God," we have explosive and dynamic power at our command!

This *dunamis* power is so strong that, when we are walking in the whole armor of God, for the first time in our lives, we are equipped to confront and pursue the enemy, rather than be pursued by him. Because of this *dunamis* power that is at our command, we become the aggressors! This is why Paul continued to say, ". . . that ye may be able *to stand against*. . . ."

The phrase "to stand" is taken from the word *stenai* (stenai), and it literally means "to stand." In this verse, Paul uses the word *stenai* to picture a Roman soldier who is standing upright and tall, with his shoulders thrown back, and his head lifted high. This is the image of a proud and confident soldier, and not one who is slumped over in defeat and despondency.

This word *stenai* ("to stand") depicts what we look like to the spirit realm when are walking in "the whole armour of God." This armor puts us in a winning position! There is no reason for us to live our lives slumped over in defeat. *We are equipped to beat the living daylights out of any foe that would dare assault us.*

Hence, we can walk boldly and confidently — with our shoulders thrown back, and our head lifted high; because we are dressed in "the whole armour of God!"

There is something else important about this word *stenai* which must be pointed out. The word *stenai* was used in a military sense to mean "to maintain a critical and strategic military position over a battlefield." Why is this so important? Because this meaning of *stenai* implies that we have a responsibility "to stand guard" over the battlefields of our own lives!

If God has called you and given you a specific job to do in the Body of Christ, then you must "stand guard" and "maintain a critical position" over that job until it is fulfilled. The devil does not want you to fulfill the call of God upon your life. He may try to attack that call from God, and turn it into a battlefield. Therefore, until the job is finished and the battle is won, you must "stand guard" over the will of God for your life. You must determine that you will not give the enemy an inch! This is your responsibility!

The most important battlefield of your life is your mind! As stated before in this book, spiritual warfare *is* primarily a matter of the mind. As long as the mind is held in check and is renewed to right thinking by the Word of God, the majority of spiritual attacks will fail. However, when the mind is left open and unguarded, it becomes the primary battlefield that Satan uses to destroy lives, finances, businesses, marriages, emotions, and so on. It is your responsibility to "stand guard" over these areas of your life!

An Eyeball-to-Eyeball Confrontation!

Notice the next word in this verse! Paul continues, ". . . that ye may be able to stand *against*. . . ." The word "against" is derived from the word *pros* and it denotes a "forward position" or "a face-to-face encounter."

By employing the word *pros* in this verse, Paul is portraying the picture of a soldier who is looking his enemy directly in the face — *eyeball to eyeball!* This is a soldier that is standing tall; his shoulders are thrown back, and his head is lifted high; he is so bold, daring and courageous, that he is now fearlessly glaring right into the eyes of his adversary. The word *pros* undoubtably depicts an *eyeball-to-eyeball confrontation!*

This clearly demonstrates that, with the power of God and the armor of God on our side, we are more than a match for the enemy! Moreover, we are a fearsome and terrible plight to his domain! Rather than shudder at the thought of what the devil can do to us, this spiritual armor puts us in a super-powerful position to make the devil shudder and tremble at the thought of what we can do to him!

With this armor of God in hand, we are so mighty and powerful in Jesus Christ, that the devil and his forces are no match for us! When we are dressed in this suit of armor, we become mighty spiritual warriors who are "dressed to kill!"

Taking a Stand Against the Wiles of the Devil

Why do we need this armor? What are we supposed to "stand against" in this conflict? Paul tells us, "Put on the whole armour of God, that ye may be able to stand against *the wiles of the devil*" (Ephesians 6:11).

What are "the wiles of the devil?"

The word "wiles" is one of three key words which you must know and understand when discussing the subject of spiritual warfare. These three key words are: (1) *"wiles,"* (2) *"devices,"* and (3) *"deception."* It is impossible to have a correct and balanced view of spiritual warfare without having an understanding of these three foundational words.

The word "wiles" (the first of these three words) is taken from the Greek word *methodos* (meth-o-dos). It is a compound of the words *meta* (me-ta) and *odos* (pronounced ho-dos). The word *meta* is a preposition which simply means "with." The word *odos* is the Greek word for a "road." By compounding these two words into one, they form the word *methodos*. Literally translated, the Greek word *methodos* means "with a road."

It is from this word *methodos* that we derive the word "method." But the English word "method" is not really strong enough to convey the full meaning of *methodos* ("wiles"). The word *methodos* was carefully selected by the Holy Spirit because it tells us *exactly* how the devil operates, and it tells us *exactly* how he comes to attack and assault a believer's mind.

The word "wiles" (*methodos*) is often translated to carry the idea of something that is "cunning, crafty, subtle or full of trickery." However, in its most literal sense, the word *methodos* means "with a road." So the most basic translation of the word "wiles" is simply "with a road."

By electing to use this word, Paul tells us *how* the devil puts his cunning, crafty, subtle, and tricky deception to work! The word "wiles" plainly tells us that the devil operates "with a road" or "on a road." *What does this mean?*

Contrary to the common belief of most people, this means that the devil *does not* have as many tricks in his bag as he would have you to believe. The word "wiles" (*methodos*) plainly means that the enemy travels on *one road*; he travels on *one lane*; or he travels on *one avenue*. In other words, he primarily has only *one trick* in his bag — and he obviously has learned to use that *one trick* very well!

"What is that one trick that the devil uses against people?" Or perhaps we should more correctly ask, "If the devil operates on one single avenue of travel, where is that diabolical road headed toward?" These questions lead us to the second important word to understand when discussing spiritual warfare: the word *"devices."*

The Devices of the Devil

In Second Corinthians 2:11, Paul gives us a clue as to where this road the devil is traveling on is headed. He says, ". . . we are not ignorant of Satan's *devices.*"

The word "devices" is taken from the word *noemata* (no-e-ma-ta), which is derived from the word *nous* (pronounced noous). The word *nous* is the Greek word for the "mind" or the "intellect." However, the form *noemata*, as used by Paul in Second Corinthians 2:11, carries out the idea of *a deceived mind*. Specifically, this word *noemata* denotes the insidious and malevolent plot of Satan to fill the human mind with "confusion."

The word "devices" (*noemata*) actually depicts the "insidious plots" and "wicked schemes" of Satan to attack and victimize the human mind. One expositor has even stated that the word "devices" bears the notion of *"mind games."* With this idea of "mind games" in mind, you could translate the verse, *". . . we are not ignorant of the mind games that Satan tries to pull on us."*

Because Paul used this word "devices" to describe attacks which he, himself, had resisted, we know that even Paul had to deal with the mental assaults of the adversary from time to time. Even Paul knew about the "mind games" which the devil tries to pull on people!

It was for this very reason that Paul said, "Casting down *imaginations,* and every high thing that exalteth itself against the knowledge of God, and bringing into captivity *every thought* to the obedience of Christ" (Second Corinthians 10:5).

The devil loves to make a playground out of people's minds! He delights in filling their emotions and senses with illusions that captivate their minds and ultimately destroy them. He is a master when it comes to "mind games."

Like Paul, we must make a mental decision to take charge of our minds and "take every thought captive to the obedience of Christ." *We must stop listening to ourselves, and start speaking to ourselves!*

The devil always tries to manipulate our emotions and senses in order to pull a "mind game" on us. Therefore, we must speak to our emotions and senses, and we must dictate to them and tell them what to believe!

By considering the words "wiles" and "devices," we have now seen two vitally important things which we *must* know about the devil's strategy to attack and victimize the human mind.

First, the word "wiles" (*methodos*) explicitly tells us that the devil travels "with a road" or "on a road." This road which the devil is traveling on is obviously headed somewhere! *Where is that road headed?*

The word "devices" clearly demonstrates that this road of the devil is headed toward *the mind*. Whoever controls the mind, also controls that person's health and emotions. The enemy knows this! Therefore, he seeks to penetrate our intellect, our mental control center, so that he may flood it with deception and falsehood. Once this is accomplished, then from this position of control, the devil can begin to manipulate that person's body and emotions.

When this penetration into the mind is accomplished, and once the adversary has paved a road into that person's mind and emotions, the process of mental and spiritual captivity is well under way. If this devilish process is not aborted by the power of God, and by the renewing of the mind, it is only a matter of time before a solid stronghold of deception will begin to dominate and manipulate that person's self-image, emotional status and his overall thinking.

This leads us to the third word which we must understand when discussing spiritual warfare: the word *"deception."*

The Deception of the Devil

Deception occurs when a person believes the lies that the enemy has been telling him. The moment you begin to believe the lie that the devil has been telling you, is the very moment when those wicked thoughts and mind games begin to produce reality in your life.

The devil may assault your mind by repeatedly telling you that you are a failure. However, as long as you resist those allegations, they will exert absolutely no power in your life.

If, on the other hand, you begin to give credence to these lies and mentally perceive them as though they are really the truth, those lies will begin to dictate to you and will dominate your emotions and your thinking. In the end, your faith in that lie will give power to it, and will cause it to become a bona fide reality in your life; *and you will become a failure*. This is completed deception.

Many marriages fail because of allegations that the enemy tries to pound into the mind. As long as those allegations are repelled, they exert no power in that marriage. However, when a spouse pays attention to those lies and begins to dwell on them, they have taken the first fatal step toward deception.

For instance, though their marriage is in tip-top shape, a spouse may begin to have unjustified questions and suspicions about their marriage. This is clearly the work of the enemy to deteriorate one's confidence in his or her marriage. At first, the husband or wife absolutely knows that this is an outright lie of the devil. Indeed, their marriage has never been better! Yet, the enemy continues to pound away at his or her mind, *"Your spouse isn't pleased with you. . ." "Your marriage is in trouble. . ." "This relationship can never last. . ." "It's too good to be true. . ."*

By listening to those insinuations and giving credence to them, this dear Christian sadly opens the door for the devil to continue pounding away at the mind and to prey on his or her emotions. After a period of time, if the mind, battered and weary from worrying, begins to believe these lying allegations, their belief in those lying emotions and suspicions may empower them to become a reality.

By mentally embracing such lying emotions, the believer opens a door for the enemy to penetrate his or her mind, and thus, the process of confusion is implemented; mind games are set in motion; and that believer's perception of things becomes twisted and bent.

If this seducing, deceiving process is not stopped at this point, it is probably only a matter of time before this weary-minded believer begins to embrace these mental lies as though they are really the truth.

What is the end result of all this? By falsely believing that his or her marriage is a failure; by falsely believing that his or her marriage is on the rocks; by falsely believing that they will die of a terminal disease; by falsely believing that they have no future; this believer opens the door for the devil to take these suggestions, and move them from the thought realm into the natural realm, where they become a bona fide reality. *Their false perception empowered the lie, and the devil uses that false belief to create!*

Perhaps the enemy has constantly bombarded your mind about sickness. Perhaps his lying allegations have repeatedly told you that you are going to contract a terrible disease and die an early death. When these lies first assaulted your mind, you resisted them and refused to believe what you were hearing. Now, however, you have begun to wonder if these thoughts may have some validity.

If this process is not stopped, it will only be a matter of time until you truly begin to feel physically sick in your body. Do not give credence to those lying insinuations! When you embrace those "mind games" and perceive them as truth, you give power to them! Thus, if you do not speak to yourself and take charge of your mind, the complete process of deception will continue working in your life, until finally, the process is complete and your fears become reality. *When this occurs, you are deceived.*

So these three things — *the wiles, devices and deception of the devil* — are extremely important for us to see and understand, especially when studying the subject of spiritual warfare.

For review, the word *"wiles"* (*methodos*) tells us that the devil operates "with a road" or primarily with "one avenue" of attack.

Secondly, the word *"devices"* (*noemata*) tells us where that avenue is headed: It is headed toward *the mind.* Once that road is paved into the mind, the enemy begins to regularly travel in and out of one's mind and emotions to confuse and scramble the mind with wrong thinking, wrong believing and false perceptions.

In the third place, *"deception"* occurs when you embrace that lie that the devil is telling you. This false perception which you have embraced will empower that lie to become a bona fide reality in your life. *This is completed deception.*

An Example of Demonic Intimidation

Perhaps the best Biblical example of *the wiles, devices and deceptions of the devil* can be found in the story of David and Goliath.

By studying the true-life story of David and Goliath, you will see all *three* of these negative forces at work, and you will see how the devil used lying allegations to intimidate the armies of Israel so that they were functionally paralyzed for forty days — until David came along with the power of God to challenge those lying allegations!

In First Samuel, chapter seventeen, the devil used Goliath to intimidate and confuse the armies of Israel for forty days. His outlandish, arrogant, boastful and proud declarations of their demise were so effective, that not one soldier from the Hebrew camp was willing to stand up to this aggressor!

The Word says, "And the Philistines stood on a mountain on the one side, and the Israelites stood on a mountain on the other side: and there was a valley between them. *And there went out a champion out of the camp of the Philistines, named Goliath, of Gath, whose height was six cubits and a span"* (First Samuel 17:3,4).

No wonder the Israelites were intimidated by Goliath! The appearance of this giant alone would be intellectually and emotionally overwhelming. Goliath was six cubits and a span tall, which is 9 feet 9 inches tall!

The next verses say, *"And he had a helmet of brass upon his head, and he was armed with a coat of mail; and the weight of the coat was five thousand shekels of brass. And he had greaves of brass upon his legs, and a target of brass between his shoulders. And the staff of his spear was like a weaver's beam; and his spear's head weighed six hundred shekels of iron; and one bearing a shield went before him"* (verses 5-7).

Goliath was armed to the max! Notice that the "coat of mail" he wore weighed "five thousand shekels of brass." As stated on page 116, five thousand shekels of brass is *the equivalent of 125 pounds!*

In addition to this helmet and this breastplate that weighed 125 pounds, he had greaves of brass and a target of brass between his shoulders! The staff of his spear was like a weaver's beam — *which means the long staff of his spear weighed at least 17 pounds.* Additionally, the scripture specifically says that the spear's head weighed six hundred shekels of iron — *which is the equivalent of 16 pounds.*

One scholar has speculated that the weight of all of these pieces of weaponry together — his helmet, breastplate, greaves, target of brass, spear, and shield — *may have weighed in excess of 700 pounds!* In every respect imaginable, Goliath was a very frightful sight! How would you feel if you were challenged by a foe who stood 9 feet 9 inches tall, and who wore in excess of 700 pounds of weaponry! If he wore weaponry that was 700 pounds in weight, imagine how much Goliath himself must have weighed!

Yet it wasn't this weaponry or Goliath's size that caused the Israelites to shrink back in fear. Then what caused the Israelites to fear? *It was the constant threats and mental bombardment that Goliath hit them with every single day. This mental harassment crippled them so that they lost sight of the awesome ability of God.*

Concerning these continuous threats of Goliath, the Word says, *"And he stood and cried unto the armies of Israel, and said unto them, Why are ye come out to set your battle in array? Am I now a Philistine, and ye servants to Saul? Choose you a man for you and let him come down to me. . . . If he be able to fight with me, and to kill me, then will we be your servants: but if I prevail against him, and kill him, then shall ye be our servants, and serve us. . . . And the Philistine said, I defy the armies of Israel this day; give me a man, that we may fight together"* (verses 8-10).

These threats from the huge and menacing Goliath were so emotionally overpowering, that the next verse declares, *"When Saul and all Israel heard those words of the Philistine, they were dismayed, and greatly afraid"* (verse 11).

Goliath mentally and emotionally immobilized the armies of Israel without ever using a sword or spear! With words alone, he incapacitated, disabled, stunned, numbed and disarmed them. His flagrant and preposterous distortion of his own greatness was so outrageous, that his words bewitched the listening Israelite army until they were spell-bound under his verbal control.

Goliath said to them, *"Who do you think you are to fight with me?"* *"Come on, just try to do damage to me, and you'll find out what I'll do to you!"* *"What's wrong? Are you afraid to face me and take me on?"*

Where do you suppose Goliath learned this kind of foul behavior? From the devil! The devil is a slanderer and an accuser! The devil seeks to incapacitate, disable, stun, numb and disarm believers today in the same way. The devil's fla-grant and preposterous allegations are so outrageous, that they often bewitch listening believers until they become spell-bound under the devil's control.

This outrageous conduct is still the mental tool which the devil still uses to assault the minds of believers. He verbally threatens them, *"I'll show you who the tough guy really is . . ."* *"I'll beat the living daylights out of you. . ."* *"I'll strike you down so hard and fast that you won't know what hit you. . ."*

These lying accusations are attempts of the enemy to beat a hole through your mind and emotions, so that you cannot think rationally. He comes to pave a road of fear into your mind, and then fills your mind with fear and confusion ("mind games"), so that you eventually will not have the courage you need to step out in faith to obey God with your life.

One slanderous accusation after another, the devil slan-ders, accuses and belittles you; he defames, maligns, reviles and smears your faith in order to drive you back into the ditch of self-preservation, where you will never do anything significant for the kingdom of God.

If you meditate and consider the devil's threats long enough, just like the children of Israel, who listened to the words of Goliath and were functionally paralyzed by fear for forty days, you will be *"dismayed and greatly afraid."* You'll

ourself living on the low side of victory, afraid to take
any new challenges — for fear that you will fail, for fear of
what others will say, for fear of potential catastrophe, for fear,
fear, fear, etc.

*The devil wants to take you captive and destroy you with the
same tools that Goliath used against the Israelites. He wants to ruin
your effectiveness with mere suggestions and lying allegations!*

The Hard Facts of Spiritual Warfare

Goliath did make one statement that was true! He said,
*"If you are able to fight me and win, we will serve you for the rest
of our lives. . . but if we win, you will serve us!"*

These battle rules that Goliath laid out were the hard
facts of warfare during David's day. Whoever challenged the
aggressor and won was the champion. Whoever fell in defeat
would forever serve the other as a slave. These hard facts of
battle are still the rules of spiritual warfare today.

If you conquer those lying emotions, slanderous accusations and deceiving suggestions that the devil tries to use in
his attempt to neutralize you, then you will be able to keep
the enemy in a subordinate position for the rest of your life.
Having pulled the plug on his intimidating threats and
boasts, he will no longer be able to take your mind captive.

If, however, you do not learn how to take your thoughts
captive, your mind and emotions will be used as a tool of
Satan to dominate your thought processes for the rest of your
life. If you do not take charge of your mind — *if you do not
learn how to speak to yourself, rather than listen to yourself* — the
devil will continue to use lying emotions and illusions to
manipulate, dominate and control you for the rest of your life.

Notice that Goliath said, *"I defy the armies of Israel this
day. . . ."* The devil is still breathing out these same blasphemous and terrorizing statements: *"Just try to walk in divine
health!"* *"I defy you to believe that your financial situation is
going to turn around!"* *"I defy you to go into the ministry!"* *"I
defy the armies of God!"*

Though the wicked Philistines never lifted a sword; they never threw a spear; and though they never budged from their encampment; they conquered the people of God — with mental and verbal terrorization and intimidation. Because Israel wrongly considered and meditated on these threats from Goliath, and allowed these thoughts to flood them with fear, they were neutralized without a ground war ever taking place.

How often did Goliath come to make these threats? The Word says, "And the Philistine drew near *morning and evening,* and presented himself forty days" (verse 16). Day and night, morning and evening, Goliath came to mentally undo the people of God.

This, of course, is how the enemy still attacks the mind and human emotions. He doesn't strike once, and then come back to strike a week later. No, instead, he strikes fast and repeatedly — again, again and again. Morning and evening he comes to try to damage faith and confidence irreparably.

The Flesh Counts for Nothing

The story goes on to say, "Now David was the son of that Ephrathite of Bethlehem-Judah, whose name was Jesse. . . he had eight sons. . . and David was the youngest: and the three eldest followed Saul. But David went and returned from Saul to feed his father's sheep at Bethlehem" (First Samuel 17:12-15).

It continues to say, "And David rose up early in the morning, and left the sheep with a keeper, and took, and went, as Jesse had commanded him [to take food to his brothers]; and he came to the trench. . . . and behold, there came up the champion, the Philistine of Gath, Goliath by name, out of the armies of the Philistines, and spake according to the same words: *and David heard them*" (verses 20-23).

Notice that it says, ". . . *and David heard them.*" This was David's first encounter with the foreboding giant! Something in Goliath's word incited anger in David's soul. What a shock it was for this young shepherd to hear a pagan Philistine insulting the God of Israel — and to see no one doing anything about it! Not only were they doing nothing about it, the next verse says, "And all the men of Israel, when they saw the man, fled from him, and were sore afraid" (verse 24).

David was so annoyed by this Philistine's verbal arrogance, that "David spake to the men that stood by him, saying, What shall be done to that man that killeth the Philistine, and taketh away the reproach from Israel? For who is this uncircumcised Philistine, that he should defy the armies of the living God?" (verse 26).

Immediately, David's elder brother was offended by David's confidence, and reprimanded him for acting too boldly. "And Eliab, his eldest brother heard when he spake unto the men; and Eliab's anger was kindled against David, and he said, Why camest thou down hither? And with whom hath thou left the sheep in the wilderness? I know thy pride, and the naughtiness of thine heart; for thou art come down that thou mightiest see the battle" (verse 28).

Quite often when young men and women of God step out to challenge the foe, they are accused of acting too boldly. Our elder leaders are correct in pointing out that there is a vast difference between boldness, rudeness and arrogance. However, there is a true boldness which the Holy Spirit gives to surrendered vessels. David was so surrendered to the power of the Holy Spirit, that this Holy Spirit-inspired confidence rose up within him, and he simply could not hold this divine anger back!

In fact, David was so filled with confidence in God, and was so stunned by the fear that huge Israelite soldiers were possessed with, that he said, "What have I now done? Is there not a cause? And he turned from him toward another, and spake after the same manner; and the people answered him against after the former manner" (verse 29).

This is the picture of David saying, *"Isn't there a cause here that is worth fighting for?"* *"Isn't there a man in this camp who is man enough to face this uncircumcised Philistine?"* *"Why aren't we fighting?"*

David apparently began to turn from one solo then to another, saying, *"How about you? Will you Goliath?"* Then he turned to another, saying, *"And how about you? Will you fight Goliath?"* Yet it is clear that no one had the faith or courage to believe this vile giant could be killed.

David's confidence and boldness immediately spread through the camp like wildfire. Likewise, you can be sure that when you determine to move in the power of God and to pull strongholds down from your life, it will make news! Everyone around you will discuss your boldness — and may even try to talk you out of it!

Notice that the Word says, "And when the words were heard which David spake, they rehearsed them before Saul, and he sent for him. And David said to Saul, Let no man's heart fail because of him; thy servant will go and fight with this Philistine" (verses 31,32).

There was a willingness in David's heart to be used of God, and to see the enemy slain. Saul was so amazed by this supernatural courage, that he said unto David, "Thou art not able to go against this Philistine to fight with him: for thou art but a youth, and he a man of war from his youth" (verse 33).

Naturally speaking, David was too young and unskilled in the natural weapons of warfare to do battle with this giant. Saul knew this. Therefore, looking on things from a natural, fleshly and worldly appearance, he knew that David — *naturally speaking* — was no match for Goliath!

But David knew the outward man — the flesh — counted for nothing when it came to moving in the supernatural power of God! He told Saul, "Thy servant kept his father's sheep, and there came a lion, and a bear, and took a lamb out of the flock. *And I went out after him. . ."* (verses 34,35).

Goliath is not the first enemy David has faced in life — he has already had an eyeball-to-eyeball confrontation with a lion and a bear! He was determined that those devourers were not going to steal one thing from his property — *not one!* David had the attitude that was necessary to defeat his enemy every time his enemy struck.

We must have this same attitude when the devil comes to manipulate our minds and emotions, when the enemy comes to strike family members with disease, when the devil clearly has come to devour our finances, or when the enemy has come to internally destroy a church or ministry.

Our attitude must be, *"Satan, you cannot have this ministry!"* *"Devil, you cannot have our finances!"* *"You cannot kill our family with sickness or disease!"* *"You cannot, cannot, cannot!"*

If the enemy does not willingly release those things when we tell him to do so, then, like David, we must "go out after him" and forcibly make him release those things which he has seized against our wills. David said, "I went out after him, and delivered it out of his mouth: and when he arose against me, I caught him by the beard, and smote him, and slew him: thy servant slew the lion and the bear. . ." (verses 35,36).

David had already experienced so much of God's power and victory in his life, that this Philistine was no threat to him! He already faced a ferocious lion — *and saw the faithfulness of God as the lion was killed.* He already faced a bear — *and saw the faithfulness of God as the bear was killed.*

Now, looking backward upon his past, and reflecting on the goodness of God that has already been bestowed upon his life, he can look straight into the face of this conflict with Goliath and say, "Thy servant slew both the lion and the bear: *and this uncircumcised Philistine shall be as one of them, seeing he hath defied the armies of the living God"* (verse 36).

David said moreover, *"The Lord that delivered me out of the paw of the lion, and out of the paw of the bear, He will deliver me out of the hand of this Philistine.* And Saul said unto David, *Go, and the Lord be with thee"* (verse 37).

Moving Beyond the Flesh

Notice Saul's response to David's desire to be used of God! The Word says, "And Saul armed David with his armour, and he put an helmet of brass upon his head; also he armed him with a coat of mail. And David girded his sword upon his armour. . ." (verses 38,39).

David had already killed the lion and the bear without the use of any natural armor or weaponry. However, because of the size of this menacing Goliath, Saul felt that David needed more than God's faithfulness!

It was as though Saul said, *"David, this fight with Goliath is going to be far more intense than your conflict with the lion and the bear, so let me help you! Let me put a helmet upon your head, and dress you in a coat of mail. Here, take my sword with you and use it as if it is your own!"*

Can you imagine how silly little David must have looked in Saul's massive armor? You can be sure that Saul's intentions were pure. He wanted David to be safe and adequately equipped with armor that was equal to Goliath's. However, Saul's counsel was extremely defective. David had never worn such armor before, and had he gone to battle with this heavy armor upon him, he would have been so weighed down by it all that he would have been unable to successfully wage warfare.

Thus, the reason that the Word continues to say, ". . . and he assayed to go; for he had not proved it. And David said unto Saul, I cannot go with these; for I have not proven them. And David put them off him" (verse 39).

Previous to this time, David had defeated his enemies without fleshly weapons. Knowing that he was unaccustomed to these kinds of fleshly weapons, and knowing that they would do him no good, he put them off and "took his staff in his hand, and chose him five smooth stones out of the brook, and put them in a shepherd's bag which he had, even in a scrip; and his sling was in his hand, *and he drew near to the Philistine*" (verse 40).

Notice it says that David "drew near to the Philistine." David, a small boy in his teenage years, charges a giant with 700 pounds of weaponry, and has nothing in hand to kill this giant, but a sling and five stones!

According to the natural man, David was not equipped to fight this kind of foe. But according to the spirit realm, David was dressed in the armor of God and was empowered by the power of God. Goliath could not see these spiritual weapons with his physical eyes. Therefore, he had no idea that David was "dressed to kill."

Verse 41 says, "And the Philistine came on and drew near unto David; and the man that bare the shield went before him. And when the Philistine looked about, and saw David, he disdained him: [i.e., he made fun of him] for he was but a youth, and ruddy, and of a fair countenance. And the Philistine said unto David, Am I a dog, that thou comest to me with staves? And the Philistine cursed David by his gods."

Goliath was expecting more! He thought the Israelites had finally found a match for him. This is the reason that the man who bore his shield went before him; this shieldbearer was to protect Goliath from the blows of his challenger. But when Goliath looked around and saw little, young David, he was shocked! Immediately, he began to mock David and mock God!

Goliath, just like the devil does today, began to use his tools of mental and verbal harassment! Attempting to intimidate David and paralyze him with fear, the Word says, "And the Philistine said unto David, Come to me, and I will give thy flesh unto the fowls of the air, and to the beasts of the field" (verse 44).

Just as the entire army of Israel had been functionally immobilized for forty days by Goliath's outrageous claims, now Goliath was proceeding in his same course of action: *to immobilize and paralyze David with preposterous and bloated boasts and lying allegations!*

If David turned his eyes from the Lord, and stopped meditating on the faithfulness of God, and hence started considering what Goliath had to say, these threats would have immobilized him as they had immobilized the armies of Israel.

Before these threats had an opportunity to take root in his soul, and thus produce paralyzing fear, David said, "Thou comest to me with a sword, and with a shield; but I come to thee in the name of the Lord of hosts, the God of the armies of Israel, whom thou has defied" (verse 45).

He continued, "This day the Lord will deliver you into mine hand; and I will smite thee, and take thine head from thee; and I will give the carcasses of the host of the Philistines this day unto the beasts of the earth; that all the earth may know that there is a God in Israel. And all this assembly shall know that the Lord saveth not with sword and spear: for the battle is the Lord's, and He will give you into our hands" (verses 46,47).

Prevailing Over the Philistines in Your Life

Once David made his declaration of war, he wasted no time. Verse 48 says, "And it came to pass, when the Philistine arose, and came and drew nigh to David, *that David hasted. . . .*"

This must have *shocked* Goliath! Most challengers ran away from him, but David *"hasted."* In other words, *when the moment of conflict finally came, David picked up his sling and his five stones and ran toward Goliath.* When David saw Goliath coming, it was almost as though David said, "Now the action begins!"

The Word continues to say, "And David put his hand in his bag, and took thence a stone, and slang it, and smote the Philistine in his forehead, that the stone sunk into his forehead; and he fell upon his face to the earth. *So David prevailed over the Philistine with a sling and with a stone, and smote the Philistine, and slew him. . ."* (verses 49,50).

But wait . . . David wasn't finished yet! While Goliath had his face to the ground and was stunned by this small pebble that had been hurled from David's sling, David seized the opportunity to make sure the job was finished!

The story continues, *". . . but there was no sword in the hand of David. Therefore, David ran, and stood upon the Philistine, took his sword, drew it out of the sheath thereof, and slew him, and cut off his head therewith. And when the Philistines saw their champion was dead, they fled"* (verses 50,51).

Are you tired of the Philistines in your life? Are you tired of being mentally harassed and emotionally tormented by the lying insinuations and slanderous accusations of the adversary? How would you like to sling a stone into the head of those accusing thoughts, drop them to the ground, stun them, and then cut off their heads so they will cease harassing you?

This is precisely why Paul urges us, *"Put on the whole armour of God, that ye may be able to stand against the wiles of the devil."*

While natural training and education is good, and we need to get as much of it as we possibly can, eventually we all come to a place where we discover that natural weapons and natural education will not help us in our fight with unseen, spiritual enemies.

In such moments, we must move beyond the flesh, over into the realm of spiritual armor. This armor will empower any believer to successfully *"stand against the wiles of the devil."*

The Devil: His Mode of Operation

It would be a great injustice to conclude this chapter without explaining what the name "devil" means. Once you have an understanding of this name, then you will know that it was the nature of the devil himself that was working through Goliath to intimidate the armies of Israel.

The name "devil" is taken from the Greek word *diabolos* (dia-bo-los), and is a compound of the words *dia* and *ballo*. The word *dia* carries the idea of "penetration" and the word *ballo* means "to throw" something, like a ball or a rock.

Literally, the word *diabalos* describes the repetitive action of *hitting something again, again, again and again,* until finally the wall or membrane is so worn down that *it can be completely and thoroughly penetrated.*

Thus, the name "devil" (*diabolos*) is not only a proper name for this archenemy of the faith, but it also denotes his mode of operation. *The devil is one who strikes repeat again, again and again, until he finally breaks down one's resistance. When this mental resistance has been broken dow he strikes with all of his fury to penetrate the mind and to take that person's mind and emotions captive.*

This is how the enemy works! He repeatedly hits you with lies, suggestions, accusations, allegations and one slanderous assault after another, another and another. He tries to wear you down, and then takes you captive in one of your weaker moments.

He tries to pave a road into your mind (*methodos*), and then confuse your emotions with "mind games" (*noemata*), and then deceives you to the point that you actually begin to believe his threats — and thus, your false perception empowers his lies to become a reality in your life.

Hence, the reason you must: *"Clothe yourself with the whole panoply* [the loinbelt, breastplate, shoes and greaves, shield, helmet, sword and lance] *that comes from God, for the sole purpose that you may have explosive and dynamic power to stand proud and upright, face to face and eyeball to eyeball against the roads that the slanderer would try to pave into your mind"* (Ephesians 6:11, *REV*).

Chapter Nine
Wrestling With Principalities and Powers

As Paul continues in the sixth chapter of Ephesians, he reveals who our battle is against. He says, "For we wrestle not against flesh and blood, but against principalities, against powers, against the rulers of the darkness of this world, against spiritual wickedness in high places" (Ephesians 6:12).

Especially notice how Paul begins this verse. He says, "For we _wrestle_. . . ." From the very outset of this verse, Paul makes a very strong, pointed and dramatic statement!

The word "wrestle" is taken from the old word _pale_ (pale), and it refers to struggling, wrestling, or hand-to-hand fighting. However, the word _pale_ is also the Greek word from which the Greek derived their name for the _Palastra_ (pa-la-stra), a house of combat sports.

The Palastra was a huge building that outwardly looked like a palace; it was a palace of combat sports, dedicated to the cultivation of athletic skills. Every morning, afternoon and night you could find the most committed, determined and daring athletes of the day working out and training in this fabulous building.

Primarily three kinds of athletes worked out at the Palastra: _boxers, wrestlers and pankratists._ These were exceedingly dangerous and barbaric sports. _Why?_ To quote from my book, LIVING IN THE COMBAT ZONE (pages 159-162):

"First, their boxers were not like ours today. Theirs were _extremely violent_ — so violent that they were not permitted to box without wearing helmets. Without the protection of helmets, their heads would have been crushed.

"Few boxers in the ancient world ever lived to retire from their profession. Most of them died in the ring. Of all the sports, the ancients viewed boxing as *the most* hazardous and deadly.

"In fact, these boxers were so brutal and barbaric, they wore gloves that were *ribbed with steel and spiked with nails!* At times the steel wrapped around their gloves was *serrated,* like a hunting knife, in order to make deep gashes in the skin of an opponent.

"In addition to this, boxers began using gloves that were heavier and much more damaging. It is quite usual, when viewing the artwork from the time of the early Greeks, to see boxers whose faces, ears, and noses were totally deformed because of these dangerous gloves.

"In studying the art of the Greeks, it is quite usual to see paintings of boxers with blood pouring from their noses and with deep lacerations on their faces as a result of the serrated metal and spiked nails on the gloves. And it was not unusual for a boxer to hit the face so hard, with his thumb extended toward the eyes, that it knocked an eye right out of its socket.

"Believe it or not, even though this sport was so combative and violent, there were *no rules* — except you could not clench your opponent's fist. That was the only rule to the game! There were no "rounds" like there are in boxing today. The fight just went on and on and on until one of the two *surrendered* or *died* in the ring.

"An inscription from that first century said of boxing: 'A boxer's victory is obtained through blood.' This was a thoroughly violent sport!

"Wrestlers, too, often wrestled to the death. In fact, a favorite tactic in those days was to grab hold of an opponent around the waist from behind, throw him up in the air, and quickly break his backbone in half from behind. In order to make an opponent surrender, it was quite normal to strangle him into submission. Choking was another acceptable practice. So wrestling was another extremely violent sport.

"They were tolerant of every imaginable tactic: *breaking fingers, breaking ribs by a waistlock, gouging the face, knocking the eyes out, and so forth.* Although less injurious than the other combat sports, wrestling was still a bitter struggle to the end. . . Wrestling was a bloody, bloody sport.

"Then there were *Pankratists.* Pankratists were a combination of all of the above. The word "pankratist" is from two Greek roots, the words *pan* and *kratos. Pan* means "all," and *kratos* is a word for "exhibited power." The two words together describe *'someone with massive amounts of power; power over all; more power than anyone else.'*

"This, indeed, was the purpose of *Pankration.* Its competitors were out to prove they could not be beaten and were tougher than anyone else!

"In order to prove this, they were permitted to kick, punch, bite, gouge, strike, break fingers, break legs, and do any other horrible thing you could imagine. . . There was no part of the body that was off-limits. They could do anything to any part of their competitor's body, *for there were basically no rules.*

"An early inscription says this about *Pankration:* 'If you should hear that your son has died, believe it, but if you hear he has been defeated and retired, do not believe it.' Why? Because more died in this sport than surrendered or were defeated. Like the other combat sports, it was *extremely violent.*"

The Survival of the Fittest

Now Paul uses this very illustration to describe our conflict with unseen, demonic powers that have been marshalled against us for our destruction. He says, "For we wrestle not against flesh and blood, but against principalities, against powers, against the rulers of the darkness of this world, against spiritual wickedness in high places."

By using the word "wrestle," which is the old Greek word *pale*, Paul conveys the idea of *a bitter struggle and an intense conflict* — which describes our warfare with demonic forces as a combat sport!

This means when you are fighting demonic foes, *there are no rules! Anything goes!* All methods of attack are legal, and there is no umpire to cry *"foul"* when the adversary attempts to break you, choke you, or strangle you.

Whoever fights the hardest, the meanest, and lasts the longest is the winner of this confrontation. Therefore, you'd better be equipped, alert, and prepared before the fight begins. (For more on how to prepare for this conflict, see pages 164-187, LIVING IN THE COMBAT ZONE.)

Notice that Paul goes on to say, "For our wrestle is *not against flesh and blood. . . .*" At first, this statement from Paul seems to be in conflict with what I have been writing in this book. In this book, I have stated that the majority of spiritual warfare *is* with the flesh and the mind.

Is there a conflict between me and Paul? *Absolutely not!* Indeed, our real adversary is an unseen host of wicked spirits that are working behind the scenes. These are the foul forces of darkness that work covertly behind every damnable disaster and moral failure. *However, they can't do anything unless flesh cooperates with them!* Therefore, they come to tempt, seduce, deceive and assault the flesh and the mind.

Thus, the reason that we must deal with the flesh before we attempt to deal with the devil! By living a crucified, sanctified life on a continual basis, we are able to neutralize any attack which the enemy would try to wage against the flesh. Why is this so? *Because dead men and women do not have the capacity to respond!* You can kick dead people, spit at dead people, curse at dead people, try to tempt, deceive and seduce dead people, but they do not respond!

Likewise, the majority of demonic attacks against us will never produce anything of any serious consequence if we are living a crucified life, and if we are reckoning ourselves to be "dead to sin" (Romans 6:6,7,11).

Principalities and Powers

Who are these evil forces that are constantly working behind the scenes to seduce, deceive, control and manipulate the flesh and the mind?

Paul continues, "For we wrestle not against flesh and blood, *but against principalities, against powers, against the rulers of the darkness of this world, against spiritual wickedness in high places.*"

Paul tells us that there are four classifications of demon spirits. He says there are (1) *"principalities,"* (2) *"powers,"* (3) *"rulers of the darkness of this world,"* and (4) *"spiritual wickedness in high places."*

Before we deal with each of these individually, first something else must be noted. Notice that Paul mentions the word "against" in Ephesians 6:12 *four times* in connection with the devil! Why is this important? Because grammatically, he could have used the word "against" once in reference to all four of these things. But rather than do this, he chose to repeat the word "against" again, again, again and again.

When a truth is repeated in scripture like this, it is always for the sake of *emphasis.* For instance, in John, chapters fourteen, fifteen and sixteen, Jesus refers to the Holy Spirit as "the Comforter" four different times. This clearly means that the Lord Jesus Christ was trying to drive a very important truth into our hearts about the Holy Spirit.

Likewise, in those same chapters of John, the Lord Jesus Christ refers to the Holy Spirit as "the Spirit of Truth" three different times. Once again, the Lord was repeating Himself for the sake of *emphasizing a very important truth.*

When God calls notable Biblical characters, He always calls them by name not once, but two or three times. For instance, when God called Moses, He said, *"Moses, Moses. . ."* (Exodus 3:4). When God called Saul of Tarsus, He said, *"Saul,*

saul. . ." (Acts 9:4). And Samuel was so important to the plan of God, that when God called Samuel, He called Samuel by name not once, not twice, but three times. God called, *"Samuel. . . Samuel. . . Samuel. . ."* (First Samuel 3:4-8).

So when God is dealing with truth that is of paramount importance, or when God calls an extremely important Biblical character, He always repeats Himself. This, of course, leads us back to Ephesians 6:12, where the Holy Spirit repeats the word "against" *four times* within the context of *one verse!* This means the Holy Spirit is telling us something *very, very, very important.*

The word "against" used all four times in this verse, is taken from the word *pros.* The word *pros* (see page 124) always depicts a "forward position" or a "face-to-face encounter." In fact, this very word is used in John 1:1 to describe the preincarnation relationship between the Father and Jesus. It says, "In the beginning was the Word, and the Word was *with* God. . . ."

The word "with" is taken from the word *pros.* A more accurate rendering of John 1:1 would be, *"In the beginning was the Word [Jesus], and the Word [Jesus] was face to face with God. . . ."*

This is the picture of the Father and Jesus so *intimate* that they can nearly feel their breath breathing upon each other's face. This clearly reveals the *intimacy* and *close relationship* that exists between the members of the Godhead.

Now this same word of intimacy, this word that is used to denote a "face-to-face" relationship between the Father and the Son, is now used to denote a "face-to-face" encounter with unseen, demonic spirits that have come to assault us.

This means at some point in our Christian experience, we will come into *direct contact* with evil forces. The word *pros* in Ephesians 6:12 could be translated, *". . .face to face with principalities, eyeball to eyeball with powers, head-on with rulers of the darkness of this world, and shoulder to shoulder with spiritual wickedness in high places."*

148

The Rank and File of the Dev↘

All serious scholars agree that the language ↘ 6:12 is military language. It seems evident tha↘ received a revelation of how Satan's kingdom ↘ aligned militarily.

At the very top of Satan's dark domain, there is a group of demon spirits whom Paul calls *"principalities."* The word "principality" is taken from the word *archas* (arch-as), an old word that is used symbolically to denote "ancient, ancient times." Furthermore, it is also used to depict individuals who "hold the highest and loftiest position of rank and authority."

By using the word *archas* ("principalities"), Paul emphatically tells us that at the very top of Satan's domain is a group of demon spirits who have held their lofty positions of power and authority since ancient times — probably ever since the fall of Lucifer.

Then Paul continues to mention *"powers"* as those evil forces that are second in command in Satan's dark dominion.

The word "powers" is taken from the word *exousia* (ex-ou-sia), and it denotes "delegated authority." This tells us that there is a lower-ranking group of demon spirits who have received "delegated authority" from Satan to do whatever they want to do, wherever they desire to do it. This second group of demon spirits have "delegated authority" to carry out all manner of evil and wickedness.

Next, Paul mentions *"the rulers of the darkness of this world."* What an amazing word this is! It is taken from the word *kosmokrateros* (kos-mo-kra-te-ros), and is a compound of the words *kosmos* and *kratos*. The word *kosmos* denotes "order" or "arrangement," while the word *kratos* has to do with "raw power."

When these two words are compounded together into the word *kosmokrateros*, they depict "raw power that has been harnessed and put into some kind of order." This word was technically used by the Greek to describe certain aspects of the military.

Why did the ancient Greeks use the word *kosmokrateros* to depict certain aspects of the military? Because the military was filled with young men who had a lot of natural ability — *raw power,* if you will. In order for that raw power to be effective, it had to be harnessed and organized (*kosmos*).

Thus, young soldiers with abounding energy were taught to be submitted, disciplined, ordered and perfectly arranged. *This is the picture of rank and file.* In the end, all of those men, with all of that raw ability, were turned into a massive force.

Now Paul uses this same idea! By using the phrase "rulers of the darkness of this world," he tells us that the devil deals with his dark legions of demon spirits like they are troops! He puts them in rank and file, gives them orders and assignments, and then sends them out like troops who are committed to kill.

It is a fact that we have more authority than the devil. We have more power than the devil. And we have the Greater One living within us. In light of this, one day I asked the Lord, "If we have more authority, and if we have more power, and if we have the Greater One living inside us, then why does it seem that the Church is full of so much defeat?"

I will never forget what the Holy Spirit whispered to my heart. He said, *"The reason the Church is experiencing so much defeat is because the devil has something that the Church does not have!"* I quickly asked, "Lord, what is that?" It was then that the Lord quickened Ephesians 6:12 to my understanding. The word *kosmokrateros* came alive in my heart, and then I understood!

The word *kosmokrateros* ("rulers of the darkness of this world") is a military term that has to do with *discipline, organization and commitment!*

The devil is so serious about doing damage to humanity, that he deals with demon spirits as though they are *troops!* They are put in rank and file, and are organized to the hilt —

while the average Spirit-filled believer doesn't stay in one church for over one year at a time!

Yes, we do have more authority than the devil has, and we do have more power than the devil has, and we do have the Greater One living in us. The Church of Jesus Christ is loaded with heaps and heaps of raw power — *but at this particular time, that power is disconnected and disjointed by a body that lacks discipline, organization and commitment!*

The Church of Jesus Christ has no power shortage, nor is the Church short of God-given authority. We simply have a great lack of discipline, organization and commitment. In order to change this, we must buckle down in the local church and begin to view ourselves as the troops of the Lord! *If we will match the discipline, organization and commitment that the enemy has in his camp, then we will begin to move into the awesome demonstration of God's power!*

Finally, Paul mentions *"spiritual wickedness in high places."* The word "wickedness" is taken from the word *poneros* (po-ne-ros), and it is used to depict something that is "bad," "vile," malevolent," "vicious," "impious" or "malignant."

It is important that Paul would save this word until the end of this verse. By saving this phrase until the last, he is telling us the ultimate aim of Satan's dark domain: these spirits are sent forth from the spirit realm to afflict humanity in a "bad, vile, malevolent, vicious, impious and malignant" way.

Revealing Names, Symbols and Types of the Devil in the Bible

All scholars of the Church, in the past ages and the present agree that we have an adversary who hates the gospel, detests the presence of the Church, and is working around the clock to discredit the message of Jesus Christ.

His entrance into the life of a believer is given primarily by way of negligence, as he slips through an uncommitted, unrenewed area of the mind — *a loophole* — and then he begins to wage warfare against the mind and flesh of the saints.

Rather than hide from this foe, we must turn our eyes to the scripture, to see what the Bible has to say about him.

There are many names, symbols and types for the devil throughout the Old and New Testaments. Each of these names, symbols and types reveals a different facet of the devil's twisted, perverted nature, and his mode of operation.

He is known as:

Abaddon (Revelation 9:11)

Accuser (Revelation 12:10)

Adversary (First Peter 5:8)

Angel of Light (Second Corinthians 11:14)

Apollyon (Revelation 9:11)

Beelzebub (Matthew 10:25; 12:24)

Belial (Second Corinthians 6:15)

Devil (Ephesians 6:11; First Peter 5:8; Revelation 12:9)

Dragon (Revelation 12:9)

Evil one (Matthew 6:13)

Murderer (John 8:44)

Prince of this world (John 12:31)

Prince of demons (Matthew 9:34, *RSV*)

Prince of the power of the air (Ephesians 2:2)

Roaring lion (First Peter 5:8)

Satan (Luke 10:18)

Serpent (Revelation 12:9)

These names, symbols and types of Satan can be divided into four categories: (1) *Satan's Destructive Bent,* (2) *Satan's Perverted Nature,* (3) *Satan's Desire To Control,* and (4) *Satan, the Mind Manipulator.*

Satan's Destructive Bent

Of the seventeen names, symbols and types given above, two are devoted to Satan's insatiable desire to destroy.

The names *Abaddon* and *Apollyon* are found in Revelation 9:11 to describe the devil. The name *Abaddon* is the Hebrew equivalent of the Greek name *Apollyon*. Both of these names mean *"Destroyer."*

In reference to Satan, Revelation 9:11 says, "And they had a king over them, which is the angel of the bottomless pit, whose name in the Hebrew tongue is *Abaddon*, but in the Greek tongue hath his name *Apollyon*."

Possessing his nature and operating on instructions given them by Satan, you can be certain that demon spirits (whom Satan rules over as a king, according to Revelation 9:11), are sent forth with their master's same destructive nature; they are sent forth to "destroy."

Satan's Perverted Nature

Of the titles given in the list above, five of them have to do with the devil's twisted, perverted nature. Those five are found in the following names, symbols and types: *Beelzebub, Belial, Dragon, Evil One,* and *Murderer.*

Beelzebub

The name *Beelzebub* was initially used by the Philistines of the Old Testament to describe the god of Ekron. It literally meant, "lord of the flies" (Second Kings 1:2-6). Originally, it was spelled *Baalzebub*. As time progressed, the Jews altered *Baalzebub* to *Beelzebub*, which added an even dimmer idea to this particular name of the devil. This new name (*Beelzebub*) now meant, "lord of the dunghill," or "lord of the manure."

Two powerful and important images of Satan are presented in these two names. First of all, he is presented as *Baalzebub*, the "lord of the flies." This is clearly the picture of Satan masquerading himself as the lord of demon spirits. Obviously, the Philistines looked upon demon spirits in the same way one would look upon nasty, dirty "flies."

Secondly, he is presented as *Beelzebub*, the "lord of the dunghill." By adding this twist to this name of Satan, the Jews told us something very important about the devil. Both he and his evil spirits, like nasty, dirty flies, are attracted to "dunghills" or environments where rotting, stinking, carnality pervades. This is the environment where Satan thrives best.

Belial

The name *Belial*, which is of Greek origination, means "worthless." This name is always used in connection with filthiness and wickedness. Whenever it is used, either in the Old Testament or the New Testament, it is used to depict extremely evil men. For instance, First Samuel 2:12 tells us that Eli's sons were "sons of *Belial*."

What an example Eli's sons were of this word *Belial*. They were fornicators, thieves, and were full of idolatry and rebellion. These terrible traits were ingrained into their character to such an extent, that God's judgment came upon them and they were removed from the scene in one day's time. According to First Samuel 2:12, they were "sons of *Belial*." They obtained this horrid behavior from Satan, who is himself the origination of the word *Belial*.

Dragon

The word *dragon* is also used in Revelation 12:9 to depict the devil. It says, "And the great *dragon* was cast out, that old *serpent*, called the Devil, and Satan, which deceiveth the whole world: he was cast out into the earth, and his angels were cast out with him."

It is clear from this verse that the terms *dragon* and *serpent* are used interchangeably in reference to Satan's twisted, demented and perverted nature. By employing both of these pictures, he is presented as a deadly, poisonous, ready-to-strike-and-kill creature.

Evil One

The next Biblical example of the devil can be found in what is traditionally called "The Lord's Prayer." In Matthew 6:13, the Lord Jesus prayed, "And lead us not into temptation, but deliver us from evil." The Greek language more accurately reads, "but deliver us from the *Evil One*."

From this usage, we know that Jesus looked upon the

devil as the *"Evil One."* No one was more familiar with Satan than Jesus; hence, it is important that Jesus, knowing him so well, would label him thus.

Murderer

It was also the Lord Jesus who told us Satan was a *murderer.* In John 8:44, Jesus told the scribes and Pharisees, "Ye are of your father the devil, and the lusts of your fathers ye will do. He was a *murderer* from the beginning, and abode not in truth. . . ."

This murderous nature of Satan was first manifest in Genesis 4:8, when he inspired Cain to slay his brother, Abel. It was this murderous nature of Satan that inspired Herod to kill all the babies in Bethlehem-Ephrata. We can see his murderous nature in the death of millions of early Christian martyrs, and still today where injustice prevails across the earth. *Murder is a part of his demented nature.*

Satan's Desire To Control

Satan's strong desire to *control* the spirit realm, the world, and every human government and human institution of the world is evidenced by the fact that the Bible calls him *"the prince of this world," "the prince of demons,"* and *"the prince of the power of the air."*

The Prince of this World

By calling him *"the prince of this world,"* even Jesus recognized Satan's temporal control over certain things in this earthly sphere.

You must remember that Satan himself personally offered Jesus the "kingdoms of this world" during Jesus' forty days and nights of testing in the wilderness. Jesus was confronted by this "prince of the world" during those forty days, and resisted the devil's power until he fled. Jesus spoke from personal experience when he referred to this temporal claim of Satan.

The Prince of Demons

In Matthew 9:34, Satan is also called *"the prince of demons."* The word "prince" is taken from the Greek word *archontas* (ar-chon-tas), and refers to "one who holds the first place" or "one who holds the highest seat of power."

The title "prince of demons" most assuredly reveals that Satan holds the highest-ranking seat among many diabolical spirits. The word "prince" denotes that there is some kind of rank and file and organization to Satan's system of things. We have already seen this in Ephesians 6:12.

Prince of the Power of the Air

The apostle Paul called Satan *"the prince of the power of the air"* (Ephesians 2:2). Again, the word "prince" is taken from the Greek word *archontas*, meaning "one who holds the highest seat of power."

This is in complete agreement with Ephesians 6:12, which states that under Satan's control there are varying degrees of spiritually wicked power. From the context of this verse in the sixth chapter of Ephesians, we know that under Satan's command there are principalities, powers, rulers of the darkness of this world, and spiritual wickedness in high places.

Satan, the Mind Manipulator

Finally, we come to the last and largest category of the names, symbols and types of Satan in the Bible. In this last category, we discover that Satan truly is *the master of mind games*.

There are six names, symbols and types of Satan that specifically have to do with his ability to twist, deceive and lie to the mind. He is called the *Adversary, Accuser, Angel of Light, Devil, Roaring Lion,* and *Satan*.

Adversary

The name *Adversary* is extremely important when attempting to understand the devil's mode of operation. It is taken from the Greek word *antidikos* (an-ti-di-kos), which is a compound of the Greek words *anti* (an-ti) and *dikos* (di-kos).

The word *anti* simply means "against." However, in older and more classical Greek, it was used to denote the mental condition of a man or woman who was "on the edge of insanity." This, in fact, was a terribly dangerous person who would do someone great harm if he or she was not restrained. Therefore, the word *anti* is quite a nasty word.

The second part of the word *Adversary* is taken from the Greek word *dikos*. *Dikos* is the root for the word "righteousness." It refers to "justice, rightness, fairness, and righteousness."

When the two words are compounded together, they portray "one who is adamantly opposed to righteousness." Because the word *anti* carries the idea of hostility, this means the devil is one who is "hostile toward righteousness" or "he is one who desires to destroy righteousness and obliterate it."

This means the devil is not just passively opposed to the presence of righteousness or righteous people; *he is actively pursuing them and doing all within his power to wipe them out!* He *hates* righteousness!

In one way or another, he mentally tries to devour them with temptation of the present, or with memories of the past. All of this is done by him in order to assault our sense of righteousness, in the hopes that we will be left high and dry with no confidence before God, devil or man.

This is precisely why Peter said, "Be sober, be vigilant; because your *adversary* the devil, as a roaring lion, walketh about, seeking whom he may devour" (First Peter 5:8).

A Roaring Lion

And this leads us to the next title of Satan. Peter says he is like unto *"a roaring lion."* What awesome command the roar of a lion draws from the heart of frail man!

In this case, the roar is more fearsome than his bite. Colossians 2:15 victoriously declares, "And having spoiled principalities and powers, he made a shew of them openly, triumphing over them in it."

By means of the cross and the resurrection, Jesus Christ stripped these demonic powers bare of the authority they once possessed, and His victory over them was so thorough that he even "made a shew of them openly" (see pages 227-229, LIVING IN THE COMBAT ZONE).

However, this has not stopped the devil from trying to sound dreadful. It is his continuous hassling of our thoughts, his insinuations about failure, his concoction of unrealistic fears in our souls, and his constant onslaught against our minds that beats believers down into defeat. This constant "roaring" in the soul is another attempt of the adversary to wear us out, wear us down, and then swallow us up in self-pity.

Notice that the object of the adversary is to *"seek those whom he may devour."* The word "seek" implies that not everyone will fall prey to these tactics.

He is not seeking *anyone* whom he may devour; he is seeking *those* whom he may devour — *he is looking for those who are weak in faith, ignorant of the Word of God, who are isolated to themselves, and are not mature enough to stand in the face of his constant, hassling allegations.*

These are the ones that this "roaring lion" is seeking after, and his object is to *"devour them."* The word "devour" comes from the Greek word *katapino* (ka-ta-pi-no), and literally means "to swallow up completely."

Angel of Light

And, of course, Satan is called an *"angel of light."* In Second Corinthians, Paul, dealing with the problem of false prophets, false teachers, false apostles and deceivers who were trying to worm their way into the Corinthian Church, says, "And no marvel; for Satan himself is transformed into an angel of light" (Second Corinthians 11:14).

This is another picture of this master mind-manipulator; Satan disguises himself to be something that he really is not! Again, this kind of attack normally comes against the mind. This is a vivid portrayal of Satan's deceptive power to twist one's thinking.

The Devil

And, of course, Satan is also called *"the devil."* As a matter of fact, the New Testament refers to him as such over forty times!

The name *"devil"* is taken from the Greek word *diabolos* (di-a-bo-los). It is a compound of the words *dia* and *balos*. *Dia* means "through" and carries with it the idea of "penetration." The word *balos* is taken from the word *ballo*, which means "I throw," as in throwing a ball or a rock.

When the two words are compounded, they depict the act of repeatedly throwing a ball or rock against something until it penetrates that barrier, and breaks through to the other side.

Therefore, in the name *"devil"* you do not only have the proper name of this archenemy, but also his mode of operation. His name means that he is "one who continually strikes, strikes and strikes again — beating against the walls of our minds over and over, and over and over again — until finally, he breaks through and penetrates" the mind.

Satan

And last, this enemy of both God and man is called *Satan*, which is taken from the Hebrew word *shatana*, and means "to hate and to accuse." It is used more than fifty times in the Old and New Testament, and often it also carries with it the ideas of "slander and false accusation."

A Prerequisite to Spiritual Warfare

It was because of this archenemy that Paul wrote to the Ephesian Church and urged them to "put on the whole armor of God" (Ephesians 6:11).

However, before he told them to "put on the whole armor of God," he urged them *"to put away lying"* (4:25); *"to speak truth with our neighbor"* (4:25); he commanded them, *"be ye angry, and sin not: let not the sun go down upon your wrath"* (4:26); *"neither give place to the devil"* (4:27); *"let him that stole steal no more"* (4:28); *"let no corrupt communication proceed out of your mouth"* (4:29); *"grieve not the Holy Spirit"* (4:30); *"let all bitterness, and wrath, and anger, and clamour, and evil speaking, be put away from you, with all malice"* (4:31).

We must not forget that a consecrated life is a prerequisite to real spiritual warfare. If these areas of our lives are left unattended, uncommitted and unsurrendered, then we have left gaping loopholes through which Satan may continue to exert his hellish schemes in our lives.

Screaming, yelling, screeching, stomping, shouting, and dancing will not accomplish one single thing if we have (deliberately, or simply by negligence) allowed "the loins of our minds" to go unchecked and ungirded. Our lack of commitment and the secret places of our lives that have never been fully surrendered will stop us dead in our tracks when it comes to dealing with the devil's attacks.

On the other hand, a holy and surrendered man, who has carefully guarded his mind and has equipped himself with the whole armor of God, is an awesome weapon in the hands of an Almighty God!

In Ephesians 6:10-18, Paul deals with key elements of spiritual warfare which we need to know and appropriate in our personal lives.

In order to successfully fight these unseen powers that have been marshalled against us, Paul tells us that a special supernatural power has been provided for this fight.

God has not left us naked before the enemy; He has provided us with spiritual weaponry that has the ability to counterattack and defeat any scheme that the devil would try to use against us.

Chapter Ten
The Loinbelt of Truth

In this chapter, we will begin to examine the specific pieces of armor that God has given to the Church. In Ephesians 6:14-18, Paul says:

"Stand therefore, having your loins girt about with truth, and having on the breastplate of righteousness;

"And your feet shod with the preparation of the gospel of peace;

"Above all, taking the shield of faith, wherewith ye shall be able to quench all the fiery darts of the wicked.

"And take the helmet of salvation, and the sword of the Spirit, which is the Word of God:

"Praying always with all prayer and supplication in the Spirit. . . . "

As stated before, the sixth chapter of Ephesians is not the first time that Paul lists spiritual armor in scripture. In the Book of First Thessalonians, the oldest book of the New Testament, Paul also lists spiritual armor.

In First Thessalonians 5:8, Paul says, "But let us who are of the day, be sober, putting on the breastplate of faith and love; and for an helmet, the hope of salvation."

This earlier version is clearly a very limited view of spiritual armor compared to the list that we find in the sixth chapter of Ephesians. Paul's earlier view was so undeveloped that he referred to the breastplate as "faith" and "love." The

---

Facing left page: A Roman soldier from the first century dressed in his loinbelt, breastplate, greaves and spiked shoes, oblong shield, helmet, and sword.

only other weapon that he mentioned in this earlier text, besides the breastplate, was the helmet of salvation.

Paul's Expanded Version of Spiritual Armor

What happened between these two texts? In First Thessalonians, Paul's list of armor is brief, but in Ephesians, he gives an exhaustive list of spiritual weaponry.

This is what happened: Through the years, the Holy Spirit began speaking to Paul, just as He speaks to us. As Paul began to meditate on the little knowledge he had of spiritual armor, the Holy Spirit began to take this subject and open it wide up for him. As the years went by, the Holy Spirit fully developed Paul's knowledge of spiritual armor.

Thus, by the time we get to the sixth chapter of Ephesians, we no longer have an incomplete view of spiritual weaponry; we see the whole picture — the Holy Spirit's full revelation of the armor God has provided for the believer.

Notice how Paul begins this text in Ephesians 6:14. He says, *"Stand therefore...."* The Greek word for "stand" is the word *stemi* (ste-mi), meaning to "stand upright." It is the image of one who is so confident that he is holding his head up high, with his shoulders thrown back.

Paul obviously has the picture of a Roman soldier in mind — a soldier who is very proud to be a soldier. This is precisely the picture that the Holy Spirit is painting for us in this verse. When you have donned the full armor of God, you have every reason to stand up straight and be confident in God!

Notice the next statement: "Stand therefore, *having your loins girt about with truth....*" Now we come to the first piece of weaponry which Paul lists in this expanded version of spiritual armor: *the Roman loinbelt.*

For Review...

On the top of his head, the Roman soldier wore a huge *helmet.* It was a very elaborate, ornate, decorative piece of weaponry, intricate in all of its parts, and interesting to look upon. That's why the Holy Spirit calls our salvation a "helmet of salvation," for our salvation is the most elaborate, ornamental, intricate thing God has ever done for us!

In addition to this, the Roman soldier wore a *breastplate* which began at the top of his neck and extended down to his hips, going past his hips as a skirt down to his knees. The breastplate was made of two pieces of bronze or brass. One sheet of metal went down the front, and the other went down the back. These sheets of metal were attached by solid brass rings on the top and sides. The breastplate looked like the scales of a fish, and it was often referred to as a "coat of mail."

As if this weren't enough, the Roman soldier wore *greaves* on his legs, and dangerously spiked *shoes* on his feet.

Notice that the Roman soldier was completely covered. He had a helmet on his head, a breastplate upon his upper torso and midsection, and he was covered with metal from the top of his knees to the bottom of his legs. He was *completely covered* by his armor.

The *greaves* were very decorative and beautiful. They were made of a piece of metal, normally bronze or brass, which was wrapped around the shin or calf of the leg and extended from the knee to the foot. A heavy piece of metal covered the top of the foot, and strong straps of hide covered the sides. On the bottom of the foot were spikes one to three inches long.

Notice how much metal this man was carrying! He was dressed in a metal helmet, his breastplate was metal, his greaves and shoes were metal, and attached to his *loinbelt*, was a little ring where he could clip his shield, which was also partially made of metal.

In addition to all of this weaponry, the Roman soldier also carried a lance or spear that rested along the ridge of his back, and sat in a specially designed pouch attached to the loinbelt.

The Most Important Weapon

Paul says, *"Stand therefore, having your loins girt about with truth. . . ."*

I initially thought the loinbelt must have been a beautiful weapon, like the others that are listed in this text. But the loinbelt was the ugliest, most boring, least noticeable piece of armor that the Roman soldier wore.

When a Roman soldier had a beautiful breastplate of brass on, who would notice his belt? If you were to describe a man's clothing, would you begin with his belt? You can hardly even see it. You would probably start out by describing his jacket, then his shirt, his necktie and even his shoes. But you wouldn't begin with his belt, would you?

The belt seems to be an insignificant little thing — until you take it off! Then you discover how important that belt really is! Take it off and you might lose your pants, and when you lose your pants, your shirt comes untucked, and when your shirt comes untucked, you look like a mess!

You fall apart when you don't have your belt on. You walk around trying to pull your pants up. You don't feel very confident, and you certainly don't want to make any fast moves!

That is precisely what the loinbelt did for the Roman soldier; it held all the pieces of his armor together. Though he would be wearing all of his great weaponry, if his loinbelt was not in place, everything would fall apart. *It was said that the loinbelt was the most vital part of all the weaponry the Roman soldier wore.*

For example, his shield was attached to the loinbelt. If the Roman soldier had no loinbelt, then there was no resting place for his massive shield. If he had no loinbelt, he had no place to hang his sword. If there was no loinbelt, there was nothing for his lance to rest upon. If he didn't have a loinbelt, then there was nothing to keep his breastplate from flapping in the wind. *The loinbelt held it all together!*

Such soldiers would have literally come to pieces, piece by piece, if they didn't have the loinbelt fixed in its place around the waist. The loinbelt was vital to the Roman soldier. Without it, he had absolutely no confidence in fighting. With it, he was assured that all the pieces of his equipment would stay in place, so he could move quickly and fight with great fury.

Thus, the Bible says, "Stand therefore, *having your loins girt about with truth. . . .*"

A Visible Piece of Armor

The majority of your spiritual armor is invisible. For instance, you can't physically see the "breastplate of righteousness." You can't physically see your "shoes of peace," your "shield of faith," your "helmet of salvation," your "sword of the Spirit," or your "lance of intercession." These are *invisible weapons.*

But you *can* see one weapon — there is only one spiritual weapon that is visible to the sight — and this is the "loinbelt of truth."

The loinbelt of truth is the written Word of God! This is the only spiritual weapon that has taken on a physical, natural form, and has passed tangibly from the spirit realm into our hands! *It is the most important piece of weaponry that we possess.*

If you saw a Roman soldier, would you begin describing his outfit with his belt? No, you would probably say, "Oh, look at that helmet! Look at those shoes and that breastplate! My goodness, look at that shield, that sword, and that lance! Oh, I almost forgot — he's wearing a belt, too."

This, however, was not the Holy Spirit's approach. He went straight to the middle of the man and began describing spiritual armor by mentioning the soldier's belt. God is making a point: God is saying that the thing that is in the middle of the man is the thing that is the most important to the man. If you take that weapon off, the man will fall apart.

Likewise, when you ignore the Word of God and cease to apply it to your life on a daily basis, you have willfully chosen to let your entire spiritual life come apart at the seams!

The Difference Between *Logos* and *Rhema*

It is important to point out that there are two kinds of the Word of God. There is the *logos*, which is the written Word, and there is the *rhema*, which is a fresh, specially quickened and revealed word from God.

Be sensible and recognize that you will not always receive a *rhema* every time you would like to receive one, but you can always receive from the *logos*, the written Word, the Bible. *When all else fails, your Bible will still be within an arm's reach!*

This may not sound as exciting as receiving a supernatural word from the Lord. But keep in mind, Paul likens the Word of God to a Roman soldier's loinbelt. It was not pretty; it was drab looking and extremely commonplace. Every soldier had one of those "old things!"

This is the way that some people view the Bible. They have so many Bibles around their house, that they have lost their appreciation for it. They toss it aside and say, "I'm not going to study this anymore. I've studied and studied it, and now I'm tired of it. There isn't anything else for me to get out of it."

Lay that Bible (your "loinbelt of truth") aside, and in time you'll begin to lose your *sense* of righteousness. Lay that loinbelt of truth aside, and you will slowly begin to lose your *sense* of peace. Lay that loinbelt of truth down, and you will feel the joy of your salvation begin to deplete. If you toss that loinbelt of truth out of your life, very quickly you will begin to lose your ability to believe and walk in faith.

You absolutely *cannot* function as a believer without the Word of God having an active and central role in your life. You may run on a little steam from the past for a while, but you won't run very far.

If you remove the loinbelt — the Word of God — it will only be a matter of time until you begin to fall to pieces spiritually. Demonic assaults will break through that invisible barrier that used to protect you, and chaos will set into your life.

The Only Way To Succeed Spiritually

God has allowed me to minister in hundreds of churches, and to speak in several thousand church services over the past few years. As we have traveled, we have made several observations.

Some have tried to build their church on praise and worship. Praise and worship is wonderful, but you cannot build a church on this alone. *Praise and worship is not the loinbelt!*

Others have tried to build churches on social gatherings. Social gatherings are good and needed in the local church, but you cannot build a church on the foundation of social gatherings. *Social gathering and church fellowships are not the loinbelt!*

Others have attempted to build their church entirely on prayer. Of course, prayer is good! We have desperately needed a new emphasis on prayer in our day, *but prayer is not the loinbelt! Only the loinbelt will hold everything together individually, as believers, and corporately, as the Church.*

The Bible is the only piece of spiritual armor that is tangible to hold and visible to the eye. It is so important for us to have the Word of God in our possession, that God permitted this divine Word to pass from the spirit realm into our world so that we could hold it in our hands, and have it in our possession. *This is an important weapon, and it is the most important piece of armor that God has given us.* Think about it: *You can actually "hold" this weapon!*

Paul declares that this "loinbelt of truth" is so powerful and crucial, that it can take the average individual and cause them to be "perfect, thoroughly furnished unto all good works" (Second Timothy 3:17).

If *you* want to walk in spiritual armor, then you must begin by taking up the Word of God, and permanently affixing it to your life; giving it a central place and a dominant role; and allowing it to be the "loinbelt" that holds the rest of your weaponry together. The Bible must be the governor, the law, the ruler, the say-so in your life.

What is your aim? Do you want to succeed spiritually? Do you want to defeat the Philistines that continually come against your life? Do you want to be spiritually equipped?

The written Word has the power to "thoroughly furnish you unto all good works." The word "furnish" is taken from the Greek word *exartidzo* (ex-ar-tid-zo), which means "to completely outfit" or "fully supply." It was used to depict wagons or ships that were "completely outfitted" with gear.

By using this word, Paul tells us that the inspired Word of God will equip us with the "gear" we need in order to walk in the power of God, and to maintain our victorious position over the devil.

How To Walk in Righteousness

When you put this loinbelt on your life and keep it on, everything else comes together. For instance, do you want to learn how to enjoy your God-given righteousness?

The writer of Hebrews says, "For when for the time ye ought to be teachers, ye have need that one teach you again which be the first principles of the oracles of God; and are become such as have need of milk, and not of strong meat. *For every one that useth milk is unskilful in the word of righteousness: for he is a babe*" (Hebrews 5:12,13).

According to this verse, by ignoring the Word of God in your life, you deliberately choose *not* to develop your understanding of righteousness. On the other hand, reverse this by spending time in the Word of God, meditating in it, praying over it, and studying it, and you will discover that a wonderful, prevailing sense of righteousness will become a part of your thought life!

Ignore the Word of God and it will only be a matter of time before you feel very condemned in nearly every area of your life. Though declared righteous by God when they are first saved, people who do not make the Word a priority in their lives are not conscious of their God-given righteousness.

So if you want to walk in the breastplate of righteousness and enjoy it, first put on the loinbelt of truth, the written Word, the Bible. The Word will furnish you with righteousness.

How To Walk in Peace

Would you like to experience more peace in your life? Paul tells us how to have this. He says, "And let the peace of God rule in your hearts. . ." (Colossians 3:15).

Naturally speaking, there are not too many people who experience this "ruling" peace of God in their hearts. Because of hectic schedules, and because of the rushed day and hour that we live in, most people experience inner turmoil and constant frustration.

Rather than have the "peace of God" ruling in their hearts, the vast majority of believers have lots of flip-flop emotions, emotions you can't depend on to lead and guide you, emotions that can deceive you. *Therefore, you must allow the peace of God to rule in your heart.*

The word "rule," used in this verse, is taken from the word *brabeuo* (bra-beu-o), and it was used to picture an "umpire" or "one who called the shots at a public game." This man was the umpire; he was the governor; he decided who won! So by employing this word, Paul is actually saying, *"Let the peace of God umpire and call the shots in your life. . ."*

How do you come to this place where peace is that prevalent in your life? How do you come to the place where your mind, emotions, fears and frustrations cease to control you?

Paul continues, "Let the word of Christ dwell in you richly in all wisdom; teaching and admonishing one another in psalms and hymns and spiritual songs. . ." (Colossians 3:16).

Especially notice the command, *"Let the word of Christ dwell in you richly. . . ."* There are two key words in this phrase: the words "dwell" and "richly."

The word "dwell" is taken from the word *enoikeo* (en-oi-ke-o), and is the Greek word which means "to take up residence." It is the idea of "settling into a house," or "to make oneself to feel at home."

The word "richly" is from the word *plousios* (plou-si-os), and it carries the ideas of "extreme extravagance" and "luxurious living."

Therefore, when Paul says, "Let the word of Christ dwell in you richly," he is actually saying, *"Let the word of Christ take up residence in your life and come to feel completely at home in you; give it the warmest, most extravagant and luxurious reception that is possible. . ."*

What happens when you give the Word of God this kind of priority in your life? *The peace of God will begin to rule, umpire and call the shots in your daily life.*

How To Walk in Strong Faith

How do you walk in strong, believing faith? How does the "shield of faith" become a daily reality in your life?

In Romans 10:17, Paul says, "So then faith cometh by hearing, and hearing by the word of God."

You say you want to walk in faith? Then get in God's Word and stay there. Give it the most important place of priority in your life! Only the Word of God can produce consistent, ongoing faith.

I hope you can see and understand why the Holy Spirit began this text on spiritual armor with the loinbelt: *If you do not have the loinbelt of truth firmly positioned in your life, you will not be able to experientially walk in these other pieces of weaponry.*

The Helmet and the Sword

Now we come to the "helmet of salvation"! The word "salvation" is taken from the root *sodzo* (sod-zo), which conveys the ideas of "deliverance, safety, preservation, soundne⸰ of mind and healing."

How would you like to habitually walk in your Christ-purchased deliverance, safety, soundness of mind and healing? Would you like that? Then you must put your helmet on! How do you put your helmet on?

In Ephesians 6:17, we are told to "take the helmet of salvation," and in First Thessalonians 5:8, we are told that salvation is a "helmet." What is the connection between the concepts of salvation and the mind?

Paul told Timothy, "And that from a child thou hast known the holy scriptures, *which are able to make thee wise unto salvation. . ."* (Second Timothy 3:15).

The power of God's Word has a way of making us mentally alert and wise unto salvation. By giving our minds to the Word of God, the Word itself begins to build a measure of deliverance, safety, preservation, soundness of mind and healing into our system.

Scripture puts a helmet on your head! As you renew your mind to the Word of God, it becomes your spiritual helmet.

In addition to wearing salvation as a helmet, the sixth chapter of Ephesians also informs us that we have a mighty and powerful sword, called "the sword of the Spirit." Would you like to wield this "sword of the Spirit" in your life on a more consistent basis? How can it be developed? *Where can you find this sword?*

Where did the Roman soldier find his sword when he needed it? It was hanging in its scabbard along his side, resting on a clip that hung from his *loinbelt!* Therefore, in order to keep his sword nearby, he had to keep that loinbelt on, because the sword was always attached to *the loinbelt.*

What is the loinbelt representative of in the sixth chapter of Ephesians? *The written Word of God.* Therefore, this tells us that most of the time that needed "word from the Lord" will come directly out of the Bible — just as the Roman soldier's sword came right out of a scabbard that hung on his loinbelt. *The loinbelt and the sword were connected.*

Many people today say, "Lord, I need *a word!* Lord, I need for you to speak to me in some special way! God, I am in this crisis. I need *a word* from you, Lord!" They run around trying to have a dream, vision, or have someone prophesy their answer to them. Or they go to church hoping that someone will have a word of knowledge or word of wisdom for them.

I praise God for dreams, visions, prophecy, words of knowledge and words of wisdom. However, there is something more *dependable* than a word of knowledge, word of wisdom or prophecy. Peter said, "We have also *a more sure word* of prophecy. . ." (Second Peter 1:19).

So you say you need a special *word* from the Lord? Do you need a *rhema*, a "sword of the Spirit?" This is how you get it: Walk in the Word and your *rhema* will most likely be quickened to you as you read and study the Word of God.

As the writer of Hebrews said, "For the word of God is quick, and powerful, and sharper than any twoedged sword, piercing even to the dividing asunder of soul and spirit, and of the joints and marrow, and is a discerner of the thoughts and intents of the heart" (Hebrews 4:12).

When you walk in the Word of God, you are in a position for the Word to cut straight to the heart. You have a sword that will "pierce even to the dividing asunder of soul and spirit, and of the joints and marrow," and it will "discern the thoughts and intents" of your heart.

What happens if you choose to ignore the loinbelt — the Word of God — and try your luck with another approach? Many saints have tried this. They've foolishly taken their loinbelt off, put the Bible down, while they said, "I've tried the Bible, and I'm weary of it. I can walk in power and authority without maintaining time in the Word of God."

By thinking this way, they just snapped the loinbelt off and put it down. You can walk like that for a while, but soon things begin to get loose. Soon you hear something jiggling and, lo and behold, your breastplate falls right off your body! That sword drops to the ground! Your lance tumbles to the floor!

What happened? You took your loinbelt off; hence, you have nothing to hold your spiritual life together. Now naked, you have put yourself in a dangerous position where the enemy may come to strike with afflictions and troubles. Never forget: *The Word supports everything else!*

Winning or Losing Is Your Choice

I want you to understand that if you are not walking daily in the power of God and the Word of God, then neither are you walking in your God-given suit of spiritual armor.

Without the Word of God operational in your life, you have no support for other pieces of spiritual weaponry. For you there is no fight. Your battle is over before it ever begins. You have forfeited your victory by rejecting the most importance piece of weaponry of all: the Word of God.

That Word holds your sense of righteousness in place — and you need your sense of righteousness. That Word holds your peace in place — and you need your peace. Peace is a major weapon, not just defensive, but also offensive.

Without your helmet of salvation to protect your mind, when the enemy comes to swing his battle ax, your mind will begin swimming with unbelief and doubt. In the end, he'll try to rob you of deliverance, soundness of mind and healing.

Some people sit in a closet in the dark, hoping to get a *rhema* from God! You will get your *rhema* when you turn the light on, pick up your Bible and begin to meditate in God's Word. Suddenly, one of those verses will leap right off the page and become a mighty blade in your hand and in your mouth.

The Reproductive Ability of God

ɔtice, too, that the loinbelt covered the Roman soldier's
Why did the soldier have his loins protected so heavily: *Because he wanted to reserve his ability to reproduce.*

Because the loinbelt is representative of the Word of God, and the loinbelt was historically a protection to the reproductive abilities of a man, this tells us yet something else very significant. *It plainly shows us that our ability to produce for God is directly tied to our relationship with the Word of God.*

You become sterile spiritually if you don't have God's Word actively operating in your life — you do nothing, you produce nothing, you produce no anointing and no healing power. *When you get out of the Word of God, you produce nothing.*

Even God creates, produces and reproduces by the Word of God. Hebrews 11:3 says, "Through faith we understand that the worlds were framed by the word of God. . . ."

God produced the worlds through His Word!

Do you know what happened to you when you were saved? First John 3:9 says, "Whosoever is born of God doth not sin; for his *seed* remaineth in him: and he cannot sin, because he is born of God."

The word "seed" is taken from the Greek word *spermata* (sper-ma-ta). It is where we derive the word "sperm."

Here we have a picture of the New Birth! Just as a woman becomes pregnant by a man's seed and conceives a child in her womb, John says that when we are born again, God injects his own divine "seed" into our human spirits.

Once that seed is placed into us, *that divine seed then immediately begins to produce the life and character of Christ within us.*

This divine "seed" (*spermata*) is the reason we cannot go on living the way we once did before we met the Lord. The life, character, nature and attributes of God are in that "seed," similar to the way that a father's eye color, hair color, and temperament is in his seed. Once the nature of God is planted into

us, that divine life forever breaks the power of canceled sin —
and the life of God begins to rule and reign in our lives!

What does the "seed" of God look like? What is the
"seed" of God? Peter tells us, "Being born again, not of corruptible seed, but of incorruptible, *by the word of God*, which
liveth and abideth forever" (First Peter 1:23).

God made the worlds with the Word of God, and he
recreated you with His divine "seed" everything God produces, He produces through the instrumentation of His Word.

The Major Mistake Believers Make

It could be that you have recently been asking the Lord,
"Why is my life such a mess?" You may have been asking,
"Where did my peace go? Where is the victory that I used to
experience?"

I believe the Lord is asking you some questions in return.
He is asking you, "Where is that loinbelt I gave you? Why
haven't you been in My Word? Who took your belt off?"

When you take your belt off, your clothes fall off! So my
solemn advice to you is, if you are going to go into spiritual
combat — don't go into this kind of fight without your belt,
because one hit from the enemy and all your armor is going
to come tumbling off.

Other believers make the mistake of thinking, "I know
I ought to spend some time in the Word today, but I really
don't have the time. I'll wait until the next church service
when I go to church. Our pastor is such a good teacher! I'll
just wait until then. I know that he'll feed me well."

Finally, the long-awaited church service comes. They go
home, and the next day they realize that they ought to spend
some time in the Word, but now they say, "Well, I'll just wait
until the next church service. That last service was *so* good!
I know the next one will be even better."

Let me ask you this question: Do you still ask your
mother to dress you? What would your mother think if you
asked her, "Mother, would you please dress me today?" She

would say, "What do you mean? You actually want me to put your clothes on you? You're not a baby anymore. Go dress yourself!"

But that is exactly what believers do! When they come to church on Sunday or to midweek service, knowing that they haven't been in the Word all week long, they say, "Preacher, would you please dress me? Would you put my belt on me? Preacher, would you please dress me?"

I want you to understand that *the teaching of the Word from the pulpit should confirm what you already heard God say personally to you through His Word during the week.*

Your pastor's preaching is not to be the *only* Word you get; it's intended by the Holy Spirit to pull the belt that is *already* on you a little tighter.

When individuals in the Body of Christ get in the Word of God for themselves every day, go to church, and the teaching of the Word comes forth, it pulls their belt tighter. Their righteousness fits even better. Their peace and everything else is locked on even tighter.

When you get these two elements of Bible study flowing together, the Body of Christ really gets dressed!

In Ephesians, chapter six, why did the Holy Spirit begin describing our weaponry by starting with the belt? Because He wanted to emphasize the absolute importance of the loin-belt of truth. Thus, through Paul, the Holy Spirit said, "Stand therefore, having your loins girt about with truth. . . ."

David on the Centrality of the Word

Perhaps no one in the Bible understood the importance of the centrality of God's Word better than David. You can hear David's love for the Word as he speaks in Psalm 119:

"Blessed are the undefiled in the way, who walk in *the law of the Lord.*

"Blessed are they that keep *his testimonies,* and that seek him with the whole heart. . . .

"Thou has commanded us to keep *thy precepts* diligently.

"O that my ways were directed to keep *thy statu*

"Then shall I not be ashamed, when I have respe<
all *thy commandments*.

"I will keep *thy statutes. . . .*

"Wherewithal shall a young man cleanse his way? by taking heed thereto according to *thy word*.

"With my whole heart have I sought thee: O let me not
wander from *thy commandments*.

"*Thy word* have I hid in my heart, that I might not sin
against thee.

"Blessed art thou, O Lord: teach me thy statutues.

"With my lips have I declared all *the judgments of thy
mouth. . . .*

"I have rejoiced in *thy testimonies. . . .*

"I will meditate in *thy precepts. . . .*

I will delight myself in *thy statutes*: I will not forget *thy
word. . . .*

"I am a stranger in the earth: hide not *thy commandments*
from me."

You can see that the Word was central to David. Do you
see how much David loved and needed the "loinbelt of truth"
for his life? David said, "I *have* to have it! I meditate on it. I
don't get away from it. Please don't hide it from me. Reveal
it to me. I promise You I will walk in it. I will think on it. I
will keep it."

The Key to Victory and Success

David understood that the Word was the key to complete victory and complete success in life. In verses 20-24,
David pleads:

"My soul breaketh for the longing that it hath unto *thy
judgments* at all times.

"Thou has rebuked the proud that are cursed, which do
err from *thy commandments*.

"Remove from me reproach and contempt; for I have kept
thy testimonies.

"Princes also did sit and speak against me: but thy servant did meditate on *thy statutes.*

"*Thy testimonies* are also my delight and my counsellors."

When you get into spiritual conflict, know that evil forces — like those who opposed David — will rise up against you. But the Word says that because you meditate in His statutes, God will remove their reproach and contempt. In other words, this "loinbelt of truth" will equip you to remove these foul forces.

In verses 57-59, David says:

"Thou art my portion, O Lord: I have said that I will keep *thy words.*

"I intreated thy favour with my whole heart: be merciful unto me according to *thy word.*

"I thought on my ways, and turned my feet unto thy testimonies."

David is saying, "Lord, your Word is going to be first and foremost in my life!"

He continues in verses 60-63:

"I made haste, and delayed not to keep *thy commandments.*

"The bands of the wicked have robbed me: but I have not forgotten *thy law.*

"At midnight I will rise to give thanks unto thee because of *thy righteous judgments.*

"I am a companion of all them that fear thee, and of them that keep *thy precepts.*"

The Word's Best Advice

Here in verse 63 is the best advice you will ever get in all your life! David said, "I am a companion of all them that fear thee, and of them that keep thy precepts."

My advice to you, and the Word's advice to you, is that your companions be people who walk in the Word. *You need people around you who understand the centrality of the Word as much as you do.*

David says, "My companions love your Word as much as I love it." Be careful to choose your friends wisely. Walk with people who walk with the Lord and in His Word as seriously as you do.

In verses 129 and 130, David says:

"*Thy testimonies* are wonderful: therefore doth my soul keep them.

"The entrance of *thy words* giveth light; it giveth understanding unto the simple."

Once again, David is proclaiming, "Lord, your Word is central in my life!"

In verses 131-134, he continues:

"I opened my mouth, and panted: for I longed for *thy commandments*.

"Look thou upon me, and be merciful unto me, as thou usest to do unto those that love thy name.

"Order my steps in thy word: and let not any iniquity have dominion over me.

"Deliver me from the oppression of man: so will I keep *thy precepts*."

Notice how much David needs the Word: He is *panting* after it! David is saying that because he keeps God's precepts, he knows that God will deliver him. Verses 135 and 136:

"Make thy face to shine upon thine servant; and teach me *thy statutes*.

"Rivers of waters run down mine eyes, because they keep not *thy law*."

David is saying, "They don't listen to your Word, and it is destroying them. They don't keep your law, and they are being killed. They are being ruined. Iniquity and sin are overtaking them!"

Why did David say this? Because David knew that keeping the Word of God central in your life saves you from destruction. Then, in verses 153-157, David says:

"Consider mine affliction, and deliver me: for I do not forget *thy law*.

"Plead my cause, and deliver me: quicken me according to *thy word*.

"Salvation is far from the wicked: for they seek not *thy statutes*.

"Great are thy tender mercies, O Lord: quicken me according to *thy judgments*.

"Many are my persecutors and mine enemies; yet do I not decline from *thy testimonies*."

In other words, people who aren't seeking the Word of God do not experience the blessings of their salvation (verse 155). It is almost as though David is saying, "In spite of them, I have refuge in your Word."

In verses 158-160, David says:

"I beheld the transgressors, and was grieved; because they kept not *thy word*.

"Consider how I love *thy precepts*: quicken me, O Lord, according to thy lovingkindness.

"Thy word is true from the beginning: and every one of *thy righteous judgments* endureth for ever."

David is saying, "I will not err from the Word of God. It is always right. It is central in my life. It delivers me, preserves me and keeps me." David's theme in Psalm 119 is the centrality of the Word of God in his life. There is no doubt about it, David had on the "loinbelt of truth!"

Many people quote Revelation 12:11, which says, "And they overcame him [the devil] by the blood of the Lamb, and by the word of their testimony. . . ."

What testimony is that? The Word of God. That's the only testimony that we have!

The Way To Win

The Bible says, "Stand therefore, having your loins girt about with truth. . . ." When you put this loinbelt of the Word on and determine to make it a priority in your life, you are on the way to winning your battles in life!

After you put the Word of God on, you may not feel righteous at first, but keep walking in the Word, and your sense of righteousness will spring up in your life!

You may not feel any peace at first, either, but the Bible promises, "Thou wilt keep him in perfect peace, whose mind is stayed on thee. . ." (Isaiah 26:3).

How do you keep your mind stayed on the Lord? By walking in the Word, and allowing the word of Christ to dwell in you richly. Then the peace of God will rule in your heart.

You say you need a sword? You need a special *rhema*, a word from the Lord? The Word of God is quick, active and operative; it's sharper than any two-edged sword.

You say that you need faith? "Faith cometh by hearing, and by hearing by the Word of God" (Romans 10:17).

You say that you need a shield? Get in the Word of God. Hear the Word of God. Meditate on the Word of God. It will put a shield into your hand.

When you have the "loinbelt of truth," you are positioned to have all these pieces of weaponry in your spiritual life. With it, nothing falls off. With it, you can move swiftly, furiously, right against the enemy.

Without it, you are in serious trouble!

If you intend to challenge the assaults of the adversary against your body, mind, family, friends, money and business, my solemn advice to you from God's Word is to pick up that loinbelt and put it on.

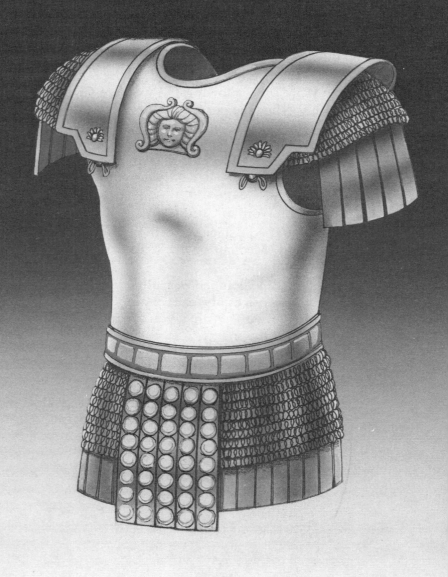

Chapter Eleven
The Breastplate of Righteousness

Paul continues to tell us what is the next piece of our spiritual weaponry. He says, "Stand therefore, having your loins girt about with truth, and having on the breastplate of righteousness" (Ephesians 6:14).

Righteousness is a weapon; it is our breastplate! You may ask, "How could righteousness be a weapon? Why would Paul call it a breastplate? In what way does it serve us as armor?"

We know that righteousness is a weapon because Paul calls it a weapon in the sixth chapter of Ephesians. He mentions it in the same context with "the loinbelt of truth," the "shield of faith," the "helmet of salvation," the "sword of the Spirit," and the "lance" of intercession. In Second Corinthians 6:7, righteousness is again referred to as a weapon. It reads, "By the word of truth, by the power of God, *by the armour of righteousness....*" Here righteousness is plainly called "armour."

Another reference where righteousness is called armor is Isaiah 59:17. Isaiah says, *"For he put on righteousness as a breastplate...."*

In order to understand *why* righteousness is called a breastplate in Paul's list of spiritual armor in the sixth chapter of Ephesians, first you must understand something about the Roman soldier's breastplate that Paul had in mind.

The breastplate was the most beautiful, shiniest, most glamorous piece of weaponry that the Roman soldier pos-

---

Facing left page: The brass breastplate of a Roman soldier from the first century.

sessed. When you walked up to a Roman soldier, you didn't notice his loinbelt first, or his shoes, his sword, or his helmet, as intricate and important as they were.

The first thing you would notice when looking at a Roman soldier was his beautiful breastplate. The breastplate began at the top of his neck and went all the way down to the knees. It was composed of two different pieces of metal. One piece of metal went down the front, and the other went down the back. They were held together by solid brass rings on top of the shoulders. Quite often, the larger sheets of metal that covered the front and the back of the man, were comprised of smaller, scale-like pieces of metal, similar to the scales of a fish.

This was the heaviest piece of weaponry that the Roman soldier wore. At times, it weighed in excess of 40 pounds. Some breastplates reportedly weighed up to 75 pounds or more! Remember, Goliath's breastplate weighed approximately 125 pounds!

The Beauty of the Breastplate

The breastplate was extremely elaborate and beautiful. It was made either of bronze or brass; usually brass. As Roman soldiers walked to and fro in their breastplates, something incredible would begin to happen.

When you rub two pieces of metal against each other for a long time, they begin to add a lustre to each other. Though these pieces of metal were already very shiny, this new lustre makes them even shinier. This is exactly what happened when the Roman soldier walked around with his breastplate on; those smaller, scale-like pieces of metal would rub up against each other, thus causing each piece to have a beautiful lustre.

Brass is a golden color, and when it is out in the sun, it shines and sparkles; especially if it is a fine piece of brass. Furthermore, the rays of the sun would reflect off the breastplate, presenting a dazzling spectacle.

So the beauty of the Roman soldier's breastplate was enhanced by using it and walking in it. Had it been stored in a dark room, and never been used, it would have been beautiful simply because it was made out of brass. But by walking in it and using it, the breastplate became more and more beautiful with time.

Have you ever been riding down the road in your car, when a piece of metal from something outside had such a glare on it, you could hardly see the road? Can you imagine a Roman soldier walking around in a breastplate to which all this shine and lustre had been added? When he walked out into the afternoon sunlight, he looked like a rainbow, casting beams wherever he went.

What do you suppose it was like when a whole legion of Roman soldiers walked out into the sunshine? The whole mountainside or valley where they were marching would begin to shine! Why? Because they were walking in those bright and shining breastplates.

Our righteousness is a weapon; a genuine weapon. It is called a "breastplate of righteousness" in Ephesians 6:14. Not only is it a *defensive weapon* to protect us from the blows of the enemy; it is also an *offensive weapon* to assist us as we assault the enemy.

Someone Wants To Hurt You

A person who is not engaged in battle does not need to wear this kind of weaponry. You wear this kind of weaponry because someone out there wants to hurt you very badly!

The Holy Spirit, therefore, tells us that we have righteousness as a "breastplate" to protect us. In Ephesians 6:11, we saw that when we have on "the whole armour of God," we are able "to stand against the wiles of the devil." The devil wants to assault you. He wants to tell you that you are *not* righteous; that you are of no value to God, or to man.

Remember, the word "devil" is taken from the Greek word diabalos (dia-bo-los), and it describes "one who strikes again, again and again, until finally, he penetrates the mind with slanderous accusations." Because of his desire to penetrate and immobilize the mind and emotions of a person, he especially delights in finding believers who do not know they are righteous. They are easy prey!

He sneers, "You're the worst believer that has ever lived. Do you think God is going to do anything with you? God can't use you, you stupid thing!"

If you don't have your "breastplate of righteousness" firmly fixed in place, those slanderous accusations will most likely penetrate you — and when they penetrate through your mind and emotions, they will deal an effective blow to you, injuring you immensely.

People who don't know they have been made "righteous" tend to habitually walk in condemnation. Why? Because the devil comes to condemn them. People who don't know they have been made "righteous" walk in guilt, because the enemy comes to throw lying accusations that penetrate their minds and make them feel like they are failures.

On the other hand, when a believer knows that God has made him righteous — when he or she has that "breastplate of righteousness "fixed firmly in place — it doesn't matter how many arrows the enemy shoots against that believer, because not one arrow will penetrate. Not one word of condemnation — not one allegation, nor guilt — will come your way if you are walking in a "breastplate of righteousness."

Unfortunately, ninety percent of the Body of Christ is walking in condemnation, with their shoulders slumped and their heads hanging low. The enemy has victimized many to the point that they can no longer pray with confidence. He has convinced others that they will never be *good enough* to be used by God.

Yet the Word plainly tells us in verse 14 of our text "to stand, throw your shoulders back, hold your head up high, and walk tall like all proud and victorious soldiers walk."

When you understand that God has freely imparted righteousness to you, and that this God-given righteousness now serves you as a gorgeous breastplate, it will affect your attitude very positively! You will find a great amount of confidence arising in your life. An attitude of righteousness imparts confidence, and it imparts tremendous authority.

With that confidence in operation, you will move out to do all kinds of things for God. Sometimes you will become so bold and confident in your God-given righteousness, that those who don't know you may not understand your new-found boldness, and may accuse you of being egocentric or arrogant.

No, you are a man or woman who has recently learned that you are "the righteousness of God in Christ Jesus" (Second Corinthians 5:21).

You have learned that God has clothed you in a gorgeous, beautiful, bright and shining piece of armor called "the breastplate of righteousness." You have just discovered that you don't have to take the devil's lying threats anymore, because you are *"dressed to kill!"*

The Correct Attitude for Warfare

When Roman soldiers went out to fight, their commanding officer told them: "Don't come back to our encampment until the enemy has been annihilated. If you're not going to kill the adversary, then don't come back and show your face here ever again."

Those soldiers were told, "It would be better for you to die on the battlefield than to come back here and tell us that the enemy won. Make sure that you come home a winner, or don't come home at all."

You can be sure that these kinds of statements affected the attitude of those soldiers. They immediately begin to mentally gear themselves up for the fight! They went into weeks and months of preparation. They did everything they could to prepare their minds and attitudes — *because your mind and attitude have everything to do with how well you perform in the midst of a fight.*

If you are mentally and emotionally defeated *before* you go into a fight, you should not go into battle! Why? Because your negative attitude has already determined the outcome of that battle. You will be defeated.

By developing an attitude of "righteousness" in your life and learning to view yourself through the work of the cross, your attitude will receive a divine impartation of confidence and boldness that will always put you on the winning side of victory!

You must become mentally prepared. This is why Peter said, "Wherefore, gird up the loins of your mind, be sober, and hope to the end. . ." (First Peter 1:13).

This is the picture of a Greek runner. In order to run faster and better, he takes hold of his skirt and tucks it up underneath his belt. By doing this, he frees his leg from getting caught in his skirt. He is *"girding up"* his skirt.

Likewise, Peter commands us to gather up all the loose ends of our minds, pull them up, tuck them under our belt, figuratively speaking, and then run our race free of encumbrances. In other words, to run this race and to fight this fight, *we must prepare ourselves emotionally and intellectually.*

In order to do this vital work of emotional and mental preparation, you need to know that you are righteous, because this knowledge will positively affect your attitude! If you really know that you have on "the breastplate of righteousness," you can fight any foe and face any enemy.

You had better know that God has made you righteous! It is of the highest importance that you make this knowledge a key part of your mental makeup. Even when you are thoroughly convinced of your right standing with God, the devil will still attempt to tell you that you are *not* righteous.

Scriptures on Righteousness

In order to establish the fact of your God-given "righteousness," we must quickly look at several verses on the subject of "righteousness."

In Second Corinthians 5:21, Paul says, "For he made him [Jesus] to be sin for us, who knew no sin; that we might be made the righteousness of God in him."

We are righteous! When you begin to meditate on this truth, and when it really begins to get into your mind and your thinking, your attitude will change. You will develop a righteous consciousness!

When your attitude is affected by righteousness — when you no longer say that you *want* to be righteous, but now realize that you *are* righteous — it gives you assurance!

Another important scripture about righteousness is found in Romans 3:21,22. These verses say, "But now the righteousness of God without the law is manifested, being witnessed by the law and the prophets. *Even the righteousness of God which is by faith of Jesus Christ unto all and upon all them that believe. . . .*"

According to these verses, a God-given righteousness rightfully belongs "unto all and upon all them that believe." What stronger statement can be made to prove that all believers are dressed in righteousness?

In Romans 5:17, Paul says, "For if by one man's offence [Adam's] death reigned by one; *much more they which receive abundance of grace and of the gift of righteousness shall reign in life by one, Jesus Christ.*"

This means that when righteousness is graciously imparted to a believer by God, and when that believer finally grabs hold of it and realizes that he or she is righteous, it *changes* him. He no longer views himself as a little, unimportant, defeated believer. He is affected in his attitude, and it gives him such assurance that he moves from the realm of being a struggler to the realm of reigning in life like a king!

You may ask, "If all believers have been made righteous and are supposed to reign in life like a king, then why do so many believers live defeated lives?"

Because their minds have not been renewed by the Word of God to this correct thinking! Because they think they are unworthy, they behave as though they are unworthy. Because they think they are of no value, they behave as though they are of no value. Because they think they are unrighteous, they behave as though they are unrighteous.

When you find out that you are righteous, you throw your shoulders back and say, "Look at me! I've got a breastplate of righteousness fixed to my life! I am the righteousness of God in Christ Jesus!"

This knowledge changes a believer!

A New Source of Confidence

When you begin to walk in your breastplate of righteousness, it will impart a new and incredible confidence to your spiritual life.

In First John 5:13-14, John says, "These things have I written unto you that believe on the name of the Son of God; that ye may know that ye have eternal life, and that ye may believe on the name of the Son of God. *And this is the confidence. . . .*"

The word "confidence" is taken from the Greek word *parresia* (par-re-sia), and it has been translated in other places as "boldness" or "openness." This word portrays the picture of a man or woman who is exceptionally "open" and "bold" about things; so "open" and "bold" that they almost appear to be "arrogant."

John continues to say, "And this is the confidence [Greek: great boldness] that we have in him, that, if we ask anything according to his will, he heareth us: And if we know that he hear us, whatsoever we ask, we know that we have the petitions that we desired of him" (First John 5:14,15).

An attitude of righteousness will affect your prayer life! If you do not know that you have a right standing with God, you cannot pray with confidence. If you aren't aware that you have been given righteousness as a breastplate, you won't be able to do anything with confidence.

People pray defeated prayers because they don't know they are righteous. In fact, you can tell when someone isn't walking in their "breastplate of righteousness" by listening to the way they pray. Their prayers are filled with defeat.

On the other hand, when someone walks in their "breastplate of righteousness," they pray with power and authority. They know that because of that breastplate, they can come directly into the presence of God and pray with great boldness.

Powerless Religion vs. Powerful Religion

In Acts, chapter three, Peter and John were going to the Temple at the hour of prayer, when suddenly, they saw a man who had been crippled for many years. It says, "Now Peter and John went up together into the temple at the hour of prayer, being the ninth hour, and a certain man lame from his mother's womb was carried, whom they laid daily at the gate of the temple which is called *Beautiful*, to ask alms of them that entered into the temple. . . ."

Notice that this man was being laid daily at the gate of the temple called *"Beautiful." "Beautiful"* was not the real name of this gate; it was an expression to describe what this gate looked like. It was an absolutely gorgeous area of the temple, so it was called the *"beautiful gate"* by the people. It was decorated with all kinds of wonderful, ornate columns and other lavish architectural details.

As beautiful as this gate was, it had never healed this man. This is a picture of a dead and lifeless religion — it had beautiful, formal buildings — and there was absolute quietness in this place for fear of being "irreverent" or "irreligious."

 all of their formality and all of their piety, the needs
 e man had never been met. This is a picture of what
 eligion has to offer — *absolutely nothing.*

⌐ he story continues to tell us what the crippled man did
when he saw Peter and John. It says, "Who seeing Peter and
John about to go into the temple asked an alms. And Peter,
fastening his eyes upon him with John, said, Look on us"
(Acts 3:3,4).

The Bible says that Peter fastened his eyes upon him.
The word "upon" is taken from the Greek word *eis* (pronounced ice), which means "into." So when the Bible says
Peter fixed his eyes "upon" the man, it is actually telling us
that Peter walked up to this poor cripple and stared straight
"into" his eyes. Once he had the man's complete attention,
Peter declared, "Look at me!"

Why did Peter say this? *Because he knew that he had something life-changing to offer this crippled man.* Once you realize
that you have been given a "breastplate of righteousness,"
you will walk around wanting to tell *everyone* to look at you,
because, like Peter, you will know that you have something
to offer that they need! This knowledge of righteousness
affects the way you deal with people.

The next verses say, "And he gave heed unto them,
expecting to receive something of them. Then Peter said, Silver and gold have I none; but *such* as I have give I thee. . ."
(Acts 3:5,6).

To translate this word "such" is a very poor translation
indeed. It should have been translated, ". . . but *Who* I have
give I thee. . . ." Peter wasn't giving that man a "such"; he
was giving that man a "Who" — Jesus Christ! Peter and John
then released the power of God into that lame man's body,
and he was healed!

Why could Peter and John move in such confidence?
Because they knew they were righteous! Righteousness
affects your attitude about yourself, and your attitude about
people and situations around you. *When you have been posi-*

tively influenced by an understanding of righteousness, it gives you the assurance you need to step out and do the work of God.

Before you run out to do warfare with the enemy, you need to have this kind of assurance in your possession. The enemy will try to slander and accuse you. He will try to tell you that you are a good-for-nothing. He will try to convince you that God won't use you, and that no one will listen to you.

That's why it is so vital for you to know that God has given you a "breastplate of righteousness." *When you walk in that breastplate, everything changes.*

Righteousness: A Defensive Weapon

Righteousness is a defensive weapon. In regard to righteousness serving us as a defensive weapon, Isaiah says, "I will greatly rejoice in the Lord, my soul shall be joyful in my God; *for he hath clothed me with the garments of salvation, he hath covered me with the robe of righteousness. . .*" (Isaiah 61:10).

Notice that this robe is going from head to foot, *covering or protecting you.* By using this expression, Isaiah tells us that righteousness will act as a defense for you.

In Isaiah 51:7,8, Isaiah announces: "Hearken unto me, *ye that know righteousness,* the people in whose heart is the law; fear ye not the reproach of men, neither be ye afraid of their revilings. For the moth shall eat them up like a garment, and the worm shall eat like wool: *but my righteousness shall be for ever, and my salvation from generation to generation.*"

When you are dressed in righteousness, you do not have to fear what the devil or man can do to you. Your righteousness will protect and sustain you — while your enemies are eaten like a moth eats a garment and like a worm eats wool. God's gift of righteousness in your life, however, is permanent; it will last from generation to generation!

When you walk in righteousness, it is a weapon of defense against the slanderous accusations and insidious strategies of the enemy.

ιe righteous are never permanently affected by afflic-
Psalm 37:17 says, *"For the arms of the wicked shall be bro-
but the Lord upholdeth the righteous."*

The righteous always outlast any attack that comes
against them. While the enemy comes to remove the influence of the righteous, Proverbs 10:30 declares, *"The righteous
shall never be removed. . . ."*

How important is it for you to walk in your righteousness? It's important if you don't want to be *"removed."* If you
don't have your breastplate of righteousness firmly fixed in
place when you begin your confrontation with the adversary,
he will do everything within his power *to remove you!*

Righteousness: An Offensive Weapon

The breastplate that the Roman soldier wore was beautiful to look and, yes, it was wonderful that it protected the soldier from attack, but it did something else very important too.

Keep in mind, the breastplate of the Roman soldier was
made of especially bright and shining golden brass. When
that soldier threw his shoulders back, and the afternoon sunshine hit that metal, it cast a blinding glare into the eyes of all
who were watching.

The brilliance of his breastplate blinded the eyes of his
opponent so thoroughly that the opponent could not see to
fight. When the breastplate was used in this way, it served as
an offensive weapon.

Similarly, when you really begin to walk in righteousness, all you have to do is to walk into a dark situation, and
that darkness will begin to flee from you. Evil forces always
flee from righteousness, because they cannot endure the brilliance that righteousness reflects into their eyes!

Righteousness will equip you not only in a spiritual way;
righteousness will affect you in the *natural* realm as well.
Righteousness will make you noticeable.

When you are dressed in righteousness, you realize you
are dressed in armor; you are dressed in the Lord Jesus Christ.

You are as brilliant and powerful as Jesus Himself when you are walking in this breastplate! With this breastplate firmly fixed in place, you have God's glory radiating from your life to all those around you.

Throw your shoulders back and be bold! You are the "righteousness of God" in Christ Jesus! You have on a "breastplate of righteousness."

Every Roman soldier owned a beautiful breastplate of brass. However, if it was going to be useful to the soldier, he had to put it on. As stated already, the more he walked in that breastplate, the more beautiful it became, as the individual smaller pieces of scale-like metal began to add a lustre to each other.

This is exactly what happens when you begin to walk in your righteousness. As you walk in your righteousness, you will experience what the Roman soldier experienced — your breastplate will begin to get more and more beautiful all the time.

Keep walking. . . keep marching. . . keep moving forward, and do not let the enemy talk you out of enjoying the benefits of your right standing with God.

As you walk in your "breastplate of righteousness," a righteous consciousness will begin to overtake your false emotions of unworthiness and condemnation. A righteous consciousness will begin to develop in your life.

As you walk in righteousness, with every step you take, you will become more and more gorgeous to the eye of God, and more and more dangerously blinding to the eye of the enemy.

Chapter Twelve
Shoes of Peace

In the sixth chapter of Ephesians, Paul continues expounding on the "whole armour of God." He says, "And your feet shod with the preparation of the gospel of peace" (Ephesians 6:15).

The Roman soldier's shoes were not an ordinary kind of shoes. In the first place, they were made out of bronze or brass — usually brass — and the shoes were primarily composed of two parts: (1) the *greave*, and (2) the *shoe* itself. These shoes were exceptionally dangerous to any foe.

The *greave* was a piece of beautifully tooled metal that began at the top of the knee and extended down past the lower leg, finally resting on the upper portion of the foot. It was made from a warped sheet of tooled metal that had been specifically formed to fit around the calf of the Roman soldier's leg. As stated earlier (on pages 116 and 117), this tube-like piece of metal caused the Roman soldier's shoes to look like boots that were made of brass!

The *shoe* itself was made of two pieces of metal. On the top and bottom, the foot was covered with fine pieces of brass. The sides of the shoe were held together by multiple pieces of durable leather. On the bottom, these shoes were affixed with *extremely dangerous spikes — spikes that were one to three inches long*. If you were involved in active combat, your spikes could be close to three inches long. *These were killer shoes!*

Facing left page: The metal greaves and spiked shoes of a Roman soldier from the first century.

Paul had these very shoes in mind when he said, "And having your feet shod with the preparation of the gospel of peace." When you see what these shoes looked like and how dangerous those sharpened spikes could be, then you can see why it is amazing that Paul would use this illustration to describe "peace."

According to Paul, "peace" is an awesome weapon; it is a *defensive* and *offensive* weapon. Peace will not only *protect* you; peace is also a brutal weapon, which when used correctly, keeps spiritual foes where they belong — *under your feet!* One good kick, and the enemy is crushed!

Notice that Paul says, "And having your feet *shod....*" The word "shod" is derived from the word *hupodeomai* (hu-po-de-o-mai), and is a compound of the words *hupo* (hu-po) and *deo* (de-o). The word *hupo* means "under" and *deo* means "to bind." Taken together as one word (*hupodeomai*), this word conveys the idea of "binding something very tightly on the bottom of one's feet."

Therefore, this is not the picture of a loosely fitting shoe; this is the picture of a shoe that has been tied onto the bottom of the foot *extremely tightly.*

Now Paul uses this same word to tell us we must firmly tie "peace" onto our lives. If we only give "peace" a loosely fitting position in our lives, then the affairs of life will knock our peace out of place. Hence, we must position peace firmly into place; we must "bind" peace upon our minds, and upon our emotions, in the same way that Roman soldiers made sure to "bind" their shoes very tightly onto their feet.

When "peace" has this firm grip in our lives, then we are ready for action! Thus, Paul continues, "Having your feet shod with *the preparation....*" The word "preparation" comes from the word *etoimasin* (e-toi-ma-sin), and carries the idea of "readiness or preparation."

However, the word *etoimasin*, when used in connection with Roman soldiers, portrayed men of war who had their shoes tied on very tightly, and hence, they had a "firm footing." With the assurance that their shoes were going to stay in place, now they were ready to march out into the battlefield and confront the enemy.

Therefore, the word "preparation" (*etoimasin*) conveys the idea of "solidity, firmness, or a solid foundation." Because Paul has carefully chosen this word to denote the action of "peace" in our lives, he is clearly telling us that when "peace" is foundational in our lives, we have a "firm footing."

This "peace" gives us a foundation so secure that we can move out in confident faith without being moved by what we see or what we hear. This aggressive peace puts us in a position to look directly into the face of the adversary, or directly into the face of a challenge, without being moved by what we see, feel, or what we hear.

Paul continues, "And having your feet shoe with the preparation of the gospel of *peace*..." The word "peace" is taken from the Greek word *eirene* (ei-re-ne), an old word that conveys the idea of a "peace that prevails or a conquering peace." As used in salutations, like Paul uses it in his epistles, it means "blessings and prosperity in every area of your life."

By using this word, Paul declares that when an individual receives the gospel message into his or her heart, it brings blessings and prosperity along with it. In fact, the word "peace" (*eirene*) implies that the blessings of God will be so strong and effective in your life, that this conquering force will remove all the former chaos you once knew, and will replace it with "peace that prevails" in every area of your life.

When that supernatural "peace" has been disturbed and chaos is attempting to regain its former place, this is a major sign that you are under seige.

However, presence of chaos and the absence of peace does not necessarily mean that the enemy has attacked you. It may be a signpost that you have violated some principle of scripture, or that you have disobeyed the will of God for your life.

Before you run out to fight the devil off your back, first look into the mirror! The devil is not always the source of your problems. Be honest with yourself and with God. Examine your life to see if *you* caused this lack of peace in your life.

Before you shift blame for a personal failure in your life to someone else, or before you scream that the devil is after your "peace," look at yourself to see if *you* left a gaping hole open somewhere along the way that gave rise to this dilemma.

God's perfect plan is that this prevailing and conquering peace will dominate your life! When this kind of peace is firmly fixed in your mind, emotions and soul, there is little the devil can do to move you! This peace gives you a firm footing. Regardless of how hard the enemy or the daily affairs of life hits you, *this prevailing and conquering peace will hold you in place!*

Two Kinds of Peace

There are two different kinds of peace that a believer can experience. First, there is *peace with God*. *Peace with God* is what a person experiences when he or she first comes to the Lord for salvation. Once repentance is complete, and the hostility of the old man is gone, a new *peace with God* comes into being.

As Paul said, "And, having made peace through the blood of his cross. . . you, that were sometimes alienated and enemies in your minds by wicked works, yet now hath he reconciled" (Colossians 1:20).

Peace with God is a spiritual condition that belongs to all believers. This *peace with God* is the condition that comes into being when the barrier between God and man dissolves, and the alienated mind comes into *harmony* with God. This, of course, is what genuine conversion is all about. This is when you first experience *peace with God*.

In addition to this *peace with God* that is the birthright of all believers, there is also the *peace of God*. It is possible to have *peace with God* without experientially knowing the *peace of God*. The *peace of God* is very different from *peace with God*.

Many people are at peace with God by virtue of their conversion experience, but they are not walking in the *peace of God*. Instead of being dominated by this prevailing, conquering peace that passes understanding, they walk in constant fretfulness, anxiety, worry, and all kinds of other turmoil.

This is the reason that "peace" has been given to us as a weapon. The *peace of God* is a *protective "peace."* It protects you from fretfulness, anxiety, worry, and everything else that the devil might try to use to disturb your enjoyment of abundant life.

Dominating Peace

Though we have covered this once already, let me repeat it again for the sake of emphasis. Paul says, "And let the peace of God rule in your hearts. . ." (Colossians 3:15).

In this verse, Paul commands us to let "the peace of God *rule* in your hearts. . ." The word "rule" is a key to understanding this overcoming, conquering and dominating supernatural *peace of God.*

The word "rule" is taken from the Greek word *brabeuo* (bra-beu-o). The word *brabeuo* was used to portray the umpire or referee who judged the athletic games in the ancient world. Why did Paul use this word to illustrate the *peace of God* ruling in our hearts?

By choosing to use this illustration, Paul tells us that there is a place whereby this *peace of God* can begin to call the shots and make all the decisions in your life, instead of fretfulness, anxiety and worry. You could translate the verse, *"Let the peace of God call the shots in your life. . ." "Let the peace of God umpire your life and your actions. . ." "Let the peace of God referee your emotions and your decisions. . ."*

The devil takes advantage of unrenewed areas of our minds and attempts to turn them into emotional roller coasters that constantly have you feeling "up" one day, and "down" the next.

Furthermore, even if there wasn't a personal devil to attack you, the ever-changing affairs of life alone would be enough to keep one continually tossed to and fro. Especially in these difficult days in which we live, we must learn to let the peace of God *"rule"* in our hearts!

When this supernatural peace rules in your heart, and when this supernatural peace umpires your life and serves as a referee to your emotions and your decisions, the devil cannot gain the foothold in your life that he desires to have; *he cannot play games with your emotions or your mind — because your emotions and your mind are governed by peace!*

Do you see why Paul included "peace" in this section of scripture about spiritual weaponry? When you are walking in the peace of God, the enemy's assaults can't affect you. They lose their power. These onslaughts are not effective against a believer who is walking in the overwhelming, conquering, and prevailing peace of God.

Peace: A Defensive Weapon

Keep in mind that Paul was using the illustration of a Roman soldier's shoes to depict "peace." To see why he does this, we must carefully consider how the Roman soldier's shoe was made, and what this dangerously spiked shoe did for the soldier. Paul uses this picture to depict "peace."

The *greave* began at the top of the knee and extended down past the lower leg, all the way to the upper portion of the foot. Why do you suppose the Roman soldier's footwear began at the top of the knee and covered the entire lower half of his legs? Why do you suppose that this *greave* was made of solid bronze or brass?

This upper portion of his footwear was very important! This piece of armor protected the soldier's legs from being bruised, lacerated or broken in battle.

A bruised, lacerated or broken leg could quickly spell disaster for a soldier. A bruised leg meant he would probably be impaired in his fighting and in his ability to swiftly respond to an attack. A lacerated leg meant he could potentially lose large amounts of blood, and become too weakened to fight. A broken leg meant he could not stand to defend himself. Furthermore, in this humbled position, it was far easier for his enemy to take his head from his shoulders!

Because of these potential dangers, the Roman soldier had to be certain his legs were protected. A damaged leg most assuredly meant the struggle would be more intense.

Commanding officers gave orders that required Roman soldiers to carry out difficult missions. At times, these dangerous missions required the soldiers to walk through *rocky places* and to scale *difficult barriers.*

Without protective guards on their lower legs, their legs would have been severely wounded and bruised as they dragged their legs past rough and sharp rocks. However, because these soldiers had greaves of brass tightly bound around their legs, they could walk through the rockiest and roughest of places — *and never get one scrape or bruise!*

Their *greaves* protected them from danger, and gave them the assurance they needed to proceed in the mission that had been given to them.

Likewise, God may give you an assignment in life that leads you through some challenging places. If you do not have this protective *peace of God* at work in your life, it is highly probable that you will be bruised by rocky relationships and rough situations.

On the other hand, when the *peace of God* is ruling in your heart, mind and emotions, you can forge your way through the rockiest of situations and never get one scrape or one bruise! Therefore, the *peace of God* enables you to successfully fulfill any mission that God will give you in this life!

Not only did Roman soldiers walk through rocky places, they were called to walk through *thorny places, too.* If you have ever been forced to walk through a large thorn patch, then you know how wicked those thorns can be! If you get caught in them, they can tear your legs to pieces!

But Roman soldiers rarely got a scratch! Their legs didn't bleed, their legs were never scuffed, and their legs were never seriously damaged by these fearsome thorns — *because their legs were completely covered and carefully protected by their greaves of brass that had been wrapped around their legs for such events.* This upper footwear protected them from being injured.

Similarly, if you make it past the rocky places in your life and are headed toward victory, the enemy may try to abort your victory by forcing you through a thorn patch. Your thorn patch may be a difficult financial situation, a bad marriage, a sick body, or a challenge against your ministry or your place of employment.

When the *peace of God* is working in your life, just as you successfully made it through rocky places, you will also make it through these sticky situations. The prevailing, conquering *peace of God* will rule to such an extent, that you can walk through those hard places in life without receiving one single prick to your mind and emotions!

Another reason Roman soldiers wore these *greaves* of brass was because a favorite tactic of the enemy was to kick their opponents in the shins, get them down on their backs where they could not defend themselves, and then decapitate them.

Very hastily, enemies would dash up to a foe and kick him so hard in the shins that it would break his leg. Once fallen to the ground, his opponent would draw his sword and decapitate him.

These *greaves* of brass protected Roman soldiers from these kinds of assaults. If not entirely impossible, it would have been most difficult to kick a *greave* so hard that it would break the soldier's legs. Those greaves were made of brass, and were specifically designed to guard the soldier's legs against such attacks. As long as Roman soldiers walked with their greaves in place, they could be assured that no enemy would ever be able to break their legs and take their heads from them.

These protective greaves enabled the soldier to walk through the rockiest of places, *and never get hurt.* These protective greaves enabled the soldier to walk through wicked thorn patches, *and never get scratched.* Because of these protective greaves, the enemy could kick, kick and kick the Roman soldier in the shins repeatedly, *but his legs would never be broken.*

How Peace Protects You

Do you see why Paul viewed peace as a weapon of defense? When you are walking in the *peace of God,* that peace protects you from cuts, scrapes, bruises and hurts. It is like a protective greave, protecting your mind and your emotions from wounds and fears that could impair your life of faith.

With the *peace of God* operative in your life, you can walk through the rockiest, most terrible, difficult times and never get bruised, cut or seriously injured.

When the *peace of God* is ruling in your life, you can walk through thorny situations that the enemy has devised to destroy you, your family, your business or your church family — such times when you wake up and realize, "I'm going through some extremely difficult times, *and I've never had more joy!* Why haven't I been more bothered by all this trouble? Why haven't I been bruised by this situation? *I seem to have total peace!*"

Because you are walking in the *peace of God,* that supernatural peace has given you the protection that you need. You can walk through horribly sticky situations, and never get one scrape if you are walking in this divine peace!

You may have known people who, naturally speaking, were going through very hard times in their personal lives, and yet, continued to display power and joy in their countenance. You may have wondered, "How are they making it this time in their lives without losing their minds? ⹂o they do it?"

There is only one answer: *the peace of God.* When you ⹂e walking in the *peace of God,* you don't even realize how difficult your predicament is! You are so insulated by the *peace of God,* that you may not realize how thorny things are. When you are walking in the protective *peace of God* (though everyone else is aware of it!), you may not be aware that the enemy is trying to fatally wound you.

How is it possible to go through all of these potential dangers without noticing it or without being hurt? Because the *peace of God,* like a Roman soldier's *greave,* is protecting you so completely that you can carry on in life undisturbed by these events.

Protection From the Devil's Attacks

You must know this one thing: The devil will try to kick you in the shins and get you down! I *guarantee* it!

Try to believe God for a healing — and see if the devil will just sit back and watch without giving you a run for your money! He doesn't want you to be healed. To keep you from receiving your healing, he may try to give you fits!

Try to believe God for prosperity — and see if the devil just sits back and watches as the blessings of God begin to freely pour into your life.

No! The devil doesn't want you to have God's best! When you begin to grow and move into these kinds of promised blessings, he will try to lambaste you and beat you down into defeat. You might say that he will try to kick you, break your legs, and then take off your head! He will come against you as hard as he possibly can.

What will protect you from that kind of a kick? What will protect your mind and emotions from that kind of onslaught? *The peace of God.* The peace of God is a weapon that will defend you and keep you in the midst of such trying circumstances.

This supernatural "peace" pulls the plug on the devil's effectiveness. If he can't disturb your peace, then he can't disturb *you!* He may try, but that peace paralyzes his efforts. He has no power to successfully attack you in such cases, because you are immersed in the *peace of God.* This "peace" is one of the most important pieces of spiritual weaponry that you possess!

You may be thinking, "My goodness, my life is falling to pieces! At the present moment, I can feel each and every single kick — and they feel *real hard!* I felt it when I walked through rocky and thorny places! As I went through those ordeals they put all kinds of scrapes and bruises on me. To this very moment, I can still feel each bruise, scrape and cut as though those thorns were still injuring my mind and emotions."

If this is really the case in your life, then you need to be clothed with the *peace of God.* It will protect you and carry you through times that are difficult and hard to bear.

As you grow spiritually, spiritual confrontations will come to challenge your new growth. Therefore, you must walk in this prevailing and conquering *peace of God* — otherwise, the enemy will move you into a mental and emotional irrationality that will destroy your effectiveness for the kingdom of God.

How To Set a Guard Around Your Heart

Along this same line of thought, Paul said, "And the peace of God, which passeth all understanding, shall keep your hearts and minds. . ." (Philippians 4:7).

The word "keep" is taken from the word *tereo* (te-re-o), and it means "to keep, to guard, to protect, or to garrison." It is the picture of a band of Roman soldiers who are standing "watch" over something that needs protection.

By using this word, Paul tells us that the *peace of God* will keep and guard your heart and mind! "Peace" will surround your heart and mind, just as a band of Roman soldiers surrounded important dignitaries and places of special importance.

Just as these soldiers kept nuisances from breaking into these special, private places, so peace keeps fretfulness, anxiety, worry, and all the other wiles of the devil from breaking into your life. When this peace is active in your life, it passes all understanding and it protects, guards, keeps and defends you.

As Isaiah 26:3 says, "Thou wilt keep him in perfect peace [i.e., "garrison him like a soldier, protect him, guard him, and defend him"] whose mind is stayed on thee."

Spikes for Standing Firmly

Have you ever felt the devil trying to drive you back from the will of God for your life? *yes*

Has God ever spoken to you and told you to stand on a certain Bible promise, only to hear the devil telling you that it will never come to pass, and that you will fail? Have you ever been mentally assaulted by the enemy in this way?

Maybe you are believing that God will work a miracle in your life, and the devil is trying to put your faith down, and keep you from moving into your land of blessing. *When you have peace on the bottom of your feet, a herd of elephants couldn't move you or knock you down!*

On the bottom of Roman soldier's shoes were extremely dangerous spikes that were one to three inches in length. They served the soldier in two very important ways.

First, these spikes helped to hold the soldier's footing in place. When one has three-inch spikes on the bottom of his feet, and those spikes are firmly planted into the earth, you become rather hard to knock over or to move!

God gives us supernatural peace to firmly plant our feet in the ground. This peace enables us to say, "Regardless of what I see or what I hear, I'm not moving! I don't care how hard it becomes; the *peace of God* keeps me here, and I'm not moving until the work of God in this area of my life is finished."

In other words, *the peace of God gives you a firm footing!* The devil may attack and attack, but a person who has the *peace of God functioning in his or her life will never move.* *That peace will hold you in place!* ~~Not~~ *move*

A person who has the *peace of God* actively functioning in his or her life, is like a tall palm tree that is blown viciously by the winds of a hurricane. The fierce winds may bend the tree over, but when the storm passes, that palm tree pops right back up to its former position. Though the storm was severe, the roots of that tree held it in place.

In Ephesians 6:14, the Holy Spirit, through Paul, said, "*Stand therefore. . . .*" In First Corinthians 16:13, Paul urges us, "*Watch ye, stand fast in the faith. . . .*" Then, in Second Corinthians 1:24, Paul says, "*. . . for by faith ye stand. . . .*"

Have you ever tried to stand in faith? Have you ever tried to stand for a miracle? Have you ever tried to stand for a financial situation to turn around? Or, have you ever tried to stand in faith for a relationship to be healed? There is a whole lot more to "standing" than first meets the eye!

It's interesting to point out that the majority of verses in the New Testament that have to do with *standing* also have to do with *faith*. When you stand in faith, the enemy will try to eliminate your faith, knowing that the elimination of faith will bring you to defeat. The enemy doesn't want you to maintain your stand of faith.

What is going to keep you in place as you seek to stand in faith? What is going to enable you to maintain your ground when vicious winds of opposition come your way?

The *peace of God* will hold you in place, just as the roots of a tree hold it in place when strong winds come against it. When you have peace on the bottom of your feet, it holds you in place.

Perhaps you have a relative who is terminally ill. The medical doctor has said he or she only has a short time to live. Friends tell you to "accept it" and work through the emotions of losing a loved one. The devil whispers into your ear and tells you that he or she will not recover.

Walk in peace

Dressed To Kill

At that particular moment — *when you are deciding to stand in faith or not to stand in faith* — every opportunity in the world will come to move you from that place of faith. You must plant your feet firmly into the soil of God's Word and declare, "I don't care what the medical reports say, and I don't care what the devil tries to whisper to me — God is going to move in his or her life. We are not moving until He does! We are going to maintain this stand of faith!"

Only the *peace of God* will keep you in that place of confidence. Why? Because every other statement you hear will try to persuade you to back away from the promise of God's Word.

Perhaps you're facing a financial crisis. Maybe you've been believing God for a miracle to turn your situation around, and the devil has been saying to you, "You're going to go bankrupt. You're going to lose your witness in the community. The whole town is going to talk about you. God isn't going to come through with this miracle you've been praying and believing to receive!

"I know you sowed money to the church! But you should have held onto that money! Now you really need it! If you hadn't given that money to the Lord, you wouldn't be in this mess right now!"

When the devil comes to accuse your mind and emotions like this, what is going to keep you in the middle of God's will? What is going to hold you in that place of faith? What is going to enable you to keep standing in faith on the Word of God? *The peace of God!*

How To Have Immovable Faith

When the peace of God is operative in your life, it puts spikes on the bottom of your feet that hold you in place! *The supernatural peace of God makes you immovable.*

The reason so many believers do not receive from God is because they don't walk in the *peace of God*. The first time they are hit with a challenge, or the first time the devil hits

212

them with a slanderous thought, they give into their emotions and throw in the towel.

They say, "Okay, devil, you can have that ground that I was trying to take by faith. You can have it. That's right, devil, my relative will never be healed. That's right, devil, I am going to go bankrupt. I'll just give up right now. I guess you're right; I shouldn't have obeyed the Word of God and given my tithes and offerings to the Lord."

Know that the devil will always try to tell you that the reason you have financial problems is because you gave money to the Lord. He will always remind you of that ten dollars you gave, as though that ten dollars would have been enough to change your situation.

There will be plenty of opportunities for you to hear the slanderous accusations of the adversary during the course of your Christian life. Therefore, you must learn how to plant your feet firmly into the soil of God's Word, and by faith, stay right where you are — unmoved and unhindered by the devil's threats and lies.

Peace is a divine weapon that will insulate you from these vicious attacks. The *peace of God* will keep you when Satan tries to shove doubt into your mind. The *peace of God* will guard your heart and mind, even when Satan is trying to make you lose your mind. *The peace of God is a keeping peace!*

Peace: An Offensive Weapon

Up until now in this chapter, we have primarily dealt with the *defensive* nature of peace; we have seen that peace is protective. Now we will see that peace is also an *offensive* piece of weaponry.

In Romans 16:20, Paul said, "And the God of peace shall bruise Satan under your feet shortly."

Notice, first of all, the word "bruise." It is taken from the Greek word *suntribo* (sun-tri-bo), and it was historically used to denote the act of "smashing and utterly crushing" grapes into wine. Have you ever accidentally stepped on a grape

213

and felt it squish out from under your heel or toes? It's rather messy, isn't it? This is precisely the idea of the word "bruise."

The word "bruise" (*suntribo*) was also used to denote the act of "snapping, breaking, and crushing bones." In fact, this is the picture of breaking bones so terribly, that they could never be mended or healed — *these are bones that have been utterly smashed and crushed beyond recognition.*

With this in mind, Roman 16:20 teaches that Satan's only rightful position is under our feet — where he has been completely subdued, squished like smashed grapes, and his bones (figuratively speaking!) have been broken and crushed to pieces!

It is important to point that that this "smashing" and "crushing" of Satan is done in cooperation with God. Alone, you are no match for this archenemy. Remember, he is a fallen angel. Even in his fallen state he has retained much of his original intelligence. He is very smart, cunning, crafty, and is extremely strong.

This is the reason that Paul says, "*. . .the God of peace* shall bruise Satan *under your feet. . . .*" In other words, this is a joint partnership between you and God Himself. By yourself, you could never keep Satan subdued. But with God as your partner, the devil has no chance of ever slipping out from under your heel!

Jesus completely destroyed Satan's power over you through His death and resurrection. Satan was utterly smashed, crushed and bruised by Jesus' victorious resurrection from the dead. Our God-given mission now is to reinforce the victory already won, and to demonstrate just how miserably defeated Satan already is!

The enemy may try to lord himself over you, and he may attempt to exert his foul influence in your life; however, most of these are merely empty threats and illusions that he is using to feed fear into your mind. If he can get you to believe his hellish tales, your faith will dwindle, your strong stand will waver, and he will truly begin to take a temporal position over you that does not belong to him. *The only place that rightfully belongs to the devil, is the small space of ground that is right underneath your feet!*

The victory is already yours! Your healing, your miracle, your financial blessing is already yours! Jesus accomplished a total, complete and perfect work at the cross of Calvary and at His resurrection from the dead!

It's Time To Do Some Walking!

Let me remind you of something extremely important. In Joshua, chapter one, God *freely* gave the children of Israel the promised land. However, in order for them to possess and enjoy this privilege, they had to go in and put their feet on that ground which God *freely* gave them. God told Joshua, "Every place that the sole of your foot shall tread upon, that have I given unto you. . ." (Joshua 1:3).

Yet the land God promised them was infested with giants and opposition. In order to possess God's promise to them, they had to do some walking and fighting. They had to fight for the kingdom of Ai, the city of Jericho, and so on. These infestations did not want to easily give up their ownership and surrender to the people of God. Yet in time the kingdom of Ai was destroyed, the walls of Jericho collapsed, and the people of God prevailed *because God was on their side!*

It may be that there are areas of your life which seem to linger on and defeat you. There may be habits that have held you for a long, long time, or personal hassles that seem impossible to overcome.

In the cross of Jesus Christ, every single one of these were resolved, and their power over your life was utterly shattered.

Now it is time for you to do some walking! Just like the Israelites of old, freedom is yours. Now you must go in and possess the land!

If the devil is foolish enough to think he can stand in your way, remember, God is right there with you! This is a joint partnership between you and Him! Therefore, march straight ahead, claim what is yours — and if the devil refuses to move, then take this as an opportunity to "smash him like grapes" and "crush him" beyond recognition. *This is your chance to demonstrate his defeat!*

With "the God of peace" on your side, you're a whole lot bigger than the devil! So throw your shoulders back, hold your head up high, and dig your heels down as deep as you can. Don't listen to Satan's hellish tales. Rather, when he whispers threats to your mind and emotions, *wiggle your heel down even deeper into the dirt to remind him that he's not coming out from under your feet!*

reinforce Satan is destroyed.

What Does "Shortly" Mean?

Paul continues to say, "And the God of peace shall bruise Satan under your feet *shortly*." Notice that Paul ends this powerful verse with the word "shortly."

The word "shortly" is taken from the word *tachos* (tachos). The word *tachos* ("shortly") depicts the picture of a large group of Roman soldiers marching down a street. The word "shortly" describes *how* they marched.

These ancient men of war were taught to take very hard, short, heavy steps when they marched in formation. Therefore, when a large group of Roman soldiers came marching through town, their noise could be heard everywhere as they stomped and pounded the cobblestone and marble pavement in the streets.

The clapping of their shoes upon that pavement served as a warning to the community. You see, these were Roman soldiers. They were very proud, and were taught that they were to stop for no one! If a little old woman fell on the ground in front of them, that was her problem, not theirs! She should have known better than to get in front of Roman soldiers.

In such events, they were instructed to keep marching, marching, and marching — all the while stomping, pounding and clapping their heavy feet and spikes upon the pavement.

Imagine what that poor old woman would have looked like after a whole group of stomping, pounding feet with spikes on the bottom of them had walked over her!

Now Paul uses this same illustration to portray our victorious position in Jesus Christ. By using the word "shortly," which depicts this stomping, pounding and short, heavy steps that Roman soldiers took, he is giving us an extremely graphic picture!

If the devil wants to stand in front of you and try to oppose you and the work of God in your life, then do not stop and ask him to move! Just keep marching! Just keep stomping and pounding as you move forward to obey the plan of God for your life, and as you move forward in faith, *do as much damage to him as you possibly can!*

As Paul said, "And the God of peace bruises Satan under your feet shortly" (Romans 16:20). There is no doubt about it! *The peace of God is an awesome and powerful weapon!*

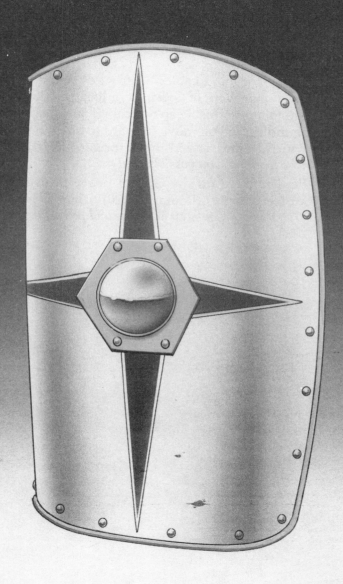

Chapter Thirteen
The Shield of Faith

After mentioning the weapon of peace, Paul immediately proceeds to our next piece of spiritual armor. Paul says, "Above all, taking the shield of faith, wherewith ye shall be able to quench all the fiery darts of the wicked" (Ephesians 6:16).

As we begin this section on the "shield of faith," it is imperative once again to point out that the shield and the loinbelt were inseparably linked to each other. The massive shield of the Roman soldier rested on a small clip on his loinbelt when it was not in use.

The loinbelt, of course, as we have already seen in chapter ten, is representative of the written Word of God, the Bible. Attached to this "loinbelt of truth" is the shield, which is representative of *faith*. *In other words, your faith is attached to the Word of God!*

If you fail to give the Word of God a place of priority in your life, it is only a matter of time before your faith will begin to dwindle and wane, because the presence or absence of faith is determined by the presence or absence of God's Word in your life. Faith and the Word of God are *inseparable.*

This is why Paul said, "So then faith cometh by hearing, and hearing by the Word of God" (Romans 10:17). Faith and the Word of God are so uniquely tied together that where there is no Word, there is no faith — and where there is no faith, it is because the Word of God is absent.

Facing left page: The leather, oblong shield of a Roman soldier from the first century.

When Paul began this text on spiritual armor, he began by listing the "loinbelt of truth" first. Why would Paul look at a Roman soldier who had a big helmet on his head, who had bright and shining armor, brass greaves, a specially tooled lance, a two-edged sword, and a large, oblong shield, and after viewing all of this armor, then begin his description by pointing to the *loinbelt* that was wrapped around the man's waist?

The Holy Spirit is telling us something very important: *The Word of God is central and foremost to everything else that we have in God.*

Your ability to walk in a wonderful sense of righteousness, hinges entirely upon the centrality of God's Word in your life. Get out of the Word, and it is only a matter of time before you will begin to lose your sense of righteousness.

Your ability to walk in peace is decided by whether or not you are giving God's Word a place of preeminence in your life. When the Word of God has such a place in your life, the peace of God is released to call the shots and keep your heart and mind. Get out of the Word, and it is only a matter of time before that wonderful sense of peace is replaced by the anxious cares of this life.

Likewise, your ability to walk in strong faith is also determined by the presence or absence of God's Word in your life. Again, Paul said, "Faith cometh by hearing, and hearing by the Word of God" (Romans 10:17). If the Word of God does not have an important place in your schedule, then it is impossible for you to grow in faith, for faith is a result of the impartation of God's Word into the human heart.

The practical outworking of your salvation is greatly affected by the renewing of your mind with the Word of God. Though born again and destined for heaven, you will not be able to enjoy the benefits of your salvation now — *in this life* — unless you permit the transforming power of the Word of God to work in your mind.

Furthermore, there will be no "sword of the Spirit" at your disposal if the "loinbelt of truth" has no place in your life. The sword of the Roman soldier rested in a scabbard that hung from the loinbelt. This is another picture of the necessity of the written Word of God in our lives. That *rhema* you desperately need will probably come directly from the Word of God as the Holy Spirit quickens a verse to your heart.

You won't always have a *rhema* to build your life upon and to give you direction in your personal life. Thank God for these special words from the Lord! When they come, they bring joy to the heart! But do not base your Christian life entirely on these "words from the Lord."

Instead, learn to base your life upon the dependable, always-present Word of God, the Bible, the "loinbelt of truth." This piece of spiritual armor will always be present and dependable. You can even touch this one! And if you have this most important weapon in hand, in time you will have everything else that you need to live a victorious Christian life.

The Shield of Faith

There were two kinds of shields that Roman soldiers owned. One was used in public parades and ceremonies, and the other was used in battle.

L. The first shield was denoted by the Greek word *aspis* (as-pis). This *aspis* shield was a small round shield that was primarily a decorative piece of equipment to be used in public ceremonies and parades.

This particular shield was absolutely gorgeous! It was decorated with all kinds of etchings, engravings and markings on the front, and often the front middle portion of this small shield depicted an artist's rendition of a previous victorious military campaign. This *aspis* shield was beautiful, but it was too small to be used in an actual military confrontation.

The second kind of shield that the Roman soldier used is the one to which Paul makes reference in Ephesians 6:16 when he speaks of the "shield of faith." This particular word for "shield" is taken from the Greek word *thureos* (thu-re-os), which was used by the Greeks for a "door" that was wide in width, and long in length. The reason that the Romans used this word to picture their battle shields was because the shields Roman soldiers carried in battle were *door-shaped.* They were wide in width, and long in length; just like the door of a house, and the opposite of the first shield, which was far too small to protect a soldier from the slings and arrows of his adversary.

The *aspis* shield would have never covered a soldier in the midst of the fray. Though beautiful and enjoyable to behold in public ceremonies and parades, such a small piece of armor would have left the soldier wide open to being struck with deadly blows.

However, *the second shield completely covered the man!* Because the Holy Spirit was careful to select this second shield (*thureos*) as the illustration of faith, rather than the first shield (*aspis*), He is telling us that God has given us enough faith to make certain we are completely covered — just like a shield completely covered a Roman soldier!

Romans 12:3 says, ". . . God hath dealt to every man the measure of faith." How much faith has God given you? He has given you enough faith to make certain you are covered in life!

Do not worry or fret that God has given more faith to others than He has given to you. Rest assured in the fact that God has imparted enough faith to you to make sure you are covered from head to toe! *That faith, like a wide and long shield, is adequate to cover any need that will ever come along in your life.*

In the majority of cases, the Roman soldier's shield was composed of multiple layers of thick animal hide that had been tightly woven together. Usually six layers of animal hide were specially tanned, and then were woven together so tightly, that they became nearly as strong as steel.

One piece of leather is tough, but imagine how tough and durable six layers of leather would be! Because the shield of the Roman soldier was made from such hides, this shield was *extremely tough* and *exceptionally durable.*

Similarly, our faith is extremely tough and exceptionally durable; more tough and durable than you have ever realized! The enemy can beat, beat and beat against your faith, and still, your faith will outlast his attack. The "shield of faith" that God has given you is a strong, lasting, and durable faith.

How To Care for Your Shield of Faith

Because the Roman soldier's shield was made of leather, it was important for the soldier to take good care of it!

Though six layers of animal hide would be strong and durable, it could become stiff and breakable over a period of time if it was not properly taken care of. Therefore, it was necessary for Roman soldiers to know how to care for their shield.

In order to keep their shields in good shape, the soldiers were given a daily schedule to maintain excellent condition of their shields. Each morning when the soldier was awakened, he would reach for his shield, and would also reach for a small vial of oil. After saturating a piece of cloth with oil, he would begin to rub, rub and rub a heavy ointment of oil into the leather portion of the shield to keep it soft, supple and pliable.

To ignore this daily application of oil, and to let his shield go without this kind of required care, was the equivalent of inviting certain death.

Because this protective shield was made of leather, without proper care it could become hard, stiff and brittle. If not correctly cared for and properly maintained, it would harden, crack when put under pressure, and fall to pieces. Therefore, the end result of a soldier's failure to care for his shield was death.

If the Roman soldier wanted to live a long life, it was imperative for him to take that vial of oil, and apply it to his shield every single day of his military life.

Because the shield is representative of our *faith*, this tells us that our faith, like this shield in Paul's illustration, requires *frequent anointings* of the Holy Spirit.

1. Oil   2. Water

Without a fresh touch of the Spirit's power upon your life, your faith will become hard, stiff and brittle. If you ignore your faith, and allow it to go undeveloped, and never seek a fresh anointing of the Spirit of God to come upon your life, when a challenge comes your way, your faith won't be soft, supple and pliable enough to stand up under attack. *A faith that is ignored nearly always breaks and falls to pieces in a confrontation.*

Many believers have made the incredible, tragic mistake of thinking they could live their Christian lives on the steam of their past experiences with the Lord. Thank God for these past experiences, but we can never rest upon the laurels of the past!

People who emphasize the life of faith are often accused of walking in presumption, instead of walking in faith. The worst presumption one can walk in is when a believer ceases to develop his or her faith, and fails to keep his faith freshly anointed by the Holy Spirit's presence and power, and then tries to move in power!

Do not assume that your faith is always in top-notch shape! *Rather, play it safe and assume that your faith always needs a fresh anointing!* By taking this approach, you will always seek to do what is necessary to keep your faith alive, active and well!

Another reason the Roman soldier's shield was made out of animal hide was, before these soldiers went out to war, they took their shields, dipped them into a tub of water, and left them there soaking in that water until their shields were completely *saturated* with water. What was the purpose of saturating their shields with water?

The enemy used arrows that carried fire! By saturating their shields with water, even if those dangerous flaming arrows hit, they were extinguished upon impact by the wet surface of the Roman shield! These water-saturated shields gave the soldier the upper hand and always put out the enemy's fire!

224

Moreover, when one keeps his or her faith dipped into the "water of the Word" (Ephesians 5:26), and completely saturates his faith with it, this "water of the Word" has the power to extinguish the flaming arrows of the adversary.

In order for Roman soldiers to keep their shields in top-notch condition, it was required that their shields had daily applications of both *oil* and *water*.

Likewise, in order to keep our "shield of faith" in top-notch condition, we must give serious attention to the condition of our "shield of faith." We must make certain that the Holy Spirit is anointing our lives in a fresh way, and we must be sure to saturate our faith with the "water of the Word."

A Word-saturated faith will always extinguish the devil's attacks! *Be dressed all. Time.*

What Does "Above All" Mean?

Some have wrongly mistaken that faith is more important than any other piece of spiritual weaponry. This *cannot* be! The "loinbelt of truth," the written Word, the Bible, is the most important piece of weaponry which we possess!

How do we know that the Word of God is more important than faith? *Faith comes from the Word of God!* How, then, could the "shield of faith" be more important than the "loinbelt of truth," the Word of God? Let's not get the cart before the horse! Yet Paul does say, *"Above all, taking the shield of faith. . . ."*

What does the phrase "above all" mean?

The phrase "above all" is taken from the Greek phrase *epi pasin* (e-pi and pa-sin). The word *epi* means "over." The word *pasin* means "all" or can be translated "everything." Rather than a statement about being more important than the other pieces of armor, the phrase *epi pasin* ("above all") describes *position over the other pieces of armor.* It could be better translated, *"Out in front of all. . . ."* Or, it could be translated, *"Covering all. . . ."*

225

This tells us that faith is supposed to be *"out front"* where it can *"cover all."* Faith was never meant to be held next to our side, or to be timidly held behind our back. Faith is designed to be *"out front"* where it can completely *"cover"* the believer.

Therefore, the phrase "above all" emphatically tells us that the "shield of faith" is meant to completely cover us and protects us from harm — especially when we are marching forward to take new ground for the kingdom of God. It is a defensive weapon that is *"out in front of all the other pieces of armor. . ."* The phrase "above all" describes *position, not importance.*

When our "shield of faith" is in this *"out front"* and *"covering"* position, it can do what God intended for it to do! This is why Paul continues to say, "Above all, taking the shield of faith, *wherewith ye shall be able to quench all the fiery darts of the wicked."*

Notice that Paul says, *". . . taking the shield of faith. . . ."* The word "taking" is from the word *analambano* (a-na-lam-ba-no), which is a compound of the Greek words *ana* (a-na) and *lambano* (lam-ba-no).

The word *ana* means "up, back, or again," and the word *lambano* means "to take up, or to take in hand." When compounded together into one word, it means "to take something up in hand, or to pick something back up again."

This plainly means our "shield of faith" can be picked up or our "shield of faith" can be laid down. The choice is ours to make. Moreover, if someone has laid his faith down at some point along the way in his life, and if he has stopped believing God to work in his life, it is not too late for him to "pick that faith up again."

No well-trained Roman soldier would have gone to battle without his shield. That shield was not optional! That shield was his guarantee that he would be guarded against deadly bombardments. Without that protective shield in front of him, there was absolutely nothing between him and his opponent. The soldier knew he was walking into his own self-imposed destruction if he went forward without a shield.

Many believers have sadly miscalculated that they could successfully live their Christian lives without giving attention to the development of their own faith. This is utter foolishness. It was for this cause that Paul told Timothy, "Holding faith, and a good conscience; which some having put away concerning faith have made shipwreck" (First Timothy 1:19).

When a believer "puts away faith," it always leads to spiritual "shipwreck." By ignoring and disregarding the significance of their faith, some of our brothers and sisters in the Lord have opted for a spiritual course that will eventually lead them to total exposure to the strikes of the enemy.

Some have criticized others for making faith too strong an emphasis in recent years. When you understand the importance of faith and its ramifications in our lives both physically and spiritually, then you can understand why it is *impossible* to over-emphasize the necessity of a life of faith.

The Purpose of the Shield of Faith

Paul continues, "Above all, taking the shield of faith, *wherewith ye shall be able to quench all the fiery darts of the wicked.*"

The word *"wherewith"* would be better translated, *"by which. . . . "* The phrase *"shall be able"* is taken from the word *dunamis* (du-na-mis), which denotes "explosive power or dynamic power." It is where we get the word "dynamite."

This phrase would be better translated, ". . . *by the use of this shield, you will have explosive and dynamic power. . . .*"

What you are seeing here is that when you have the "shield of faith" — and when that "shield of faith" is anointed by the Holy Spirit and saturated with the Word of God — it positions you to move in power. It positions you to move in "explosive and dynamic power."

Peter declares we ". . . *are kept by the power of God through faith. . .*" (First Peter 1:4,5).

227

There is an unseen connection between the power of God and the operation of faith in your life. When these two are working hand in hand, they build a wall of defense against the tactics of the enemy that is impenetrable. In other words, *when the power of God and faith get together, they become a shield to the believer!*

When you have these two elements working together in your life, you become fortified, invulnerable, and armed to the teeth! Power and faith working together will spiritually equip you to hold an ironclad position against the enemy without taking any serious blows to yourself!

When the power of God and faith are operative in your life, you are like a tank; you have the ability to move your position forward without taking any losses!

This doesn't mean the devil won't try to stop you, because he will try! This is why Paul says, ". . . that ye may be able to stand against *the fiery darts of the wicked."*

Fiery Darts of the Wicked

You may ask, "What are the fiery darts of the wicked?"

The Greek word used to describe these particular "darts" is a very specific word of warfare that is very historical. Thucydides, the ancient Greek writer, used the same identical Greek expression to depict especially terrible "arrows that were equipped to carry fire."

There were three types of arrows used by the military of New Testament times. First, there were plain arrows that were similar to the arrows that one would shoot from a bow today. Next, there were arrows that were dipped into tar, set on fire, and then shot through the air. Last, there were arrows that contained combustible fluids that burst into flames upon impact.

The arrows in Ephesians 6:16 are called "fiery darts." Because Paul's word usage is identical to that of Thucydides, the early Greek writer, we know exactly what kind of arrows Paul has in mind.

228

Paul is thinking of "arrows that carry fire"! Specifically, he is picturing those arrows that were made from long, slender pieces of cane, and were filled with combustible fluids which exploded upon impact.

These particular arrows were the greatest terror of the day. To the natural eye, they looked like minimally dangerous arrows. The natural eye could not see that these arrows had been filled with combustible fluids. Only after impact, and after a great fire had begun, could one know for certain whether or not these arrows had been equipped with the potential of fire and disaster.

These fluid-filled arrows were not used in normal combat situations. Regular arrows were sufficient for those kinds of confrontations. These fire-bearing arrows were reserved to inflict damage upon a fortified place; an encampment.

If an army had fortified its position so that the enemy could not easily break in to destroy it, then the enemy would revert to using these deadly arrows of fire!

One by one, the opposing forces would turn these long pieces of slender cane in an upright position, and then would begin pouring *explosive fluids* into them. Once these kinds of arrows were filled to the brim with this potential death, they were sealed and disguised to look like normal, minimally dangerous arrows.

Since the enemy could not physically break into the encampment and personally destroy the entrenched army, they took these arrows — *which were disguised to look very harmless* — and shot them over the walls of the army's fortified position. Because these arrows looked harmless, those inside the encampment often made the fatal mistake of ignoring these attacks. *Until...*

Troops were shocked and taken off guard when those arrows hit inside the walls of their fortress and burst into raging flames! Once those terrible flames had begun and the troops were taken off guard, the enemy would shoot another, another and another arrow into their encampment. Each arrow came equipped with the same surprising deadly capabilities. You might say these arrows were the *bombs* of the ancient world!

It is this very picture that Paul has in mind when he says, "Above all, taking the shield of faith, wherewith ye shall be able to stand against *the fiery darts of the wicked.*"

Fire That Stirs the Vilest Passions

This is the kind of arrow that the enemy wants to send your way! When the enemy has no easy access into your life, he may try another more covert route to come against you.

He may shoot a fire-bearing arrow into your emotions! When they hit, they have the potential of arousing the worst and vilest of human emotions and passions!

When a flaming arrow from the enemy hits its target — your emotions — it can throw the emotions into rage, anger, anxiety, unbelief, worry, and so forth. These flaming arrows come to do something vile and horrendous in your mind and emotions. They come to hit you and enrage you like a fire that is hopelessly burning out of control.

Have you ever been hit by an arrow from the enemy? Many believers are hit by the enemy's arrows every day — because they are not walking with their "shield of faith" where it belongs! If that "shield of faith" was anointed by the Spirit and saturated with the "water of the Word," it would keep those arrows from getting through to them.

The "shield of faith" must be "*out front*" so it can completely "*cover*" your life and protect you from these "fiery darts."

I Pet 1:4/5

Who Is Responsible for Failure?

The devil and his hosts are *never* your real problem! The Lord Jesus Christ spoiled them through the work of His death and resurrection!

The reason you continue to be controlled by habitual hangups and hassling problems is foremost because *you* have not made the decision to submit your flesh and mind to the sanctifying work of the Holy Spirit.

If your "shield of faith" was properly anointed by the Holy Spirit — and if your "shield of faith" was saturated in the Word of God — these arrows would be instantly *extinguished* upon impact!

The fact that these arrows have been effective in throwing you into rage, anger, anxiety, unbelief, worry and so forth, is evidence that *you* failed somewhere along the way! It is apparent that *you* failed to deal with wrong attitudes and thoughts in your mind; hence, *you* allowed an open door through which these arrows could pass!

If *you* were living in the presence of God on a daily basis, the Holy Spirit's anointing would have been upon your faith! The absence of the Spirit's oil upon your faith has caused your faith to become hard, stiff and brittle. The reason those arrows broke through your "shield of faith" is because *you* didn't do what was necessary to keep your faith supple, pliable and durable.

Likewise, if *you* had given the Word of God a place of priority in your daily schedule, your "shield of faith" would have been so saturated with the "water of the Word," that your Word-saturated shield would have instantly extinguished those flaming arrows!

As I stated on page 22, human nature loves to shift the blame for failure to someone else. The truth of the matter is that God has given us everything we need to stand against the wiles of the devil. If we have been wounded, *we are responsible.* We must assume responsibility for this failure, and stop shifting the blame to someone else.

It is very important that you live in the presence of God, give the Word of God a place in your daily schedule, and live the crucified life. By keeping your "shield of faith" anointed with the oil of the Spirit and saturated with the "water of the Word," you will ensure that these fiery darts will miserably fail.

By dealing with the unseen areas of your life and mind (which may only be known to you, God and the devil) *you are ensuring that there are no open doors through which these arrows may pass to pierce through your emotions, and thus, throw you into a fit of raging carnality!*

God has provided a way for us to avoid being hit by these "fiery darts." He has provided a way for us to *escape* their destructive impact.

Paul said, "There hath no temptation taken you but such as is common to man: but God is faithful, who will not suffer you to be tempted above that ye are able; but will with the temptation also make *a way to escape,* that ye may be able to bear it" (First Corinthians 10:13).

The "shield of faith" is your *"way of escape"* from the *"fiery darts"* of the adversary. When your faith is *"out front"* and *"covering"* all, it quenches every temptation and every fire-bearing arrow that the enemy would send your way.

When you are carrying your "shield of faith," those arrows lose their power and fall to the ground. Thus, *you escape!*

Quenching, Extinguishing and Ricocheting Faith

What the enemy wants to do is to lodge an arrow of unbelief in your mind that will eventually destroy you!

Perhaps that arrow says, "You are going to die of cancer!" Or, "Your marriage is going to fail." Perhaps the arrow that has lodged in your mind says, "You are going to go under financially!"

If that arrow lodges in your mind, and you begin to *believe* it, your false belief in that lie will most likely empower it to become a reality!

If an arrow of unbelief lodges in your mind and tells you that you are going to go broke, you may really go broke if you don't get rid of that lie!

If an arrow of unbelief lodges in your mind and tells you that there is no hope for your marriage, and you *believe* it, your marriage may really begin to deteriorate as your false faith empowers that demonic accusation to become a reality.

The "shield of faith" enables us to quench, extinguish and ricochet these lying accusations! This is why the Word of God commands us, "Casting down imaginations and every high thing that exalteth itself against the knowledge of God. . ." (Second Corinthians 10:5).

How much trouble are those fiery darts going to do if you have cast them down? They can't do much harm to you if they are lying on the ground around your feet! Hence, the "shield of faith" puts the fire out, and knocks those hellish tales down to the ground where their deceptive powers cease to influence you!

When you are walking in faith, you can confidently say, "Here comes another arrow from the evil one," lift up your "shield of faith" — and watch as that arrow bounces right off you! *When you walk in faith, you are not affected mentally, emotionally or physically by the "fiery darts" of the enemy.*

Because the Roman soldier anointed his shield with oil, it was *slippery*. Thus, when he walked with his shield held high, even if those fiery arrows hit his shield, they slipped right off it. Often the arrows would hit and ricochet back into the face of the enemy, exploding in his own face!

Likewise, when you are walking in faith that is anointed, it defends you. It puts you in a place where you are guarded; a place where you will not be successfully attacked by the assault of the wicked one.

Faith will quench, thwart, and extinguish anything that tries to hit you!

You may ask, "Just how evil are these arrows that are going to try to hit me and slow down my spiritual growth?" Ephesians 6:16 says, ". . . wherewith ye shall be able to quench all the fiery darts *of the wicked.*"

The word "wicked" is taken from the word *poneros* (pone-ros). This word comprises all of these words: "sorrow," "pain," "evil," "malignant," "malicious," "ill," or "vicious."

This explicitly tells us that these are vicious arrows, evil arrows, arrows that have potential sorrow in them, arrows that have potential pain in them, arrows that are actively involved in spreading the flame and fire of wickedness, evil, and suffering.

I hope you see from this why it is important that your faith is *"out front"* where it belongs! If your faith is ignored and allowed to go undeveloped, you will soon find out for yourself that these arrows have the capacity of producing sorrow and pain. When they hit, they are malicious.

Furthermore, these lies that the devil shoots into the mind are not intended just to wound you; they are intended to hit you with their full destructive force. When they hit, they *explode!*

The purpose of the devil is to seize your mind, paralyze it with fear, and then flood it with allegations that are not true. If he can captivate your thinking and reasoning processes, and if he can coax you into believing that those allegations are true, then those arrows will begin to release their damnable destruction in your life and mind!

For example, some years ago we were ministering in a church where a prominent woman had died of cancer. Her death really shook the faith of that particular congregation. As a result, the entire congregation concluded, "Healing is not for us today!"

The enemy shot an arrow of cancer and suffering into that woman's body. From her, that deadly fire began to spread into the whole church body. Because their "shield of faith" was not *"out front"* where it belonged, protecting and covering them, they were mortally wounded! When that arrow hit, it released its destructive powers. It didn't come just to kill one woman; it came to kill a whole church!

Corporate Faith in the Local Church

While a Roman soldier could carry a shield to fight one enemy by himself, he and his shield were not big enough to take on an entire army! He could defend himself for a while, and perhaps could even make a little headway, *but what is one man against a whole army?*

Therefore, when Roman soldiers were threatened by a mass of opposition, they would walk very close to one another in one long line, side by side. Link up

On the sides of their massive shields were small hinges. One at a time, these soldiers would begin fastening their shield to the next soldier's shield, and then to the next soldier's shield, and then to the next and the next.

After all their shields were securely fastened to one another, they would begin marching in unison toward the opposing forces. Because their shields were connected, it looked like a huge wall of armor was moving across the field toward the enemy! *Therefore, when shield was attached to shield, these soldiers had a massive wall of protection in front of them.*

When soldiers marched together like this (with their shields connected) it positioned them to march right up against the enemy, yet rarely lose one of their own.

Similarly, when the Church of Jesus Christ learns to march in unison and to walk with each other, it will position us to make advances and inroads into the enemy's territory that have never been made before! need help

Thank God, your faith will work for you personally; but we must also thank God that when we join our faith to the faith of others, it corporately positions the Body of Christ to make some significant gains as a whole!

When you've got your shield out front like the Roman soldiers did in such events, it doesn't matter how many of the enemy there are out there to oppose you. *You can steadily, aggressively move forward and press in on that enemy because you've got so much corporate faith working alongside of you!*

Does Your Shield Have Cracks?

If you ignore this "shield of faith" — if you never seek a fresh anointing of the Spirit's presence upon it — and if you do not soak your faith in the Word of God — you had better not try to take on any big challenges. Your shield is not in the best of shape!

A faith that is ignored becomes hard, stiff, and brittle. If you run out to challenge the adversary with a hard, stiff, and brittle faith, it will crack in the midst of conflict. If you wave a cracked shield in the enemy's face, you're going to end up in heaps of trouble!

If, however, your faith is intact — if the presence of God's Spirit is active upon your faith, and if your faith is saturated in God's Word — then you can wave that faith in the face of the enemy like a shield, and every dart that he tries to use against you will fall to the ground.

If Your Faith Needs an Anointing

If your faith needs a fresh anointing, you must go before the Great Anointer and allow Him to give you a fresh anointing of the Holy Spirit.

This is precisely what David was referring to when he said, ". . . I shall be anointed with *fresh oil*" (Psalm 92:10).

The word "anoint" comes from the Greek word *chrio* (chri-o). It was originally a medical term. When a patient with sore muscles came to see his physician, the physician would pour oil upon his own hands, and then would begin to rub that oil into the sore muscles of his patient.

Technically, the word "anoint" has to do with the "rubbing or smearing" of oil upon someone else. I call the anointing *a hands-on situation.*

Thus, when we speak of a person who is anointed, we are actually saying that the hand of God is upon that person, and God is rubbing the strong presence of the Holy Spirit into that man or woman's life or ministry.

If a sermon is anointed, it is anointed because the hand of God is upon it. If a song is anointed, it is anointed because the hand of God is upon it.

The presence of the anointing tells us that God has laid

His hand upon that person. The anointing comes when God has laid His hand upon something; the anointing is a result of God's hand personally imparting the strong presence of the Holy Spirit into something.

Therefore, if you need a fresh anointing of the Holy Spirit upon your faith, then you must come before the Great Anointer! He alone can give what you need. Open your heart to Him, and allow Him to lay His hand upon your life and faith in a new way

When the hand of God comes upon your life and upon your faith, a strong anointing will follow! This is *guaranteed!*

In Conclusion

When you walk in the "shield of faith," you are in a position to storm the enemy's lies and allegations without fear of being hurt.

Perhaps you tried to act in faith in the past, and got disappointed. Perhaps you didn't get healed, but only got worse, and this discouraged you into thinking that your faith won't produce results. Perhaps, because of this, you are afraid to step out to believe God again.

Perhaps you have felt those evil arrows of the enemy hit you because your faith was not "out front" where it belonged. They are malignant, bringing sorrow, pain, suffering, mental distress, and so on.

These arrows come to assault the soul realm; they hit the mind and the emotions. *Again, the devil knows that the mind is the strategic control center of your life. If he can seize your mind, then he can begin to wage warfare against the other parts of your being.*

In order to keep your mind from being struck by one of these vicious "fiery darts" that come to deceive and destroy, it is imperative that you pick up that "shield of faith" again!

Chapter Fourteen
The Helmet of Salvation

There is perfect balance in the armor of God. There are three offensive weapons, three defensive weapons, and one neutral weapon.

The breastplate, the shield, and the helmet are *defensive* weapons. These are weapons that protect you and give you confidence and assurance so that you can move forward in your spiritual growth.

The three *offensive* weapons are the shoes, the sword and the lance. These are weapons that enable you to demonstrate Satan's defeat.

The neutral weapon is the loinbelt, which is representative of the Word of God. It is the central piece of weaponry that holds all of these other pieces together. Without this central piece of spiritual armor, the written Word, these other pieces of weaponry cannot function properly in your life.

Let me remind you that these pieces of weaponry come *from God*. To walk in them and to see them work in your personal life, mandates that you live in the presence of God.

Just as you draw your power *from Him*, and just as you draw your nature *from Him*, so also you must draw this weaponry *from Him*. He is the source of origination for everything we have — *including spiritual armor.*

The Helmet of Salvation

In this chapter, we will deal with the "helmet of salvation." Paul continued in his list of spiritual armor by saying,

---

Facing left page: The ornate helmet, cheek pieces and plume of brightly colored horse hair of a Roman soldier from the first century.

"And take the helmet of salvation. . ." (Ephesians 6:17).

The helmet was a fascinating piece of armor. It was a flamboyant piece of weaponry, very ornate and intricate.

The helmet of the Roman soldier looked more like a piece of artwork than a helmet! His helmet was *beautiful!* Rather than a simple piece of metal that had been formed to fit the head of a soldier, the helmet of Roman soldiers was highly decorated with all kinds of engravings and etchings.

It was not uncommon for pastoral farm scenes, with all kinds of animals, to be depicted on the helmet of a Roman soldier. Frequently the entire helmet of the Roman soldier was fashioned to look like the head of an elephant, the head of a horse, or other animals.

Some helmets had engravings and etchings with fruit on them. Think of how odd some of these helmets must have been to behold! To look at some soldiers was like looking at a fruit basket on a man's head! Others looked like they had elephants and horses on their heads! Thus the reason that these helmets looked more like a piece of sculpture than they looked like a piece of armor.

Furthermore, as if these fabulous engravings and etchings were not enough, a huge plume of brightly colored feathers, or brightly colored horse hair, stood straight up out of the top of the helmet. If the helmet was one to be used in a public ceremony or parade, this brightly colored plume could be very long; long enough to hang all the way down the back of the soldier.

The helmet was made of bronze and was equipped with pieces of armor that were specifically designed to protect the cheeks and jaws. It was extremely heavy, and therefore, the interior of the helmet was lined with sponge in order to soften the weight of the helmet upon the head of the soldier.

This piece of armor was so strong, so massive and so heavy, that nothing could pierce it — not even a hammer or battle-ax.

It would be very hard to walk past one of these soldiers without noticing them. You would definitely take note of a man who had a piece of sculpture on his head! You would notice a man who had a brightly colored plume standing straight up on the top of his helmet! *These helmets made the Roman soldier noticeable!*

God's Most Gorgeous Gift

Why would the Holy Spirit take a piece of weaponry like this and compare it to salvation? It's because *your salvation is the most gorgeous, most intricate, most elaborate, most ornate gift God ever gave you!*

Paul calls this marvelous gift "the helmet of salvation." Moreover, he used the example of a Roman soldier's helmet to make his point.

He likened salvation to one of these flamboyant helmets that were worn on the head, where everyone would notice it! And to make *sure* everyone noticed it, there was a plume of feathers standing straight up out of the top of it.

By using this example, Paul is telling us something very important. When a man or woman is confident of his or her salvation — and when he or she is walking in the powerful reality of all that salvation means for them, they are *noticeable people!*

The word "helmet" is taken from the Greek word *perikephalaia* (pe-ri-ke-pha-lai-a). The word *peri* means "around" and the word *kephalaia* is the Greek word for the "head." When you compound these two words into one, you discover that the word *perikephalaia* denotes a piece of armor that fits very tightly "around the head."

Why did a Roman soldier need a helmet? Because his opponent carried a short-handled ax called a battle-ax, and when battle-axes were used, heads rolled!

If the Roman soldier did not have a helmet on when he went out to fight, he could be absolutely sure he would lose his head! So the Roman helmet was not merely a beautiful piece of weaponry; it was something intended to save a man's head.

That's exactly what salvation will do for you when you wear it like a helmet on your head! If you don't walk in your salvation and all that your salvation entails, you may feel the brunt of the enemy's battle-ax coming to attack your mind and steal your victory.

If your salvation — like a helmet — is not worn tightly around your mind, then the enemy will come to chop the multiple benefits and blessings of your salvation right out of your theology. He will wack away at your foundation, trying to tell you that healing, deliverance, preservation of mind and soundness were not really a part of Jesus' redemptive work on the cross.

By the time the enemy is finished with your mind, the only thing he will leave you with is heaven. By exposing your unprotected mind to his insinuations, you are placing yourself in a position to be deceived.

To face the adversary without your "helmet of salvation" is the equivalent of *spiritual suicide!*

Many believers try to do the work of God without making it a personal goal to walk in the full knowledge of their salvation, and they are spiritually slaughtered.

You must have this helmet on if you are going to be useful to the kingdom of God.

How is the enemy going to attack you? How is the enemy going to try to wage warfare against you? How is he going to try to do you in? *The devil comes to attack the mind!*

He knows that this is the control center for your life. He knows that if he can seize this area, then from this position of control, he can begin to manipulate your emotions, he can begin to send sickness and disease into your body, and so on.

To protect us from such attacks, God has given us a "helmet of salvation." The fact that Paul likens salvation to a helmet, means we must know our salvation and all that it includes, inside and out!

We must spend time studying what the Bible has to say about healing; we must spend time studying what the Bible has to say about our deliverance from evil powers; we must spend time studying our redemption and the consequences of it.

Our intellectual understanding and comprehension of salvation and all that it encompasses, must be ingrained into our minds. When our minds are convinced of these realities, and when our minds are trained and taught to think correctly in the terms of our salvation, that knowledge becomes a helmet in our lives!

At this point, it doesn't matter how hard the devil hits and tries to wack away at us, because we know — *beyond any shadow of doubt* — what Jesus' death and resurrection purchased for us! Once this knowledge becomes a part of us, the enemy can no longer attack our minds as he did in the past.

The knowledge of salvation and all that it is, puts a helmet on our heads!

Armed and Dangerous

Remember, Paul's command was to "Put on the whole armour of God. . ." (Ephesians 6:11).

When God sends you forth to reinforce the victory of Jesus Christ over Satan in various areas of your life, He doesn't send you out naked. He gives you armor! Without the helmet, you will be attacked by the "wiles of the devil" (Ephesians 6:11).

Because it is so important to understand how the wiles of the devil work against us, we must quickly review the words "wiles," "devices," and "deception" (for more on this, see chapter eight). These three words are foundational to our understanding of how the devil successfully defeats believers.

For review, the word "wiles" is taken from the word *methodos* (meth-o-dos), which is a compound of the word *meta* (me-ta), which means "with," and the word *odos* (pronounced ho-dos), the word for a "road." The word *odos* is where we get the word *odometer*, like the odometer in your car that measures how many miles you have driven on the road. Taken as one word, *methodos* literally means "with a road."

What is God's Word saying? It is saying that the devil, when he works against a believer, does it *"with a road."* There is only one entrance into the life of a believer — he uses only one road, one avenue, or one lane of attack.

There is no creativity or variety in the devil. He has only one way to work, and he always attacks believers the same way. He uses one lane into the life of a Christian. But we know that roads go *somewhere*. Where do you suppose this road goes?

This leads us to the word "devices." Paul said, ". . . for we are not ignorant of his [Satan's] *devices*" (Second Corinthians 2:11).

Here we have come to the second word which has to do with how the devil works in the life and mind of a believer.

What is a "device?" The word "device comes from the Greek word *noemata* (no-e-ma-ta), which is from the root *nous* (pronounced noous), the word "mind." However, the form *noemata* could be translated as "a scheming of the mind."

Playing Mind Games With the Devil

A modern-day translation of this could read: ". . . we are not ignorant of *the mind games* that the devil tries to pull on us." *Mind games!* Have you ever experienced a mind game with the devil?

When we put these first two words together, we see that the devil works with a "wile," or he works "with a road." Where is that road headed? *It is headed for your brain!* And if the devil can get a foothold *inside* your brain, he is going to pull a "device" on you. Once he has a road into your brain, he is going to begin to mess around with your mind.

Now we come to the third word which has to do with the way the devil works in the life and the mind of a believer. It's the word "deception," which is taken from the word *dolios* (do-li-os). The word *dolios* doesn't mean to deceive accidentally or haphazardly; it means to "deceive with purpose." This word can be found throughout the New Testament in verses that are connected with the devil's deceptive abilities.

The word *dolios,* in its most literal sense, means to "bait" someone, as in setting "bait" in front of a fish. By putting these three words together, we see exactly how the devil works in the life and mind of a believer.

He comes with a "wile," which means "with a road." That diabolical road is headed for the mind. If the devil can beat down a believer's resistance, then he can begin to wage warfare in their minds with a "device" or "mind game." Once the "mind games" are in full motion, he "baits" the believer with lying accusations and slanderous allegations. With those lies, he "baits" the believer.

If the believer perceives these lies to be true, and bites the bait, then the process of deception will be fully implemented in his or her life.

What Is a Stronghold?

It was for this cause that Paul said, "For the weapons of our warfare are not carnal, but mighty through God to the pulling down of strongholds" (Second Corinthians 10:4).

He continues, "Casting down imaginations, and every high thing that exalted itself against the knowledge of God, and bringing into captivity every thought to the obedience of Christ" (verse 5).

Especially notice that Paul says spiritual weapons are effective at pulling down *"strongholds."* There is a lot of talk today in the Body of Christ about "strongholds." In light of this, we must ask, "What is a stronghold?"

The word "stronghold" comes from the Greek word *ochuroma* (o-chu-ro-ma). It is one of the oldest words in the New Testament, and it originally used to describe a "fortress." By New Testament times, this same word depicted a "prison."

A more accurate rendering of the word *ochuroma* would be, ". . . to the pulling down of *fortresses.*" Or, you could even translate it, ". . . to the pulling down of *prison houses.*" Both of these are correct and convey two powerful messages to us about strongholds.

In the first place, this tells us that a stronghold is like a *fortress.* A fortress is a fortified place; a citadel, a fort, or a castle.

Fortresses have exceptionally thick, impregnable walls to keep outsiders from breaking in. To assure that outsiders will not scale the walls and come in, the walls of fortresses were built very high. Such walls were intended to keep intruders *outside.*

The word "stronghold" was later translated as the word "prison." What does a prison do? A prison serves just the opposite purpose of a fortress. While a fortress keeps outsiders from *getting in,* a prison keeps insiders from *getting out!*

Prisons are places of detention; holding tanks; places like dungeons and jails. Like fortresses, they also have fortified walls. Even more, prisons have bars of steel to keep prisoners in captivity.

The fact that the word "stronghold" can be translated as both the words "fortress" and "prison" tells us some important things about strongholds.

In the first place, this emphatically means that when a man or woman has a "stronghold" in his or her life, mentally and emotionally, they have walls around them that are so thick, that others who could help them, cannot seem to break through that barrier to get through to them. *Those invisible walls keep outsiders from getting in!*

Like impregnable, invisible walls, strongholds are rooted in the mind and emotions to keep people from getting too close to us. This is a trick of the devil to keep people isolated, and far removed from those who could help bring freedom to their lives and minds.

Please understand that these strongholds do not suddenly pop up in our lives overnight. You can be sure that when the adversary first began to attack your mind and to fill it with immobilizing fear, the Holy Spirit tried to warn you about it.

Because you allowed these lies in the mind to go unresisted, and because you permitted wrong thinking and wrong believing to go unchallenged, step by step, day by day, and hour by hour, the devil began to use those lies, insinuations, and unrealistic fears to build thick, impregnable walls around your life. Finally, you were sieged and taken captive mentally and emotionally by the lying allegations of the devil.

Unrealistic fears of rejection keep you from developing relationships in your life. Unrealistic fears about the future of your marriage hinder you from functioning in the marital relationship as God intended. Unrealistic fears about potential failure will keep you from stepping out to do something worthwhile with your life.

In such cases, the devil's claim upon your mind and emotions must be commanded to leave. However, there is another step that must be taken first.

The first step to eradicate strongholds in your life is to recognize your responsibility in the matter. You permitted your mind and emotions to get into this mess! Therefore, repentance for allowing this mess to mentally and emotionally develop in your life is absolutely essential — *before all else!* Until you have taken this first step, nothing else will occur.

After you have done this, the power of God will cooperate with you as you seek to renew your mind daily with the Word of God to right thinking and right believing again.

Those same walls that keep other people from getting in, also keep you from breaking out and becoming all that God meant for you to be. Like the steel bars of a prison, that mental stronghold has falsely told you that you will fail, that no one wants you, that you're not worth anything, and so on.

Individuals who have a stronghold in their lives have been taken captive *mentally and emotionally.* The enemy has located some open door in their lives, and upon locating it, has passed through that entrance into their minds, where he has begun to take their thoughts captive.

Two Kinds of Strongholds

There are two kinds of strongholds: rational and irrational. The rational strongholds are the hardest to deal with — because they usually make *sense!*

Paul refers to these rational strongholds when he says, "Casting down *imaginations. . . .*" The word "imaginations" is taken from the word *logismos* (lo-gis-mos), and it is where we get the word "logic" as in "logical thinking."

Thank God for a good, sound mind, but even a good, sound mind must be submitted to the sanctifying work of the Holy Spirit — otherwise that mind, like a stronghold of reason, will begin to dictate to your life.

I wonder how many people have been called by God to go into the ministry, but didn't go because they rationalized away the call of God. I wonder how many have heard their minds tell them, "You can't go into the ministry! You've got a wife, three children, a house payment, and a car payment to make. You can't obey God!"

The logical mind, though necessary and wonderful, will work against your spiritual life unless it is submitted to the control of the Holy Spirit. The unsubmitted mind will always try to talk you out of obeying God. If the rational mind is not taken charge of, it will begin to completely dominate and control one's obedience to God.

People who are "thinkers" are prone to fall prey to such rational strongholds. Because they are rational thinkers anyway, they are naturally inclined to allow their minds to dominate them and to conquer their faith.

In addition to rational strongholds, there are irrational strongholds. Everyone has fallen prey to these irrational strongholds from time to time.

Irrational strongholds primarily have to do with fears and worries that are completely unrealistic. These are strongholds such as a fear of disease, a fear of dying early in life, an abnormal fear of rejection, a fear of financial collapse, and so forth.

These irrational strongholds in the mind, emotions and imagination will normally play their course, and then dissipate. After a time, it becomes apparent even to those who are dominated by them, that such fears are ridiculous and unfounded. Frequently these ridiculous, yet captivating thoughts, lose their power instantly when you tell a friend or spouse what you have been thinking.

Irrational strongholds are so ridiculous that eventually you wake up to realize this is a trick of the enemy to enslave you and keep you from functioning normally. Such is the case with irrational strongholds.

If these harassing thoughts persist in your mind and insist on controlling you mentally and emotionally, you must obey the Word of God and deal with them straightforwardly.

This is why Paul said, "Casting down imaginations, and every high thing that exalteth itself against the knowledge of God, and bringing into captivity every thought to the obedience of Christ" (Second Corinthians 10:5).

Notice that Paul doesn't say one thing about the devil in this verse! He doesn't say "...and bringing *the devil* into captivity. . . ." Rather, he says, "...and bringing into captivity *every thought* to the obedience of Christ." The truth is, if you do not take your thoughts captive, then your thoughts *will* take you captive!

Let me draw your attention to the phrase "bringing into captivity" for a moment. This phrase is taken from the Greek word *aichmalotidzo* (aich-ma-lo-tid-zo). It is a brutal word which means "to take one captive with a spear pointed into his back."

By electing to use this word, Paul lets us know that our thoughts are not going to be taken captive easily. We must decide to take them captive. *We must be brutal with ourselves, and forcibly seize control of our minds.* If our minds and our emotions try to get away from us, then we must grab hold of them and force them into subjection!

And guess what! The word "thought" (i.e., "bringing into captivity every *thought*. . . .") is taken from the word *noema* (no-e-ma), which has the same meaning as the word "devices" (*noemata*) that we saw in Second Corinthians 2:11. Paul is talking about "mind games" again!

Paul continues to tell us that these "mind games" must be brought ". . . to the *obedience* of Christ." The word "obedience" is from the word *hupakoe* (hu-pa-ko-e), which is a compound of the words *hupo* (hu-po) and *akouo* (a-kou-o).

The word *hupo* means "under" and the word *akouo* means "I hear or I listen." The word *akouo* is where we get the word acoustics. This is the picture of *"forcing someone into a subordinate position, and then making them listen!"*

Remember, Paul is talking about mental strongholds and mind games that attempt to manipulate and control us. Rather than listen to these lying emotions and slanderous accusations, we must lay hold of our minds and tell them to submit and listen to what the Word of God has to say!

When we choose to do this, this is the very moment that the renewing of the mind begins to work wonders in our lives! This is when real *mental renovation* begins!

What Is Oppression?

On the other hand, if we choose to let our minds and our emotions continue dominating and controlling us, we will inevitably become *oppressed*.

What is oppression? The word "oppression" is found in Acts 10:38. In his sermon to the household of Cornelius, Peter says, "How God anointed Jesus of Nazareth with the Holy Ghost and with power; who went about doing good and healing all who were oppressed of the devil; for God was with him."

The word "oppression" is taken from the word *katadunasteuo* (ka-ta-du-na-steu-o), which is a compound of the words *kata* (ka-ta) and *dunamis* (du-na-mis). *Kata* denotes something that is "dominating" or "manipulating." *Dunamis* refers to a "power" that is "explosive."

Oppression is a force that comes to "powerfully dominate and manipulate." It was technically used to portray a wicked tyrant or an evil king who forcibly imposed his will upon his subjects. He told them what they would eat, where they would live, and what kind of money they would make. He imposed his will upon them — against their wishes.

Therefore, when a person is oppressed, his mind and emotions are dominated by an outside source. The enemy, like a wicked tyrant, comes to oppress him by telling him what his future will and will not be, what his self-image is, and whether or not he has any hope of advancement in life.

When a stronghold in the mind is unchallenged, it eventually turns into a serious case of oppression. When oppression sets in, the end result is hopelessness.

Salvation Protects Your Mind

When salvation is wrapped tightly around your brain — when it is fitly in place — these strategies of the devil to take you captive cannot work! That is why salvation is seen here as a defensive weapon. It's a weapon that protects your mind from such assaults.

When salvation is wrapped around your mind, you will never again fall prey to these tactics. When salvation is wrapped around your mind, your mind is in safekeeping. You are protected.

The devil knows that if he is going to attack you, he must begin his attack in your mind — which is the strategic control center of your entire being. If the enemy can get a foothold in your mind, then he can get a foothold in your body. If he has no say-so in your mind then he has no say-so in your body, in your family, or in your finances. That mind of yours is important!

251

God gave you a brain, and He didn't give it to you so you could set it on the back burner. God wants you to use your mind. Your mind is important.

That's why First Peter 1:13 tells us to "gird up the loins of your mind." God is saying, "Gather up the loose ends of your mind and get your mind into good shape."

If the devil can weary you in your mind, you will lose out in the long run. If the devil plants a seed of unbelief in your mind, and you allow it to grow, you will end up in a dismal condition. That mind of yours is important, and God did not leave it unprotected; God gave us a helmet and called that beautiful, gorgeous, elaborate, ornate, intricate helmet "salvation."

In your "helmet of salvation" you have several things: You have salvation from sin, you have salvation from hell, you have protection, you have preservation, you have healing, you have soundness of mind — all kinds of God-given attributes.

What Is a Sound Mind?

A primary emphasis of this chapter is to see what the "helmet of salvation" does for us. In Second Timothy 1:7, the Word of God says, "For God hath not given us the spirit of fear; but of power, and of love, and of a *sound mind.*"

What is a sound mind? One translation says, "sensible thinking." What is sensible thinking? The word for "sound mind or sensible thinking" is taken from the Greek word *sophroneo* (so-phro-ne-o). It is a compound word. The first part of the word is derived from the word *sodzo* (sod-zo), which means "saved or delivered." The word *phroneo* (phrone-o) refers to "intelligent thinking."

Put the two words together, and it means to have a "saved mind or a delivered mind." In other words, this describes a mind that has been set free and is thinking correctly. You might say this is a picture of *saved brains!*

When your mind is guarded and renewed by the Word of God, you will think saved thoughts. When you have a renewed mind, *it sounds perfectly logical to walk in faith*. When you think with a renewed mind, *it sounds perfectly logical to obey God with your money*.

It is as though Paul says, "Timothy, why are you allowing fear to control your mind and emotions? God hasn't given you this spirit of fear, but of love, and of power, and He has given you a mind that has been delivered."

When you are walking in the knowledge of your salvation, you walk and talk like a saved man. When your mind is renewed with the Word of God concerning all the blessings contained in your salvation, *you walk and talk like a saved man*. When your mind is filled with the goodness of God, because salvation is wrapped around your mind, *you think like a saved man*.

Some people have been saved for years, but they do not think like saved people. Some saved people have more unbelief in what God *can't* do than they have faith in what God *can* do. This is what happens when saved people do not walk in the knowledge of their salvation.

On the other hand, when a believer meditates on the Word of God, and begins to comprehend the multiple blessings contained in his or her salvation, all he can think about is what God *can* do!

You think differently when you walk in your "helmet of salvation."

Why is this important? Because when you begin to live a life of faith — when you reach out to do the impossible — the enemy will try to assault you mentally and emotionally in an attempt to stop your progress.

The devil may speak to your mind and say, "You can't do this! You can't do that! This doesn't make sense! Don't you know that you have a car payment to make! What will your family and friends think of this?"

He may try to pave a road into your mind, play mind games with your head, and then deceive you. Thus, play it safe and make certain that you are growing in the knowledge of your salvation. Take care to guard your mind with the Word of God, and wear your "helmet of salvation" by filling your mind with the Word of God.

When you walk in your "helmet of salvation," you think like God thinks, you reason like God reasons, you believe like God believes, and you act like God acts!

In Romans 8:6, Paul says, "For to be carnally minded *is death. . . .*"

In Titus 1:15, Paul restates this again when he says, ". . . unto them that are defiled and unbelieving is nothing pure; but even their mind and conscience *is defiled.*"

Though these verses are about a lost man's mind, there are plenty of believers out there who still walk around with their natural, carnal minds controlling them.

It doesn't matter how many years you have been saved, if you take that "helmet of salvation" off, and if you don't walk in the knowledge of your salvation, you will end up with a mind that is contaminated and defiled.

Do not underestimate the importance of filling your mind with a proper understanding and knowledge of your salvation. Salvation is a powerful piece of weaponry. If it is allowed to function correctly in your life, it will defend your mind from attacks!

However, when you take your "helmet of salvation" off, the devil is going to hit your mind and emotions, toss you here and there, and you will become similar to a person with multiple personalities — believing God and doubting God at the same time.

You will become like a spiritual deformity if you do not walk in your "helmet of salvation." Do you want to be spiritually deformed? If not, you had better put that "helmet of salvation" around your mind!

What Does the Word "Salvation" Mean?

Now let's look at the word "salvation." The word "salvation" literally means "saved or delivered." In the broadest sense of the word, it means "to be brought into a safe place." It is taken from the Greek word *soterios* (so-te-ri-os), which means "to be saved, to be delivered from danger, and to be brought into a safe place."

Here you see that when a man or woman is "saved," they are "delivered from danger and brought into a safe place." The knowledge of the gospel sets your mind free!

When a man or woman is saved, they are rescued from a place of danger. Being lost is a dangerous condition to be in, for you are under the dominion of Satan. But when a man is saved, he is brought out of that dangerous place, and is brought into a place of safety.

It is very pertinent that salvation was viewed by Paul to be like a helmet upon the mind, because, when you were saved, God rescued you — not just spiritually, but *God rescued you mentally.*

A Transformed Mind

Prior to your salvation, you were a member of Satan's slave market and your mind was accustomed to thinking just like the rest of the world (for more on Satan's Slave Market, see pages 48-60). By nature, the Bible says we were all the "children of wrath" (Ephesians 2:3). The word "wrath" means that we were bent out of proportion. What a plight we were in!

What the devil had done to us was incredible. He left his marks and scars all over the minds and the emotions of those who were previously under his control.

Now that you have been ". . . delivered from the power of darkness, and translated into the kingdom of his dear Son" (Colossians 1:13), you must allow the power of God to work in your mind and renew it to right thinking; *saved thinking.*

God doesn't want one area of your mind to think like the world, the way it used to think. God doesn't want one cell in your brain to have unbelief in it. That is not the will of God: God intends for every cell in your mind to be dominated by your New Birth. God intends for your mind to think like a mind that is controlled by the Holy Spirit.

You may ask, "How do I get my mind into this condition?"

First, get in touch with the power of God. That's the prerequisite to walking in spiritual armor. Ephesians 6:10 says, ". . . be strong in the Lord. . . ." When that strength comes to you, it will clothe you with spiritual armor.

But there is a second thing you have to do. In Ephesians 6:17, Paul says, "And *take* the helmet of salvation. . . ." The word "take" is translated as the word "receive" forty times in the New Testament. Thus, the verse would be better translation, "And *receive* the helmet of salvation. . . ."

God is not going to force a renewed mind on you; you have to *receive* this "helmet of salvation." This means you have a part to play in the saving of your mind.

How do you do that? You *put on* salvation. You put that "helmet of salvation" on your head by studying what the Bible has to say about salvation. Know it inside and out. Know what the Bible teaches about Jesus' redemptive work to deliver, heal, preserve, and give a sound mind to you.

Wrap that knowledge of salvation around your brain, and let it protect your mind. You will be transformed as you do this. You will no longer walk like an individual who is constantly sick. You will no longer think and walk like an individual who is poor. You will no longer walk like an individual who is defeated, because your mind is being filled with the knowledge of salvation, and *this new knowledge will begin to change your conduct and your experience.*

The devil wants to rob you of every blessing that God has prepared for you. He wants to take every good thing from you that he can, so fill your mind with all God has done for you. Let that knowledge of salvation and all of its benefits become like a helmet of bronze upon your head to protect your mind from the battle-ax of the enemy.

By letting the Word of God work in your mind to this extent, your mind will be renewed. You will become so convinced of your salvation and all of its benefits — salvation will become so *real* to you — that your mind will be secure in your salvation; your mind will no longer be able to be penetrated by doubt and unbelief.

Those questionable areas in your mind that the enemy used to attack regularly , will no longer be attackable! For now you are completely surrounded — *mentally and emotionally* — by a "helmet of salvation."

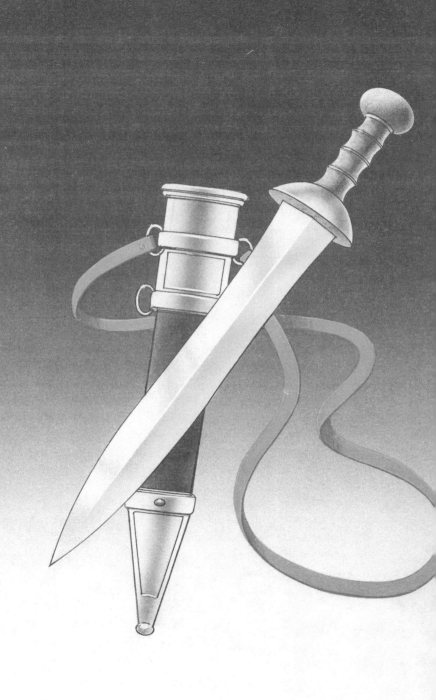

Chapter Fifteen
The Sword of the Spirit

Spiritual battles are just like natural battles. Nations do not engage in warfare constantly; they fight when a problem comes along. Afterwards, their soldiers return home, experience a time of peace and refreshing, and do not fight again until there's a reason to fight.

This book is not designed to make you run around looking for the devil; it is designed to help equip you so that when battles do come, you will be prepared to stand against them.

Battles *will* come, but they won't come every day. God has given us this weaponry so that when they do come, you will be prepared to maintain your victorious position over Satan.

In this chapter, we are going to look at one of the most aggressive, offensive weapons that God has given to the Body of Christ — the "sword of the Spirit"! Our text is Ephesians 6:17, which says, "And take the helmet of salvation, and the sword of the Spirit, which is the word of God."

The Swords of the Roman Soldier

Of the five different kinds of swords that Roman soldiers used in confrontations with enemies, the Holy Spirit carefully selected one of them to illustrate our "sword of the Spirit." But first, let's look at each of these swords individually.

The *first sword* of the Roman soldier was called the *gladius* sword. It was an extremely heavy, broad-shouldered sword

Facing left page: The two-edged machaira sword and scabbard of a Roman soldier from the first century.

with a very long blade. Of all these swords, the *gladius* was the most aesthetically beautiful; however, because of its weight, it was also the most cumbersome and awkward to use.

This particular sword was so massive that it was referred to as a *two-handed sword*. In other words, it was so heavy that the soldier had to use both hands to use it. This powerful, heavy tool had to be swung with all of one's might.

Furthermore, this first sword was sharpened only on one side. The other side of the sword was blunt and dull. After suffering a terrible defeat from the hands of the Carthaginians, the Romans abandoned these large swords, adopting another version similar to the ones the Carthaginians had used to defeat them.

The *second sword* was shorter and narrower. It was approximately seventeen inches long and about two and one half inches in width; hence, it was lighter than the swords they previously used. This newer version rapidly grew in popularity throughout the empire because it was so much easier to carry and swing.

The *third sword* used by the Roman army was even shorter than the second sword. In fact, it was so short that it looked more like a dagger than a sword. This dagger-like sword was carried in a small, hidden scabbard beneath the soldier's outer coat; it was used to inflict a mortal wound into the heart of an enemy or an aggressor.

The *fourth sword* Roman soldiers used was a long and very slender sword. This sword was primarily used by the cavalry, as opposed to the more durable swords that were carried by the infantry. Additionally, this long, slender sword was also used in a sport that was similar to modern-day fencing. No soldier would have wanted to enter into combat with this sword; this was not the kind of sword that you would use in battle.

The *fifth sword* was the type of sword that Paul had in mind when he wrote about spiritual armor in the sixth chapter of Ephesians. He said, ". . . *and the sword of the Spirit, which is the word of God."*

This particular word for "sword," used in this text, is taken from the Greek word *machaira* (ma-chai-ra). This brutal weapon of murder was approximately nineteen inches long and was razor-sharp on both sides of the blade. Because both sides of this sword were razor sharp, it was much more dangerous than the other swords. The very end of the sword turned upward, causing the point of the blade to be extremely sharp and deadly.

This two-edged blade inflicted a wound far worse than the other swords. Before the Roman soldier withdrew this particular sword from the gut of his enemy, he held his sword very tightly with both hands, gave that sword a wrenching twist inside his enemy's stomach, and withdrew the man's entrails as he pulled the sword from his enemy's body.

Of all the swords available, this was the most dangerous sword of all. While the other swords were deadly, *this one was a terror to the imagination!* This sword was not only intended to kill, but to completely rip an enemy's insides to shreds — it was *a weapon of murder!*

What Is a *Rhema*?

Here, in Ephesians 6:17, Paul uses the word *machaira* to describe our "sword of the Spirit." By doing so, he declares that God has given the Church a weapon that is just that brutal! God has given us a weapon that has the potential to rip our foe to shreds. *This weapon is called the "sword of the Spirit."*

Paul continues to give more information about this sword. He says, ". . .the Sword of the Spirit, *which is the word of God."* Paul says that this "sword" is "the *word* of God."

The expression "word" is taken from the Greek word *rhema* (rhe-ma). The word *rhema* is one of the most familiar Greek words used in the New Testament. It describes something that is "spoken clearly, spoken in unmistakable terms, spoken vividly, spoken in undeniable language, or something that is spoken in unquestionable, certain, and definite terms."

In the New Testament, the word *rhema* carries the idea of a "quickened word," such as a word of scripture or a "word from the Lord" that the Holy Spirit supernaturally drops into one's mind, thus causing it to come alive supernaturally and impart special power to that believer!

These *rhemas* are so powerful, that when the Holy Spirit supernaturally "quickens" such a word or Bible verse in a believer's heart and mind, he knows, *really knows,* that he has heard from the Lord! There is no doubt about it!

Jesus referred to this quickening work of the Holy Spirit in John 14:26, when He said, "But the Comforter, which is the Holy Ghost, whom the Father will send in my name, he shall teach you all things, *and bring all things to your remembrance, whatsoever I have said unto you."*

When the Holy Spirit drops a "word" into our hearts, or supernaturally reminds us of a verse, or when He puts us in remembrance of a Bible promise, that word, verse, or promise floods our entire being with faith! *He speaks to us in a way that is clearly spoken, unmistakable, undeniable, unquestionable, certain, and definite.*

Therefore, a *rhema* is a specific word which the Holy Spirit quickens in our heart and mind at a specific time and for a special purpose.

Therefore, when Paul says, ". . . the sword of the Spirit, *which is the word of God,"* he is referring to the Holy Spirit's ability to make a "word" vividly come alive in your heart and mind at a moment of need.

One expositor has translated this, ". . .*the sword that the Spirit yields, as He draws forth a special word from God."* This kind of word from the Lord gives you *"sword power"* in the spirit realm.

The Sword and the Loinbelt

Like the other pieces of armor that God has given us, *the sword and the loinbelt are inseparable.*

Just as the shield rested on a clip on the right side of the loinbelt, the sword dangled down from a clip on the left side of the loinbelt. Just as the loinbelt was the support for the shield, it was also the resting place for the sword.

As we have seen before, the loinbelt is representative of the written Word of God, the Bible. This written Word of God is the primary source for a *rhema* from God. A genuine *rhema* — a word or verse which the Holy Spirit quickens in your heart at a specific time and for a specific purpose in your life — is so strong and powerful, that it is like God has put a supernatural sword in your hand.

With that sword in hand, you have a powerful weapon with which to repel the attacks of Satan. These "words" are given by the Holy Spirit — and they are supernaturally empowered by Him to enable us to withstand the mental, emotional, spiritual and physical attacks of the adversary.

The "sword of the Spirit" is a word that the Spirit yields! It is a specially "quickened word." This is the Holy Spirit's rebuff to the devil's attempt to penetrate the mind with slanderous lies and accusations!

Have you ever experienced the "sword of the Spirit" before? Have you ever been in a precarious situation, when suddenly, the Holy Spirit reached into that reservoir of scripture that you had stored up in your heart through study, prayer and meditation, and He quickened one of those verses to your mind at a point of need?

Have you ever been empowered by a verse from the Bible that seemed to drop from out of nowhere into your mind at just the right moment? Naturally speaking, you weren't even thinking of that verse. Yet, it seemed to pop right up into your mind? When that verse came into your mind, then you knew that things were going to be all right.

A verse that leaps off the pages of the Bible and into your heart carries a special measure of power in one's life! It is as though God speaks *only to you* through such life-transforming words.

You might say the written Word, the Bible, is like the *gladius* sword of a Roman soldier; it is like a broad-shouldered and extremely heavy blade. This huge blade is capable of making a sweeping blow against the enemy. On occasions, however, we need a specific word — a smaller sword — a two-edged sword — *a rhema* — to deal the enemy a fatal blow!

We need to stab the enemy! This will require a *rhema,* or a "specifically quickened word" from the scripture that the Holy Spirit has placed into your heart. With a *rhema* from God like this placed into your heart and hand, you do have "*sword power!*"

Vegetius, a Roman historian from circa A.D. 380, said, ". . . A stroke with the edges, though, made with ever so much force, seldom kills, as the vital parts of the body are defended by both the bones and armor. *On the contrary, a stab, although it penetrates but two inches, is generally fatal*" (for more of Vegetius' historical description of Roman soldiers, see pages 123-152, LIVING IN THE COMBAT ZONE).

It is not the sweeping action of a sword that kills, but on the contrary, it is the stabbing action of a sword that mortally wounds a foe. Vegetius tells us that a stab that penetrates two inches is all that is required to kill an adversary.

Many people have miscalculated that they must have the entire Bible memorized before God can use them or speak to them. While the memorization of scripture is good, and we should seek to commit as much scripture to memory as possible, it is not necessary to know the entire Bible in order to have the "sword of the Spirit" at our disposal.

Please know that it is not necessary to receive a prophecy that is ten pages long in order to have the "sword of the Spirit" in your hand. I have received numerous so-called "words from the Lord" from people over the years. I will never forget one man who wrote and asked me to verify that his "word from the Lord" for his personal life was accurate.

As I looked at this "word," I saw that it was nearly twenty pages long. It was so outrageous that I wondered how in the world anyone could have led himself to believe that it was really a valid word from the Spirit of God.

Do not think your *rhema* — a specifically spoken "word from the Lord" — must be pages and pages long in order to be valid. I meet many people who have pages and pages of prophecies and "words" from the Lord concerning their ministries, their businesses or their families. Most of these lengthy words are so complex and difficult to follow that they wouldn't be able to obey them if they tried. Most of the time, they can't even figure out what they mean!

It is true that the Spirit of God can speak a lengthy personal word to our hearts about our lives, but this is the *exception,* and not the *rule.* On the contrary, by studying history it is clear that most great men and women of God who have earned a place on the pages of history, have done so by obeying *a single, simple word from God.*

Noah received a very relatively short word from God that saved him and his family from destruction (Genesis 6:13-7:4). Considering the ramifications of the flood and the history-making consequences of Noah's obedience, the Lord's word to him was quite brief and simple. This history-making and life-saving word from the Lord must have lasted at least a whole ten minutes!

Likewise, when God called Abraham to leave Mesopotamia and to start his walk of faith, his word of instruction from the Lord was a whole three verses long, and a mere seventy-five words (Genesis 12:1-3). This extremely brief word from God led to the establishment of the Jewish people, and ultimately to the walk of faith we all now enjoy.

Joseph received a word from God about his personal life through two dreams. Through these two short dreams, the Holy Spirit vividly spoke to Joseph and revealed his future to him (Genesis 37:6-9). These encounters with God eventually put Joseph in a position to care for his family and the whole nation of Israel.

While tending sheep on Mount Horeb, the angel of the Lord appeared to Moses in a burning bush, unmistakably revealing that he had been chosen by God to lead Israel out of Egyptian captivity (Exodus 3-4). By obeying this relatively short word from the Lord, Israel's captivity was reversed and Moses became one of the greatest prophets of all time.

Mary, the mother of the Lord Jesus Christ, received a word from God that is still working wonders in the world today. The angel Gabriel delivered a very brief, yet life-changing word to Mary. *That most important word from the Lord was only eight verses long* (Luke 2:28-33,35-37). Because Mary's heart was receptive to this word from God, she was chosen to give birth to the Lord Jesus Christ.

The ministry of the apostle Paul was constantly influenced by specially given words from the Lord. A word from God was spoken to him at the time of his conversion in Acts 9:4-6. Furthermore, a special word from God was given to Ananias concerning Paul's salvation in Acts 9:10-16. Another word was spoken to him by the Holy Spirit at the time of his "sending forth" into public ministry. A word from the Lord was given to him in Acts 21:11 to prepare him for a period of persecution that he would experience in Jerusalem. He, likewise, received a word from the Holy Spirit in Acts 23:11 concerning his ministry in the city of Rome.

The list of modern-day men and women who received a simple, succinct word from the Holy Spirit and obeyed it is too long to cover in this book. By obeying simple, single words from the Lord, men and women of God have altered history. It is because of these who obeyed such simple, specially spoken words from the Lord that we enjoy many of our spiritual blessings today.

Without exception, these historical figures received words from the Lord that were simple to understand and right to the point. These "specially spoken, vividly given, unmistakable, undeniable words" from God changed the history of mankind!

You might say these men and women stabbed the domain of darkness by responding to *a word* they had heard from God concerning the purpose of their lives. Though these words from the Lord were brief and straight to the point, they did great damage to the domain of darkness.

Remember, a two-inch penetration by a sword is all that is required to fatally wound an enemy. When the Holy Spirit puts a sword — a *rhema* — in your hand, it will probably be short, concise and succinct. The Lord knows that a long word would be confusing to the majority of us. Therefore, He speaks clear, vivid, unmistakable, undeniable, certain, definite, and easy-to-understand words to us.

In the majority of cases, that *rhema* which you desperately need will come right out of the Bible, as the Holy Spirit supernaturally makes a verse to leap right off the pages of the written Word and into your heart where it begins to release great amounts of power.

When that verse jumps off the pages of the Bible and into your heart, that freshly given, freshly spoken word from the Holy Spirit — that *rhema* — yields a mighty blade in your hand that is capable of mortally wounding the work of the devil in your life.

What Is a Two-Edged Sword?

Two-edged swords, such as the sword that Paul refers to when he writes about the "sword of the Spirit" in Ephesians 6:17, appear all over the New Testament!

When the apostle John received his vision of Jesus on the isle of Patmos, he said, "And he had in his right hand seven stars; *and out of his mouth went a sharp two-edged sword. . .*" (Revelation 1:16).

A "two-edged sword" came out of Jesus' mouth!

The phrase "two-edged" is taken from the Greek word *distomos* (di-sto-mos), and it is unquestionably one of the oddest words in the entire New Testament.

Why is the phrase "two-edged" so odd? Because it is a compound of the word *di*, meaning "two," and the word *stomos* (sto-mos), which is the Greek word for one's "mouth." Thus, when these two words are compounded into one (*distomos*), they describe something that is "two-mouthed."

Therefore, a "two-edged" sword is really a "two-mouthed" sword. You could accurately translate Revelation 1:16 to read, ". . . *and out of his mouth went a sharp two-mouthed sword. . . .*" John tells us that this was a sword that had *"two mouths!"*

A similar statement is found in Revelation 2:12, which says, "And to the angel of the church in Pergamos write: These things saith he which hath the sharp sword with two edges."

The phrase "two edges" is once again taken from the Greek word *distomos*. As before, the word *distomos* would be translated better as "two mouths." Thus, Revelation 2:12 could be translated, ". . . *a sharp sword with two mouths.*"

The same identical phrase is also found in Hebrews 4:12, a verse that is very crucial to this chapter on the "sword of the Spirit." The writer of Hebrews said, "For the word of God is quick, and powerful, and sharper than any two-edged [*distomos*] sword [*machaira*, the same word that Paul uses in Ephesians 6:17 to describe the "sword of the Spirit"] . . . ."

Why is the Word of God repeatedly referred to as a "two-edged sword"? Or even more correctly, why does the original Greek text actually say that the Word of God is a "two-mouthed sword"? What is the difference between a "two-mouthed sword" and "two-edged sword"?

Keep in mind that the Romans had previously used a very large sword that was sharpened only on one side. The other side of the blade was dull and blunt. To use this *gladius* sword effectively, you had to swing it perfectly and you had to make certain that you were swinging with the correct side of the blade exposed toward your foe.

If you hit your foe with the blunt side of that blade, though it would certainly lay a bruise on him, it would not kill him. Therefore, this kind of sword was not entirely effective in battle.

The *machaira* sword, however, was sharp on both sides of its murderous blade. Even more than this, the blade of this special sword, because it was sharpened on both sides, made deeper gashes and wounds than the *gladius* sword. It was terribly sharp and pointed at the tip; hence, if the soldier wrenched the blade just right inside his opponent's stomach, when the sword was withdrawn, it pulled the man's entrails out of his body.

This deadly, two-edged sword always left the enemy lying on the ground in his own puddle of blood. This murderous weapon, a two-edged sword, when used correctly, always left the foe in a position where he would never bother you again!

Now the Holy Spirit tells us that the Word of God is just like that! It is like a sword that has two edges, cutting both ways and doing terrible damage to an aggressor.

One sharpened edge of this sword came into being when the Word of God first initially proceeded from the *mouth of God.* The second edge of this sword is added when the Word of God proceeds out of *your mouth!* Thus the reason the original text calls the Word of God a *"two-mouthed sword."*

When God first spoke His Word and inspired Biblical writers to record it, it was a *one-mouthed sword — it had only come out of one mouth at that time!* Yes, it was the Word of God, and yes, it was a sword — a mighty sword at that! However, it had only come out of one mouth, God's mouth, at that time, and therefore, it was a *one-mouthed sword.*

You might say that the Word of God was like a *gladius* sword, sharp on one side, but dull on the other. However, when you willfully took that Word into your spirit, and willfully began to meditate on it and give it a place of priority in your life, you took the first necessary step to give the Word of God a second edge in your life.

As you are confronted by a challenge from the demonic realm, the Holy Spirit is now able to reach down into that reservoir of the Word of God that you have stored up on the inside of you; He is able to pull one of those verses or Bible promises right up out of your inner man! When those verses, which the Holy Spirit draws up out of your spirit, begins to fill your mind and comes out of your mouth, it then becomes *a two-mouthed sword!*

First, that powerful Word passed through the mouth of God, thus giving it one sharp edge. Second, that powerful Word rose up from your spirit, invaded your understanding, and then proceeded out of your mouth. When that Word came out of your mouth, a second edge was added to it. God's mouth put one sharpened edge on that sword, and your mouth added the second sharpened edge!

Meditation and Confession

I hope you can see from this why it is important to meditate on the Word of God, and why it is vital for you to confess the Word of God with your mouth!

By meditating on God's Word, you allow the Word to do its marvelous work in you! Hebrews 4:12 continues to say, "For the Word of God is quick, and powerful, and sharper than any two-edged sword, piercing even to the dividing asunder of soul and spirit, and of the joints and marrow, and is a discerner of the thoughts and intents of the heart."

When God's Word begins to work inside of you, it cuts through the muck and mire of your mind and emotions, and goes straight to the heart of the matter. In other words, it pierces asunder soul and spirit, it divides between the joints and marrow, and it discerns the thoughts and intents of the heart.

You could figuratively say that *the Word of God has eyes!* It sees what the human eye cannot see, it knows what no human knows, and once received into the heart, it immediately begins working to renovate those areas of our soul realm that are off-base and wrong.

This is precisely the reason why the writer of Hebrews continues to say, "Neither is there any creature that is not manifest in his sight: but all things are naked and opened unto the eyes of him with whom we have to do" (Hebrews 4:13).

Meditating on the Word of God releases its dividing and discerning work inside us. Ignoring the Word of God leaves us in a position where our wrong thinking and bondages from the past will continue to exert authority over us.

But when we willfully take the Word of God into our lives and allow it to do its supernatural work in us, *that Word, like a divine blade, slices right to the heart of the matter* — it does what no spouse, friend, pastor, teacher, psychologist or psychiatrist could ever do. It divides asunder the soul and spirit, and the joints and marrow, and correctly discerns the thoughts and intents of the heart.

When the Word has done this extraordinary work in us, *we are inwardly changed!* Furthermore, we become *filled with faith* when we allow the Word of God to work in our lives. Why? Because "faith cometh by hearing, and hearing by the Word of God" (Romans 10:17).

Once that Word has taken root inside of you and your mind and emotions have been changed by its power, then you are in a position to speak the Word of God from deep down inside of your being! Finally, your renewed mind will cooperate with your faith, and you can speak the Word of God boldly with no doubt whatsoever!

One reason people have no results when they confess the Word of God is because they speak before the Word of God has personally done its life-transforming work in them! Before the Word has had time to take root in them and to renew their minds, they hastily mimicked what someone else confessed, or what someone else did. Because it was not yet personal revelation to them, it produced no lasting results.

Do not underestimate the importance of studying, meditating and praying over the Word of God. This vital work of studying, meditating and praying releases the Word to become a part of your own inner being.

When the truth of God's Word takes root in your soul like this — and when it begins to release its transforming power in you — then you are positioned to confess the Word of God in a manner that will release tremendous amounts of spiritual power. A confession like this is truly the equivalent of raising a two-edged sword in the face of your adversary!

When the Holy Spirit reaches into that reservoir of scripture inside of you, and quickens one of those verses to your memory — *when he yields one of those verses like a mighty sword* — it comes up from your inner man, past your mind and through your mouth! *As it proceeds from your mouth, a second deadly edge is miraculously added to it!* At that very moment, that Word becomes a "two-edged sword" — a "two-mouthed sword."

Some have said, "I have the Word down in my spirit. But there is no need for me to confess the Word of God with my mouth. I'll just keep the Word to myself."

To stop short of confession will keep you from the victory you desire. It's good to meditate on the Word — that is how the mind is renewed. You should get as much of the Word in your mind as you possibly can. The Word will make you inwardly rich!

However, if this is all you do, then you have a single-edged sword, not a two-edged sword. Because it has only passed from the mouth of God into your heart, and has not come out of your mouth yet (the second mouth), it will be like a blade with only one sharpened edge.

To be sure, that Word will work in you *personally*, but it will never release its full power until it comes out of your mouth (the second mouth), thus adding *a second fatal edge to that sword!*

When God drops the Word into your spirit, and then it comes up out of your spirit and you speak it out, you've got a sword with two edges on it. It is powerful. It has had opportunity to produce faith in you, and hence, when it comes out, it comes up out of your mouth with *force!*

It is interesting to note that Jesus, who *is* the Word of God, is described as having a sword coming out of His mouth. Notice the sword is not in His hand; *it is in His mouth!*

How To Hear From God

The sword of the Roman soldier hung down from the loinbelt in a beautiful scabbard that was made of either leather or specially tooled metal. The sword hinged entirely on the soldier's loinbelt.

Likewise, your *rhema,* that word that you need from God today, hinges entirely upon the presence or absence of the written Word of God, the Bible, in your life. In other words, that *rhema* you need to receive from God, will be received because you have the written Word at your disposal.

Some people go out, sit on a rock, and wait for God to speak to them. Some have been sitting on that rock for years and years, wondering why they have never heard from God!

God speaks through His Word! The "sword of the Spirit" hangs from the loinbelt! So if you want a "sword of the Spirit," get in the Word. Until you have the Word, there will be no "sword of the Spirit" available to you. Let me repeat it again for the sake of emphasis: *The sword and the loinbelt are inseparable.*

If you are in the Word — if you are walking in the loinbelt of truth — it doesn't matter what problem you are facing; the Spirit of God will yield exactly the word you need when you need it!

That *rhema* is going to come directly up out of that Word you have been studying, meditating, and praying over. After you have meditated on it and permitted it to become a part of you, the Holy Spirit will exercise His option to use that verse as a sword against the enemy.

You will not have a *rhema* from God — you will not have a sharp, two-edged sword — you will not have a blade that will put the devil on the run — by simply sitting on a rock somewhere waiting for God to speak to you mysteriously!

Psalm 119:130 says, "The entrance of thy words *giveth light....*" Isaiah 8:20 says, "...if they speak not according to this word, *it is because there is no light in them.*"

These two verses explicitly teach that when people do not have the Word of God, they have no light. If people do not have the Word of God, they sit in darkness. Why? David said, *"The entrance of thy words giveth light. . . ."*

When the Word of God gets in your heart and mind, that Word begins to impart light and direction to you. That Word will rise up from within as a sword; as a word of direction. It doesn't matter how dark it is; *when this sword comes up out of your spirit, it will show you the way to go.*

It doesn't matter what lies, accusations, and allegations the devil may try to use against you; when this divine light of the Word is working in your spirit and mind, that light will rise like a mighty blade right out of your mouth, and it will give you the very words and direction you need to overcome the devil's attacks at that precise moment.

Your ability to walk in this kind of supernatural direction and revelation is completely determined by *how much Word* you have inside of you. People who receive frequent *rhemas* from the Lord are people who have made the *logos*, the written Word, a central part of their lives.

When Jesus Needed a Sword

In the fourth chapter of Matthew, we find the story of Jesus' temptation in the wilderness. For forty days and forty nights, Jesus was inordinately and intensely tested by Satan. Because this testing of the devil was so extreme and intense, the Lord Jesus Christ needed a *rhema*, a "sword of the Spirit," to withstand these attacks from the Evil One.

Matthew 4:1-3 says, "Then was Jesus led up of the spirit into the wilderness to be tempted of the devil. And when he had fasted forty days and forty nights, he was afterward an hungered. And when the tempter came to him, he said, If thou be the Son of God, command that these stones be made bread."

274

Jesus faced the enemy in the same way that we face the enemy in life. In this portion of scripture, the devil was saying to him, *"If* You are who You say You are, show me!"

How did Jesus answer Satan? The next verse says, "But he answered and said, *IT IS WRITTEN. . . ."* The Holy Spirit, in all of His power and might, yielded a verse in due season! He drew a scripture right up out of Jesus' spirit, speaking it with great power and authority — *yielding it like a mighty blade* — and the enemy could not stand against it!

Why was the Holy Spirit able to pull a sword up and out of Jesus' inner man? Because the Lord Jesus Christ had spent time studying, meditating and praying over the Word of God! As a child he had been reared in the synagogue, hearing the Word of God week after week. Over a period of time, Jesus, in His humanity, had taken the Word deep into His soul.

Thus, when the Lord Jesus Christ needed a "sword of the Spirit," the Holy Spirit reached directly into that reservoir of scripture stored up inside of Jesus, and quickened one of those verses to His mind. When that Word passed through His memory and out of His mouth, it became a two-edged, two-mouthed sword which the enemy, even though he tried, could not withstand!

Notice that Jesus said, *"It is written. . . ."* What passage of scripture was Jesus quoting? He was quoting from Deuteronomy 8:3 — *a verse which the Lord had obviously committed to memory at some earlier point in His life!* Because this Word was a part of Him, when He needed a two-edged sword to attack the adversary, the Spirit of God simply brought that Word to the forefront of His mind and used it to repel this attack.

Notice what else was happening! The devil attempted to pull a "mind game" on Jesus, just like he tries to pull mind games on you! The devil said, *". . .If* thou be the Son of God, cast thyself down. . . ."

Keep in mind that Jesus had just stabbed the enemy with the Word of God! Jesus had just said, *"It is written. . . ."* How did the devil react to this stabbing action of the Word of God? What did the devil say in response to Jesus? The devil threw the Word of God right back into Jesus' face. The devil himself said, *"It is written. . . ."*

Talk about a mind game! The devil started quoting scripture! He said, *". . . for it is written, He shall give his angels charge concerning thee: and in their hands they shall bear thee up, lest at any time thou dash thy foot against a stone. Jesus said unto him, It is written AGAIN. . ."* (verses 6,7).

Jesus had to know the Word of God; otherwise, He would have been deceived by this deceptive ploy. The devil can quote the Bible better than any believer on the face of the earth! The fact that Jesus knew the written Word and its discerning power was at work in Him, kept Him on course when dealing with these temptations.

The Word of God had better be in you — *living, active, and powerful.* Moreover, it had better be more than mere head knowledge, because if all you have is head knowledge, the devil is going to confuse you and ultimately pull you down into defeat.

The devil knows how to use the Bible! He knows how to teach you the Bible the way *he* wants you to know it. The devil is a very good Bible teacher! He will tell you everything that's *not* in there, and then he will send someone along to supposedly "scripturally prove" every one of his lies!

Don't be deceived! The devil is well able to declare, *"It is written. . . ."* He will teach you the Bible just the way he wants you to know it, filled with error and misunderstanding that will rob you of the blessings of God. Thus, you must allow the Word of God to get down inside of you. When that Word is down inside you, and your mind becomes renewed by it, you can discern these lies and mind games that the devil would try to use against you. *The Word of God is a discerner!*

The devil tried to pull a mind game on Jesus by quoting the Bible to Him incorrectly. Jesus, knowing that these scriptures had been misquoted, said, "NO, IT IS WRITTEN

AGAIN. . . ." It was as if Jesus said, "Satan, listen to what the Word of God *really* says. . . ."

Jesus told the devil, "It is written again, Thou shalt not tempt the Lord thy God." How did Jesus know to quote that scripture from Deuteronomy 6:16? This was clearly another verse which the Lord had committed to memory at some earlier point in His life. Because Deuteronomy 6:16 was already stored up inside of Him, the Spirit of God could draw it out of Him like a deadly blade!

The story continues, "Again, the devil taketh him up into an exceeding high mountain, and sheweth him all the kingdoms of the world, and the glory of them" (verse 6).

The gospel of Luke records this same scenario. However, Luke tells us, "And the devil said unto him, All this power will I give thee, and the glory of them: for that is delivered unto me; and to whomsoever I will I give it" (Luke 4:8).

Talk about an invitation — the devil gave Jesus the most inviting invitation anyone has ever been offered! The glory of the earth — the authority of the earth — all of this had been handed over to Satan by Adam. That's why the devil said all of this has been "delivered" to him. The word "delivered" is taken from the word *paradidomi* (pa-ra-di-do- mi). It describes the act of "handing something over" to someone else. By disobeying God, Adam handed the earth and the authority of it over to Satan.

Jesus had come to seize the control of the earth and mankind from Satan's hands. This is why the apostle John said, ". . .For this purpose was the Son of God manifested, that he might destroy the works of the devil" (First John 3:8).

The Lord Jesus Christ knew He was going to face the cross. He knew He was going to take sin and sickness upon Himself and die a sacrificial death. In an effort to appease Jesus' flesh, the devil said, "Hey, Jesus! You can skip every bit of that and I'll give You this whole place — *if You will just worship me. I'll give it to You without your ever having to be crucified!* I'll give it to You *without your ever having to go to the grave!* I'll give it to You *without your ever knowing what sin is!"*

Talk about a mind game — that would be an invitation hard to refuse! How did Jesus respond to this seducing temptation of Satan? Jesus said, "Get thee behind me, Satan. . . ."

What empowered Jesus to resist this temptation? *The Word of God!* Jesus said, "For it is written, thou shalt worship the Lord thy God, and him only shalt thou serve." Once again, Jesus told the devil, *"It is written. . . ."* The Spirit of God withdrew another deadly sword to answer the devil's offer.

After the Spirit of God had continually drawn on the reservoir of Word that was stored up in Jesus — causing that Word to come alive — raising that Word up like a terribly dangerous sword — the Word says, ". . . and [the devil] departed from him for a season."

A Sure-fire Guarantee!

When you begin to reach out into the spirit realm in order to take new territory for the kingdom of God, the devil will try to stop you! When you begin to grow in your knowledge of God's Word and begin to make spiritual progress, the enemy will try to slow you down! He doesn't want you making any progress in your spiritual life!

Most believers sit around and allow the devil to batter them to pieces. They forget that they don't just have *defensive armor* at their disposal; they also have *offensive armor*. God has given you a "sword of the Spirit," but it will not work for you until you've taken the first steps to get the written Word of God down into your heart.

If you permit the written Word to have an authoritative role in your life, then when you do face the wiles of the enemy, the Spirit of God will have a vast reservoir of scripture within you from which to draw the exact needed sword to repel these attacks.

Rather than being beaten down into defeat by the devil every time he comes with his lies and accusations, you should allow the Holy Spirit to wield the Word of God — *like a mighty blade of a sword* — and send him on his way.

Therefore, if you want to be guaranteed of a "sword of the Spirit" to answer the devil's mental assaults, you must position the "loinbelt of truth" firmly in your life. That Word is the source from which your sword will be drawn!

Remember, like the Roman soldier of old, your "sword of the Spirit" hinges upon the presence or absence of God's Word in your life.

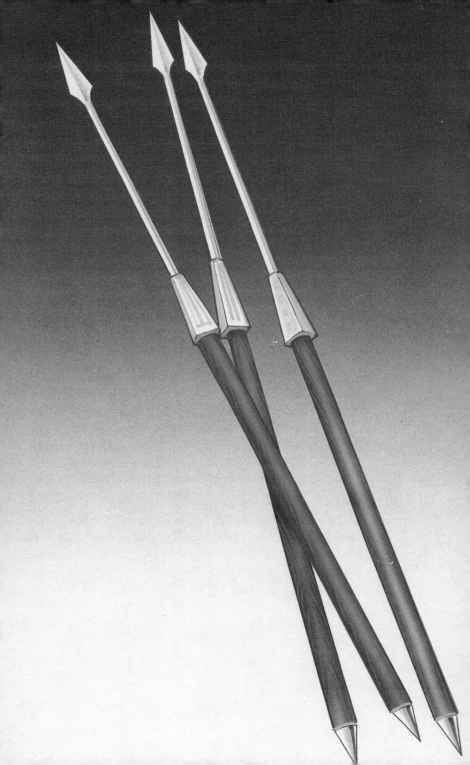

Chapter Sixteen
The Lance of Prayer and Supplication

Up until now in this book, we've covered the "loinbelt of truth," the "breastplate of righteousness," the "shoes of peace," the "shield of faith," the "helmet of salvation," and the "sword of the Spirit." Now we come to the last piece of weaponry which Paul lists in Ephesians, chapter six.

Paul says, "Praying always, with all prayer and supplication in the Spirit, and watching thereunto with all perseverance and supplication for all saints" (Ephesians 6:18).

As I studied these verses about spiritual armor, I was perplexed when I came to the end of this text. I was particularly puzzled by what most commentators and expositors had to say at this point. While all of them agreed that the Roman soldier had seven pieces of weaponry in his suit of armor, they all said Paul's list of armor was incomplete, stopping short of one weapon, the Roman soldier's *lance*.

The reason I was so puzzled by the absence of the lance was because Paul commanded us, "Put on the whole armour of God. . . ." If this was true that the lance was not a part of our armor, as commentators and expositors claimed, then it would not be possible for us to put on the whole armor of God, for the lance was a strategic part of a Roman soldier's weaponry.

Though the lance is not specifically mentioned by name in these verses, the lance *has* to be in this text; otherwise, we do not have the whole armor of God. However, the lance *is*

Facing left page: The lance used by a Roman soldier from the first century.

included in this set of spiritual equipment; it can be found in Ephesians 6:18: "Praying always, with all prayer and supplication in the Spirit. . . ." I call this last weapon *"the lance of prayer and supplication."*

When "the lance of prayer and supplication" is wielded by a believer, this powerful prayer tool is thrust forward into the spirit realm against the malevolent works of the adversary. By forcibly hurling this divine instrument into the face of the enemy, you have the power to stop major obstacles from developing in your personal life.

Various Kinds of Lances

When Paul came to the conclusion of this text about spiritual armor, he had the images of lances and spears in his mind. It is quite possible that Paul was able to physically look just beyond himself, to the other side of his prison cell, where his Roman guard had propped all kinds of lances and spears of different sizes up against the wall.

The lances used by the large and diverse Roman army varied greatly in size, shape, and length. Over the course of many centuries, these various lances were modified substantially. The Roman soldier used all kinds of lances.

The old Greek lances, used during Homer's time, were normally made of ash wood, and they were about six to seven feet long, having a solid iron lance-head at the end. Like the lance itself, the iron head of the lance varied tremendously in form; often it resembled a leaf, a bulrush, a sharp barb, or perhaps simply a jagged point like the lance-heads used on spears today.

Some lances were small; others were extremely long. The smaller, shorter lances were used for gouging and thrusting an enemy up close, while the longer lances were used for hurling at an enemy from a distance.

Most Roman soldiers carried both lances, short and long. With the aid of the shorter lance, they thrust through the body of their enemy from close range — what a morbid death this was! With the longer lance they struck their adversary with a deadly blow from afar. After successfully hitting an enemy with this longer lance, the Roman soldier withdrew his sword and ran to finish the enemy off by taking his head from his shoulders while he was wounded.

In addition to these, there were many other kinds of lances. For instance, during Xenophon's day, the armed forces carried a whole myriad of lances — *short lances, long lances, narrow lances, wide lances, pointed lances, dull lances, jagged lances, multiple-blade lances, and so on.* The average soldier in the infantry carried five short lances and one lance that was long.

Of all the lances in the ancient world, the Macedonians used the longest. The lance they used in battle was twenty-one to twenty-four feet long, or the length of a telephone pole! Imagine the awkwardness of using such a lengthy weapon of war. Such a lance would require the user to be amazingly strong! This was not the only lance the Macedonians used. The Macedonian cavalry used other lances that were much shorter.

The Roman army used a lance called the *pilum,* which was primarily used for throwing at an enemy from a distance. These *pilum* were used when an opposing force came to attack the Romans' fortified position or encampment. Rather than wait for the enemy to come upon them and then begin their fight, thus taking many losses, they hurled this extremely heavy lance through the air toward their foes. By doing this, they could strike their foes to the ground before they were able to penetrate the encampment of the Romans.

The length of the *pilum* by New Testament times was about six feet long, with the iron lance-head at the top of the lance and the iron shaft at the bottom each being approximately three feet in length. Thus, six feet of these *pilum* were made of solid iron. Many of these lances have survived to this day and can be viewed in museums of antiquity around the world.

Vegetius, the Roman historian who wrote about the military institutions of the early Romans, told of another lance which the Roman soldier used. This lance, Vegetius says, was about five and one half feet long, with a three-pointed lancehead that was between nine inches and one foot long. It was later modified to be three and one half feet long, with a lancehead that was five inches in length.

If the soldier desired to inflict a massive and terrible wound upon his enemy, then he made sure to load his lancehead with extra iron. The heavier the instrument, the more deadly the wound. Furthermore, this heavier load of iron helped to carried the lance farther when throwing it at a great distance.

There were many different kinds of lances and many variations of each one of them. In fact, there were so many kinds of shapes, sizes, lengths and variations of lances, that on this subject we could write and study for pages and pages to come.

Various Kinds of Prayer

What does all of this have to do with spiritual armor? Why do I make such a point about these various shapes, sizes and lengths of lances?

It is because Paul sees a whole range of lances and spears in his mind when he comes to the issue of prayer. Now, by revelation, he begins to compare these various lances to the various kinds of prayer that God has made available to us.

This is why Paul said, *"Praying always, with all prayer and supplication. . . ."*

Especially notice the middle portion of this verse, where Paul says, ". . . with all prayer. . . ." The term "all prayer" is taken from the Greek phrase *dia pases proseuches* (di-a pa-ses pros-eu-ches), and it would be better translated, *". . .with all kinds of prayer. . . ."*

As he moves toward the end of this text on spiritual weaponry, Paul urges us to pick up our final weapon: *prayer.*

He uses the imagery of these different kinds of lances to portray different kinds of prayer. Just as there were all different types of lances that Roman soldiers used in battle, Paul now begins to enlighten us to the fact that there are many forms of prayer available for us to use in our fight of faith.

For instance, there is *the prayer of faith, the prayer of agreement, the prayer of intercession, the prayer of supplication, the prayer of petition, the prayer of thanksgiving, united prayer,* and so forth. There are many forms of prayer, and we are instructed by Paul to use each form of prayer that has been made available to us as it is needed.

Just as the Roman soldier had a short lance for thrusting an enemy at close range, there is nothing to compare to a prayer of faith that is filled with authority! A prayer like this is well able to deal a mortal wound to an unseen foe who has come into too close a range.

Similarly, just as the Roman soldier had a long lance to hurl at his opponent from afar, preventative intercession, like a lance loaded with deadly weight, can deal a wound so fatal to the domain of darkness that it will hinder the devil's deadly devices from becoming a reality in our lives, families, businesses, churches and ministries.

Unseen spirits desire to bombard the flesh and hassle the mind. Because of these wicked spirits who hate the presence of Jesus Christ and His Church in the earth, prayer is indispensable.

Regardless of how skilled we think we are when it comes to the issue of spiritual conflict, or how bold and courageous we think ourselves to be, we simply cannot maintain a victorious position apart from a life of prayer. Without prayer we can be sure of absolute and total defeat.

As we look to God through prayer, we can be certain that we shall continue victoriously reinforcing Jesus Christ's triumphant victory over Satan — and we shall continue to gloriously demonstrate Satan's miserable defeat. Our victory has already been won, but by seeking God's direction, God's will and God's power for our daily living, we will be assured of continued victory.

To assist us in maintaining this victorious position, God has given the Church various kinds of powerful prayer. This is why Goodspeed translated Ephesians 6:18 to say, *"Use every kind of prayer. . . ."* The Amplified Bible says, *"Pray. . . with all manner of prayer. . . ."* The New International Version says, *"Pray. . . with all kinds of prayer. . . ."* Another expositor has translated this verse to read, *"Pray. . . with all kinds of prayers that are available for you to use. . . ."*

There is no doubt about it, Paul has the picture of various lances in his mind as he writes about various kinds of prayer. He sees long lances, short lances, wide lances, narrow lances, sharp lances, dull lances, multiple-blade lances, and so on.

Just as there were many kinds of lances for the soldier to use, Paul says, *"Pray. . . with all kinds of prayers that are available for you to use. . . ."* None are better than the others; they each serve a different purpose and are necessary for the life of faith.

How Often Should We Pray?

Before we get into a discussion about the wide range of prayers that have been made available to us, first we must back up for a moment and ask, "How often should we pray?"

Notice how Paul begins at the the very first of Ephesians 6:18. He says, *"Praying always. . . ."*

The word "always" is taken from the phrase *en panti kairo* (en pan-ti kai-ro). The word *en* would be better translated "at." The word *panti* means "each and every" It is an all-encompassing word that embraces everything, including the smallest and most minute of details. The word *kairo* is the Greek word for "times or seasons."

When all three of these words are used together in one phrase (*en panti kairo*), as Paul uses them in Ephesians 6:18, they would be more accurately translated, "at each and every occasion." It could be translated to read, "at every opportunity, every time you get a chance, at every season, or at each and every possible moment."

The idea is, "anytime you get a chance, anytime there is an opportunity, no matter where you are or what you are doing, use every opportunity, every season, every possible moment — seize that time to pray."

This clearly tells us that prayer is not optional for the Christian who is serious about his spiritual life. Unfortunately, prayer is the most ignored piece of weaponry which the Body of Christ possesses today. People find it more exciting to talk about the "shield of faith," the "sword of the Spirit," or the "breastplate of righteousness" than to talk about prayer.

Yet the "lance of prayer and supplication" is equal in importance to these other pieces of armor. Prayer is a part of our spiritual equipment. In fact, this piece of weaponry is so crucial, that Paul urges us to use it continually and habitually — "at every possible moment."

Six Kinds of Prayer for the Believer

Paul says, *"Praying always, with all prayer and supplication in the Spirit, watching thereunto with all perseverance and supplication for all saints."*

The New Testament uses six different Greek words for prayer that are available for our use. Some sources may list more than this; however, these additional words primarily have to do with worship, or are prayer words that were only used by the Lord Jesus Christ. God has given six kinds of specific prayer that pertain to us.

Each one of these six forms of prayer is specific and different from the others — each is just as varied and different as the multiple lances of the Roman soldier — and each is at our disposal to use in our fight of faith.

The six types of prayer found in the New Testament can be categorized as: (1) Prayer of Consecration, (2) Prayer of Petition, (3) Prayer of Urgent Need, (4) Prayer of Thanksgiving, (5) Prayer of Supplication, and (6) Prayer of Intercession.

Prayer of Consecration

The most common word for "prayer" in the New Testament is taken from the Greek word *proseuche* (pros-eu-che).

word, and its various forms, is used approx-
times in the New Testament. It is this very word
aul uses in Ephesians 6:18, when he says, *"Praying
ys, with all prayer. . . ."* In both instances, the word
prayer" is taken from the word *proseuche.*

The word *proseuche* is a compound of the words *pros* and *euche.* The word *pros* is a preposition which means "face to face." We have already seen this word once before to portray the intimate relationship that exists between the members of the Godhead.

John 1:1 says, "In the beginning was the Word, and the Word was *with* God. . . ." The word "with" is taken from the word *pros.* By using this word to describe the relationship between the Father and the Son, the Holy Spirit is telling us that theirs is an *intimate* relationship. One translator has translated the verse, "In the beginning was the Word, and the Word was *face to face* with God. . . ."

The word *pros* is also used in Ephesians 6:12 to picture our "close contact" with unseen, demonic spirits that have been marshalled against us . Nearly everywhere it is used in the New Testament, the word *pros* carries the meaning of a close, up-front, intimate contact with someone else.

The second part of the word *proseuche* is taken from the word *euche* (eu-che). The word *euche* is an old Greek word which describes "a wish, desire, prayer, or vow."

The word *euche* was originally used to depict a person who made some kind of a vow to God because of some need or desire in his or her life. This individual would vow to give something of great value to God in exchange for a favorable answer to prayer.

A perfect example of this can be found in the story of Hannah, the mother of Samuel. Hannah deeply desired a child, but was not able to become pregnant. Out of great desperation and anguish of spirit, she prayed and made a solemn vow to the Lord.

The verse says, "And she vowed a vow, and said, O Lord of hosts, if thou wilt indeed look upon the affliction of thine handmaid, and remember me, and not forget thine handmaid, but wilt give unto thine handmaid a man child, then I will give him unto the Lord all the days of his life. . . " (First Samuel 1:11).

The story continues to tell us, "And they [Hannah and her husband, Elkanah] rose up in the morning early, and worshipped before the Lord, and returned, and came to their house in Ramah: and Elkanah knew Hannah his wife; and the Lord remembered her. Wherefore it came to pass, when the time was come about after Hannah had conceived, that she bare a son. . . " (verses 19,20).

In exchange for this son, Hannah vowed that her young boy would be devoted to the work of the ministry. By making this commitment, she gave her most valued and prized possession in exchange for answered prayer. Technically, this was a *euche* — she made a vow to give something to God in exchange for answered prayer.

Quite frequently, persons seeking an answer to prayer would offer God a gift of thanksgiving in advance — this was their way of releasing their faith in the goodness of God. This was their way of thanking God for His favorable response to their prayer request.

Before prayer was made and the prayer request was verbalized, a commemorative altar was set up and thanksgiving was offered on that altar. Such offerings of praise and thanksgiving were called "votive offerings" (from the word "vow"). These votive offerings were similar to a pledge; a promise that once his prayer had been answered, the person would be back to give additional thanksgiving to God.

All of this is in the background to the word *proseuche*, used more than any other word for "prayer" in the New Testament. Keep in mind that the majority of Paul's readers were Greek in origin; hence, they understood the full ramifications of this word. What a picture this is of prayer!

This tells us several important things about prayer. First, the word *proseuche* tells us that prayer should bring us *"face to face* and *eyeball to eyeball"* with God in intimate relationship. Prayer is more than a mechanical act or formula to follow; prayer is a vehicle to bring us to a place whereby we may enjoy *a close, intimate relationship with God!*

The idea of *sacrifice* is also associated with this "prayer" word. This word portrayed an individual who desired to see his prayer request answered so desperately, that he was willing to surrender everything he owned in exchange for answered prayer. Clearly, this describes an altar of sacrifice and consecration in prayer, whereby our lives are yielded entirely to God.

While the Holy Spirit may convict our hearts of these areas that need to be surrendered to His sanctifying power, He will never forcibly take these things from us. Thus, this particular word for prayer tells of a place of decision; a place of consecration; an altar where we freely vow to give our lives to God in exchange for His life.

Because the word *proseuche* has to do with this type of surrender and sacrifice, this tells us that God obviously desires to do more than merely bless us; *He wants to change us!* Thus, this type of prayer primarily has to do with the concepts of surrender and consecration.

Because *thanksgiving* was also a vital part of this common word for "prayer," this tells us that a genuine prayer, offered in faith, will thank God in advance for hearing and answering. Thus, when we come to the Lord in prayer, it is imperative for us never to stop short of giving Him thanksgiving in advance for answering our prayers.

The word "prayer" (*proseuche*) that is used most often in the New Testament is more than a simple prayer request. This word demands surrender, consecration and thanksgiving from our lives.

This is the first "lance of supplication and prayer" that God has placed into our hands. By learning to use this powerful prayer tool, we place our lives into the hands of God in a very consecrated fashion.

The idea of *proseuche* is, *"Come face to face with God and surrender your life in exchange for His, making consecration an ongoing part of your life and be sure to give Him thanks in advance for moving in your life. . . ."*

The possible references for the word *proseuche* are far too many to list here. I suggest that you study many of the 127 occurrences of this word in the New Testament.

Prayer of Petition

The second most often used word for "prayer" in the New Testament is taken from the word *deesis*. The word *deesis* and its various forms are translated "prayer and petition" more than forty times in the New Testament.

Paul uses this word in Ephesians 6:18, when he says, "Praying always, with all prayer and *supplication*. . . ." In this verse, the word *deesis* is translated as the word *"supplication."*

Deesis is taken from the verb *deomai*, which most literally describes a "need or want." This is the picture of a person with a kind of "need or want" in his or her personal life.

As time passed, the word of "need" begin to take on the meaning of prayer, the kind of prayer that expresses one's basic needs and wants to God. This word, however, has to do with very basic needs, not wants, such as larger homes, more expensive cars, etc. Rather, the word *deesis* has to do with the basic needs which must be met in order for a person to continue in his or her existence.

You could say that a *deesis* is a petition, *a cry for God's help, that exposes your own insufficiency to meet your own needs.*

We find that Jesus prayed in this manner in Hebrews 5:7, "Who in the days of his flesh, *when he had offered up prayers and supplications with strong crying and tears unto him that was able to save him from death*, and was heard in that he feared."

The word "prayers" in this verse is taken from the word *deesis*. This plainly tells us that the Lord Jesus Christ was very aware of the weakness of His humanity. Recognizing His need, and the Father's ability to provide strength for Him, He prayed deeply from His heart and soul, asking the Father to provide divine assistance to help Him in His humanity.

The Lord was so aware of His own need, that He "prayed" (*deesis*) with strong crying and tears. Some would try to make "strong crying and tears" a new method of prayer and then try to teach it as doctrine to others. This, however, was no formula or new method of prayer. This was the cry of Jesus' heart to the Father, crying out for God to empower Him and to meet His most basic needs of strength and power.

The word *deesis* is used again in James 5:17, where the Word says, "Elijah was a man subject to like passions as we are, and *he prayed earnestly. . . ."* The phrase "prayed earnestly" is also taken from the word *deesis.* Hence, Elijah, though a great and mighty man of God, recognized his own inability to do anything significant for God. Out of this deep sense of need, he prayed earnestly (*deesis*), asking God to intervene on his behalf.

This kind of prayer stems from someone who is very aware of his or her own great need in life. The word *deesis* almost always portrays a cry for help. A person praying this kind of prayer (*deesis*) appeals to God from his or her humility, requesting God to grant some kind of special petition — to provide such things as spiritual power to minister, or power to resist temptation, and so forth.

Whereas the word *proseuche* had to do primarily with surrender and consecration, the word *deesis* has to do with humility. Again, this is the picture of believers who recognize their utter dependence upon God, and therefore, knowing of their inability to meet their own need — and knowing of God's ability to meet it, they pray earnestly — sincerely beseeching God from the deepest part of their spirit and soul to graciously provide on their behalf — to meet some type of want or need in their lives — whether it be mental, emotional or spiritual.

This intense prayer stems from one's awareness of his or her own human frailty. *This is prayer that exposes our own insufficiency and continual need for God.*

The word *deesis* is used in Ephesians 6:18. In this verse, the word *deesis* is translated as the word "supplication." The *King James Version* says, "Praying always, with all prayer and supplication [*deesis*]. . . ." A better rendering would be, *"Praying always, with all prayer and earnest, sincere, heart-felt petition. . . ."*

For other examples of *deesis*, see Second Corinthians 8:4 and First Thessalonians 3:10.

Prayer of Authority

The third form of prayer used in the New Testament is taken from the word *aiteo* (ai-teo). The word *aiteo* is used approximately eighty times in the New Testament, making it the third most common word for prayer.

The word *aiteo* means "I ask or I demand." At first glance it seems to be a strange word for prayer. Why is this so? Because the word *aiteo* does not refer to one who humbly requests something from God, but rather, this word describes someone who prays authoritatively, almost demanding something from God! This person knows what he needs, and he is not afraid to boldly ask that he receive it!

Unlike the word *deesis*, which has to do with spiritual need and want, the word *aiteo* primarily has to do with tangible needs, such as food, shelter, money, and so forth.

How can one approach God with such frankness, commanding and demanding that his needs be met by God? Jesus gave us the key to understanding this word *aiteo* in John 15:7. The Lord Jesus said, "If ye abide in me, and my words abide in you, ye shall *ask* what ye will, and it shall be done unto you."

The word "ask" is taken from the word *aiteo*. The verse could be translated, ". . . ye shall demand when ye will. . . ." Some are disturbed by this notion of "demanding" something from God. However, it is not so disturbing when you keep it in context with the entire verse.

At the first of the verse, the Lord Jesus said, "If ye abide in me, and my words abide in you. . . ." Notice the word "abide" is used twice in this verse. In both instances, the word "abide" is taken from the word *meno* (me-no), which means "to stay, to dwell, to lodge, to remain, to indwell, to continue, to remain in constant union with, or to take up permanent residency."

In light of this, you could translate the verse, "If you permanently and habitually lodge, dwell, abide, and remain continually in Me, and if my words permanently and habitually lodge, dwell, abide, and remain continually in you, strongly ask for whatever you wish for, and it will happen to you."

The Lord Jesus knew that if His words took up permanent residency in our hearts and mind, then we would never ask for something that was out of line with His will for our lives. Hence, when a believer allows the Word of God to permanently and habitually lodge in his or her heart, that Word so transforms their mind to the Word of God, that when they pray, they pray in accordance with the Word of God.

When you know you are praying in the will of God, you do not have to sheepishly utter your requests — rather, you can boldly assert your faith and expect God to move on your behalf! As the writer of Hebrews stated, "Let us therefore come boldly unto the throne of grace, that we may obtain mercy, and find grace to help in time of need" (Hebrews 4:16).

The word *aiteo* is also found in First John 5:14,15. In those verses, John says, "And this is the confidence that we have in him, that, if we ask any thing according to his will, he heareth us: and if we know that he hear us, whatsoever we ask, we know that we have the petitions that we desired of him."

Notice the first part of this verse, where John says, "And this is the *confidence*. . . ." The word "confidence" is derived from the word *parresia* (par-re-sia), and it always depicts someone who is exceedingly "bold or courageous." It is as though John says, "If you want to know why we are so bold, courageous and outspoken when we pray, here is the reason why. . . ."

The verse continues to say, ". . . that, if we ask any thing *according to his will,* he heareth us: and if we know that he hear us, whatsoever we ask, we know that we have the petitions that we desired of him."

Notice especially that John says, ". . . that if we *ask* any thing according to his will. . . ." The word "ask" is once again taken from the word *aiteo.* It must be pointed out that the word "ask" (*aiteo*) is once again used in connection with knowing the will of God for one's life. You could paraphrase John's verse to say, ". . . if we strongly request anything that is according to His desire for our lives. . . ."

Just like he had said in John 15:7, now John again says that if the Word of God permanently dwells in us, and if we pray according to that indwelling Word, we can come into the presence of God and make our requests known with great boldness, courage and confidence.

God is clearly not offended by this type of outspoken prayer. John continues, ". . . and if we know that he hear us, whatsoever we *ask,* we know that we have the petitions that we desired of him." The word "ask" is once again taken from the word *aiteo.*

If the Word of God dwells in you — if the Word of God has lodged in your heart and mind and has taken up residency in your life — then you will not pray prayers that are out of line with His plan. Thus, when you pray, your prayers will be accurate and in line with His predetermined plan for your life.

You will be praying God's will! When you move in this kind of accurate knowledge, you can be very bold and courageous in prayer! As a matter of fact, God wants us to move forward boldly and courageously in prayer to seize His will for our lives, and to bring it into demonstration!

By allowing God's Word to take an authoritative role in your heart and mind, you are giving that Word the freedom to transform your thinking. Because your mind is renewed to God's will, when you pray, you will pray in accordance with God's plan for your life.

When you are in this position, you are ready to experience this *aiteo* kind of prayer. With this "lance of supplication and prayer" at your disposal, you can boldly, courageously, and confidently move into higher realms of prayer to obtain the petition you desire of Him!

For other examples of the word *aiteo,* see Ephesians 3:20, James 1:5-6 and First John 3:22.

Prayer of Thanksgiving

The fifth most common form of prayer in the New Testament is taken from the word *eucharistia.* The word *eucharistia,* and its various forms, is used fifteen times throughout the New Testament.

The word *eucharistia* (eu-cha-ris-tia) is a compound of the words *eu* (pronounced eu) and *charistia* (cha-ris-tia). The word *eu* describes something that is "good or swell." It denotes a general good disposition or feeling about something. The word *charistia* is from the word *charis,* the word "grace."

When compounded together into one word, the word *eucharistia* refers to "wonderful feelings and good sentiments that freely flow up out of the heart in response to something." It is primarily used in Paul's epistles when Paul joyfully thanks God for someone or for some group of individuals.

For instance, when Paul wrote to the Ephesian Church, he was so overwhelmed with the grace of God in their midst, that freely, up from the depths of his heart, he said, "I. . . cease not *to give thanks* for you, making mention of you in my prayers" (Ephesians 1:15,16). The idea is, "I can't help but thank God for you. My feelings concerning you cannot be contained. I thank God for you!"

In Colossians 1:3, Paul prays the same way for the Colossian Church. He says, "We *give thanks* to God and the Father of our Lord Jesus Christ, praying always for you."

In First and Second Thessalonians, he prays similarly for the Thessalonian believers. He prays, "We give thanks to God always for you all, making mention of you in our prayers" (First Thessalonians 1:2). He likewise prays, "We are bound *to thank* God always for you, brethren. . . " (Second Thessalonians 1:3).

Furthermore, Paul used the word *eucharistia* in First Thessalonians 5:18, when he tells us, "In every thing *give thanks:* for this is the will of God in Christ Jesus concerning you."

According to this verse, it is God's will that we use the prayer of thanksgiving in every respect of our lives. Paul says, "In every thing. . . ." The Greek could be better rendered, "In every occasion and in every way possible. . . ." This plainly means a spirit of thanksgiving should play a dominant role in our lives.

Especially when praying for others, stop for a moment, and reflect on all that God has done in those persons' lives. Though they may still have flaws that are disturbing to you, they have made great progress from where they used to be! When you are reminded of what God's grace has already accomplished in them and how much they have changed, you will be able to freely, joyfully, and unreservedly thank God for His transforming work in their lives.

This "lance of supplication of prayer" is extremely important in our spiritual lives. While most would prefer to talk about supplication, intercession and other forms of prayer, the prayer of thanksgiving is also a vital part of our spiritual weaponry.

For other examples of the word *eucharistia,* see Second Corinthians 4:15, 9:11,12; Philippians 4:6; Colossians 2:7, 4:2; First Timothy 4:3,4; and Revelation 7:12.

Prayer of Supplication

The sixth form of prayer used in the New Testament is taken from the word *enteuxis.* The word *enteuxis* and its various forms (including its root, *entugchano*) are used only five times in the New Testament.

The word *enteuxis* is taken from the root *entugchano*, which is a compound of the word *en* (pronounced in) and *tugchano* (tug-cha-no). The word *en* means "in or into." The word *tugchano* means "to happen upon." When these two words are compounded into one, it means "to fall into a situation" with someone else, or to "happen into a circumstance" with someone else.

This word *enteuxis* and its various forms (*entugchano*) are usually translated as the word "intercession" in the New Testament. However, *enteuxis* does not necessarily refer to intercession like most people think of intercession (i.e., prayer for other people). The word *enteuxis* rather carries the idea of one who comes to God in simple, childlike faith, to freely enjoy and fellowship in the presence of the Lord. One expositor has said that this is prayer in its most individual, simple form.

It literally means "to fall into or to happen upon." The idea is, "to fall into the presence of the Lord." Or, "to come into wonderful relationship in prayer." In some places it has been translated as the word "supplication."

Indeed, this is the idea: to "supplicate" with the Lord. The word *enteuxis* was used in some classical writings to depict a love relationship between two lovers — two individuals who had happened upon each other, who had found or discovered each other, and now were sharing their lives together.

This is wonderful and intimate prayer whereby we come before God in childlike faith, learning to freely express ourselves and our desires, and to unreservedly enjoy His wonderful presence. Furthermore, this is that special time in prayer when God, by His Spirit, showers us in love and life-changing, life-transforming acceptance!

Thank God for this glorious privilege that He has extended to us in prayer! For other examples of the word *enteuxis*, see Romans 11:2 and First Timothy 2:1; 4:5.

Prayer of Intercession

The seventh word for prayer that is used in the New Testament is taken from the word *huperentugchano* (hu-per-en-tug-cha-no). The word *huperentugchano* is found only one time in the entire New Testament, making it the rarest of prayer words.

The only usage of *huperentugchano* in the New Testament is found in Romans 8:26. However, it is not used in connection with us; rather, it is used in connection with the Holy Spirit.

Romans 8:26 says, "Likewise the Spirit also helpeth our infirmities: for we know not what we should pray for as we ought: but the Spirit itself [Himself] maketh intercession for us with groanings which cannot be uttered."

Did you notice who was doing this particular work of intercession? *The Holy Spirit!* Paul says, ". . . but the Spirit itself [Himself] maketh intercession. . . ." Therefore, this word for intercession, *huperentugchano*, is not an intercessory work which we do, but a work which the Holy Spirit does on our behalf. Thus, the reason that this word is only used once in the entire New Testament, and that is here, used in reference to the Holy Spirit.

The word "intercession" (*huperentugchano*) is an old word which means "to fall in on behalf of someone else." It is what we would call a word of "rescue." For instance, if someone fell deep into a cavern, you would have to descend down into that cavern along with them in order to get them out and to rescue them.

This is precisely the idea of this word of "intercession." By using this word, Paul tells us that this is a special work of intercession — done by the Spirit Himself — when He supernaturally joins us in our circumstances, shares our emotions and frustrations, and then begins working a plan to get us out of that mess!

The true intercessory ministry of the Holy Spirit occurs when you are at a loss of words and do not know how to pray. Suddenly and supernaturally, the Holy Spirit falls into that place of helplessness and joins with you in the rhythm of prayer.

The Holy Spirit, in all of His wonderful attributes and personality, feels everything you feel. He understands the complete inadequacy that you experience. He understands the battles that you are facing. He willingly falls into that circumstance with you, feeling each emotion and frustration. Then He begins a plan of rescue!

The word "intercession" means "to fall in with someone else" — not just so you can be down in the dumps together, but so you can be rescued, renewed and delivered from that predicament. This is what the intercessory ministry of the Holy Spirit is all about.

Who experiences this type of supernatural intercession and divine intervention? The first of Romans 8:26 says, "Likewise, the Spirit also helpeth our infirmities. . . ." Especially pay heed to the word "infirmities." One great expositor has said this could be translated, "Likewise, the Spirit helps those who know they are weak and infirm. . . ." This is exactly the idea that Paul had in mind!

It is when we recognize our own human weakness, that we open our hearts and souls up to this intercessory ministry of the Holy Spirit. Really, until we recognize our need, He is limited in regard to how much freedom He has to move in our lives.

When, however, we come to grips with our need for supernatural assistance, and open our hearts to His help, this liberates the Holy Spirit to release all of His power in us — and this liberates Him to begin doing His supernatural work of intercession in our lives. (A soon-to-be-released book by this author will deal with this supernatural intercessory work of the Holy Spirit in great detail.)

A Final Word

In this book we have thoroughly searched the scriptures to grasp a fuller understanding of spiritual weaponry. We have studied the scriptures to see what the Bible has to say about our victorious position over Satan.

When you finish reading this book and pass it on to someone else, keep in mind that real spiritual warfare has to do with taking authority over your mind and your flesh, as well as taking authority over the works of darkness.

If you are living a holy and consecrated life, the bulk of spiritual warfare in your life already will have been settled. To deal with the other attacks, you must begin to apply the Word of God to your situation on a daily basis.

Paul said, *"Wherefore, take unto you the whole armour of God, that ye may be able to withstand in the evil day, and having done all, to stand"* (Ephesians 6:13).

Additional copies of this book and other book titles
from ALBURY PUBLISHING are
available at your local bookstore.

Albury Publishing
P. O. Box 470406
Tulsa, Oklahoma 74147-0406

To order tapes by Rick Renner,
or to contact him for speaking engagements,
please write:

Rick Renner Ministries
P. O. Box 472228
Tulsa, Oklahoma 74147-9994

Other Books by Rick Renner

Dream Thieves
Dressed to Kill
Merchandising the Anointing
Living in the Combat Zone
Seducing Spirits and Doctrines of Demons
Point of No Return
The Dynamic Duo

2 COR 10.:3/4 Warfare — not flesh.

James 4:7 submit to God
Resist . devil & he will flee run fr you